By day **Maggie Wells** is buried in spreadsheets. At night she pens tales of intrigue and people tangling up the sheets. She has a weakness for hot heroes and happy endings. She is the product of a charming rogue and a shameless flirt, and you only have to scratch the surface of this mild-mannered married lady to find a naughty streak a mile wide.

Two-time *RITA*® Award–nominated author **Linda Warren** has written over forty books for Mills & Boon. A native Texan, she's a member of Romance Writers of America and the RWA West Houston chapter. Drawing upon her years of growing up on a ranch, she writes about some of her favourite things: Western-style romance, cowboys and country life. She married her high school sweetheart and they live on a lake in central Texas. He fishes and she writes. Works perfectly.

TRIAL IN THE BACKWOODS

MAGGIE WELLS

COLTON 911: FORGED IN FIRE

LINDA WARREN

MILLS & BOON

First Published in Great Britain 2021
by Mills & Boon, an imprint of HarperCollins*Publishers* Ltd
1 London Bridge Street, London, SE1 9GF

www.harpercollins.co.uk

HarperCollins*Publishers*
1st Floor, Watermarque Building,
Ringsend Road, Dublin 4, Ireland

Trial in the Backwoods © 2021 Margaret Ethridge
Colton 911: Forged in Fire © 2021 Harlequin Books S.A.

Special thanks and acknowledgement are given to Linda Warren for her contribution to the *Colton 911: Chicago* series.

ISBN: 978-0-263-28354-9

0921

MIX
Paper from
responsible sources
FSC C007454

This book is produced from independently certified FSC™ paper to ensure responsible forest management.

For more information visit: www.harpercollins.co.uk/green

Printed and Bound in Spain using 100% Renewable Electricity at CPI Blackprint (Barcelona)

TRIAL IN THE BACKWOODS

MAGGIE WELLS

For my Super Cool Party People—
my life would truly suck without you.

Chapter One

The town of Pine Bluff hadn't changed much in the weeks since Alicia Simmons packed her bag and headed back to Atlanta, but she had. Only a couple of months ago, she'd been riding high on the arrest of one of the most insidious heroin traffickers in the southeastern United States. Heck, one week ago, she was the kind of woman who had a handle on exactly who she was and what she wanted. Sure, the promotion she'd thought was hers went to yet another member of the boys' club, but she couldn't honestly say she was shocked. Her path to section chief was littered with the prone bodies of men who thought they were better than she was. Time and again, she proved them wrong.

But she hadn't counted on getting pregnant.

So here she was, back in Pine Bluff, a million butterflies and one tiny embryo swirling in her belly. She hadn't intended to make the drive south. Now she sat parked at the curb in front of Harrison Hayes's neat ranch-style house.

She'd made a somewhat awkward call to her old friend Ben Kinsella to get the address, burbling something about wanting to add Hayes to her Christmas card list. The former DEA agent turned county sheriff threw her for a loop when he complained about how he'd never received a Christmas card from her in all the years they'd been acquainted. The torment had been cut short, though. Ben's girlfriend, Marlee Masters, had snatched the phone from the nosy sheriff and provided Hayes's address with a minimum of fuss. Marlee, being the smart woman she was, also rattled off Ben's, though Alicia was fairly sure the other woman suspected no cards were being mailed.

Warm air blasted through the vents. December was only a couple of days off and the South Georgia evening had turned cool. Of course, this close to the Florida state line, it rarely ever got truly cold. Or if it did, not for long. Unlike the vicious winters she'd endured growing up in Wisconsin.

Drawing a bracing breath, she turned off the engine and opened the door. The brisk wind stung her cheeks and made her eyes water. Then again, they'd been watering nonstop since the day she realized she'd missed a period. Not because she was sad or even upset. More, she was surprised. She wasn't the type to enjoy surprises.

Pulling her jacket close around her, she circled the hood of the car and stepped onto the brick walkway leading to the small porch. She had a vague recollection of her previous visit. She'd been one too many tequila shooters in to appreciate the softness of the gunmetal-gray shutters against the white brick. What looked to be window boxes affixed to the front of the house held a few scraggly purple-and-yellow pansies. The lawn was mowed and edged. A smattering of crisp fall leaves dotted the expanse of yellowing green. Alicia figured they had to have blown in from a neighbor's yard, because the tall poplar planted in the center of Hayes's lawn was mostly bare.

Harrison Hayes was the orderly type. Not a shock. So was she. Normally. At least she wouldn't be the only one whose world was about to be shaken like a snow globe.

Stepping onto the porch, she shoved her hands deep into her pockets, giving herself one last chance to dissect her own motivation in coming here with news like this. She hadn't gotten pregnant on purpose. And though they both may have been tipsy the night eccentric millionaire Samuel Coulter was formally arraigned on drug-and-human-trafficking charges, neither of them was anywhere close to being incapacitated. They'd willingly fallen into bed with each other. They were both aware of the added risk of having unprotected sex.

After all, they were adults. Responsible adults in positions of authority. More than most, they saw the day-to-day ramifications of bad choices. Why had they thought they were impervious?

Before she could change her mind, Alicia jerked her right hand out of her pocket and jabbed her index finger at the doorbell. A shiver ran down her spine. Something crackled under her foot. She looked down and spotted a brown mailing envelope left on the welcome mat. She swooped down to pick it up, peeking through the sidelights for any sign of occupancy. There were lights on in the house and a BMW parked in front of the closed garage door, but the presence of the car didn't necessarily mean he was home. In a town the size of Pine Bluff, residents often walked to their destinations. He could've taken a stroll downtown or—

The door opened and Harrison Hayes appeared, breathless and rumpled, wearing only a faded University of Georgia T-shirt, black gym shorts and an expensive-looking pair of athletic shoes. Alicia took in the sight for a moment. Harrison Hayes all sweaty and pumped up was something a woman should take time to appreciate.

"Alicia," he panted, his eyes widening. "What are you doing here?"

A valid question. All the way down from Atlanta, she'd debated her approach. One option would be to play it casual. Use the old "Oh, I was in town" line, but she dismissed the idea because neither of them was the type to simply drop by someone's house.

On the other end of the spectrum, she could blow in like a woman on a mission. As a special agent for the US Drug Enforcement Agency, storming in was a modus operandi she was far more familiar with, but she wasn't certain he deserved to have his life raided. Yes, choices were made, but they were made on both sides. She wasn't about to square off and demand he have answers for questions she hadn't fully wrapped her head around yet.

Tucking her chin to her chest, she slumped down into the collar of her coat, then gave her head a bewildered shake. "I, uh—"

A line formed between his dark brows, but there was no hesitation when he reached for her arms. Grasping her biceps, he pulled her into the house. Heat closed in around her, and for the first time since she'd seen the plus sign appear on the stick, something warm blazed low inside her.

"Are you okay?" he asked, running his hands up and down her arms like he might ward off any chill she might have caught.

"I'm fine," she replied. But it was a lie.

If she were fine, she wouldn't be there. If everything

were okay, she'd be in Atlanta. If her whole world hadn't shifted on its axis, she probably never would have seen Harrison Hayes again. But here she was.

She thrust out the envelope she'd been clutching and pressed it to his chest. "You had a delivery."

"Come on inside," he ordered, gesturing toward the living room beyond the small foyer. He gently removed the envelope from her grasp, then guided her into the room. "I'm sorry it took me a minute to answer. I heard the doorbell but figured it was a warning."

"A warning?"

He gave a mirthless laugh. "Around here, doorbells are more a formality than anything. People ring them, but they usually walk on in. I figured you were Ben or Simon, but when you didn't come to the back, I thought I'd better check."

She let her gaze travel down over his workout attire. "You have a gym in the back?"

He shrugged. "I have a treadmill and some weights. Not exactly a gym, but it keeps me busy on cold nights." He pinched the fabric of her jacket between his thumb and forefinger. "Where are my manners? May I take your coat?"

Her lips quirked up. She forgot he was like this. The courtly Southern gentility must have been drilled into him growing up. And though she never got used to it, Alicia was surprised to discover she actually liked his old-fashioned demeanor. There was no condescension in him. No pretense. He simply wanted to make her more comfortable.

"Thank you," she said, slipping the jacket from her shoulders.

He caught it and held the collar as she extracted her

arms. With the jacket draped over his forearm, he gestured for her to have a seat on a sleek low-slung sofa.

"Can I get you something to drink? Water? A beer? Or maybe you'd like something hot. I have coffee, but I don't think I have any tea in the house."

Her eyebrows rose. "No tea in the house? How will you ever survive?"

He chuckled. "I have iced tea, but no hot. There's a gallon of Bubba's in the refrigerator if you'd like iced tea."

The offer made her laugh. Only a true Southerner kept cold tea on hand at all times. Everywhere else in the world, it was a summer drink, but down here it was a way of life. And, according to Marlee Masters, only a single Southern man would buy the stuff they sold in the grocery store by the gallon.

Alicia desperately wanted a cup of coffee, but she didn't dare expose her unborn child to her caffeine addiction any more than she already had. "Water would be nice, thank you."

"Coming right up."

She watched him disappear around a corner to what she assumed was the kitchen. Asking for a drink was a stalling tactic, but she was having a hard time feeling ashamed. Seeing him again had thrown her.

In her mind, Harrison Hayes was no different from any other lawyer. Another brown-haired man in a nice suit with polished shoes and a briefcase. Line him up with a handful of other upper-middle-class businessmen and he'd blend right in.

Or so she'd thought.

She'd forgotten about the flecks of green and gold in his hazel eyes. She'd forgotten the way his square jaw looked covered in a true five-o'clock shadow. He was a clean-shaven man who fought a battle against growth lesser men cultivated and manicured with clippers. He was courtly and gallant, but he was also all man.

It was no stretch to imagine Hayes tromping off to the woods outfitted in camouflage and carrying a hunting rifle. Most of the men around these parts were avid hunters, inclined to spend their every autumn weekend buried deep in the deer woods or hiding out in a duck blind.

When he reappeared a moment later, she tried to gather her thoughts, but her runaway mouth betrayed her. "Do you hunt?"

He drew up short beside her seat, his brow creased into extremely attractive furrows of concentration when he bent forward and offered her a glass of water.

"Do I hunt?" he repeated.

Feeling foolish, but unable to abandon the line of questioning she'd begun, she said, "I wondered..." She glanced around the comfortably furnished living area and saw no evidence of trophy animals, but for all she knew, the man might have a rec room decorated with duck paneling and dozens of mounted deer heads. "I mean, it's hunting season in a lot of places," she continued. "I was only...asking."

The corner of his mouth quirked up, but rather than tease her about the odd inquiry, he simply shook his head. "No. I mean, I have hunted, but it's not my thing. I prefer fishing."

Alicia nodded, digesting this information and filing it away for future use. "I enjoy fishing too," she blundered on, happily latching on to any excuse not to approach the subject at hand. "Of course, I mainly fly-fish.

Though I have also hauled in some crappie and walleye."
He watched her with a bemused expression.

Hayes took a sip of his own water and smiled. "Then
we have something in common. Except for the walleye.
Don't see many of those around these parts."

Wetting her lips, she stiffened her spine and marshaled all of the nerve she usually reserved for storming
into drug dealers' lairs. "I came here because I need to
tell you something," she began haltingly.

Placing her glass on the coffee table, she leaned forward, rubbing her palms together between her knees
and searching for the right words. "Hayes, I realize we
don't know each other—"

She was called up short when he raised his hand and
interrupted. "Harrison. Or Harry, if you prefer." She
looked at him blankly, and he gave a wry smile and a
shrug. "We may not have spent much time learning everything about one another, but we *have* seen one another naked. Seems odd not to be on a first-name basis."

"Right." She barked a laugh. "Of course." Alicia drew
to an abrupt stop, her momentum lost. She looked up
at him from under her lashes, wondering exactly how
she was going to break this kind of news to a man so
forthright.

But then, forthright was the answer. She simply
needed to tell him straight-out.

"Harrison," she tried, then winced at the formality.
"Harry," she amended, and he smiled encouragingly. "I
need to talk to you about something pretty important."

"I figured it would take something big to bring you
to my doorstep." He took the seat opposite her, then
nodded. "Go on."

She looked up and this time met his gaze directly. "I'm pregnant."

He froze. She'd seen deer standing in the middle of a busy highway looking completely nonplussed compared to the otherworldly stillness of Harrison Hayes. She couldn't blame him. She didn't think she moved a muscle for five full minutes after seeing the plus sign show up in the tiny window on the over-the-counter pregnancy test. Then, when she did spring into action, it was to repeat the process with the two other tests she'd bought. Each time, she'd read the results with the same bewilderment currently breaking through his immobility.

"Excuse me?" he managed to croak.

"I'm pregnant," she responded, purposefully keeping her tone even. One of them had to remain calm, and she'd already had hours to freak out. It was Harry's turn now.

"But—" He huffed a laugh and scrubbed a hand over his face. "I was going to ask how, but I have a grasp on the mechanics of it."

Alicia watched him warily, all the while trying not to think about how unmechanical it had been between them. *Explosive. White-hot. Reckless. Hungry.* Those words might have fit better. But she was hip to what he was asking. Even in their tequila-fueled throes of passion, they'd paused long enough to have "the talk." They were adults, after all, not hormonal teenagers.

They'd left the celebration at Coulter's former defense attorney Simon Wingate's house and gone back to the place she'd rented for less than two full weeks. Like this baby's conception, Samuel Coulter's arrest and arraignment happened faster than anyone anticipated. Neither had a condom handy, but both swore they were in good health. She'd been diagnosed with polycystic ovarian syndrome in her early twenties and given birth control pills to help regulate her hormones. But even without the pill, her condition carried a high risk of infertility.

All of this added up in her head to mean she was meant to have this baby. Driving down to Pine Bluff, informing Harrison Hayes of his impending paternity and absolving him of all adjacent responsibility seemed reasonable. Possibly even noble.

"You're pregnant," he stated flatly, breaking into her reverie.

"Yes."

He blinked as if he still couldn't quite believe what he was hearing. "I assume you're here to tell me I'm the father?"

"Yes."

"Yes," he repeated dully. Then he threw his hands wide, absolute incredulity contorting his handsome face into an almost comical leer. "You're pregnant and you're saying I am the father."

"I'm pregnant and you absolutely are the father," she confirmed, keeping her tone even and nonconfrontational.

"Holy—" He shot from his seat and began to pace, plowing one hand through his rumpled brown hair. He wrapped the other around his middle and swung away from her. "I can't… Are you…? Well, of course you are, or you would never have driven all the way down here, right?"

She let him ramble, bracing herself so it all rolled off her. Words spoken in shock could and should not be held against a person.

"I took three tests," she informed him. "I haven't been to the doctor yet, but all three were pretty clearly positive." She paused, then gestured toward the foyer. "I have them out in the car. I can go get them and show you," she offered.

He held up a hand to stop her when she began to rise. "No." He wagged his head hard. "I believe you." Then, settling his hand on the back of his neck, he kneaded the muscle there. "God help us both, I believe you."

"I didn't plan for this to happen," she started.

Harry whirled, his hazel eyes glinting gold when they met hers. "Of course you didn't, but it did, and now…" His long strides ate up the floor space. He stopped in his tracks when he spotted the envelope she'd collected from his welcome mat. "What's this?" He snatched the envelope from the chair where he'd dropped it. "Did you bring legal papers or something?"

Alicia recoiled. In all their previous encounters, she'd pegged Hayes as a cool cucumber. A man so watchful and laid-back, he hadn't even batted an eyelash when Samuel Coulter assaulted his own attorney. But she'd managed to get such a levelheaded man utterly riled up one night, and it was a memory she reveled in for weeks after. But now, as she watched him grasp the craft-paper envelope in both hands and pull it apart at the seams, she wondered at her own powers of agitation.

"That wasn't mine—"

The first thing she noticed was the sheaf of blank white papers tumbling to the floor at his feet and scattering on the polished pine floors with a whoosh. When she looked up, she saw a dissipating cloud surrounding Harry's head and the streaks of white powder clinging to his clothes.

"Don't move," she shouted, springing to her feet.

"Don't come near me," he barked at the same time, thrusting his hands out to keep her at bay.

"Don't talk. Don't move, but don't hold your breath," she ordered, her training kicking in. "Breathe carefully. Keep it slow and shallow." She saw his chest expand and contract and moved directly into his line of sight, but outside the reach of his outstretched arms. "Let go of the envelope. Open your fingers and drop it."

To her relief, his fingers unclenched and it fell to the floor with the blank pages.

"Okay. Stay calm and don't move," she said in the same deliberately steady tone she'd used to deliver her big news. The soothing cadence employed by people who specialized in hostage negotiation.

"I'm not moving." But even as he spoke, he started to curl his arms in as if to reach for his shirt.

"Keep your arms as far away from the rest of your body as you can, but lift them over your head," she said, reaching for her purse.

"What? Why?" He shied away, but she plunged her hand into her bag and fumbled past her gun and credentials for a pair of the disposable gloves she always carried.

"Hold still." She wriggled her hands into the gloves and slid her fingers under the T-shirt, pushing her palms over his chest, spreading her wrists wide when she reached the neckband. She stretched the cotton until the threads popped. "Close your eyes. Close your mouth. Don't breathe. I have to get this over your head."

"What are you doing?"

"I've got to get you out of these clothes," she said urgently.

Chapter Two

In the weeks since Alicia Simmons blew out of Pine Bluff with her biggest bust to date on her résumé, Harrison Hayes had thought about her far more than he cared to admit. Their night together had been, for want of a better word, unforgettable.

They didn't simply have chemistry together. They created spontaneous combustion. But it didn't slow her roll. Barely forty-eight hours after the arraignment celebration ended with the two of them tangled in faded floral sheets, she was gone.

Now she was back. Here. Claiming to be pregnant. Next moment, there was white powder exploding all over his face, and she was trying to strip him naked in his own living room.

"You need to what?" he asked again, partially because he wasn't sure he'd heard her quite right, but mainly because he wanted her to have to say it again.

Despite the emotional tsunami her announcement had stirred, he couldn't say he was entirely opposed to her removing his clothes. Sure, she'd bruised his ego when she left without saying goodbye. But he had gone a long time without meeting anyone half as intriguing as she was, so he had no regrets. To pin his visceral reaction to her strictly to a lack of female companionship would be a lie. And Harrison made it a point not to lie to himself. Nor was he inclined to let her make a fool of him.

"Cooperate, please."

"Stop groping me," he ground out.

"Your face and clothes have been dusted with a suspect white powder," she said, speaking slowly and deliberately. Like he didn't have the brains to grasp his current situation. And she may have been justified in doing so. He wasn't having a hard time hearing her. Hell, he could hear his shirt tear when she stretched it farther and farther with the backs of her hands. He couldn't believe after all these weeks, she'd come into his house wanting to strip him naked, and it wasn't for recreational purposes.

"We need to get you out of these clothes and into the shower ASAP." She looked him dead in the eye. "Now, close your eyes and mouth, and do your best not to breathe in. I'm going to lift this over your head. We want to get it off without any more of the powder coming in contact with your skin if we can."

Comprehension finally overtook his bewilderment. He slammed his eyes shut, and she carefully lifted the shirt over his head. He stood stock-still, barely breathing and waiting for her next command.

"Okay," she murmured, and he wasn't sure if she was talking to him or to herself.

Cracking one eyelid, he peered at her through his lashes. "Okay what?"

"Shorts off," she said brusquely.

He opened his eyes to find her folding the shirt in on itself. Tucking his chin to his chest, Harry looked down and saw white streaks flowing down the front of his gym shorts. He hooked his thumbs into the waist-band and then cautiously pulled the elastic away from his body so he could lower them to the tops of his shoes without the fabric turning inside out.

Alicia nodded her approval and offered her arm to him. "Steady yourself and step out of them. Then toe out of your shoes. Try not to disturb the stuff on the floor any more than you have to."

Harry did as she instructed, leaving the shorts in the pool on the floor and his running shoes a step behind them. He stood clad only in his boxer briefs and a pair of no-show socks, but before he could start to feel self-conscious about his seminudity, he realized the woman collecting the clothing possibly covered in a toxic sub-stance also happened to be carrying his child.

Allegedly.

His gaze fell to the shirt she held clutched in one hand. "Hey, you need to drop the shirt," he told her.

Alicia looked up, lines of puzzlement bisecting her arched brows. "What? No. I have to preserve the scene if I can." She looked down at the sheets of paper scat-tered around them like debris from an explosion. "Step out of the area and head straight for the shower. Soap and water, nothing more," she ordered briskly. "Wash everything. Your hair, under your nails, everything. Lather, rinse, repeat. A few times if necessary. I'll call Ben Kinsella."

At the mention of the sheriff's name, Harry jolted. Reality came crashing into this bizarre daydream. He hadn't fully registered what was happening, but now he got it.

"You're pregnant," he murmured under his breath.

"We'll talk about it later. Right now, you need to go hit the shower."

He nodded dumbly. "Okay. Call Ben, but you need to put those things down and go wash up too. I mean it." Feeling better having gotten some of his own orders in, he slowly stepped out of the field of debris.

Alicia placed his folded shirt atop his shoes and stepped away. "I'll be fine. It didn't get any on me."

"You still breathed it in," he shot back. "And you touched my shirt. You should trash those gloves and wash your hands right away," he said with an emphatic nod. "There's a guest bath in the hallway. You go wash everything too."

"I'm fine."

"But you've been touching me," he pointed out. Harry gestured to the corridor leading to his bedroom at the end of the hall. "I'm going to the shower, but please at least go wash up." He jerked back, recalling the most salient point of the conversation they'd been having when the evening became even more surreal than he could possibly imagine.

"You're pregnant."

"Right." She nodded once, then looked down at her glove-covered hands. "I'll wash up, then call Ben. You get to the shower."

He did as he was told, because holy hell, what was it? Anthrax? Ricin? Rounding the corner into the master bath, Harry had to resist the urge to wet his now parched lips. He'd seen and heard enough about threats made on prosecutors. They weren't always empty. No matter how tempting it was, he couldn't risk it.

He didn't wait for the water to warm. He simply turned on the spray and stepped in, boxer briefs and all. He blindly washed his face three times before he dared to lick the shower's spray from his lips. Then he scrubbed his entire body from head to toe. Twice. On the third pass, he let his mind off the leash.

Alicia Simmons was in his living room. Alicia Simmons was pregnant. Alicia Simmons believed her baby was his. His baby.

But how?

The question was ludicrous on the surface, but it kept circling around in his brain. They hadn't gotten carried away in the back of a car like teenagers turned loose on a summer night. Okay, so they hadn't used a condom. Not the most responsible decision he'd ever made, but they'd talked. Frankly. Openly. Like adults. There had been informed consent. Both his and hers. A serious discussion about sexual health and birth control. She'd said she was on the pill. Tequila or not, he remembered one vital bit of information clearly. But there was only one truly foolproof form of birth control, and abstinence hadn't even seemed like an option at the time.

Switching off the water, Harry stood in his shower dazed and dripping. And somehow, he was still wearing his underwear. Scowling, he shucked off the soap-soaked briefs, turned the water back to full blast for a quick rinse, then twisted the knobs again. He shivered slightly when the water running from his shower head slowed to a rhythmic drip.

Placing both hands flat on the smooth tile, he hung his head and took three slow breaths to steady himself. White powder in an envelope. Slashed tires. Obscenities etched into his car doors with a key or other metal object. He shouldn't be shocked. These things happened when a person was prosecuting someone with a following. Heck, the vehicular vandalism wasn't a first for him. Of course, he hadn't been driving a new German-made sports sedan at the time. And his previously impugned Chevy had been considerably older than the tiny new model he'd driven home a scant four months ago. He hadn't cracked the spine on the owner's manual, and the new-car smell still lingered.

"She was only a baby," he murmured on a heavy sigh.

The last word lingered on his lips. Straightening his spine, he shook his wet hair back from his face. He opened the glass door wide enough to snare a towel from the bar and quickly wrapped it around his waist. Still dripping, he padded from the bathroom into his darkened bedroom. Light spilled down the hall. The low hum of hushed conversation drifted back to him.

Part of him wanted to rush out there. He needed to check on Alicia. Find out if they could tell exactly what the powdery substance was once the shock of it had worn off. But he needed clothes first.

After closing his bedroom door, he let the towel come loose as he strode to his closet. He ran the damp terry cloth over his head, then used it to dry himself from head to toe. Pulling a fresh pair of briefs from his dresser, he set to work putting his thoughts in order while he dressed.

These types of threats rarely involved actual toxins. Logically, he was aware it was likely a hoax. But there was always the chance. Besides, logic and statistics were standing firmly outside his circle of trust. He yanked a T-shirt from another drawer and shrugged into it. Sure, logic and statistical analysis might give him some comfort in regard to the contents of the package, but they failed when it came to calculating the probability of Alicia Simmons showing up at his house out of the blue to tell him he was about to become someone's daddy. Stepping into a pair of clean jeans, he hiked them over his hips and fastened them. He decided to forgo socks and shoes in favor of getting a few answers.

When he reached the end of the hall, he found Deputy Lori Cabrera crouched over the scattered papers and holding up the torn envelope with a pair of long tweezers. She wore gloves and a disposable respirator mask. So did Sheriff Ben Kinsella, who stood next to his deputy holding a plastic evidence bag open wide.

"Hey." He spoke the greeting softly, not wanting to startle them in the midst of their work.

Lori looked up, her big brown eyes warm and reassuring. "Pretty sure we have a cornstarch situation."

Her words were slightly muffled by the mask, but he read her loud and clear. They'd still have to get the substance tested, though, which was the real damage done. Not only was it costing the sheriff and his deputy their time, but the crime lab would have to analyze the powder, the envelope and all the contents for proper identification and clues as to who might have sent it.

"No postage," Lori reported. "Someone hand delivered these season's greetings."

Great. Whoever had done this had dropped their package of doom directly on his front doorstep. "Anything in the papers?" he asked, hopeful, but not expecting much.

To his surprise, Ben nodded. "Actually, yes."

He gestured to the pile, and Lori raised one of the sheets of paper. Someone had drawn a picture in pencil but carefully erased it. The lines were faint, though he could make out the crude rendering of a coiled snake with the words Don't Tread on Me printed beneath it.

"Oh, well, no points for subtlety," Harry said as he ran his hand over his face, suddenly drained.

"No," a husky voice agreed from behind him.

Harry jumped and turned to find Alicia standing in the kitchen area. There was dark amusement in her tone. In truth, her wry cynicism was what had drawn him to her two months before. Now it rankled. Someone had left an envelope addressed to him and filled with mysterious powder at his front door. Cornstarch or not, this was getting out of hand.

"Step back." Ben shooed Harry toward the kitchen, then opened more evidence bags. Lori steadily and methodically worked her way through the papers, bagging each one individually in hopes the lab might be able to lift a print or two. "So, we're assuming this is related to Samuel Coulter's case," the sheriff said gruffly. "Anything else happening? Any new developments?"

Biting the inside of his cheek, he cast a sidelong glance at Alicia. He wasn't too keen on the idea of spelling out all the mini-and macroaggressions he'd suffered since Samuel Coulter and some of his compatriots were brought up on charges of drug and human trafficking, but it wasn't like she wouldn't hear about it all eventually. This would be one topic of conversation among many, he figured.

He shrugged, trying to play it cool, but one of the threats had made it into his house. He felt shakier than he cared to admit. "The usual. Threatening calls. Callouts on social media. Some minor vandalism."

Ben's eyes narrowed. "I saw your car. They scrape it up here or at the office?"

Harry raised his brows, a sardonic smile tugging at the corner of his mouth. "You mean here or four blocks away from here?" Beside him, Alicia snickered softly. He was embarrassed to admit how much he liked hearing it. "It happened here."

Alicia pivoted then. "Someone damaged your car?"

"Punctured a couple tires one night, keyed the paint job another," he reported, his tone dispassionate. Turning his attention back to Ben, he said, "Those incidents both happened here."

"So, it's someone who has your home address," Alicia mused.

Harry couldn't contain his bark of laughter. The same amusement danced in Lori's eyes before she refocused on her task. Only Ben refrained from showing how entertaining the question might be to anyone accustomed to small-town life.

"Most everyone in town knows where he lives," Ben explained. Harry couldn't determine if the note of apology he detected in his friend's tone was because he was tuned in to how ridiculous life in a town like Pine Bluff could be, or because he was a onetime city dweller with an urbanite's casual assumption of anonymity. "This town is pretty small, and Harry is the sucker who gives the kids the big candy bars at Halloween."

He shrugged again. "Someone has to do it."

Beside him, Alicia hummed her disapproval. "I'm surprised you're not more careful. There's always a chance someone looking for some payback might search you out."

For the first time since he'd opened the door to find her standing on his welcome mat, it occurred to Harry she must have done the same—searched him out. After all, they hadn't come back to his place when they left Simon's party. No, they'd gone to the rental house she'd lived in for less than a month. But somehow, she had found him.

"How'd you get my address?"

"Why don't you park in your garage?" she asked simultaneously.

Time stood still for a second. Somewhere, in the back of his mind, he couldn't help thinking two people who were having a child together should have the answers to these types of questions. But they didn't. They were virtual strangers who'd come together high on victory and drunk on tequila.

"I, uh, I use the garage as a gym," he said at last.

"Ben gave up the goods on your address," she admitted, shooting her friend an apologetic glance. "But it's not his fault. I told him I wanted to send you a Christmas card."

"A Christmas card," he repeated blankly.

She smirked. "Seemed a good excuse."

Harry went on high alert the moment Ben Kinsella turned his flat cop stare on him. "I guess she decided to deliver your card in person, Harry."

"None of your business, boss," Lori murmured, scooping white powder into vials to be sent into the crime lab. Harry let out a gusty breath when Ben swung his glare toward his insubordinate deputy. But Lori returned it, unperturbed. "Unless you think our friendly DEA agent was the one to send our district attorney an envelope full of fake anthrax."

Alicia laughed, and Ben's stony expression softened. "No, I feel pretty confident Alicia sends her messages more directly."

"You've got that right," the woman in question replied, unfazed by the turn the conversation had taken. "I am here because I wanted to talk to Harry about some things."

Ben's cop face returned with a vengeance. "Things I need to be aware of?" he asked, his tone sharpening.

Alicia shook her head. "No. If they were, I would have come to you. This was information specifically for Mr. Hayes."

For one minute, Harry was afraid she might blurt out her reason for being there. Thankfully, Deputy Cabrera rescued him.

"There. I think we have enough."

Harry eyed the dusting of powder coating his living-room floor. "And you're sure it wasn't anything dangerous?"

"We're sure," the three answered in almost perfect unison.

They chuckled, and Harry was forced to crack a smile at last. "Okay, well, all right." He clapped his hands together. "I guess I should break out the old Shop-Vac."

Ben nodded, then pulled an individually wrapped mask and gloves from the kit Lori was repacking. "Here. To be on the safe side," he said, thrusting the personal protective equipment at Harry.

"And poof! My warm fuzzy feeling is gone," Harry grumbled.

Chapter Three

The moment Harry closed the door behind Ben and Lori, Alicia's nerves rushed to the surface of her skin. She stood in the kitchen doorway, feeling twitchy as a teenager on her first date. But she was way beyond her teenage awkwardness. She and Harry may not have ever had a first date, but they had a baby coming. And someone was threatening him.

God, what a night.

Harry stood in the foyer, his hands braced on his hips and his head bowed. His posture made him appear both thoughtful and vulnerable. A quality she recognized as one of the reasons she'd been so attracted to him to start. He was confident, but not cocksure. A potently powerful combination.

And his winning vulnerability made her ache to reassure him.

"Harry, I don't want to mess up your life," she said, injecting an abundance of sincerity into the sentiment. "I'm a grown woman. I have a good job, and I can take care of myself and this baby. I didn't come here expecting you to upend everything you've built for yourself because we got reckless one night."

"Reckless," he repeated softly.

"But you see, the odds of this baby ever happening were so microscopically slim…" She trailed off with a laugh. "I have a complicated medical history, and this might be my one and only chance. And while I think I'm ready to grab hold of it, I want you to understand I absolutely do not expect you to alter any of your plans for the present or future."

He lifted his head at last. "Then why come here to tell me?"

There was no accusation in the question. He asked purely out of curiosity. Unfortunately, she didn't have a truly satisfactory answer. She had no idea why it had seemed so important to tell him. She could've gone on with her life and he never would've been the wiser. But doing so felt dishonest. She didn't want to make her baby a secret. Treat her child as something to be ashamed of. And the last thing Alicia wanted was for this baby to come into a world doubting they were wanted whole-heartedly.

"Would you have rather I made it a secret?" she asked, needing reassurance she'd done the right thing. "I thought no, but maybe I was wrong. Was I wrong?"

His hands fell away from his hips, and he raised one to scrub his face and smooth his hair back into place. "No, you weren't wrong."

He stated his position with such clarity, she couldn't help but smile with relief. "Listen, this night has been, well, a lot," she said with a laugh. "Let's take some time and maybe talk again in a day or two?"

He eyed her carefully for a moment, then nodded. "Probably a good idea."

"I'll leave you all of my contact information," she offered. "You can use it or not. No hard feelings either way."

"No hard feelings," he echoed, his tone hushed with disbelief.

"I mean it. I meant it when I said I could handle this on my own. I can, and I will. Actually, going it alone was my intention all along. My coming here was more of a...courtesy." She stepped out of the kitchen and into the open-plan living area. The place was still an utter mess. "Would you like me to help you clean up?"

He shook his head. "I've got this."

Her mind played back the discussion he and Ben had about the damages done to his car. "Do you often get threats against you?"

He cocked his head and it was clear from his expression he considered her question slightly ridiculous. "I'm a prosecutor. People are seldom happy when I bring charges against them. Even more unhappy if I win. And even if they go to jail, those people often have family members who are happy to carry their unhappiness for them." He shrugged. "This is all part of the territory."

"But do they usually strike so close to home? Literally," she said, gesturing to the mess on the floor.

He didn't bother trying to deny it. Instead, he shook his head and cast a mournful gaze at his dust-covered floor. "No, not this close."

"Coulter has friends. He has some unsavory friends," she said pointedly.

"I'm aware."

"If this gets to be too much, if this escalates in any way, you need to ask for protection."

"Protection," he said with a soft snort. "If we were going to pick a word of the night, right?"

Alicia couldn't stifle her laugh. Gallows humor was often the refuge of law enforcement, and it appeared their counterparts on the judiciary side of things were no different. "In both cases, I think the horse is out of the barn, but you can take steps to protect yourself."

"I'll take your recommendation under advisement," he said dryly. Alicia watched him draw a deep breath in and then let it out slowly. At last, he took a step closer to her and looked her in the eye. "Are you planning to drive back to Atlanta tonight?"

She nodded. "I planned on it. Why?"

"I'm not sure." He rolled his shoulders back and torqued his head to the side to stretch his neck. "It's late," he said.

Alicia glanced down at the sports watch strapped to her wrist. "It's seven twenty-two."

"I mean, it's dark…and cold…" He trailed off. "You're traveling alone."

"I often do," she said briskly. "Again, I'm a grown woman. I can take care of myself. And if anyone tries to mess with me, I have a gun, remember?"

He reared back. "On you? I've never seen you carry."

"That's because I don't wave my gun around. It's either in a holster or in my bag. Tonight, it's in my bag," she said, lifting her brows and fixing him with a pointed stare. "Would you like to see my concealed carry permit?"

"No." He shook his head, then had the good grace to laugh at himself. "I never thought of you carrying a weapon. Every time I've seen you, you've been more on the command side of things, I guess. I thought you were a suit. Like me," he added with a winsome smile.

"I am," she said, amused. "But I'm also armed at all times. The suit helps cover the holster."

He chuckled and shook his head, running a hand over his mouth, a hint of color touching his cheeks and the tips of his ears. "I'm not sure if I should be terrified or turned on," he admitted.

"I recommend both," she answered without hesitation.

"Sorry, I didn't mean to imply you were any less of an agent because..." He shot her a look from under his lashes. "It never occurred to me."

"It's because I'm so feminine," she said with an edge of sarcasm.

His brow crinkled. He was working hard to determine if she were joking or not. "You are."

She snickered. "Don't fret, Counselor. I'm not going to shoot you."

He looked up into her eyes and his gaze never wavered. He studied her, searching for a clue as to whether he'd stuck his foot in some kind of a trap. "But you are. Feminine, I mean. From where I've stood, you always have been. Both strong and feminine," he said with a decisive nod.

Alicia was so disarmed by his mild stammering, she decided to let him off the hook easy. "Thank you. I am. I never could understand why some men think a woman can't own her sexuality as well as a SIG Sauer."

This time, he let out a full-blown laugh. Country raised, he couldn't help appreciating a woman who was more comfortable talking about handguns than handbags. "Okay, now you are definitely trying to turn me on," he accused.

Alicia felt her own cheeks warm with a flush of pleasure. On impulse, she reached for his hand and gave it a squeeze. She would not think about how good those hands had felt on her. She had more important matters to focus on now. A baby. Her baby.

"I'll go to the doctor to get things verified. The due date will be pretty easy to calculate, since there's no wondering about the date of conception…" She snapped her mouth shut and inhaled deeply through her nose. Once she felt more in control, she gave him a wan smile. "I should have more information by the end of the week."

Reaching into her bag, she pulled out one of the business cards she kept loose in an inside pocket. "I never got a chance to give you this before I left Pine Bluff, but here's all my contact info."

He scissored the proffered card between his fore and middle fingers but made no move to pull it from her grasp. "Would you have?"

His voice was rough. Gravelly with exhaustion and emotion. She recognized it from the long hours they'd spent working together to make sure he had every scrap of evidence he needed to bring Coulter in front of a judge and ask that the millionaire be held without bail because he was a flight risk. A federal prosecutor had been assigned to the case, but Alicia convinced him to take Harrison as his second chair. Since he'd been born and raised in Masters County, she'd thought Harry might hold more sway with a jury in rural Georgia. But then Coulter had thrown them all for a loop by waiving his right to trial by jury. Now Harry was a hanger-on in a case scheduled to be heard by a federal judge in another town, but receiving threats from the slimebags who lived in his own backwoods.

"I'd planned to, but then you got busy and I got busy and we never, uh…"

"Got busy again?" he supplied, taking the card from her at last.

She nodded. "Yeah." She hiked the strap of her bag up on her shoulder. "Then I got a call saying I was needed back in Atlanta, and, well, I guess it felt awkward," she confessed.

To her relief, he nodded. "I get you."

"But the card has all my numbers plus an email address." She indicated the card. "You don't have to use them if you don't want to." She raised both hands to ward him off. "If you want to be a part of this baby's life, I will do everything in my power to make it happen, but if you choose not to be, no judgment. The only thing I ask is you take some time to think it over before you decide."

He nodded, but she had to press on with the hard part before he got too agreeable.

"Harry, I need you to be certain. If you opt out, I will ask you to relinquish all rights. Not to be spiteful, but because I don't want to leave things open to chaos and confusion later. Do you understand where I'm coming from?"

"Yeah," he croaked.

"Take your time, okay?" She smiled and gave her still-flat stomach a pat. "It's a big decision, but we have time to figure it all out."

"Right." He cleared his throat, then nodded more emphatically, dragging his gaze from her hand. "Definitely. Yes. Not something to make rash decisions about, for sure."

They stood there, eyeing each other, waiting for the other to make the first move. Never one to shy away from diving in, Alicia gave him a quick nod, let her hand fall away from her belly, then stepped toward the door.

"Wait," Harry blurted, reaching out to take hold of her arm.

Alicia instinctively looked down at his hand before lifting her gaze to his. The moment their eyes met, he released his hold. "Yes?" she asked, tamping down the flicker of hope flaring where their baby nestled in her womb.

"Have you eaten?"

The question was so far from her train of thought it might have parachuted in from a plane. "What?"

"Dinner. Have you eaten?" he asked again, his tone slightly more persistent.

She shook her head. "No, I haven't, but I'm not sure I will," she said with a grimace.

"You need to eat," he insisted. "Because you're pregnant."

She gave a soft laugh, tipping her head to the side as if conceding his point, then shaking it firmly. "This isn't a good time for me."

"Not a good time? Are you in a hurry or something?" he asked, a note of irritability creeping into his tone. "Anxious to drop your bombs and fly off into the rising sun or something?"

"Rising sun?"

"Tactical maneuver. Blinds people trying to take you out with antiaircraft fire," he said with a shrug.

"Are you former air force or something?"

"Or something," he replied. When she let the silence stretch, he huffed out a breath. "I like war movies, video games and stuff," he said with a dismissive wave of his hand.

"Ah," she breathed. "A nerd."

He narrowed his eyes. "I appreciate a strategic assault. Like to employ them too."

"Do you now?"

"Some people use weapons—I use words." He crossed his arms over his chest. "Coulter and his new attorneys think a bench trial will get a good chunk of the evidence against him thrown out on technicalities. They're banking on not needing to appeal to a jury. They want to slip through loopholes in the letters of the law."

"Do you think he can?"

Harry exhaled long and loud, turning away. "Maybe. He'll wriggle out of at least some of them. Like you're trying to wriggle out of sitting down to eat a meal with me."

"I'm not..." She started and stopped, not sure why she was trying to play it coy all of a sudden when she'd come through this man's front door with a proverbial battering ram. "I, uh... Morning sickness is a misnomer," she finally said.

"Excuse me?"

"I don't get sick in the morning. Or as sick, I should say. It's morning, noon and night sickness for me, but it seems to hit me harder at night," she explained, lifting her chin a notch, practically daring him to tell her she and her body were being ridiculous with their refusal to follow the rules.

His face went blank for a second. Then realization dawned. "Oh."

"So, yeah, I've mostly been eating crackers at night. I thought it was a stomach bug at first, but then the smell of soup set me off. A colleague's wife was the same way. I remembered her, and it made me think maybe..." She gave him a shaky smile.

"I can make something easy, like some plain pasta," he offered.

"You're sweet, but I think we both may need those couple days," she said gently. "This is new for me too, and though I am sure I want this baby, I haven't had much time to process it."

Again, he scraped a hand over his face. "You're not going to…disappear again, right?"

"I gave you all my contact information," she reminded him.

"Calls can go unanswered, and emails can be trashed. And something tells me I'm not going to be able to score your home address by saying I want to send a Christmas card."

Her smile widened. "I think I've already blown my chance at remaining a woman of mystery. Plus, I came here to tell you, didn't I?"

"Promise you're not dropping this bomb and heading for the horizon," he persisted. "This whole night has been beyond wild. I need you to give me your word we will talk again."

Alicia sobered in an instant. "I give you my word."

He nodded in concession. "Can I give you anything for the drive back? Water? I don't have any fancy crackers, but I think I have some saltines. You did say you can eat crackers, right?"

"Right. And yes. A bottle of water and some saltines would be great," she said, sensing it would give him comfort and provide her with something to settle her rebellious stomach.

Harry nodded. "Be right back."

She moved toward the door, her hand hooked around the strap of her bag, but her gaze strayed to the streaks of powder trailing into the hall. Guilt twinged in her gut. If she hadn't picked the stupid envelope up and brought it inside, some richly deserving porch pirate might have swiped it and gotten a poof in the face and an hour of panic for their perfidy.

"You're sure you don't want help cleaning up?" she called toward the back of the house.

"No, I'm good." Harry reappeared, a plastic grocery sack dangling from his fingers. "I had some electrolyte water. It might help. I threw it in with a couple bottles of regular water. And the crackers, of course."

Alicia accepted the offering, a smile tugging at the corners of her mouth when she spotted an entire box of saltines nestled in with three large bottles of water. "It's only a little over three hours' drive." She let the grin grow. His hazel gaze was sincere. "If I drink all this, it'll be over four hours with stops."

Harry rolled his eyes. "Sip, don't guzzle."

He moved past her to open the front door. She stood there a moment, taking in the sight of his handsome face bathed in the warm light. The night beyond him was dark and still. The breeze had died down, but the air was now crisp and cool. Beyond his front porch, the citizens of Pine Bluff were all nestled in for a long winter's evening of television and other indoor activities.

She was about to say something insane about what a pretty street he lived on when she heard a sharp crack and saw a puff of brick and mortar explode beside his head. Alicia dropped the bag and grabbed the front of his jeans—the first handhold she could get on him—and yanked him down to the floor.

Rolling her body on top of his, she flailed a foot out to kick the door closed. The heavy oak swung shut on well-oiled hinges. The moment of breathless suspension was shattered by the crack of another shot. Through the glass pane set in the top of the door, they watched as Harrison's porch light exploded in a shower of sparks.

Chapter Four

Gunfire. Someone was shooting at his house. They were under fire. And he was under Alicia.

Alicia Simmons was covering his body with hers while one of the unhinged hillbillies he'd dealt with his entire life took potshots at his house. Again.

Alicia thought she was saving him. She thought she was saving him by dragging him down to the floor and covering his body with hers. Her much smaller body. Her pregnant body.

The second the thought popped into his head, his body reacted. Hooking his leg over both of hers, he wrapped his arms tight around her and rolled until their positions were reversed.

"What are you doing?" she asked, breathless.

"What do you think you're doing?" he panted back.

"There's someone shooting at the house."

No sooner were the words out of her mouth than a rain of pellets sprayed the house and the narrow pane of glass beside his front door splintered into a spider-web of cracks.

"What the hell?" Alicia huffed, straining to look toward the door. "Get off me."

"No." He backed his refusal with action. Digging his

bare toes into the floor, he slid them about three feet away from the door.

"Damn it, Harry, someone is shooting at your house."

Beneath him, she wriggled and squirmed, and at one point balled up her fist and struck his shoulder. He shook his head, and she retracted her arm again. Thankfully, she telegraphed her punch by staring too hard at his jaw. He ducked his head at the last second and her knuckles glanced off the side of his skull.

"Ow! Damn it, Harry, let me up."

"Not on your life," he muttered.

His foot brushed something solid, and he looked back to see it was her purse. Flexing his foot, he caught the bulk of the bag and scooted it toward his outstretched hand. He could feel her body coil and tensed for another blow. "Hang on a sec," he ordered. "I have your purse."

"Good," she huffed. "I need my gun."

Harrison felt his eyebrows shoot up, but as he groped around in the soft leather bag, he hoped he didn't grab hold of a firearm. The moron spraying the front of his house with birdshot wasn't looking for a firefight. They only wanted to get his attention. A gun was the last thing they needed, but he didn't trust himself not to fire back if the weapon fell into his hand.

He stilled for a moment, listening closely. No more shots fired. Whoever it was had probably run for the woods. Probably feeling triumphant. After all, they'd taken out a perfectly good porch light and a whole window. He was shaking with rage when, thankfully, his hand closed around her cell phone.

"Here," he said, shoving the instrument into her flailing hand. "Call Ben. Tell him someone is using the house for target practice again."

"Again?"

He looked down to find her staring up at him, her eyes wide with alarm. Nodding, he said, "I'm guessing buckshot this time. Someone used birdshot before, and it didn't do much more than mess up the paint on the porch."

To his relief, he saw her thumbing the screen. "Does this happen often?"

He heard the quaver in her voice, and something in him unraveled. "No, not often," he assured her. "It's just...there's been some trouble. I won another motion today. It's not unusual for tensions to escalate as we get closer to opening arguments. People don't need much of an excuse to get riled these days, and Coulter has kicked over more than a few dead logs around here."

"You weigh a ton. Get off me," she complained, but then Ben must have picked up because she jerked her attention to the call. "No. Uh, not you, Ben. Listen, someone is shooting at Hayes's house." She listened for a moment, her face slackening in incredulity before she rolled her eyes. "Yes, again. He says to tell you it looks like buckshot this time, but I'm pretty sure something higher caliber took out the porch light," she said, sliding a pointed glare at Harry. "The first two shots were rifle fire."

He pressed up on his hands, relieving her of some of his weight, but not enough for her to slip out from under him and start running down the street with her gun in hand. To make her feel better, he conceded her point with a nod. "Could have been more than one of them. These guys rarely fly solo on missions."

Alicia's forehead puckered as she listened to Ben issuing opinions and instructions. "Okay. Yeah. Okay, I'll

stick." She ended the call and met Harry's eyes again.
"He said you're probably right—he's going to cruise out
to somebody called Arnie Smithson's place, and I'm to
hang here until he calls back."

"Good idea." Pressing into a full push-up, Harry
lifted a hand and flipped over off her. Alicia immediately scuttled into a sitting position, but he had trapped
her handbag behind him against the foyer wall. "No need
for the gun," he informed her, his voice calmer than he
felt in his gut.

She glowered at him as she crossed her legs like a kin-
dergartner and pushed her hair away from her face. "I am
a trained law enforcement officer," she reminded him.

"I'm aware. You also just told me you're pregnant,"
he retorted a shade too sharply.

"It's not a disability. I can still do my job," she shot
back.

He raised both hands in surrender. "I'm only saying
you might try to remember the change in status the next
time you throw someone to the floor and cover them
with your own body."

Her cheeks flushed a pretty pink, but Harry refused
to be drawn in by it. At least, he did his best not to. Lord,
she looked beautiful with the color riding high on her
cheekbones and her eyes gleaming with determination.

"I could always use the whole 'My body, my decision' argument."

He narrowed his eyes. "It was your decision to come
here and make sure I was aware of what was happening with your body."

"But I didn't give you a say," she countered.

He leveled his most stern "speaking directly to one
juror" stare on her. "I'm asking you, please do not do

anything to place you or your baby in harm's way on my behalf."

She seemed to sag, the fight seeping out of her bones. For the first time since she'd stepped through the door, he noticed how tired she looked. Dark smudges under her eyes. Her skin pasty under all her bluster. The starch in her spine softened and all traces of defensiveness disappeared. Maybe because he referred to the child she was carrying in the singular possessive? He wasn't sure. As long as it kept her from charging out his front door and into the night, he didn't care.

"There are some groups of people who go looking for trouble," he said quietly. "They're loosely organized gangs of thugs, but Ben refers to them as militia. Coulter made friends with a couple of them, and now they feel the need to take up the fight for him."

"Oh."

The single syllable slipped out of her on a whisper, but it spoke volumes in understanding. He nodded, confirming every scenario he feared might be running through her head. Ben had clued in to the big picture fast enough when things started getting personal in the past few weeks. But the fact that the envelope had been dropped on his doorstep on the same night someone else decided to do some target shooting disturbed him.

The thugs Arnie Smithson ran with were not the brightest bulbs, but they were savvy enough to spread their mischief out over a stretch of time. Make it last. Rotate perpetrators so no single person could be brought in on multiple charges. Harry and Ben understood what many city slickers failed to grasp. The people they were dealing with might be uneducated and uncouth, but they were far from stupid.

"Ben is a good cop. We need to sit tight and let him do his job."

Not surprisingly, Alicia reached into her bag again and came up with her gun and a slim leather ID case. "It's my job too," she said, lifting a challenging eyebrow.

He wasn't entirely certain if he wanted to hug her or shake her. Instead, he stared her down, though it took almost every ounce of energy he had not to reach for her.

"Listen, Dirty Harriett, unless you spotted someone doing a deal on my front doorstep, you have no jurisdiction here." He extended the first two fingers of his right hand and pushed the barrel of her firearm to the side. "I have more right to discharge a weapon on these premises than you do."

To his relief, the corner of her mouth lifted in a smirk. "Dirty Harriett? You need to get some movie references from this century... Harry."

Her pointed emphasis of his name made him smile in return. "You understood the reference," he retorted.

To his relief, Alicia shoved her weapon and credentials back into her bag. "Do you keep a .44 Magnum handy, in case some punk feels lucky?"

"No, but I have my granddad's old .22 for when I want to put the fear of God into a few squirrels."

"You hunt squirrels?" she asked, wrinkling her nose. "I thought you said you didn't like hunting."

He found the girlish reaction oddly enchanting. She was such a straightforward, capable woman. It was funny to think of her getting grossed out by anything. "I haven't since my granddad passed, but I think I can manage to defend the homestead if the need arises."

"How do you defend against stuff like this?" she

asked, her voice rising with exasperation as she gestured toward the front porch.

"By putting bad guys behind bars," he replied without missing a beat. At her skeptical snort, he shrugged. "Those yahoos are simply looking for something to get riled about. The Coulter case—and me by extension—is their flavor of the week. Don't worry. They're bound to latch on to whatever is the latest conspiracy theory coming out of news talk radio, and by next week they'll have forgotten all about me."

"The blessings of the twenty-four-hour news cycle," she said dryly. "I don't see how you can stand it."

"Stand what?"

"Living out here with all these rebels," she said derisively.

"You forget—I am one of these people." He crossed his arms over his chest.

She snorted. "Hardly."

"I went to school with Andy Smithson, Arnie's younger brother. I was born here. These people have been my neighbors my whole life."

Alicia exhaled long and loud, but her gaze never wavered. "Hard to believe. Anyhow, yes, Counselor, unless I'm in a bathing suit, you can believe I'm carrying. Even then, I probably have a gun in my beach bag."

He shrugged, then nodded to her purse. "I'm afraid to ask what else you have in there."

Her hair swung forward, partially shielding her face as she opened the purse wide for his perusal, then rummaged around in its cavernous depths. "Nothing unusual. Lipstick tubes, a Glock, a compact, my wallet, zip-tie cuffs, phone charger, granola bar, cond…" Her voice trailed away, and the last syllable hung there unspoken.

A beat passed. Then he ran his hand through his hair with a harsh choke of laughter. "Sure, now you have protection."

"I bought them at the pharmacy downtown, uh, the morning after," she said quietly. "I didn't want to get caught without again."

He swallowed hard, a thousand unanswered questions bubbling up inside him, fighting to burst out. But he kept the lid clamped tightly. He swooped down and snagged the handles of the plastic bag he'd given her mere minutes before. Gesturing to the kitchen, he said, "Come back in and sit down. It's going to be a bit until Ben sounds the all clear, and we need to talk."

Seated at his kitchen table with bottles of water and a package of saltines open in front of Alicia, he asked the one question swirling in his mind. "How do you think this happened? And not the technical stuff. I mean, we discussed birth control…"

She nibbled a bit of cracker but didn't drop his gaze. "I cut my finger slicing lemons. I didn't think much about it, but a couple days later I noticed it was red and tender. I had an infection, so the doctor gave me antibiotics. I was taking them when I came down here."

Her pointed stare told him she thought she'd imparted sufficient explanation, but for the life of him, Harry was having a hard time connecting the dots. Tired of trying to figure things out, he made a motion for her to continue.

"Antibiotics can sometimes impact the efficacy of birth control pills," she explained, her delivery flat. "It's usually recommended people use some form of backup contraceptive—"

"Like a condom," he interjected.

She inclined her head. "Like a condom," she conceded, "if they plan to have intercourse."

"I see."

"I didn't plan to have intercourse, nor was I overly worried about the birth control failing because I have a condition... It makes my chances of conception lower than average," she said, opening her hands in a helpless motion.

"You mentioned something about a complicated medical background," he prompted. "What condition?"

"Yes, well..." She paused. "It's called polycystic ovarian syndrome, but it's kind of a moot point now, isn't it? I'm pregnant, so what I thought couldn't happen, or at least wouldn't happen easily, has actually, uh, occurred."

She ducked her head for the first time, and all of a sudden, Harry was struck by how much it must have cost her to come here and tell him this news. She could have kept her secret, and he would never have been the wiser. Would being oblivious have been better or worse? He wasn't sure.

"I swear I would never have done something like this intentionally. I mean, you remember the whole discussion we had about consent, right?"

Remember it? He still chuckled each time he thought about it. She'd been the initiator. At first. But the minute he'd caught up with her seduction and thrown himself into the action, she'd pulled back. She'd pulled back and spelled out what was about to happen between them in no uncertain terms. Then, unsatisfied with his eager nodding, she'd demanded verbal assent. They'd gone through the same routine again when they realized they didn't have a condom close at hand, with the addition of a curt briefing on medical and sexual history.

As though she could read his thoughts, Alicia spoke. "It was an accident, Harry. It sounds lame, but it's the truth." She reached across the table and gave his hand a squeeze. "It's a shock. I get it. Truthfully, it is for me too, but it's a happy accident for me. It may not be for you, and I understand." She closed her eyes as if mustering the strength to speak words she wasn't entirely certain she could. "In truth, happy or not, my head is in a whirl. I have no idea what I'm going to do." She gave him a wry smile. "I only want you to believe me when I say I have no intention of trying to derail your life. You may want nothing to do with this child once it's born, and no matter what, I will respect your choices."

"How could you think I'd want nothing to do with my own child?" The words were out of his mouth before he'd even had time to process them. And since he'd always been a man to go with his gut reaction, Harry didn't quibble with himself. "Wait. No. I retract the question. Of course, you couldn't know how I would react. I wouldn't have guessed how I'd react," he said with a laugh.

"We don't know each other well at all." She gave his hand another squeeze and he looked down at their clasped fingers. "Except in the biblical sense."

He chuckled at her blunt assessment, then shook his head. "I wish I'd reacted better."

"I think we could both use some time to let this… unexpected turn of events settle." She gave him a shaky smile. "Probably not gonna happen tonight, though, right? We need time to be practical…think rationally about all aspects of what this can mean for both of us. And tonight isn't turning out to be a night for calm consideration."

This time, his laugh came easier. Pinching his temples, he rubbed his forehead. "It's been a doozy." Turning his hand over, he gave her fingers a warm squeeze in return. "Can we agree to table any further discussion until we've both had the opportunity to think things through?"

"Absolutely."

Alicia gently slipped her hand from his. Harry felt the loss of her warmth immediately. He lowered his hand to his lap and clenched it into a loose fist to keep from reaching for her again. "Would you consider spending the night? I mean, I have a guest room…"

"Oh, I'm not sure."

He understood her hesitation. She obviously hadn't come prepared to spend the night in Pine Bluff, but a small irrational part of him wanted to make sure she never opened his front door again. People using his house for target practice aside, the thought of watching her walk out the door and her driving back to Atlanta made him uneasy. Not because he didn't think she was fully capable of making it home safely. He had too much confidence in her capabilities.

She'd done what she thought was the right thing by telling him about her condition. But now he had been informed, and she could decide to go back to Atlanta and her life there without giving him a chance to determine how he might fit into her new reality.

"Stay tonight," he said gruffly. "I'll pull out a frozen pizza, and you can have the crackers, and we can spend some time getting better acquainted—in a non-biblical way, I mean."

Alicia eyed him with wary skepticism. "Thank you for the offer," she began. "But I'm not sure it's a good idea."

An odd sensation slithered through him, leaving him

feeling inexplicably bereft. Unsure what else to do, he stepped back and lobbed a Hail Mary of an attempt at keeping her there. "Are you really going to leave me here all by myself with a bunch of crazies shooting at my house?"

Her eyebrows rose. "Are you really asking me to stay the night in the house under siege? You think it's better I stay here and risk being taken out by someone who thinks your house is a shooting arcade?"

Harrison couldn't help but laugh. When viewed from her position, his request sounded even more unreasonable. He understood. He was a man who weighed his options, calculated the odds and angled for the best possible outcome. All he could hope for here and now was to keep appealing to the same sense of ethics that brought her to his door. "Safety in numbers?"

"Speaking of safety," she said, then pressed her lips together as if she was fighting the urge to go on.

"Yes?"

"Have you considered taking a step back from the Coulter case?" She asked the question in such a rush, the words almost piled up on each other.

"No."

"I mean, it's not like you're the lead on it," she persisted. "But since you do live here locally, it's obviously more of a risk to you."

"Do you plan to?"

She blinked in surprise. "Do I plan to what?"

"You're slated to testify. You are the DEA's main witness. Tell me, do you plan to take a step back?"

The question wasn't exactly fair, but he couldn't help asking, if only to make his point. Clearly, she'd never considered walking away from the case. And if it weren't for the news she'd given him earlier, he never would have asked. But now...

"You're pregnant."

She sat up straighter. Harry could practically see her hackles rising. "So?"

He rolled his eyes at the lame comeback. "So, you're not only putting yourself in harm's way."

Her mouth tightened, but she didn't look away. If anything, her intense gaze burned brighter, likely fueled by the perceived challenge to her autonomy. Heaving a sigh, Harry dropped his voice and did his best to de-escalate the discussion. "Okay, not entirely fair, but there's more at stake today than there was even yesterday. I'd like us to be able to talk about this."

"I will testify at the trial. Nothing is going to change my mind," she retorted. "This is my case. Has been from the start."

"And I have been waiting for the chance to go after Coulter since the man moved to town," he replied, keeping his tone even. "But I'll back down if you will."

The offer made her flinch. "Are you saying you'd walk away from this case if I did?"

"It's not only about you or me anymore, is it?" he challenged.

"We're getting way ahead of ourselves," she said, waving his arguments off with wide swoops of her hands.

"We are," he agreed.

"I'll go back to Atlanta and set up an appointment to confirm everything. I'm going to need—" her voice tangled, but she pressed two fingers to her throat and carried on "—I'm going to figure out how I'll be handling things on my end. In the meantime, maybe we should refrain from making any hasty decisions."

"I think taking some time is a great idea." He fixed his gaze on her and held steady. "Promise me one thing."

"Okay," she agreed cautiously. "What?"

"Promise me you won't go back to Atlanta and never speak to me again," he said, his voice hoarse with churning uncertainty. "Promise me you're not going to drop this bombshell on my life and then disappear. If this is what's happening, I need to be…" He paused, searching for the correct word. "I need to be informed. I need to be able to make informed decisions, and I need you to respect me enough to let me be a part of those decisions."

"Harry," she said, staring straight into his eyes. "I came here."

"Right." He swallowed hard, then nodded as if by doing so he might convince himself. "Right."

Her phone lit up with an incoming call. Harry didn't need to check the display. It would be Ben on the line.

He listened with only half an ear as she took the call, speaking to the sheriff with the same economy of words cops seemed to pride themselves on. She ended the call, and Harry let his gaze follow as she rose from her seat.

"Ben's on his way back to take our statements. He said to tell you Arnie was home when he went by, and his wife… Annelle, is it?" she asked. When he nodded, she continued. "His wife and kids all swear he's been there all night. This Arnie guy also says he has no idea who might have shot up your house."

"Right. Of course he doesn't."

"Harry?"

"Yeah?"

"Would you mind if I took you up on the offer of your

guest room? If we're going to do another round of statements, I'm not sure I'm going to be clearheaded enough to drive home after."

"I don't mind at all, as long as you don't mind if I go ahead with the pizza."

"Ugh, pizza." Alicia pushed the package of saltines aside and bolted from her chair.

When he heard the door to the guest bath close behind her, Harry winced. "So it's a no on the pizza." He got up, snagged a jar of peanut butter from a cabinet and a knife from a drawer, and sat back down with the abandoned sleeve of saltines.

Chapter Five

"Thirty-eight?" Alicia repeated into the phone.

"According to the Southern Poverty Law Center's map as of last year," Ben Kinsella responded.

Alicia decided there was no better way to pass the early-morning drive from Pine Bluff to Atlanta than to pick the sheriff's brain about the rabble-rousers who inhabited Masters County.

"Of course, those are only the hate groups organized enough to be recognized," he continued.

"Right," she drawled.

"You can't be too surprised," he prodded. "The political climate around here is a tinderbox. People seem to be looking for a reason to be angry these days."

The truly sad part was, she was surprised, even though she shouldn't have been. Alicia was glad he couldn't see her slack-jawed expression through the phone. She made every effort she could to check her privileged status, but there were times when the truth about the world they lived in jumped up and slapped her. There were thirty-eight known, organized hate groups in the state of Georgia alone. Groups so active in promoting their particular brand of radicalized thinking they were kept on a watch list. They had no idea how many independent-minded vigilantes were hiding deep in the pine woods.

"You think some of them have adopted Coulter as their poster boy?" she asked.

"Oh, they have. Subtlety isn't exactly their strong suit," Ben said with a mirthless chuckle. "Speaking of subtlety... Christmas card? Really? I can't believe Marlee fell for such a lame ploy."

She snickered, flexing her fingers on the steering wheel. "Marlee didn't fall for anything. I promise you she knew I was trying to get in touch with Harry."

"Why? Does it have something to do with the Coulter case?"

Alicia took a deep breath in, then let it out slowly. She wasn't a fan of other people digging into her business, but if there was anyone in Pine Bluff she trusted, it was Ben Kinsella. They'd trained together when they first started with the DEA. And later, she'd been equally impressed and outraged on his behalf when the agency hung him out to dry. Ben had been forced to give up both his career and his life in Atlanta when he got crossways with one of the most influential gang leaders in the state, but he'd landed on his feet. Now she was staring down the possibility of needing to start from scratch, and not sure she'd handle it as gracefully.

"No. Um... Let's say there's some unresolved personal business between Harrison Hayes and me and leave it at that," she said cagily.

Ben let out a bull-like snort. "I may not have twigged to the Christmas-card thing, but I figured the rest out on my own."

"Yeah, well, I don't think it's the right time or place

for me to give you the details, so let's file this under It's Complicated."

"Okay," Ben said cautiously. "But you're all right, correct?"

"Other than exposure to a fake toxin and someone mistaking me for a buck in season?" she asked tartly.

"Yeah, other than those things."

"I am." She let her head fall back against the headrest as she scanned the miles of empty state highway ahead of her. "I'm actually more than okay. I think."

"As clear as mud," Ben grumbled. "But I guess you'll tell me what's going on in your own time."

"I will." She drummed her fingers on the steering wheel and then sat up straighter in her seat. "I'm heading into the office in Atlanta this afternoon, but I expect I may be spending some more time in Pine Bluff as we get closer to the trial."

"Oh? I would have figured you'd moved on to another case by now," Ben said, a note of concern creeping into his voice.

"Yeah, well, Bronson has me working on a number of cases," she said, hoping the frustration she'd been feeling for the past couple of months didn't ring through in her tone.

"How are things with the new section chief?"

Alicia avoided pressing any harder on the accelerator as she felt the tension creep from her shoulders up to her neck. Funny, in the past twelve hours she'd been shot at, tackled a guy, been flipped and pinned down and thoroughly dusted in what they all hoped was nothing more than cornstarch, but she hadn't felt this kind of searing tension the mere thought of her new boss conjured. It still galled her Andrew Bronson had snagged the section-chief job. It should have been hers, and they both knew it. Ticked her off even more he had the power to assign her to tasks that were essentially a waste of her time and talents. Heaven forbid she might show him up.

"About as you'd expect," she said briefly.

Ben knew better than anyone how bad things might end up being for her. The agency had used him up and tossed him aside once his cover was blown. Alicia had no illusions about her own position. There were people gunning for her. Had been since she'd been promoted ahead of most of the guys she came up with. Andrew Bronson was more than old-school. He was almost a throwback to another era. The era where men did not welcome women into their ranks.

And he had her sighted in his crosshairs.

"Don't worry about me," she said to Ben. "He's not the first jerk boss I've ever had. He won't be the last."

"If he doesn't value his best agent, then he's an idiot," Ben grumbled.

Alicia smiled. Her personnel file had to gall Bronson. She had more commendations and better performance reviews than any of the male agents in his section. Every day, he found some sneaky way to make it clear he didn't like women on the job. More than once he'd alluded to the supposed emotional instability of females. Of course, he'd always been talking about the women caught up on the other side of their cases. In an odd way, Alicia couldn't help thinking Bronson liked women best when they were pawns or unwitting witnesses. He saw most women as nothing more than tools used to bring big men down. It certainly irked him to believe a mere woman might be able to see through him, much less outmaneuver him.

Six months ago, she wouldn't have worried over her job for one minute, but now… Now her present situation felt more precarious. Once he found out she was pregnant, it would be open season on her career. As much as she hated what was happening to Harrison Hayes and his Podunk town, Alicia couldn't help but see the threats being made against him as an opportunity for her to step out of Bronson's line of sight long enough to figure out her next move.

"I'm going to gather more in-depth information on what you've given me and put it together with what we have on file for Coulter. The last thing Bronson wants is for such a high-profile collar to slither out from under these charges, so I'm going to see if I can make a case for staying in Pine Bluff for a few weeks."

"I see." Ben spoke the words quietly and with almost no inflection, but she knew he understood what she was saying.

Alicia had been one of the few agents to reach out to Ben after the agency turned its back on him. She needn't spell out her situation for him. If she was willing to duck out of the Atlanta office and all of the plum assignments she could be snagging, Ben would twig to the notion everything wasn't as peachy as she'd like it to be.

She gripped the wheel tighter and shrugged, even though Ben couldn't see her attempt at bravado. "Maybe Bronson will be happy to have me out of sight and mind for a while."

"I can ask Marlee to see if the house we set you up in last time is still available," he offered.

Alicia's memory flashed on the pretty brass bed tucked under the eaves of the bungalow she'd invited Harrison Hayes to one cool autumn night, and a prickle of perspiration tickled her hairline. She swiped the back of her hand across her forehead.

"Thank you, but I think I'm gonna stick closer to Hayes if I can," she replied, trying to keep her tone light and casual, but all too aware he could see through her casual tone.

"Exactly how close are you planning to stick?" Ben pressed.

"His guest room is pretty comfortable. Nice plush pillow-top mattress," she said with a small smile. "The rest of the decor is a bit austere. More a monk's cell than a guest room, but I guess one can't expect much more from a confirmed bachelor."

"You plan on staying at Hayes's house?"

The disbelief in his voice gave her a moment to pause, but she'd lain awake half the night thinking this plan through. She could move in. She would be able to keep a closer eye on Harry, plus it would give them the opportunity to talk through what needed to come next for them. She could help keep him safe and acquire a legitimized hole for her to hide out in until she figured out exactly how to approach her career conundrum.

"Is Harry in on this, or did you make a unilateral decision to move into his place?" Ben's question jolted her from her thoughts.

"He isn't on board yet, but I don't think he's going to object too strenuously," she said with a confidence she didn't quite feel. "Anyway, I can't do anything until I get back to the office to assess our situation, add these notes to the file and run it past Bronson."

"You'll keep me updated?" the sheriff asked.

"Ten-four," she replied succinctly.

"Be safe, Alicia. Don't worry about things here. We're

keeping a close eye on Harry. I truly believe most of what's happening is meant to scare him more than harm him."

"It scared me, and this is not the first time I've been under direct fire," she reminded him. "You guys may believe this is nothing but a bunch of the hayseeds blowing off steam, but I'm looking at it as something more serious. Hopefully, between the two of us, we'll get it right."

"Call me after you talk to Bronson. If we need to, I can have Marlee apply some pressure to have agency representation here. We can also get Representative Wingate to weigh in if we need to."

Ben's girlfriend, Marlee Masters, ran Timber Masters, the county's largest employer. She was a powerful woman with a lot of pull. Pull Ben had no trouble taking advantage of when it served the greater good.

"Keep your big guns holstered for now, Sheriff. I'll send up a flare if I can't handle the chief myself," she promised. Alicia ended the call and blew out a long breath. If she wasn't misreading him, she'd bet anything Bronson would be as happy to get rid of her for a while as she would be to get lost.

SHE WAS WRONG in her assessment. For a split second, Andrew Bronson looked to be ecstatic at the prospect of having her out from under his feet for a while. Then he remembered if he said yes, he'd be giving her what she wanted, and shut her down.

"You are working on a number of crucial cases for us," he said officiously.

Alicia wanted to sneer. He had her sifting through raw video footage and unedited audio collected from undercover operatives in hopes of unearthing nuggets of gold. A task which would keep her tied to her desk and mired in the minutiae of a handful of cases, rather than letting her sink her teeth into one.

Her former chief was Bronson's polar opposite. Waterson appreciated her doggedness, but also allowed her to run with her gut instincts. When she'd made the connection between some of the jailhouse ramblings of deceased Atlanta drug kingpin Ivan Jones and indications that heroin was moving through the rural parts of the state using the loose network of locals, she'd started poking around to see if she could locate the source of distribution. And there he was: Samuel "Cottonmouth" Coulter. Eccentric millionaire, friend to some of South Florida's most elusive importers, exotic snake collector and general bad guy.

She'd led the charge down into Masters County. She'd collected the evidence against him, following every single breadcrumb Coulter had dropped since he moved from Miami to Jacksonville and then finally into Georgia. She was the one who made this happen. She didn't need some jackass coming in at the eleventh hour telling her she couldn't do her part to keep the prosecutorial team safe.

"Understood," she said, keeping her response to a minimum so she wouldn't risk mouthing off. "But, Chief, I'm still connected in the area. I have contacts who will set me up. I can keep a low profile, mostly undercover. I want to do whatever I can to help the local authorities apprehend these troublemakers before things can get too serious."

"Don't they have law enforcement there?" He raised his eyebrows in challenge. "I thought I heard your old friend Ben Kinsella had landed down there? He's county sheriff now, isn't he?"

Alicia heard the derision in the man's tone but refused to be baited. "Yes, Ben is about to be elected to a full term and seems happy in Pine Bluff," she replied, as if responding to a polite inquiry.

"Well, then, I'm sure someone as…capable as your friend Ben can keep a lid on things."

Unwilling to be dismissed so easily, she pressed on. "I looked into a few of the groups operating in the area and some have crossed paths with us on previous occasions. If the brass need justification beyond keeping the people working Coulter's case safe, we can tell them I'm looking into deeper connections between some of the militia groups in the distribution network."

"We are already looking at them." It was a lie, but she couldn't call him on it. He was her superior, and if he said it was under control, she was supposed to accept his word at face value. Bronson tapped the top of his desk, then nodded to the door. "Don't you worry about it. All you need to do is be prepared to testify when the time comes. Otherwise, I need you here. You're the best I have when it comes to finding those tiny needles in the haystacks."

Alicia shot up out of her chair and made a beeline for the ladies' room. It had been all she could do to keep her breakfast down through her chat with her boss.

She didn't dare take more than five minutes to rinse her mouth, wash her hands and shake a few mints out of the container she'd started carrying in her pocket. It was ridiculous, but being the only female in her section made her self-conscious about anything the men she worked with might consider feminine. She needed to figure out a way to get back to Masters County. Preferably in some sort of official capacity so she didn't have to worry about burning up leave she could be banking for the weeks after the baby was born. But she wasn't going to get anything done by hiding out in the ladies' room.

Winding her way through the warren of low-walled cubicles, she turned a corner to find Alan Campbell hovering nearby. She eyed the other agent warily as she approached. Campbell had transferred from another division and wasn't as entrenched in the desire to outpace her as some of the men she'd come up with seemed to be. Still, they weren't exactly friends. It had taken only a few weeks under Bronson's command to make it clear she was the agent on the outside looking in at the good old boys' club. She wasn't entirely certain where Campbell fell on the scale of tolerable to insufferable.

Slowing her steps, she forced a small smile because heaven forbid she come off as unfriendly or uncooperative. "Hey, Campbell," she greeted him. "Something you needed?"

The other agent nodded. "The chief said I might want to send you some files to listen to."

Alicia clenched her teeth in her effort to keep her smile in place. This was the kind of garbage detail she'd been getting lately. Of course, whenever anyone pressed Bronson about why his most decorated agent was spending her time culling through hours of grainy footage or muffled voice recordings, he simply beamed and told anyone listening she was the *absolute best* when it came down to *fine detail* work, and he was only making sure he put his *ace* on the job.

For his part, Campbell seemed completely oblivious

to her agitation. "There's something there. I can feel it. There's something I'm hearing, but not quite getting."

He ran a frustrated hand through already rumpled hair, and she lowered the flame under her indignation. The appeal in his eyes made it clear he actually had come to her in hopes she might be able to ping on exactly what it was he was missing. Inhaling deeply through her nose, she moved past him to her desk and dropped into her chair.

"Oh yeah? What have you got?"

"We've got a guy who's been in with some of the local low-level operatives." The section chief's preferred term for gang members who worked the trade on the streets. "A couple of them were members in the southeast crew we thought were scattered to the winds a couple years ago."

Alicia sat up straighter, fighting to keep her mask of casual indifference firmly in place. She was excited by a connection he might have to the mostly disbanded gang, but refused to let it show. For years, the Southeast Atlanta gang had been ruled by a man named Ivan Jones. Ivan liked to think he was the drug kingpin of the southeastern United States, though there were many in the underworld who would argue the title shouldn't apply to anyone who moved low-grade inventory like methamphetamine.

Still, Ivan and his network had been a big deal to the DEA. So big, Ben Kinsella, former DEA agent and current Masters County sheriff, had once been deeply embedded in the man's organization. But Ben's mission to take Jones down barely qualified as a success. Sure, they'd locked the guy up in the end, but a number of people were killed, and Ben's cover had been blown wide open. Poor Ben had watched his best friend die during the raid to take Jones down. He'd also ended up with a bounty on his head, making him expendable to the agency.

"What makes you think they could be connected to the Southeast gang?" she asked Campbell.

"They said so," he said with a shrug.

"Then what do you need me for?"

"I think whatever they have going is connected to something bigger."

Intrigued, she gestured to the single guest chair she kept nearby. "Connected in what way?"

"They said something about Ivan's lawyer and some land downstate." He shrugged again. "They were talking about how the guy had died and left everything all, uh, screwed up, but then someone stepped in."

"Someone stepped in where?" she asked.

He shook his head. "I'm not exactly sure. And I may only be drawing all these lines in my head, but I was wondering… What was the name of the town where you arrested Samuel Coulter?"

Chapter Six

Dusty's Barbecue was a Masters County mainstay. Nestled in a notch cut out of timber-company woods, the shack near the highway overpass had served some of the best smoked meats in South Georgia for over thirty years. It was also the only place in the county with a liquor license allowing for on-premises consumption. After having his place busted up a couple of times in the early days, Dusty decided to limit his alcoholic offerings to long-necked bottles of beer and a couple of cheap wines no one ever ordered, but his wife seemed to like.

Since dining options in the area were severely limited and the barbecue joint was the only public place a body could walk in and order a cold beer, most everyone visited Dusty's at some time or another. Harry made his way there on the night after Alicia Simmons dropped her bomb on his life.

Behind the bar, Dusty's daughter Selena pulled a bottle from the ice bath and uncapped it with a quick flick of her wrist. When he was a boy, Harry had thought she was incredibly strong. Now he knew she kept a small metal bottle opener practically embedded in her palm as she worked her shift.

"Thanks, Sel," he said as she slid the bottle in front of him.

"You eating?" she asked, propping her knuckles on her hip and eyeing him speculatively. "Ribs are long gone, but we have the pork sandwich plate on special today."

Twirling the bottle until the label faced him, Harry considered the meager options in his fridge, then gave her a nod. "Sounds good. Beans and slaw for my sides, please and thank you."

"Coming right up."

Bottle in hand, Harry spun on his stool and took a moment to peer into the wood-on-wood gloom of the place. Signs advertising beverages or food specials provided the only color. Aside from the patrons. Dusty's was a veritable treasure trove for a person who enjoyed people watching. And Harry did. Now, with the workday wrapping up, the restaurant and bar was as full as it would ever be past the lunchtime rush.

Most of the men who worked the mills in the area stopped at Dusty's for a cold one on their way home. Harry recognized a good many of them. There were a couple of strangers in leather biker gear lounging at a table in the corner. They had the wind-beaten cragginess of men who spent a great deal of time on the road. He spotted Darleen Sheridan from the Daisy Drive-In sitting with Patti Cummings. Patti's overprocessed blond hair shone like a beacon as the two women huddled close, their expressions avid. There must be hot news in town, Harry concluded. He made a mental note to prime the gossip pump with a trip to the Daisy the next day. People tended to dismiss gossip as petty and avoid the town busybodies, but he didn't. The lumber mills provided the residents with a livelihood, but Pine Bluff's thriving gossip mill kept track of everything and everyone else in their lives.

Harry knew Arnie and Andy Smithson were regulars at Dusty's. Sure enough, when he scanned the patrons scattered around the scarred wooden tables, he spotted the brothers. It would have been hard to miss them. They were seated with a whole crowd of people wearing Timber Masters logos on their uniform shirts and jackets. They'd pushed three tables together to make one long one stretching across the rear wall of the building. The Smithsons sat with their backs to the wall and their gazes locked on him.

He braced his elbows on the bar and let the beer bottle dangle from his fingers. The scrape of chair legs on the wooden plank floor didn't bother him. Nor was he afraid of the large man stretching himself to his full height. As he'd explained to Alicia, he had known Arnie and his younger brother Andy his whole life. Regardless of Arnie's somewhat checkered past and reputation as a hothead, Harry found it hard to be afraid of someone he knew so well.

He quirked a smile as the mountain of a man approached. Arnie's curling gray-brown beard had grown out a bit. Harry couldn't help wondering if the foreman was stretching the limitations on Timber Masters safety policies concerning facial hair. Maybe he'd mention something to Marlee in passing. A joke about old Arnie gunning for Santa Claus's job or something. 'Twas the season, after all.

Harry lifted his bottle of beer a couple of inches in salute when the other man drew to a stop a few feet away. "Evening, Arnie."

"Heard you got your house shot up," Smithson replied, crossing his bulky arms over his barrel chest.

Harry gave his head a rueful shake. "You know, I got the porch repainted in September. Makes me mad when people make me do work twice."

"Yeah, well, I don't know what theories you and your friend the sheriff have cooked up, but it wasn't me or mine," Arnie replied resolutely. "So if you're here thinking you can shake us down for some kind of confession, you're barking up the wrong tree."

"Shake you down," Harry said with a laugh. Raising the bottle of beer to his lips, he kept his eyes fixed on the bigger man as he took a pull of the icy cold brew. "Seems foolish for a man like me to try to shake a man like you, and we both know I'm not foolish." Harrison maintained eye contact. "You may not have pulled the trigger, but I'm willing to bet you know who did."

"I'm not allowed to gamble these days," Arnie replied. "You know Annelle would have my head."

Harry smirked. Once upon a time, Arnie had been busted for trying to knock over a Prescott County gas station with a pointing finger in his jacket pocket. Apparently, he put some money on a football game, and Arnie couldn't pay up when his team hadn't pulled through. Unfortunately, he was wearing his work coat with his name embroidered on the front. A lenient judge gave him six months for the attempt. But for nearly a decade, the man had to endure the jokes about finger-pistol desperadoes.

"Annelle is a smart woman. I always wondered what she saw in you," Harry said, tossing off the insult with a friendly smile.

"You can keep on wondering," Arnie said, his smile

not quite as friendly but still there. "Let's say she doesn't love me for my brains."

"That much has been obvious for years." He took another sip of his beer.

"I wanted to come over and tell you man-to-man it wasn't us," Arnie said, jerking his head toward a small knot of men seated at his table. "You know if we had a beef with you, we'd come right at you."

He quirked an eyebrow. "Did I hear you threaten an officer of the court?"

Arnie was smart enough to shake his head. "Nope. I was very careful to pose a hypothetical."

Pleased with himself, the big man pivoted and walked back to his table of friends. Harry studied each of them for a moment. A couple of faces were familiar, though he couldn't quite put names with them.

If they became a bigger concern, he could put some feelers out with Marlee Masters and see if her supervisors hadn't heard any rumblings about them.

His gaze connected with Andy Smithson, and the two men who had known each other their entire lives, gone through twelve years of school together and even gotten drunk in this very bar together, shared a moment of unspoken communication. When Andy raised his eyebrows, Harry could do nothing but nod in acquiescence. He believed them. Which made it worse, because now he had absolutely no idea who might be taking potshots at his house.

Sighing, Harry took a long pull on his bottle of beer. A plate clattered onto the bar behind him. He spun on the stool to find a sectioned plate piled high with piping-hot barbecue waiting for him, and his stomach growled its approval.

He flashed another smile at Selena and swung around on his stool. "Looks good."

She deposited a tightly wrapped bundle of silverware and a couple of packets containing moist towelettes beside the plate, then wiped her hands on a dishcloth. "Best damn barbecue around," she replied flippantly before returning to the kitchen.

Harry focused his attention on the heaping plate of food in front of him. The scent of hickory smoke and tangy sauce made his mouth water. Picking up the roll of silverware, he unfurled a napkin he knew would be unequal to the task at hand and placed it on his lap, then grabbed his fork.

Sauce-drenched pulled pork stood high and proud atop the bottom half of an oversize bun. He shoveled up a heaping helping of slaw, dumped it on top of the meat and smooshed the top half of the bun down until the good stuff oozed out the sides.

Pleased to get his hands dirty with something other than criminal matters, he picked up the sandwich and took a healthy bite. Harry could feel the sauce smears clinging to his lips and cheeks, but didn't bother swiping them away. There'd only be more where those came from, and he liked to wait until the job was done to clean up right.

As he worked his way through the sandwich, he tried to let his mind drift, but it kept jolting over the speed bumps set out by the previous evening's events.

He'd been happy to see Alicia Simmons at his door. As happy as he'd been sad when she left Pine Bluff without saying goodbye. Not heartbroken, but maybe mildly disappointed? They were both grown-ups and knew going in what they would be to one another. Or thought they knew.

Pregnant.

The word kept popping into his head like one of those plastic moles you tried to beat down with a foam mallet at an arcade.

His chewing slowed and Harry set the sandwich carefully back on the plate. He had to swallow hard to get the food down. Alicia Simmons was pregnant with his child. Oddly enough, he'd never really doubted her word the baby was his. He had a hard enough time wrapping his head around the existence of a baby at all. But Alicia was nothing if not a straight shooter. He'd believed her the minute it all came tumbling out. He simply didn't know how to process the information.

He was gonna be a father. Thoughts had ricocheted around in his mind all day, but he hadn't been able to grasp one of them long enough to figure out how he felt about it. He planned on being a father one day. It might not have been happening in the way he expected, but this wasn't a bad thing. Most things didn't come about the way a person expected. He sure wouldn't have counted on being the last member of his family left in Pine Bluff, for one thing.

But here he was, back in the place he once yearned to escape. Back by choice, not circumstance, like Marlee Masters. He'd moved back with this brand-spanking-new law degree and happily taken the job as the assistant district attorney for the area.

His parents had been shocked. His sister incredulous. He had no way of explaining to them what had caused the change of heart because he wasn't quite sure himself. All he knew was when he saw the job posting pop up, he jumped at it without hesitation.

Harry rocked back on the stool and sucked the barbecue sauce off each of his fingers before reaching for the napkin on his lap to dry them. He sighed and ducked his head, bracing his forearms on the edge of the bar. The fact was, the minute Alicia had said she was going back to Atlanta, he'd wanted to protest, though he knew he didn't have a right. He wanted her here, even if it was irrational to think she'd stay. Alicia had a career there. A damn good one. She had decorations and commendations. He assumed she had a life there, as well. He wasn't exactly the social butterfly of Masters County, but he had friends. She likely did too. And those friends certainly weren't going to be pointing her in the direction of a small-time prosecutor who chose to live in the middle of nowhere.

After picking up his fork, Harry scooped up some baked beans and shoveled in a few mouthfuls. He ate on autopilot, oblivious to the noise and commotion around him. Within a few minutes, he'd demolished the beans and what was left of the slaw and the sandwich, not giving them the appreciation they deserved.

"Must've been good," someone commented gruffly.

Harry jerked and his head swiveled. Ben Kinsella stood behind him. Still chewing, Harry eyeballed the sheriff. "Evening," he said, but with more warmth than he'd given Arnie Smithson. He took in the jeans, flannel and ball cap the other man wore and nodded to the empty stool beside him. "I take it you're off duty tonight?"

Ben gave a brief nod as he straddled the stool. "Picking up some barbecue. I find it helps to have food on hand if I hope to lure Marlee away from the office any-time before seven."

"Smart thinking." Harry tore open a wet wipe and used it to give his face and hands a thorough cleaning. "Had a chat with Arnie," he said, gesturing toward the long table before the sheriff could ask. "I don't think it was them."

Ben bobbed his head, then smiled at Selena as she approached. "Hey, Selena. I need two of the specials with potato salad and beans to go."

She nodded and made a note on her pad. "Want a drink while you wait?" she asked, pointing her pen to Harry's beer bottle.

"Don't mind if I do."

She uncapped a cold one and slid it in front of the sheriff. "Another, Harry?"

He shook his head. "I'm good. I'm driving, and I hear the law around here is pretty vigilant."

Ben smirked as he lifted his bottle and toasted them both with it. "It's a tough town. Somebody got his house shot up last night."

Selena, who'd started for the kitchen, stopped short, spun on her heel, then marched back over to them. The stern expression on her face had Harry and Ben pulling up straight as she leaned in to speak to them under the din. "What did you say?"

Ben lowered his bottle to the bar, then spoke with deliberation. "Someone took a few potshots at Harry's house last night. Took out the porch light. Almost took out a friend of ours."

A deep furrow appeared between Selena's brows. She glanced over at Harry, her expression surprising him.

She looked torn between incredulity and anger. "Are you kidding me? Actually shot at your house?"

Ben spoke before Harry could. "Yes."

She planted her hands on her hips and rocked back on her heels, clearly weighing something in her mind. At last, she pitched forward again. "I wasn't going to say anything because, you know, I hear things—all sorts of things—but I never know what's true or not."

"We understand," Ben prompted, glancing over at Harry as if looking for confirmation of his presumption.

Harry nodded. "Anything you've heard might help." He balled up the wrapper from the wet wipe and tossed it onto his empty plate. "I'd appreciate it. I really liked my porch light."

She scowled so fiercely Harry was afraid he'd pushed too hard, but then she shook her head, clearly disgusted. "Not those two in the corner," she said, flicking a glance toward the bikers seated at the corner table. "But I'm seeing more and more guys from that, uh, club come through these days."

Neither Harry nor Ben was dumb enough to look, but Harry recalled the men he'd spotted when scanning the room. "The bikers?"

"The Outriders," she said with a sneer in her voice. "Not even a good name."

Her commentary coaxed a reluctant laugh from Harry. "Aw, come on. It's not bad."

"Only saying they could have done better," Selena said, raising her hands as if to ward off an argument.

Ben wasn't as easily distracted. "The Outriders," he murmured as he automatically reached for the notebook he kept in the breast pocket of his uniform shirt.

Unfortunately, the patch pockets on his flannel were empty. "Damn."

Harry pulled his phone out of his pocket and sent a text message with the name. "There. And I want it noted technology saved the day for you in this case. You're the only person I know who is even more low-tech than I am."

Ben rolled his eyes, then checked his own phone to be sure he had the information. Lifting his bottle, he flashed Selena a smile so mild they might have been exchanging recipes. "How many would you guess you've seen lately?"

Selena pursed her lips and shrugged. "At least a half dozen, but likely more. Usually come in twos or threes. No big groups, like a club out for a cruise, you know?"

"Gotcha. Thanks, Sel. We'll put some feelers out." He took a sip of his beer as she headed back to the kitchen again.

But Harry saw a spark of something restless in Selena's eyes. On impulse, he called after her. "Hey, Selena?" When she spun around, quirking one perfectly arched brow, he gave her the winsome smile he used to woo a jury. "I, uh—" he made a motion to imply she should keep their conversation on the down low "—appreciate your help."

Running her tongue over her teeth, she marched back over to them, tore a ticket from her pad and said, "Put your money where your mouth is, Mr. District Attorney."

Laughing, Harry reached for his wallet as the swinging door swooped back and forth in her wake. "She's gonna start nosing around," he said without looking at Ben.

Ben nodded, then tossed off Harry's worry with a

shrug. "You know as well as I do service personnel are some of the best sources any investigation can have."

"I don't want her asking too many questions and getting unwelcome attention. Selena has her hands full running this place and trying to keep old Dusty from working himself to death. She doesn't need to be doing our jobs, as well."

"Well, for your information, I *have* been doing my job, Counselor." Ben grasped the neck of his bottle and tipped it toward him, rolling the edge of the bottom back and forth. "I've identified a handful of credible leads as to who might have you in their sights."

"Oh yeah?" Harry threw a twenty down on top of the ticket to cover his meal, the single beer and allow for about a 60 percent tip.

A minute later, Selena came through the swinging door again holding a tightly wrapped plastic bag with two food containers. She swept Harry's ticket and the twenty from the counter. "Need change?"

"Doubt I'd get it even if I said yes," he answered with a smirk.

She flashed a smile. "Have a good night," she said dismissively, then slapped a ticket down in front of Ben.

Harry clapped a hand on Ben's shoulder as he rose. "Wow. No freebies for the law around here."

"No freebies in Dusty's at all," Selena retorted. "Never have been, never will be."

The sheriff shook his head as he pulled out his wallet and extracted a card. "And worth every penny," he said with an affable smile. "Night, Harry."

Harry let his gaze drift to the table along the back wall before sweeping the room. The two biker guys in the corner were still there, their table littered with wad-ded napkins and several empty beer bottles, and their gazes fixed on the sheriff. Harry figured they'd let Ben get a head start before mounting their rides. Probably hoping to evade any chance at being pulled over.

Pushing through the door, he hunkered into his suit coat, though the worsted wool did little to inhibit the chilly wind. He was halfway to his car before he spotted the trouble. There she sat, his poor, abused car. Her shiny—if slightly marred on one side—paint job gleaming in the floodlights illuminating the parking area. All four of his tires were flat.

There was a short burst of noise and clatter as someone came out the door, but soon the evening quiet closed in around him again. Before he managed to pick which swear word to use, a heavy hand landed on his shoulder.

Anger and frustration roiled inside him as he saw Ben staring mournfully at his BMW. "Come on," the other man said gruffly. "I'll give you a lift home."

Chapter Seven

It took everything she could glean from Campbell's recordings plus the information she'd received from Ben Kinsella, but Alicia was finally able to convince Bronson to let her head back to Pine Bluff. A well-placed word in his superior's ear hadn't hurt either. At last, he set her free to see for herself what was happening with her case down in Masters County.

She pulled to a stop in front of Harry's house exactly where she'd parked mere days before. The neighborhood looked much the same. A few people had started decorating for Christmas, giving the street a boost of much-needed color as the days grew shorter and the nights longer. She noted Harry had compensated for his broken porch light by stringing white Christmas lights along porch rails and pillars. They should have cheered her, but the thought of him standing out there hanging those lights, open to any crackpot with a gun, made her stomach flip over.

Slamming the car door, she strode around to the trunk and hefted the suitcase she'd barely touched since her last trip to Pine Bluff. Once upon a time, she rarely fully unpacked from any trip. Before Bronson had become her chief, she was hardly in the office for more than two days together. She'd come home, send out a batch of dry cleaning or run a couple of loads of laundry, then put everything back into the same suitcase and go.

But whether Bronson clipped her wings or not, those days were over for her. Or at least they would be soon. Soon, she would be planted. She'd finally let her roots sink into the soil so her child would know who he or she was and where he or she came from and never face the sort of displacement she had as an army brat.

After setting the suitcase on the asphalt, she extended the handle and dragged it up over the curb with a grunt. She noted the lack of car in the drive, but figured the lights on inside were a good indicator. Maybe Harry had finally decided to use his garage as an actual garage. The luggage wheels bumped over the grassy berm until she reached the walkway leading to his front door. At the foot of the steps, she abandoned the extension and reached for the handle attached to the top of the case to heft it up the four shallow stairs.

The weight of the case hitting the wooden floorboards must have alerted Harry to a caller, because the foyer light went on. She pressed the bell, but the door swung open before she could retract her finger.

"Alicia," he said gruffly. "What are you doing here?"

She took a moment to appreciate the view. He wasn't wearing a suit coat, but he wore gray pin-striped trousers and a white shirt with his polished wing tips. His collar was open, and any evidence of a tie had been eradicated. Dark stubble shadowed the distinct lines of his jaw.

Alicia smiled, recalling how upon meeting him for the first time she'd decided his slightly pointy nose kept him from being too blandly handsome. Harrison Hayes was one of those men who snuck up on you. His charm and appeal lay as much in his sharp mind, quick wit and sly smile as it did his good looks. One might be tempted to dismiss him as simply yet another clean-cut Southern man with his neatly trimmed hair and solemn hazel eyes. But dismissing Harry for any reason was a mistake. It took Alicia about twenty-four hours to realize the district attorney grew far more potent as one got to know him.

"I'm coming to stay for a while," she announced.

He rolled a pointed glance down at the suitcase beside her and raised an eyebrow. "So I see."

"I mean, I'm coming to stay with you," she said, clarifying.

His head jerked up and he looked genuinely surprised by the notion. "Coming to stay with me?"

She gave a brisk nod. "May I come in? It's cold out here."

Ever the gentleman, Harry unlatched the screen door and pushed it open. Then he stepped back, allowing her to pass. When she reached for her suitcase, his hand closed over hers. "I'll get your bag."

She didn't fight him, because mainly she was tired of wrestling with the damn thing. If he wanted to be all chivalrous about things, she wasn't about to stop him. Once they were inside with the door closed firmly behind them, Harry glanced down at the large suitcase again before looking her dead in the eye.

"You think you're going to stay with me?"

"Ben offered the house I had before, but I don't see much point since I plan to stick pretty close to you the next couple weeks."

His jaw dropped and his eyes opened so wide she almost laughed. He was the very caricature of a man in shock. "You do?"

"I've been assigned to investigate some of the threats being made against you in the weeks leading up to the Coulter trial."

"Everybody and their brother is already investigating most threats. Why did they need to send you?"

"You act like you aren't happy to see me." She planted a hand on her hip and thrust it to the side as she studied him directly. "Would you prefer I leave?"

He shook his head. "No."

His answer came quick enough to assure her it was his gut reaction, so she rolled with it. "We've come across some indicators leading us in a different direction when it comes to identifying the forces behind the perpetrators of these crimes."

"Crimes?" He gave a brief, bitter laugh. "Around here, we call it mischief and vow to get even with whoever it was later."

"Where I'm from, it's called terroristic threatening." She smiled then. "Potato, po-tah-to."

Harry ran his hand through his hair, rumpling its styled perfection. The nervous habit had been one of the things that first drew her to him. Alicia found tousled Harry so appealing she'd once reached over and smoothed his hair in the middle of their postinterrogation recap. She wanted to mess him up now, but doing so wouldn't be appropriate. Which was ironic, considering they knew each other a lot more intimately now than they had then.

"Come in," he said, gesturing toward the living room. "I'll, uh, put this in the guest room."

She smiled to herself as he wheeled her bag away. In the living room, she took a minute to drink in the details of the room she hadn't bothered noticing the night they were under fire.

Framed family photos were arrayed atop side tables and on a couple of floating shelves attached to the wall. The room was furnished with comfortable, masculine pieces upholstered in leather. An old refinished trunk served as the coffee table, and an upright piano was installed against the far wall.

"Would you like something to drink?" Harry called from the hallway.

"Water is fine, thank you."

A moment later he reappeared with two bottles of water in hand. He loosened the cap on one before handing it to her. Alicia smiled, once again amused. "Thank you. I never would've been able to open a bottle on my own."

"Oh, sorry. Habit," he said with a shrug.

"You often go around handing out bottled water?" She eyed him as she lifted the bottle to her lips and took a quick sip, trying to figure out this somewhat inscrutable man.

He shook his head. "No, but my mama taught me to serve people a certain way. I wouldn't dare hand a can of Coca-Cola without first popping the top."

Alicia laughed. "I see. Yes, heaven forbid we risk a broken fingernail."

He smiled as he joined her on the sofa, leaving the cushion between them open, but angling his body to face hers. "I know you're tough, but like I said, old habits."

"I understand." She gestured to the array of photos. "Does your family live nearby?"

He shook his head. "My sister and her family live in the Chicago area. My parents retired to Florida."

"It always kind of tickles me when people move from Georgia down to Florida. Doesn't seem to me like there'd be a whole lot of difference."

"Maybe not from Atlanta to Florida, but there's a whole world of difference between Masters County and most cities in Florida."

"Your father was a doctor, right?"

He raised his bottle to her in silent salute. "You've been doing your research." He took a drink, then nodded. "My father was general practitioner here in town, and my mother was a homemaker, though she wasn't much interested in housework. She spent most of her days down at the beauty parlor catching up on the latest. My sister is also a doctor, as is her husband. I am the black sheep."

A laugh burbled out of her. "If the black sheep ends up being a successful district attorney, I'd say your family is doing quite well."

He shrugged. "Anyway, they all seem happy, and I'm happy here, so I guess we're all winning at life." He propped his elbow on the back of the sofa and rested the bottle on his thigh. "How about you? Where's your family?"

Alicia's smile faded. "Let's see." She tipped her head back. "At the moment, my parents are in Germany, but they're due back into the Washington, DC, area sometime after the first of the year." She straightened and eyed him directly. "My father is expected to take an appointment with the Joint Chiefs of Staff"

He did a comical double take. "Joint Chiefs of Staff? Wow. Cool."

"The culmination of a lifetime of work."

"Which branch?"

"Army."

"Any siblings?"

She shook her head. "No, only me. They found out pretty quickly a child can slow a person down when one is trying to march up the ladder."

"I see." His face softened.

Alicia shrugged his sympathy off. There was no sense fretting over it. Her childhood was long over. She had her own life and her own career to worry about. Her relationship with her parents was fine, if somewhat distant. Frankly, it suited her as well as it suited them. And there was no sense dwelling on the past when she had a future to plan.

"So, I did go to the doctor, and the pregnancy is confirmed." He sat back, and his face went blank. She didn't know if his sudden reserve was due to the subject matter or the abrupt shift in conversation topics, but if they were going to work out any sort of relationship, she believed they needed to have all their cards out on the table. "I didn't count right, though. I'm actually almost eight weeks along, but everything seems to be right on target."

Her brisk summation earned her a slight change in expression, but for the most part, he was still unreadable. This was the problem with dealing with lawyers—their poker faces were too damn good.

"I thought you should know," she said, opening her hands in a gesture she hoped he'd read as simple frankness.

As if snapped from a trance, Harry ran his hand over his face, a gesture she was coming to recognize as his way of grounding himself before speaking. "Okay. Well, wow." He chuckled. "I guess it shouldn't come as such a shock to hear again, but it does." He cocked his head and gave her a crooked smile. "You're pregnant."

She nodded solemnly, a responsive smile quirked at her lips. "I am indeed."

"Have you thought any about how you're going to handle it work-wise?" he asked.

"I have," she replied thoughtfully. "I'm not going to lie. It's going to be complicated."

"To say the least," he said with a laugh. As if the situation were only dawning on him, his whole face brightened. "Wow. I can't believe this is happening."

She narrowed her eyes. "Going by your facial expression, I'm guessing this isn't an entirely unwelcome turn of events in your life?"

He shook his head. "No. It isn't. Unexpected, yes. But I've had time to digest…and not unwelcome."

She took a moment to absorb his assurance. "Does this mean you *do* want to be involved in some way?"

He answered without hesitation. "Yes."

She almost jumped out of her skin when he reached across and took her free hand in his.

"Alicia, I know the situation isn't ideal, and was unplanned, but I thought about it a lot over the past couple of days, and one thing I am *not* is unhappy. As a matter of fact, given everything going on around here, this may be the best news I've had in weeks."

His sincerity unleashed a flood of warmth she hadn't realized she was repressing. Flipping her hand over, she gave his fingers a gentle squeeze. "I'm glad you're happy. Like I told you before, this might've been an accident, but it's a happy accident, in my book. I'm glad it's one for you too."

He let out a nervous laugh as she released his hand

and drew back. She watched as he laced his long, grace-ful fingers together and let them dangle between them. "Okay, so you're here. You're here working. You're preg-nant, and you intend to live in my house while you're here working." He shot her a sidelong glance. "Have I got everything right?"

"Right on the nose, Counselor."

He nodded. "Well, in terms of logistics, it's no prob-lem, but I think we haven't discussed how we're going to present this to the world at large."

She reared back. "Present what?"

"You living in my house, to start," he said without hesitation.

She frowned. "Do you need to clear it with someone? I'm sorry—I didn't even ask. I'm assuming you're still single, but maybe you're not?"

He shook his head hard. "Yes, still single. But this isn't Atlanta, Alicia. Around here, people will notice if I have a woman living in my house. People will notice, and people will talk."

"Is gossip a problem for you?" she asked, trying to keep the note of challenge from her tone, but failing.

"Not a problem, per se, but it's not going to go unno-ticed." He smiled at her wanly. "You forget how it is in small towns. Everybody's business is everybody's busi-ness. So, for the sake of saving ourselves a whole lot of explaining and for providing you with cover for being here, I suggest we let people think we're a couple."

This time, Alicia pulled back. "A couple?"

"Together."

"Together?"

He sighed. "Alicia, I'm not saying it has to be the re-ality, but I think we should..."

"Put on an act?"

"...let people believe what they want to believe," he finished. "Trust me—it would be so much easier to deal with the Nosy Nellies if we let them think we're romantically involved."

"Won't we be inviting even more questions?"

He shook his head. "Relationships they understand. We might get some blowback about living together after so little time together, but only from a few of the holier of the holy rollers. Trust me—you don't want to try to explain a one-night stand while celebrating the arrest and arraignment of the county's most infamous criminal, then us going our separate ways only to discover you're pregnant. Add in the bit about how I've got somebody trying to scare me away from even sitting in on this case, and it's a whole lot of talking on our part." He shrugged. "I say let them draw their conclusions and do their talking on their own."

"Well, when you put it in those terms..."

He inclined his head to her. "Exactly. Much easier to say we met when you were here and started dating long-distance. You've got time off and have come down to stay with me. That's all there is to it."

She sat back and eyed him closely. "For a guy who spent his life trying to ferret out the truth, you're awfully good at the subterfuge."

He chuckled. "The company I keep," he answered brusquely. "Now, I know this may be an unwelcome question, but are you hungry?"

"Starving, but I don't think I could manage much more than toast," she said with a tired smile.

"Toast I can handle." He jerked his head toward the kitchen and rose from the couch. "Come on—let's get something in your stomach and we can talk some more about what's really brought you here."

Alicia laughed, scrambling up from the sofa as he led the way to the kitchen. "There's no subterfuge with me, Counselor. I'll tell you straight up everything I know."

He stopped in the kitchen and surveyed his surroundings. Running a hand over the top of his head down the back of his neck, he snuck a peek at her before glancing at the fridge. "I can handle the toast, but will it bother you if I make myself something to eat?"

She wrinkled her nose. "This is your house, Harry. You don't need my permission to make yourself a meal. If I can't handle it, I'll leave the room."

He gestured toward her stomach. "I don't want to do anything to set off any kind of adverse reaction."

"Okay, well, can you survive on sandwiches for a while?" she asked. "It's mainly cooking smells getting to me right now. I can stomach the scent of toast, but any kind of meat cooking is a no go… It sort of hits me wrong."

"I love a good sandwich." He nodded toward the kitchen table, where they'd sat a few nights before. "Make yourself comfortable."

Alicia watched as he moved from the refrigerator to the counter, reaching easily into drawers and cabinets for whatever he needed to construct what looked to be a sandwich straight out of a cartoon. "Wow, you don't mess around."

He slid a plate with two slices of dry wheat toast in front of her. "Butter? Jam?"

"No, thank you. Dry is best right now."

He brought two more bottles of water over to the table, then carried his thick sandwich over to join her.

He sat across from her as if poised to spring up if necessary. "Is this okay?"

She smiled. "Harry, you don't need to walk on eggshells. I'll get through this, and so will you."

He smiled back at her, then picked up half of the monster sandwich he'd built. She watched his teeth flash white before they sank into the bread. But the moment he started to chew, the quiet of the kitchen was obliterated by the smash of glass and the soft whoosh of a fire igniting.

Harry and Alicia both leaped from the table and ran toward the living room. A cool breeze blew through a broken window. A glass Mason jar lay on its side, spilling liquid onto the hardwood floor, and about a foot away, a scrap of flaming cloth blazed too close to the curtains for comfort.

Chapter Eight

Harry's first instinct was to act, not to think. He ran into the living room, carefully jumped over the puddle spreading across his floor and stomped on the flaming rag as the fire licked at the bottom of the sheer curtains his sister had insisted he needed.

"Harry, stop," Alicia shouted, but he couldn't.

Cold air poured in through the broken window, but his blood ran hot. Thankfully, he hadn't yet taken off his shoes. The soles heated and the leather flexed as he stomped on the rag.

"Are you crazy?" Alicia demanded. "You're going to catch your pants on fire. Get out of there."

Harry kept his gaze fixed on the charred bit of rag he'd stomped to pieces, then yanked the curtains up to make sure they hadn't caught a spark.

"I think I got it out," he called back to her.

"There's a river of gasoline flowing toward you, and if you don't get away from the window, I'm gonna tackle you," she warned him.

He looked up and saw her poised inside the living room, her arms spread as she crouched, ready to launch herself at him.

"No need for tackling," he assured her.

"Be careful—it's spreading," she ordered.

He eyed the liquid spilling from the heavy jar. The pool was indeed spreading, but the flow ran straight in his direction. Damn this old house for not having level floors, he thought as he dragged the rag away from the encroaching liquid with his foot. Not taking his eyes off the gasoline, he asked, "Am I missing anything? Is it out?"

"Yes, you idiot. It's out."

He barked a laugh. "Tell me how you really feel about me," he joked as he stepped off the wad of incinerated fabric and moved back toward her.

"Someone threw a Molotov cocktail through your front window and you want to make jokes?"

Her sharp tone caught his attention. He stopped in front of her and placed both hands on her upper arms, drawing her up to her full height. "Sorry. Defense mechanism," he admitted gruffly. "My mother always said I tend to get flippant when I'm freaking out."

She stared back at him. He liked her height. Loved looking her straight in the eye and knowing she could meet him head-on in every way.

"Are you freaking out?"

"Someone threw a really bad Molotov cocktail through my front window." He gave her a wry half smile. "Safe to assume I'm freaking out."

"But you charged right in there and put it out," she countered. "With your feet."

"I'm wearing shoes."

She sighed, and he felt her entire body sag. "Well, I guess we should be okay as long as we don't light any matches."

He nodded, still holding her gaze. "Right. We're okay."

Alicia pulled back enough to peer around him at the mess. "We can go on believing we're not dealing with professionals."

"How do you figure?"

"Someone who knew what they were doing would have made it impossible for the wicking to come out. We got lucky."

He opted not to point out her choice of pronoun and simply nodded. "We did. Thank God for ineptitude." He gave her arms a gentle rub, then steered her back to the hall. "Would you call Ben for me?"

Giving him the side-eye, she asked, "What are you going to do?"

He nodded toward the kitchen. "Neither of us need to be standing by those fumes, broken window or not." He moved past her and went to the door to the garage. "I'm going to see what I have to soak up some of the kerosene, then find something to cover the window, otherwise it's going to get pretty chilly in here pretty fast."

"We need the ventilation," she said.

He stepped down into the garage he'd converted into a home gym. "Then we'll get it cleaned up."

"I don't suppose you have a cat," she said from too close behind him.

He whirled to find her standing in the open doorway. "A cat?" He shook his head. "No."

"Too bad, because I think you need kitty litter to tackle this spill." She held up her cell phone. "I'll ask Ben to pick some up on his way over."

He hesitated, then spoke his greatest worry aloud. "Staying here isn't the best idea for you."

Her spine stiffened. "Don't try to shield me. I'm no delicate flower for you to protect. I can take you out about nine different ways before I even have to reach for my gun."

"I believe you, but circumstances being what they are—"

"I don't run from danger—I run to it," she continued.

"I don't want you endangered on my account," he insisted.

"Tough."

The simple, somewhat adolescent response would have made him laugh if he weren't so damn frustrated and worried. Still, he kept his cool. Like he would a hostile witness, he needed to lead her to the conclusion he wanted her to make. "Again, circumstances, Alicia."

"I make my own decisions."

"Yes, but you're making them for two now," he pointed out.

"You can do whatever you want to do," she snapped back.

Her knee-jerk reaction and momentary oblivion startled a sharp laugh out of him. He walked back toward her, holding her belligerent stare every inch of the way. "I wasn't talking about you and me. I meant you and the baby."

Hectic color rose in her cheeks, and she shook her head hard as if she could dismiss his concerns with simple negation. "It doesn't matter. I'm not going anywhere," she said, thrusting her chin up as she crossed her arms over her chest.

He studied her for a moment, but rather than argue about it, he gave in. "All right. Then call Ben for me, will you? Tell him we need another damn hazmat cleanup."

DEPUTY MIKE SCHAEFFER caught the call. A tall, borderline-gangly guy with an easy smile and good old-fashioned Southern manners, he'd shown up with the requested hazmat kit and an enormous bag of cat litter.

"It really is the best thing, but you have to get the kind with clay in it," he explained as he dumped the litter directly onto the kerosene. "The problem is, takes forever to get the smell out. Of the kerosene, I mean." He shook his head, a rueful smile on his lips. "My cousin knocked over a heater at our hunting cabin, and I swear we had to air the place out for weeks."

Harry made an unintelligible grunt in response. Which wasn't fair. He liked Mike. The guy was a good cop, down-to-earth and thorough. Qualities Harry usually appreciated. But his front window was broken and the cool December air was gushing in. Harry was damn tired of people taking out their petty complaints about his job on his house.

They wanted him to quit the case. What they failed to realize was, with or without him, Samuel Coulter's day in court was coming. He'd spoken to Marcus Zeller, the federal prosecutor who'd serve as first chair on the case, the day before and filled him in on what was happening. Zeller assured him he was needed on the case, and if he wasn't put off by what he termed *pregame theatrics*, he still wanted Harry on the litigation.

Rather than making him want to give up his second-chair position, these assaults made him want to get Coulter to court even faster. He longed to be there to help US Attorney Zeller nail the smuggler to a wall. He needed to show these thugs he wasn't afraid of them.

Then, when everything was said and done, he could go back to prosecuting domestic disturbances, property damage issues, and small-time drug peddlers spread through the backwoods of Georgia as thick on the ground as kudzu. He'd prosecute people who keyed cars and slashed tires for criminal mischief. But this stuff—the shots taken at his house and now this home-made hand grenade—it elevated things to terroristic threatening levels.

A Molotov cocktail, he thought, incredulous. Scrubbing a hand over his face, he searched for something to say to the young deputy who was working so hard to help with the mess in the living room. "Not the best time of year for airing things out," he managed at last.

"No, sir," Mike responded affably. "It's a chilly one tonight."

The deputy rocked back and pursed his lips as he surveyed the mess they'd spread upon mess. Rubbing the back of his neck, Mike shrugged one shoulder. "I guess you can try some lemon. My mama always said it was best for neutralizing odors. But you might wanna check the internet first. I'm not exactly sure what the best solution might be. Citrus can be awful acidic, you know."

Harry was almost overtaken by the urge to smile at the remark, but he held back. He appreciated the young man's need to be helpful. Instead, he clapped the deputy on the shoulder as they took in the clumps of granulated litter now covering his living-room floor. "Thanks, Mike. You went above and beyond, and I appreciate it."

"It was no big deal," Mike said with a shrug. "A quick run into the Stop & Shop on my way over. Sheriff should be here shortly."

"Okay. Yeah, I guess I shouldn't have called him into this. You have it well in hand," he said to the deputy.

Mike only chuckled. "I know the sheriff, and I can tell you he wants to be in on this."

No sooner were the words out than there was a sharp

rap on the front door. As usual, Ben let himself in after waiting only a moment. Stopping dead in the middle of the entrance, the sheriff stared at the two of them, amazed disbelief written all over his face. "A Molotov cocktail? Are you kidding me?"

As if on cue, Alicia stepped out of the kitchen, where he'd left her propped up against the counter, snacking on a sleeve of saltines. "Not a very good one. They used a canning jar but no lid or anything to hold the fabric in place to ignite the fuel."

"Thank God for small favors," Ben replied.

"And idiotic assassins," Alicia added dryly. When both Ben and Harry swung their heads around altogether, she shrugged and asked, "Too soon?"

"Yes," Harry replied tersely.

"Got it." Alicia nodded. "I'll stow the cop humor until later."

Ben smiled and shook his head. "I've got a couple good ones in mind. Remind me later, when Harry finds his sense of humor again."

"I'm ready to give my statement," Harry snapped.

Not missing a beat, Ben pulled his trusty notebook and pen out of the back pocket of his jeans and nodded toward the kitchen. "We'll step in there so we can stay out of the fumes." He glanced over at the living room. "Thanks for running interference on the hazmat, Mike," he said with a nod to his deputy. "I called the fire chief, and he said litter was the right thing to use." Shifting his attention back to Harry, he added, "He also said to call them if we want them to come out and take a look."

"Fire's out," Harry said flatly. "Let's get this over with."

While Mike gathered his gear in the living room,

Harry pulled out his wallet and extracted a twenty. "Here." When the deputy tried to wave him off, he shook his head. "For the litter. Thank you."

"The least I could do," Mike responded, taking the bill with a nod. "Night."

After seeing Mike out, Harry joined Alicia and Ben in the kitchen. They took the same seats at the table they'd claimed a few nights before. The second they were settled, Harry began to talk without prompting.

"Alicia and I were here in the kitchen talking when we heard something come through the window. When we ran in there, I saw the jar and makeshift wick had separated, so I extinguished the fire by stepping on it. The fire didn't spread to anything else, but now I have a living room soaked with kerosene."

"I'm not going to bother asking you if you have any ideas who might've done this," Ben murmured as he made notes on the page. "Can you give me the time frame?"

Harry and Alicia exchanged a look as they both scrambled to pinpoint the sequence of events on a clock. "I think I got here at about six thirty," she said slowly.

Harry nodded. "We talked for a while, and then I was going to make something to eat," he continued. "I'm pretty sure the clock on the stove showed after seven when I got up."

Alicia shrugged and nodded. "It's coming on eight, so it couldn't have been after seven."

Ben's head swiveled as he switched his gaze back and forth. "Narrows it down some." He flipped his notebook shut, placed his hands on the table in front of him and zoomed in on Alicia. "Didn't expect to see you back in town so soon," he said in a conversational tone. "Did you come to sing Christmas carols this time?"

"She came to see me," Harry said, hoping to put the kibosh on any teasing. He wasn't in the mood for games.

His strident tone did the trick. Ben sat up straighter and shifted the full force of his attention to him. "I'd assumed as much."

Their eyes met and held. It was all Harry could do to resist shifting under the sheriff's unblinking gaze, but he held it together. Barely. Ben glanced over at Alicia, saving him from having to come up with a better story than the "we're together" plan they'd settled on minutes before the night went all to hell.

Thankfully, Alicia was better at this stuff. She met Ben's perusal with a smirky smile, daring the sheriff to pry. When the tension stretched so taut Harry thought he might have to spill the whole story to exonerate himself, she spoke.

"We're together."

Harry blinked, surprised to hear their plan spoken aloud and with such simplicity it made any further probing seem like an overreach.

"Ah," Ben said. He had the grace to nod as if he hadn't put one and one together on his own, then tapped the top of his notepad. "I, uh, figured something was going on."

"You're so smart," Alicia cooed, letting her smirk stretch into a teasing smile.

Ben smiled back, but slid his attention back to Harry so quickly he wasn't able to plaster one on in time. The sharp glint in the sheriff's eyes said he hadn't missed the moment of hesitation, but he was merciful enough to let the lack of deeper explanation slide.

"Marlee will be glad to hear it. Since Simon and Lori

are dating, she seems determined to see everyone she knows paired up," Ben said dryly.

"Of course. No one loves love as much as a lover," Alicia said, her smile so wide Harry felt his own cheeks ache.

Harry wondered if she realized she'd thrown the *L* word out there like a live grenade. Still, he needed to get himself together. Pull his weight. If they were going to make the citizens of Pine Bluff believe there was something going on between them, there was no better place to start than with the county's top cop.

"We, uh, got to know each other when she was here a couple months ago," Harry said, warming up slowly.

"Obviously," Alicia said with a laugh.

She reached over and put her hand over his, but Harry got the feeling she was trying to quell him rather than show affection. He must be worse at this than he thought.

"We've talked some, but with the reorg at work, I haven't had a chance to get back to Pine Bluff until the other night."

Harry couldn't help but stare at her. He could only hope his admiration was coming across as something more romantic than appreciating her skill at embroidering the truth. Other than the announcement of their "together-ness," she hadn't lied. Judging by the size of the suitcase he'd rolled into the guest room, they actually would be together for the foreseeable future. How other people defined the word wasn't their problem, was it?

No. Their problem was something far more sinister than whether he and the DEA agent who'd brought Samuel Coulter down had something going on.

"Back to this thing tonight," Harry said, hoping to

refocus the conversation. "I think we can all agree this is an escalation."

Ben and Alicia both nodded. "Undoubtedly," the sheriff said.

"And not a tactic we'd expect anyone from around these parts to employ," Harry continued.

"Which is why I came here tonight," Alicia interrupted.

Caught off guard, Harry's head swiveled in time with Ben's.

"Oh?" The sheriff slipped open the notepad again. "What have you found?"

Something about the way Ben asked the question clued Harry in. Ben knew Alicia was looking into the threats against him. She must have talked to the sheriff in the days since she'd left Pine Bluff, but she hadn't bothered to call him. A surge of jealous anger sliced through him, but he bit the inside of his cheek to keep from saying anything.

"I put out feelers about the groups you identified and a couple more I pulled from our own database, but couldn't come up with anything tying them directly to Coulter or that would give me a reason why they'd be interested in his case."

"Yeah, I've been coming up empty too," Ben admitted. "We have a lead involving a motorcycle club called The Outriders, but nothing concrete on them yet."

"A couple of their members were at Dusty's Barbecue at the exact same time all four of my tires were slashed."

Her head whipped around. "Your tires were slashed?"

Harry nodded, a grim frown tugging at his mouth. "Yes. Again. While I was eating dinner last night."

"But no one saw those guys move," Ben pointed out.

"I questioned them myself, then asked everyone who was there if they'd seen either of them budge from their table, and came up empty."

"Maybe they messaged some friends," Harry tossed out.

Ben shrugged. "It's possible, but even if they said, *Hey, Harry Hayes is here, come and slash his tires!* we wouldn't be much closer to the root of the problem. I can't help going back around to thinking there's a local connection. Your guy at the US Attorney's Office hasn't had any trouble like this."

She shook her head. "Nothing out of the ordinary. I agree with you, Ben. Someone has taken up Coulter's cause, and they're making it personal with Harry."

The sheriff found his gaze again. "I don't suppose you'd consider—"

Harry didn't let him finish. "No. I'm not backing off."

"I already tried," Alicia said with a wry smirk.

"Of course you have," Ben answered smoothly. He blew out a breath and tapped his pen on the pad. "So you're coming up empty too?"

"I didn't say I came up empty," Alicia corrected, smooth as silk.

This time, when both men focused on her, she looked at Harry. "Did you know Ben spent a good deal of time undercover for the agency? He was what some people call an embedded asset."

Across the table, Ben sat up straighter. "What are you getting at?"

Alicia wet her lips before answering. "We have another agent working deep with The Disciples. It seems they picked up a couple of former Southeast members."

Ben went completely still but said nothing, so Harry waded in. "Southeast members?"

"A gang based out of Southeast Atlanta. Called themselves SEATL. They ran a lot of crystal meth," she explained. To Ben she said, "I listened to some audio our operative gathered and there's talk of getting the old gang back together again. One of the guys they mentioned was Anton Brooks."

"Anton?" Ben repeated, as if mesmerized by the name.

"Who is Anton Brooks?" Harry asked, tired of being on the outside of this conversation looking in.

At last, Ben snapped out of his trance. "Anton Brooks is the younger brother of Andre Brooks...my best friend growing up. He's dead. Andre, I mean," he said gruffly.

"I'm sorry," Harry said, the response automatic, but genuine.

"Andre was the right-hand man to SEATL's leader, Ivan Jones," Alicia explained. She looked at him as if the name should mean something to him. Which it didn't. But it clearly meant something to Ben.

"Jones is dead too," he said flatly.

She nodded. "Yes. But you know there's always someone willing to step in."

"You're telling me Anton Brooks is trying to revive the operation?" Ben pressed, leaning forward.

Alicia nodded. "Rumor has it, he was handpicked by Ivan's partner before he died."

"Ivan or the business partner?" Harry interrupted, still trying to grab the tread of the conversation.

Alicia shrugged. "Well, they're both dead, but his business partner was the one to pick him. This is where it gets interesting," she said, her eyes sharp. "You might not know Ivan Jones, but I bet you've heard of his partner, Harry. He was an attorney named Jared Baker."

"Jared Baker?" He swung his gaze to Ben, who looked about as shocked and confused as Harry felt. "He was the guy tied to all the murders set up to look like suicide. Clint Young, Bo Abernathy—"

"And Marlee's brother, Jeff," Ben finished for him. Pushing up from his chair, the sheriff ran a hand across the back of his neck. "So Baker bestowed little Anton," he murmured. "But I can't imagine any of the other players are going to let him waltz in and take back what they gobbled up of Ivan's empire."

"Seems unlikely, doesn't it?" Alicia said, watching him warily. "But it looks like they may have a new moneyman. Someone with enough clout to make them all play nice together. At least for the moment."

"Any idea who?"

"Nothing for certain," Alicia hedged. "But I did come across something interesting when looking into Baker."

"What?" Harry asked, making a mental note to make her stitch this all together for him the minute Ben left.

"I was poking around to see who some of his old clients were, and guess whose name I came across?"

Harry's stomach sank and his heart rate kicked into overdrive. "No."

She nodded, unwilling to let him cling to his oblivion for more than a minute. "Yes. It appears Baker was the attorney of record when Samuel Coulter purchased a large parcel of timberland located in Masters County, Georgia."

Chapter Nine

Alicia stood in line at the bakery the next morning, bleary-eyed and her stomach rumbling at the sight of all the pastries in the case. Harry had left a note welcoming her to help herself to whatever she'd like, but she still wasn't feeling comfortable enough to make a mess in his kitchen. The previous night had proved to be enough of a mess for both of them.

After Ben left, they had sat at the table nibbling on crackers and cheese and talking about, well, everything. Harry filled her in on the spate of suicide-murders in Masters County in the previous year, all of which were connected to Attorney Jared Baker and the methamphetamine trade in the area.

She filled Harry in on Ivan Jones and the bounty the gang leader had put on Ben's head, even though the man had been behind bars. With his cover blown and a price on his head, the DEA considered Ben more of a liability than an asset. The biggest bust of his career had also ended up costing Ben his job and his home. No place in Atlanta was safe for him. He'd had to leave, which was why he ended up taking the job as sheriff of Masters County.

Sipping from bottles of water, they had sat in the

quiet. Alicia marveled at the realization that their lives had been unknowingly and loosely intertwined for many months before they'd actually laid eyes on one another. When she could no longer stifle her yawns, he insisted she go to bed and get her rest. By the time she woke, he'd already left for work. And despite the note written in neat block letters and left on the kitchen table, she'd wager he hadn't made himself breakfast. There were no dishes in the sink or even a crumb on the counter. He was likely afraid to light the gas stove. The house still reeked of kerosene.

The kitchen window had been cracked about an inch, letting in a steady stream of cool air, but without opening another to create a cross draft, it was doing nothing to help disperse the smell. Alicia had peeled back the plastic on the broken window enough to allow it to vent a bit in hopes of encouraging dissipation. Then she'd headed for the bakery she remembered had the best coffee in town.

Unfortunately, the real stuff was off her menu now, but she was still counting on decaf and self-delusion to rev her system. And a pastry. A body needed fuel, after all.

As she walked the two blocks to the business district, she took the time to survey her surroundings more carefully. She found it easier to brainstorm when she had the setting fixed firmly in her mind.

Who was behind these assaults on Harry's property? She couldn't imagine anyone hating him enough to do these things. Verbal threats, sure. And maybe the envelope thing, she conceded. But shooting up a man's house was something entirely different. But the failed Molotov cocktail? Whoever was doing this had gone a bridge too far. This wasn't someone local. Or not entirely. But there had to be some locals involved somehow, didn't there? Perhaps Coulter had sunk his roots deeper into Masters County than anyone realized.

If there was anyone local involved, there was no better course of action in a small town than putting one's ear to the ground. She remembered Brewster's Bakery with its pink awning from her previous stay in the area. It and the neon-lit Daisy Drive-In were the spots where locals congregated. Her stomach growled, and though she considered drinking decaf a step above drinking a brown crayon melted in hot water, she saw no better place to start her day than the bakery.

A bell above the door announced her arrival. As she stepped into the sugar-scented warmth of the café, she glanced around, hoping to spot a familiar face seated at one of the small tables. Sadly, she came up empty. Not a big surprise. She didn't know many people in Pine Bluff, and most of them were either attached to the sheriff's department or the local attorneys. All people who'd likely been at their desks for a couple of hours.

When she stepped up to the counter, she smiled engagingly at the woman with salt-and-pepper hair standing poised to take her order.

"Good morning," Alicia said briskly but with what she hoped was a friendly smile. "I'd like a decaf Americano, and one of those chocolate croissants."

The woman nodded and spun away to prepare her order. Seconds later, a paper cup and a white bakery bag appeared on the counter, and the woman started punching numbers into the cash register.

"Coffee and croissant comes to six forty-nine."

Alicia glanced over her shoulder at the tables where

people were drinking their coffee from oversize mugs and eating off of mismatched china plates with real silverware. "Oh, I'm sorry. I should've said it was for here."

The older woman paused, her expression neutral but unwavering. "Oh, well, you're welcome to eat here if you'd like. Six forty-nine," she repeated.

Alicia raised her eyebrows as she handed over her debit card. The woman swiped it, punched in the amount of the charge and waited for the ancient printer to spool out a receipt.

Desperate to establish some rapport, Alicia nodded to the outdated credit-card machine. "Still swiping, huh?" The other woman looked up at her, the bland expression she wore hardening. A moment too late, she realized the woman probably found her comment insulting. "I mean, most places have a chip reader or even one of those scanners where you tap the card…"

She trailed off as the woman yanked her receipt from the machine and pushed it across the counter.

"Yes, well, this one works fine, and when I need a new one, I'll get a new one. Thank you. Have a nice day," the woman responded curtly.

She leaned to her left and peered at the customer behind Alicia in case she hadn't gotten the hint. Alicia stepped away, and the woman behind the counter smiled so broadly it transformed her entire face. "Good morning, Carolee. I wasn't expecting to see you in here. What can I do for you today?"

Taking her cup and to-go bag, Alicia moved to an open table nestled against the far wall. From there, she watched people come and go from the busy bakery.

Almost everyone stopped to chat with at least one or two people on the way in or out. The place seemed to be humming. High on the exchange of information as much as the sugar, she suspected. Unfortunately, the mishmash of soft-spoken Southern accents made it hard to pick out any particular tidbits.

She took a sulky sip of her coffee and tore the corner of her croissant into bite-size pieces, arranging them on top of the sheet of wax paper it came wrapped in. She couldn't take her eyes off the woman who'd taken her order. She was speaking to an immaculately dressed blonde woman who looked like she'd never touched a doughnut in her life.

Alicia popped a bite of buttery pastry into her mouth and tried to pick apart the sudden surge of resentment she felt as she watched the easy exchange between the two women. She slumped lower in her seat and watched them through narrowed eyes when a familiar voice interrupted her ruminations.

"Hello, Alicia."

Sitting up straighter, she jerked her head up to find Marlee Masters beaming down at her.

"Ben told me you were back in town."

Alicia dropped the hunk of croissant she was smashing between her thumb and forefinger and quickly wiped her hand on a paper napkin from the dispenser on the table. "Oh, yes. Hello. Nice to see you again."

Marlee's smile widened as she waved to someone across the room. "May I?" she asked, gesturing to the empty seat across from her.

"Please."

"I snuck away from the office. I swear, some days it's a meeting about a meeting about when to schedule a meeting to have a meeting," she said with a laugh. She nodded her head toward the woman at the counter.

"Over there's my mama. Carolee Masters," she added. "She wanted to come down here to order some pastries for bridge club, and had gone by the house to talk to Daddy, so I volunteered to be her chauffeur."

"I thought you said you were in meetings," Alicia pointed out.

Marlee shook her head. "No, I said today was all about meetings, but I didn't say I was participating in them. One of the perks as boss."

She said the last with such an engaging smile, Alicia couldn't help reciprocating. "It must be nice."

"I'll go back after I drop Mom off again," Marlee said, waving her hand dismissively. "But in the meantime—" She looked up and, as if on cue, the woman who had waited on Alicia so brusquely a few minutes before appeared beside the table.

She held a large cup and saucer, and a plate with what appeared to be a breakfast sandwich made out of a fluffy biscuit. "There you go, Miss Marlee," the woman practically cooed.

Marlee gazed openmouthed at the food.

"Thank you so much, Miss Camille. This is a treat."

"I made it with egg whites like your mama likes, so you don't have to feel guilty about anything."

"Thank you for looking out for me." Marlee managed to say the last bit without even a hint of sarcasm.

Alicia found herself staring at Marlee in shock. Wasn't she insulted about the implication of watching her weight? Apparently not.

Marlee simply smiled. "I'll see you at Tuesday night's Slim Session?" she asked, her voice sweet as honey.

The woman called Miss Camille pulled a face and blushed. "I suppose I should come, but I have to tell you my weigh-in won't be any good. I've been sampling more of the wares than I should lately."

Marlee shook her head. "You know it's not all about what the scale says—it's about how we feel. If you'd like to attend, and you need support, we'll be there for you."

When the other woman walked away, Alicia looked at Marlee agog.

"Slim Sessions?"

Marlee chuckled. "The name is kind of a holdover from my mom's days, and we don't do the whole diet thing like they used to do where they eat nothing but a couple leaves of lettuce. I'm trying to help it to evolve into something more…holistic. Diet, exercise and generally what we're doing to make ourselves feel good these days. More of an all-around support group, I guess." She frowned as she picked up the layered breakfast biscuit. "We really do need to think of a better name," she murmured before taking a hefty bite.

"At least you got a plate," Alicia pointed out, gesturing from her crushed bag and wax-paper place mat to Marlee's plate, cup and saucer.

"Oh." Marlee's brows knit as she chewed, eyeing the bag and paper cup. "I think Mrs. Brewster assumes people who are not from here are passing through." She hesitated for a moment. "I'd tell you not to take it personally, but in truth, I think she means it to be personal."

Marlee's candor made Alicia laugh out loud. The sound drew the attention of the few people seated around them, but Alicia didn't care. There were worse things than being seen laughing and enjoying breakfast with the town's biggest mogul.

"I was hoping to put my ear to the ground and pick

up some gossip while I was here, but it doesn't look like I'll have much luck," Alicia said, wrinkling her nose.

Marlee chewed thoughtfully, then took a sip from the enormous mug. "Small towns can be tough to crack."

"An understatement," Alicia said wryly.

"No doubt." Marlee chuckled. "But I understand why people are wary. Pine Bluff is small, but we've had a lot of trouble in the past few years. More trouble than any town this size should. Right now, people are stuck in some kind of nostalgia loop." She set her biscuit back down and pulled a paper napkin from the dispenser to wipe her fingers. "There's a whole contingent of them who think we were living in a damn Norman Rockwell painting before all this 'trouble,'" she said, using air quotes, "came to town. But I grew up here, and I can tell you this was no paradise before."

"This is Georgia, not Utopia," Alicia said with a nod.

"Exactly. Ben tells me you're looking into drawing some connection between the group who was after him in Atlanta and whoever's doing these things to Harry," Marlee said, lacing her fingers together and leaning in as she spoke softly. "I want you to know I will help in whatever way I can."

Alicia was smart enough to know this was no small offer. Marlee was a Masters of Masters County. She ran the timber company founded by her great-great-grandfather. The company was the largest employer in the area, which made Marlee a powerful woman. If she pledged her support, it wasn't a token gesture.

"I appreciate the offer," Alicia said sincerely. "And I want you to know I always thought Ben had been treated very unfairly by the agency. They should have done more for him. They should've found a way to protect their own."

Marlee nodded. "I agree. But I'm also glad they didn't, otherwise he never would've landed here."

"Things have a way of working out, regardless of what we plan," Alicia said, almost to herself.

"They do indeed." Marlee sat up straight again, picked up her sandwich and bit into it. "Oh!" she said through stuffed cheeks. Cupping a hand over her mouth, she continued to speak. "Sorry. I was thinking we need Lori. Lori will help," she said, her voice garbled.

"I'll take any help I can get, but why wouldn't people talk to Lori? She's from here too," she pointed out.

Marlee nodded vigorously as she chewed, then swallowed hard. With another slurp of her latte, she swiped the napkin from her lap and wiped her mouth. "But she's the law. Some people get hung up on the badge."

"I see." Alicia popped another bite of croissant into her mouth and chewed slowly. If some locals wouldn't talk around Lori because she was a cop, then surely others would clam up around Marlee since she likely held the keys to their livelihoods, but maybe between the three of them…

Marlee wiped her mouth again, then nodded. "Don't you worry. Between Lori and me, you'll have an in about anywhere you want around here. And between the three of us, surely we can hear something."

"You read my mind." Marlee laughed, but Alicia was not entirely convinced. "What makes you think we can get any further than Ben has gotten?"

Marlee snorted. "Listen, I love the man, so I'm admittedly not the most objective person when it comes to him, but I can tell you this—people like Ben, but he's an outsider." She shrugged. "They might start letting him in here and there, but he's never going to have the network of information someone who is born and raised here would have. Heck, even Mike Schaeffer has an advantage on him," she said, referring to one of Ben's deputies.

"I see," she repeated.

"Don't worry—he knows it," Marlee said, picking a bit of the biscuit off and lobbing it into her mouth. "I like to tease him and say he keeps me around because I'm his golden ticket."

Alicia eyed the radiant blonde seated across from her and laughed. "I'm pretty sure that's not why he keeps you around. I've never seen a man more smitten."

A peachy blush colored Marlee's cheeks. "Well, the feeling is entirely mutual, in case you were wondering," she said with a pointed look.

"I wasn't wondering. It's crystal clear."

"Marlee, honey," her mother called from across the room. "Come on—I need to get back to your daddy."

Marlee glanced mournfully down at the remainder of the breakfast biscuit and tossed her paper napkin on the table. "Coming, Mama." She rose, lifting her coffee cup in one fluid motion. "Let me get a to-go cup for my latte."

Carolee Masters shook her head when she spotted her daughter's abandoned plate. "Marlee, you know how it is with biscuits—two minutes on the lips and forever on the hips."

"Well, now, Mama, you know we don't think about food in those terms anymore," Marlee said with a toss of her golden hair. "Food is fuel. It's all about making the right choices at the right time. And I can tell you at this very moment my belly was craving a biscuit, and I am not gonna apologize to my hips."

Alicia fought the urge to applaud. She watched as Marlee sashayed up to the counter and handed over her unfinished coffee to be poured into a paper cup. When her mother approached, Marlee leaned in and kissed her cheek. Clearly there were no hard feelings generated by their exchange.

Alicia watched heads swivel as the Masters women made their way to the door, calling out goodbyes and wishing various people nice days and asking to be remembered to other people as they passed.

When the bell above the door jingled, she stared down at the remnants of the bacon-and-egg biscuit. Probably what she should have ordered. She was pregnant. She needed to start eating like a grown-up, not a teenager, she admonished herself. More protein. Maybe some leafy greens, she thought, barely suppressing a shudder.

Miss Camille appeared at her table to clear Marlee's place. "Can I get you a top-off on your coffee, sugar?" she asked in a markedly friendlier manner.

Alicia glanced down at the plastic dome of the coffee cup and figured more decaf couldn't hurt. "Yes, please. I'm drinking decaf."

"Be right back," Camille Brewster replied. Then she bustled away.

Alicia managed a couple more bites of croissant and a sip of her now lukewarm coffee. Even though the coffee tasted the same as regular, she missed the kick of caffeine. The combination of a lack of stimulant and what the doctor termed early-pregnancy exhaustion was going to be crippling.

Ms. Brewster startled her from her thoughts when she

placed the cup and saucer down on the table with a clatter. Alicia stared, her eyes fixed on the heavy porcelain cup. "Thank you," she managed. "What do I owe you?"

The older woman simply shook her head. "Refills are on the house."

Alicia watched in astonishment as the woman who'd barely acknowledged her a short time before made her way back to the counter.

Determined to make a good impression, Alicia cleaned up scraps of her croissant and brushed every last crumb into the bag she'd revived. All in all, not a bad trip to the bakery, even if she didn't overhear anything about Harry's tormentors. She was more than happy to take advantage of Marlee's generous offer to help her break through some of the small-town barriers, but would also take heed not to be fooled into thinking she belonged because people didn't treat her like a stranger. Marlee's words about Ben and his ability to fit into Pine Bluff society resonated with her.

As a military kid, Alicia had been an outsider her entire life, moving from post to post, never making deep, decades-long friendships. Having gone through life without forming attachments had served her well when she went to work for the agency. She hadn't always been partnered with the most forward-thinking people, nor had some of her bosses been as enthusiastic about having her in their ranks as one would hope. Bronson was a good example. But she'd survived others like him, and she would figure out a way to carry on. She would be the one in control of her destiny with the agency.

She sipped until she'd depleted the second cup of coffee. When she was done, she gathered the paper goods as well as her cup and saucer and carried them back to the counter.

"Oh, let me get those," Camille said, snatching the bag from Alicia's hand, looking slightly abashed. She put the cup and saucer into a black tub behind her. "Everything okay, I hope?"

"Everything was delicious, thank you." Alicia hesitated for a moment, then decided if she was going to make a go of her time here in Pine Bluff, she needed to go all in. "Mrs. Brewster, I don't suppose you could tell me what it is Harry Hayes prefers or how he takes his coffee?"

Camille Brewster's eyebrows rose almost to her hairline. "Harry Hayes?"

Alicia nodded and did her best to look bashful. She wasn't sure if she was pulling it off, given the look of consternation on Mrs. Brewster's face. "Yes. You see, I'm staying with him and I'd like to take him something at the office, but I wasn't sure what he prefers."

"Staying with him?" Camille Brewster repeated.

Alicia fought the urge to smile. She knew the information would go out on the wire before the door closed behind her. "Yes."

The confirmation seemed to snap the other woman from her trance. "Oh, well, Harry doesn't like anything particularly fancy. A doughnut every once in a while. Glazed or twist, usually, but sometimes he goes for the cream-filled."

"Great. I'll take one of each. And a coffee," she added. "Whatever he usually orders."

The woman looked at her blankly for a moment. "Coffee? Harry doesn't drink coffee."

Alicia gaped at the woman, struck silent for a moment. "Doesn't drink coffee?"

The other woman laughed. "I know, right?" She shook her head. "Occasionally, he'll buy a bottle of orange juice, but mostly I think he sticks to water."

Alicia goggled at the woman. "No caffeine at all?"

Camille Brewster's lips drew tight, and for a moment Alicia thought she might've stepped over the line, but then she shook her head in bewildered dismay. "No. None. I honestly don't know how the man makes it through the day."

Chapter Ten

Harry walked into his office to find the place deserted and a fat stack of mail piled at the center of his blotter. His ADA, Danielle, was likely across the hall talking to Julianne in the sheriff's department. The intern they'd hired from Albany State University, Layla, had mentioned running to the Piggly Wiggly for break-room supplies. Ever since the debacle with the envelope delivered to his house, he'd insisted he open his own mail. The last thing he wanted was for the people who worked for him to open anything dangerous or even questionable.

If someone was coming after him, they needed to keep him and him alone in their sights.

Sighing, he dropped his briefcase onto the desk and used the corner of it to push the pile around a bit. It looked like a mishmash of number-ten business envelopes and Christmas cards. There were a couple of larger manila envelopes. Dropping into his chair, he closed his eyes and gave himself a minute to process what had transpired in Judge Nichols's chambers.

At any other time, he would not have thought anything about a twenty-year-old kid getting busted for possession, but now every single drug-related incident in Masters County felt personal to him.

He'd been there when the DEA's methamphetamine raids had decimated the town. He'd been there when the power struggle resulting from those arrests led to a series of heartbreaking murders made to look like suicides. Then Samuel Coulter moved in and changed the face of it all. Wealthy and urbane, Coulter had been an object of curiosity, and yes, even admiration to some, when he first moved to Masters County. Judging from the gossip he heard around town, some of the women considered the man handsome, but Harry could only figure they'd never seen him up close and personal.

His own dealings with Coulter left him feeling cold inside. Like he'd swallowed an ice cube whole and it landed in the empty pit of his stomach and refused to melt.

The man was off. He'd seen it from the moment they met. But getting a hinky feeling about someone and being able to prosecute them for a crime heinous enough to put them away for a good long time were two very different things.

Earlier, he'd given Judge Nichols a brief rundown of all the incidents involving his property. Harry and the judge had worked closely for a number of years, and since his office was adjacent to the judge's chambers, he felt the man should be in the know. He also wanted someone in a trusted position, someone who wasn't law enforcement or had any personal vested interest in seeing Coulter convicted beyond a thirst for justice, to know what was happening.

In the event something should happen to Harry.

Judge Nichols, always a fair and patient man, had listened calmly, taken notes and assured Harry if the worst ever came to pass he would throw the full weight of his

influence behind flushing out who was responsible for
these misdeeds.

Harry had felt comforted for the five minutes it took
to walk from Judge Nichols's chambers back to his own
office.

The stack of mail had undone his sense of calm.

Pulling a letter opener from the center desk drawer,
Harry leaned closer to the pile and began to shift it with
the tip of the blade to survey the contents. The number-ten envelopes were likely simple correspondence
from law firms in the area. He saw the logo from Wendell Wingate's firm, now run by his grandson Simon,
printed on the corner of one. The names on the Christmas cards were all familiar to him. Mostly colleagues,
but a few friends from college, and a couple of locals
who knew the best way to get him was always at work
rather than home.

He snared the edge of one envelope with the tip of
the opener and pushed it from the pile. The sticker in
the corner showed it was from Lourdes Cabrera. He had
only seen Lori in passing since the night of the mystery
powder scare, but the sight of the card made him smile.
He pulled the envelope out of the stack and slit it open.
Deputy Cabrera had sent him a Christmas card. Mailed
it, even though they worked directly across the foyer
from one another. He couldn't wait to prod Lori's boyfriend, Simon, about making her list.

When he removed the heavy card stock from the envelope, he saw it wasn't simply a card but an invitation. A tastefully designed holiday party invitation. He
smiled at the sight of it. Elsewhere in the world, emails,
texts and phone calls might be enough, but here in South

Georgia, when a person was throwing a soiree of some import, paper invitations were still the done thing.

Harry rocked back in his seat smiling as he read the details. Lori may have mailed the invitation, but the holiday party was to be held at Simon's house. His eyebrows rose when he noted the date. It was set for this coming Saturday, which meant this had been thrown together at the very last minute…or he'd been an afterthought on the invitation list. The second notion made him frown. In the past few months, Harry had come to consider Simon, Ben and Lori some of his closest friends. He preferred to assume the party was arranged last minute, and not that he was on the B-list.

No sooner had the thought entered his mind than a text message buzzed on his phone. He extracted it from his suit pocket and read the screen. It was from Simon Wingate.

Did you get the invitation?

Harry smirked. The impatience was typical for Simon. Thumbs flying, he texted back.

Just opened it. Did you forget to mail mine in the first round?

The three dots appeared and Harry found himself partially holding his breath as he waited for his friend to reply.

This is the first round, Simon said in the first bubble. It's kind of a last-minute thing. I was going to text, but Lori wouldn't let me.

Harry snickered, but before he could reply, another bubble appeared.

Can you make it?

I don't see why not, he typed back.

The three dots appeared again, and then the answer to Harry's next question magically appeared.

And Alicia? Are you bringing her?

Apparently, he was expected to bring his guest. A flashback of hot, hungry kisses ignited in his mind. The last time he and Alicia had attended a party at Simon's house, the evening had not only ended with them tangled in the sheets, but also…a baby.

If she wants to come, he eventually typed.

There was a longer pause as the ellipses blinked on the screen. A larger text bubble appeared.

Good, because we're having this thing since Lori heard Alicia was back to stay for a bit and you two are together. I think she might have a girl crush on Alicia. Either way, any excuse for a party, right?

Harry chuckled, tickled by Simon's reasoning.

This way, you get to be the first people in town hosting a Christmas party.

May have crossed our minds, Simon replied. Another bubble appeared a moment later. See you Saturday.

Setting his phone aside, Harry decided to start in on

the rest of the Christmas cards to see if they also had surprises in store. Alas, they were the usual assortment of family photo collages, winter landscapes or variations on jolly old St. Nick.

Next, he opened the correspondence from the law firms, unfolded the papers and gave them a quick scan before putting them in his outbox for his assistant to pick up and add to the appropriate files.

Only the two manila envelopes were left.

He prodded each one with the tip of the letter opener. One looked to be filled with paperwork and appeared to have been sent by the Prescott County district attorney. The other appeared to have some sort of item enclosed in a hard square, like a picture frame. The return address showed it was from his sister.

Curious as to why Sarah would be mailing something to his office rather than to the house, he slipped the package open and peered inside. There was a framed photo and a note. Harry smiled, expecting to see another artfully casual shot of his nephews romping in a park or rolling in the snow or some such thing.

He pulled the frame from the envelope and the folded sheet of paper covering the glass fluttered. He picked it up, but rather than his sister's hurried cursive, he saw a single typed sentence.

"Next time it won't be a rock."

He stared at the paper for a moment, willing his brain to absorb both the unexpected message and the import. As it was, all he could do was catalog the facts as he saw them. Plain white copier paper. Standard Courier font, no bigger than twelve point. A threat. Mailed from his sister's address.

"What the—"

He bit back the profanity and dropped the piece of paper atop the frame once again and grabbed the envelope. It was postmarked in Atlanta. Not mailed from his sister's address. It was a ploy. A way to get him to open the damn thing without a second thought.

He snatched the piece of paper from the frame and found himself staring down at a photograph of Samuel Coulter. It had been inscribed, autograph style. "I've been framed, S.J. Coulter."

Harry dropped the frame like it was hot. His mind raced. Rock? What did they mean *rock*? Oh, damn. What if Layla had opened this? It was one thing to come after him. He shot out of his chair and took off for the front of the office at a run.

"Layla! Dani!" He shouted their names though he knew the office was empty. He was almost to the door when he looked through the plate-glass windows and saw a small cluster of people gathered near the drained fountain in the center of the atrium. Among them were Layla and Danielle, Deputy Lori Cabrera and Julianne Shields, the sheriff's department's dispatcher.

"What happened?" he demanded, breathless. "What's going on? Is anyone hurt?" he said, scanning each woman for injury as he skidded to a halt near the group.

Layla swiveled, her eyes wide and frightened. "Someone threw a rock through the window."

Harry rushed over to them. Shaking his head, he gazed down at the shaken young woman. "Are you okay?"

"I'm fine," she said a shade too quickly.

"What window? I didn't see any broken glass."

"It was in the break room," Danielle informed him.

"I was up at the county clerk's desk, but Layla was in the office."

Lori Cabrera spoke up. "We think they meant to throw through your office window but miscounted."

Harry blinked at her. This was a perfectly reasonable explanation. At least as reasonable as anything was these days. It would be easy to get it wrong. The municipal building had been built in the 1960s. The floor-to-ceiling windows on the interior were meant to allow light to shine inside, but the exterior windows were built high on the walls and embedded in brick. A person couldn't simply walk by the building and peer inside. Such windows kept things bright enough while keeping the relentless South Georgia heat out. They also provided security for the law enforcement and legal professionals who worked in those offices.

"Where is this rock?" Harry demanded.

Lori held up a large zip bag with a smooth brown river rock about eight inches in diameter inside. "There was a note rubber banded to it," she reported.

"Of course there was," Harry snapped, unable to keep the snarky edge out of his tone. "I bet it said something to the effect of 'Free Coulter!'"

Before Lori could confirm or deny, Layla nodded like a bobblehead doll. Harry swallowed his anger and impatience. He couldn't get worked up. He needed to remain calm so all those around him did so too.

He gave Layla's shoulder an awkward pat. "Were you in the break room when it happened?"

She shook her head. "No, but I was in there like two minutes before," she said with a shudder. "I was restocking the fridge with water, because I thought you'd be back from Judge Nichols's office soon. I made myself a cup of coffee. I'd just gone back to my desk."

Harry clenched his jaw, but he looked her directly in the eye when he spoke. "I'm glad you aren't injured, and I'm sorry you're scared." He gave her a wan half smile. "You said you wanted to get some experience in a DA's office before you started law school. I know this isn't exactly what you had in mind, but sometimes this is the reality of it, Layla." He straightened and glanced around their group. "Sometimes, stuff like this comes with the territory. We prosecute bad people. Bad people associate with other bad people, and sometimes they think they can intimidate us out of doing our jobs, but they can't."

He snapped his mouth shut and shifted his gaze from one person to the next.

"I realize I am not the lead on this case, but for some reason they are singling me out, and I refuse to back down," he said firmly. "Having stated my intention to make my stand, the last thing I want to do is put any of you in danger." Locking eyes with Layla, he said, "If either of you wish to take a leave of absence or find a way to try to do some of your work remotely, I have no issue with giving you some flexibility."

He then zoomed in on his assistant district attorney. "Same goes for you. But I want you both to know I won't be scared into quitting." He rolled his shoulders back and took a deep breath. "I am scared, but I'm not quitting."

"We've got your back, Harry," Deputy Cabrera said gruffly.

He nodded, then shifted his attention to the two women who worked for him. "There's nothing wrong with being scared. But if this is the career you want, if this is the path you're going to choose to take, you're going to have to find a way to tamp down your fear, as well. I don't mind admitting I'm scared. I don't like having my home and office violated. I don't like having the people around me frightened and intimidated. If I could do my job in a way where I wouldn't have to deal with these sorts of things, I would. Do you understand me?"

The two women nodded, then stepped out of the small knot of people. He glanced at Lori. "Have you got enough of a statement?"

The deputy nodded, and Julianne, the dispatcher, reached over to pat Layla on the shoulder.

"I think we're good here, Harry," Lori said. "Keep watching your step. Let us know anytime anything happens. Anything at all," she ordered.

He nodded and then gestured for the two other women to follow him back into the justice side of the law-and-justice center. As he reached for the door handle to hold it open, he spun around and called out to Lori Cabrera.

"Oh, and, Deputy?"

Lori drew to a stop. "Yes?"

"I'd like to RSVP for Saturday," he called across the atrium, holding up two fingers.

The exterior door opened and Alicia walked through holding a white bakery bag. "Hey," she said, dividing the greeting with a glance between himself and Lori. "What's Saturday? Am I missing something?"

Lori suddenly tucked the evidence bag behind her leg, then shot a pointed look at Harry. "Nothing Harry can't fill you in on. See you guys on Saturday, and hopefully not before."

The moment the door to the sheriff's department whooshed closed behind Lori, Alicia looked at him questioningly. "Well, I guess she told you. What's Saturday?" she asked again.

He forced a smile but knew it wasn't quite enough. "We've been invited to our first Christmas party."

Alicia's eyes narrowed as she approached him. "A Christmas party? Isn't it still a bit early for those?"

Harry shrugged. "It's after Thanksgiving, so I think any Saturday is fair game," he said, trying to inject a note of lightness into his tone. But Alicia wasn't fooled.

"What's going on?"

"The usual," he said dismissively. "I got a rock thrown through the break-room window this morning and a framed photograph of Samuel Coulter sent to me by someone using my sister's return address."

Alicia, in all her wisdom, zeroed in on exactly what was bothering him most. "Your sister's address?"

He tipped his head in the affirmative. "Exactly. But postmarked in Atlanta."

"So whoever this is either actually knows you and your family or has enough knowledge of you to get access to personal information."

Sighing, he released the door and let it swing shut, leaving them alone in the echoing atrium. "It isn't too hard to get personal information. You don't have to be much of a computer hacker to dig up people's addresses these days."

Alicia pondered for a moment. "No, probably not. But unless you've got a bunch of programmers who decided they were born to be wild, it might discount your biker gang."

He sent her an arch look. "Aren't you being presumptive? For all you know, each one of those guys has a PhD."

Alicia nodded in concession. "You're right. I was typecasting. In my defense, I haven't had any caffeine and I'm not sure my brain knows how to function without it. Speaking of caffeine, I think I blew our cover."

"How so?"

"I didn't know you don't drink coffee. Mrs. Brewster had to tell me."

"Ah, yeah, well, it's kind of new. I broke the habit a year or so ago."

She pulled a face. "Sorry. She may be suspicious now. If we were in a real relationship, I'd know you were a freak of nature."

"You can tell her I've been hiding my dirty secret from you. Camille loves to be in the know."

She frowned as she looked down at her hand and then back up at him, lifting it as if she'd completely forgotten she was holding a white paper bag. "I brought you something."

Sheer surprise made his heart skip a beat. "You did?"

She nodded solemnly. "I bought all three because I didn't know which one you would prefer, but now I'm thinking you probably need all of them."

He took the bag from her and unrolled the top. Peering inside, he saw three doughnuts. One glazed, one cinnamon twist and one cream-filled. This time, there was no holding back his smile. "I think you've mistaken me for a police officer."

"Now who's typecasting?"

Harry chuckled, then gestured toward the door. As he pulled it open for her, he said, "You forget, I've watched Ben Kinsella demolish a box of doughnuts."

She looked back at him over her shoulder as she

passed him and led the way toward his office. "Good. Then you won't mind if I eat the cream-filled."

Harry sobered instantly. "Have you not had any breakfast yet?" He took two quick steps to fall in beside her. "I told you to help yourself to anything you wanted."

She shot him a sidelong glance. "You operate under the assumption I know how to cook. Now we're back to the typecast thing again."

"You could be typecast yourself by claiming you are a woman so focused on her career, she never bothered to learn how to cook."

She smirked as she waltzed into his office and plopped into one of the guest chairs. "Another case of a cliché coming true."

Harry dropped the doughnut bag on his desk, then held up a finger. "Hang tight—I'll be right back."

When he stepped back out of his office, Layla was hanging up the phone. "Maintenance is going to be right up to put some plywood over the window," she reported.

Harry nodded. "Thank you for calling them. Are you sure you're okay?"

"I'm fine. I was freaked, you know?" she said, tucking her hair behind her ear.

Harry let out a bitter laugh. "Yeah, I know."

"If you don't mind, I think I will head home for the day," she said cautiously. "I only need—"

He held up a hand. "No need to explain. Go ahead and take the day. Call or text me to let me know how you're doing, okay?"

She nodded, then reached into the bottom drawer of her desk for her purse. "I will."

Harry stood back for a moment watching as the young woman gathered her belongings. She left with a self-conscious wave. When she was gone, he walked toward the break room. On his way, he poked his head into Danielle's office. "Are you sticking around today, or do you want to head out too?"

Danielle released an indelicate snort. "Not scared of rocks, Harry."

"Neither am I, per se," he said pointedly. "But there have been other threats—one implying it may be more than a rock next time. If you wanted to avoid the office until we figure this out, no one would blame you."

She inclined her head. "Noted, boss. For now, I think I'm going to finish this motion and keep moving ahead." She made a swimming gesture with her hand. "You know I'm a shark."

He smiled. "I know you are."

He crossed into the break room to grab a few paper napkins and a plate. The cool December breeze poured in through the hole in the window. Harry scowled but refused to give it more than a moment's notice. Hustling back to his office, he entered to find Alicia standing in front of his desk staring down at the pile of mail he had opened in the moments before discovering this last bout of vandalism.

"Snooping?" he asked as he strode into the room.

"Admiring the fan art," she replied, nodding to the framed photo of Samuel Coulter. "We need to bag those as evidence."

"I know."

He made a slow circle, then spotted the plastic grocery bag from the Piggly Wiggly in his trash can. "This will do for now. I'll call Lori and have her come get it." Using the letter opener, he finagled the note, envelope and framed photo into the bag, then dropped it on his credenza.

"I wonder if this is his handwriting," Alicia mused as she dug into the bakery bag.

Harry shrugged and handed over the plate and a paper napkin. "I couldn't tell you, but I'm sure someone will be able to."

"I had a nice talk with Marlee Masters this morning. She said she and Lori Cabrera were going to help me get in good with some of the ladies around town," she said with a saucy smile. "Apparently, folks around here don't cotton to strangers," she said, exaggerating her drawl.

He laughed, then extracted the cinnamon twist from the bag, wrapping it in a napkin as he sat down in his desk chair. "I'd like to say it isn't true, but I don't wanna be a liar." He took a giant bite of the doughnut, then, using his free hand, extracted the printed invitation to Simon's Christmas party from the pile. "I believe they concocted this plan without getting you to sign on first," he said, waving the heavy card stock in her direction.

Alicia looked up, the cream-filled doughnut held aloft between her thumb and middle finger. "Oh?"

"We've been invited to a Christmas party, remember?" His smile grew sly as he rocked back in his chair, peeling back the napkin and preparing to take another bite of his doughnut. "I believe Ms. Masters and Deputy Cabrera have arranged your debutante party."

Chapter Eleven

"Come in, come in!" Simon Wingate said, standing back to wave Harry and Alicia across his threshold. Alicia blinked at the man's effusive greeting. His whole demeanor seemed lighter and brighter since Coulter, his former client, had been arraigned and held without bail. Taken aback, but not willing to show it, Alicia plastered a smile on her face as their host gave Harry's hand a hearty shake. She stepped into the warmth of the foyer and nearly jumped out of her skin when Simon whipped a bunch of broccoli from behind his back and held it over her head.

"What do you know? Mistletoe, right here in the entry. Almost doesn't seem fair," he said, leaning in and tapping his cheek to indicate she should kiss him.

Harry snorted, pulling Simon back a couple of steps to give her some room. "Watch it. She can take you down in more ways than you can count."

To his credit, Simon appeared mildly chastened. Offering Alicia a weak smile, he said, "Sorry. Not well done of me. I was trying to get under Harry's skin."

"Well, it worked," Harry growled. "Has to be the lamest excuse for mistletoe I've ever seen," he added derisively. "I can't believe Lori's letting you get away with that."

"Lori's not letting him get away with anything," the woman in question said, entering the foyer. She snatched the broccoli from Simon's hand and threw it directly at the man's forehead. "For someone so smart, you sure do like to act a fool sometimes."

Lori turned to Alicia and offered an apologetic smile. "I'm so sorry. Somebody gets overexcited when he hosts social gatherings and forgets about important things like consent and personal space. I'm sending him to obedience school next week."

"I'm not a dog," Simon retorted, tossing the broccoli back to Lori.

She snagged it midair. "Stop acting like one." She rolled her eyes at her boyfriend's antics. "You're going to scare her off. She's not used to obnoxious men like you."

Simon let out a snort and closed the front door. "I don't think I could scare this woman if I tried. And how do you know what kind of men she's accustomed to being around? I'm willing to bet some of those federal agents are downright obnoxious." He turned to Alicia. "Am I wrong?"

She gave a chuckle. "I can absolutely say you are not wrong." She thrust the bottle of wine they'd brought with them into Simon's hand. "He wasn't nearly this rambunctious the last time I saw him."

Lori rolled her eyes. "He was regretting his god-awful taste in clientele," she said, glaring at Simon while making the pronouncement. "Weren't you?"

"I rue the day," Simon responded, his expression sober. "Can we all forget my past indiscretions and move on knowing I am the charming and lovable guy you see standing in front of you?"

Alicia shrugged. "If she can forgive you, I think any of us could."

Which was true. When Alicia first came to Pine Bluff, Lori and Simon had an intense sort of vibe between them. It was obvious to anyone with eyes there was an attraction, but Lori was hell-bent on bringing Simon's most important client down. It took some time and careful maneuvering for Simon to wriggle out of his attorney-client relationship. Alicia was glad to see the enmity she'd witnessed between the deputy and the defense attorney morph into something happier. By the time she'd left town, there was no doubt Lori and Simon would end up together, and now here they were.

Simon smiled, and Alicia nearly had to take a step back. He was almost as blindingly handsome as Marlee Masters was golden. No one could blame Lori Cabrera for falling hard for a man she didn't entirely trust. She'd fought it. In the end, Alicia gave the younger woman credit for going with her gut. Wingate was one of those guys who could talk the bark off a tree. Unlike Harry, whose good looks and approach to life were shades more understated. But not any less appealing. At least, not to her.

"Where do you want us to throw our jackets?" Harry asked, and Alicia exhaled some of the tension she hadn't realized she was holding.

His pragmatism was a balm to her. His calm in the face of Simon's exuberance made her grateful to have him by her side. For a woman who prided herself on keeping an even keel, she was beginning to feel a bit scattershot in the face of Harry's unshakable cool.

Through everything happening to him in the past few weeks, she'd only seen him lose his temper in brief flare-ups, though she knew the man had to be raging inside.

As was she. Bronson had sent her a text. Apparently, he was regretting sending his favorite minion away and insisted she be back in the Atlanta office Monday morning. When she explained what was happening to Harry, he told her the protection of a local district attorney was outside the scope of her job, and unless she had something solid leading to further drug-trafficking arrests, he would see her in his office or she'd find herself on disciplinary leave.

"You may want to hang on to them," Lori said, waving them toward the back of the house. "Everyone is in the kitchen or on the patio. We have a fire going," she explained. "I will show you where the refreshments are."

Harry slipped out of his leather jacket. Ever the gentleman, he held the collar of her coat so she could shed it more easily. Lori took their jackets and led them to the back of the house.

In the kitchen, she offered Harry his coat again and he blinked at it in confusion. She gestured to the sliding doors to the patio. "Most of the men are out there. They have made fire. They must stand by fire and drink beer as men do," she said, grunting each word in a bad caveman impression.

Harry rolled his eyes. "Gee, thanks. I love being classified by my gender as a Neanderthal. For the record, I cook, and I cook well."

Lori laughed. And Alicia watched as her hostess casually tossed her coat onto a mound piled on a bench near the back door. "You can complain to us about gender inequalities in about two or three hundred years. In the meantime, scram. I want to talk to Alicia and I don't want you around," Lori said, tipping her chin up and defying him to contradict her.

"You're a lot bossier here than you are at work."

"I'm not the boss of you at work," Lori shot back without missing a beat.

Harry checked with Alicia, silently making sure she was okay with the plan. She nodded vigorously. This was exactly how she wanted the evening to go. Alicia had taken Marlee's words at the bakery to heart.

Divide and conquer. She would let Marlee and Lori pave the way for her with the women of Pine Bluff. There was no better way to know the pulse of a place than to get in with the locals.

"Run along. Don't set yourself on fire," she said dismissively. "We've had enough excitement for one week."

"I concur," Harry said dryly. He lifted a hand in farewell and made his way toward the patio.

The second the sliding door was pulled shut, Lori took Alicia by the elbow and escorted her to the hall. "You have had a heck of a week. Are you sure you're up for a party tonight?"

"I am most definitely up for a party tonight," Alicia stated, meeting the other woman's gaze directly. "And I'm counting on you to tell me who I need to get to know."

Lori's eyes narrowed, but her lips curved up and she gave an appreciative nod. "Marlee will be here soon, and between the two of us, we're going to introduce you to everybody who's anybody in Pine Bluff."

"And will those everybodies who know anybody have any clue as to who might be doing some of the things happening to Harry?"

"If they don't know them directly, they will have knowledge about them," Lori declared. "We haven't told too many people what you do for a living," she said quietly.

Alicia quirked an eyebrow. "Cool. Thank you."

"It's a good idea," Lori said. "First of all, you're a Fed, and people around here are still wary of the DEA. The methamphetamine busts a couple years ago threw the town into a tailspin. There have been ongoing repercussions for a lot of families. They are also wary around me and Ben because we're 'the law,'" she said, using air quotes. "Country folks get a bit touchy about people nosing in their business. Even people they know." She sighed. "They're going to be even more on their guard if they know you're with the DEA. So for our purposes tonight, I'm going to be introducing you as Harry's girlfriend."

Alicia startled, taken aback at hearing the label spoken out loud.

"If they ask how you met, be vague. Tell them you consulted on a case or something—don't get too specific," Lori said in a low voice. "They'll want to pry, but they want to pry more about you personally and professionally."

Alicia swallowed hard, and a small knot of panic tightened her stomach. "Personally? Like what kind of personal stuff?"

Lori dismissed Alicia's worries with a wave. "Like the romantic personal stuff. And it's none of their business. But they want the story, so make up a good one. Go with the old 'Our eyes met across a conference table and I couldn't resist him.'" She circled a hand to indicate this was enough to get the ball rolling. "The next thing you knew, the two of you were throwing down."

The notion was so ludicrous, a laugh burbled out of Alicia. "Throwing down."

Lori grinned. "I know it's silly, but people around here like a juicy story, so don't be shy about embellishing. The more they think they know about you, the more they'll be apt to tell you about themselves. People in small towns are like eggs. They have a tough shell, but once you crack the outer coating, it's all going to come spilling out."

Two HOURS LATER, Alicia could say without a doubt Lori wasn't lying.

She'd been introduced to everyone from Simon's grandfather Wendell—a dapper older man whose honey-eyed drawl made Alicia think of porch rockers, seersucker suits and mint juleps—to a woman named Susie Troutman, who obviously prided herself on being the town's font of information. Alicia didn't know exactly how it happened, but she found herself squished into a love seat in the living room with a hairdresser named Shelly on one side, Susie the talker on the other and a shrewd woman named Trudy parked in a nearby armchair, watching Alicia like a hawk.

Harry had popped into the room, she assumed to check on her, and all the women cooed. It turned out, Harry was a natural at this whole "act like we're together" thing. He strolled in with a beer in one hand and a bottle of water for her. Their audience watched appreciatively as he handed over the water and asked if she needed anything from the overburdened buffet set up on the dining-room table. He oh-so-casually pressed a kiss to her forehead before wandering away again. When he was out of earshot, they pounced, demanding to know how they had met.

She and Lori exchanged an amused smirk before she cautiously started to spin a tale. "Well, I knew Ben in Atlanta." She paused, not wanting to say they worked together because someone might be able to add one and one and come up with the DEA. "We kinda ran in the same circles," she added with a wave of her hand. "Anyway, I came down here to visit a few months ago."

When they all nodded, she faced Marlee. With a slight incline of her head, Marlee signaled her to say whatever needed to be said. "The truth is, I was single, and I was hoping to find Ben was too when I came down here," she confessed, leaning closer to Susie. She fixed Marlee with a playful glare. "Unfortunately, I was too late."

"You snooze, you lose," Marlee called back.

"I guess so. Anyway, I had been laid off at my job, and Marlee and I got to talking, and the next thing I knew, she offered me a position with Timber Masters. I'm telling you, it was a godsend," she said, shifting her attention to hairdresser Shelly.

Almost on cue, the other woman pressed her hand to her chest and opened her eyes wide. "Nothing short of divine providence," she said with a nod, prompting the others to agree.

Alicia did her best not to smile when she saw a few other heads bob in agreement. "She's a saint. I met Harry through Ben and Marlee." She ended with a shrug, but a sharp elbow from Lori told her the story wasn't going to cut it in terms of being juicy enough. Thankfully, Marlee picked up the baton.

"She came down here to try to steal my man," she said

with a broad smile. "I had to explain to her how those of us who grew up here in Masters County protect what's ours, but I was taught to be generous with what I have, and I try to be. With everything except my man," she added with a playful glare.

There was a general murmur of laughter and good-natured agreement. Alicia ducked her head, and her cheeks warmed. She hoped the blush was visible.

"Honestly, I wasn't trying to steal anybody's guy. Last I'd known, he was fair game."

"I was afraid she'd start making eyes at Simon," Lori interjected.

Alicia's eyebrows rose right along with everybody else's. "I did not."

"Only because I was onto you." Lori sniffed and rolled her shoulders back, assuming the confident posture of a woman who knew she had her man wrapped up tight. "But I can't blame you. The man is hot."

There was another general murmur of agreement as a couple of other women drifted over from other conversations, deepening the circle around the love seat.

"Y'all are making me sound desperate and man-hungry," Alicia argued. She turned to Shelly the hairdresser. "Do I give off some kind of man-hungry vibe?"

The other woman pursed her lips as if giving the question serious consideration. "No. I think if you were man-hungry, you'd have had some highlights done or something."

Alicia barked a laugh. "Exactly."

As if summoned, Simon Wingate appeared in the doorway to the living room. "Did I hear somebody in here is man-hungry?"

There was a general chorus of nos and orders to go

away. Chuckling, he raised his hands in surrender and backed out of his own living room.

"You already have more woman than you can handle, mister," Lori called after him.

Simon's response floated back to them. "Don't I know it."

"I didn't come here to steal anyone's man. You know how it is when your whole life is turned upside down," she said, turning to the skeptical woman in the chair nearby. "I wanted a fresh start."

"But you didn't stick around long," Marlee said with a chuckle. "I know it's hard to find good people these days, but usually people stay in my employment for longer than three weeks before they get a better offer and move on."

Alicia rolled with it. "Aw, you know I'm sorry about having to leave so quickly. It was too good to pass up," she said with a helpless shrug. Turning back to Susie, she explained, "I was recruited by a headhunter for a big firm back in Atlanta. They were offering the sun and the moon, and I was already at the point where I was going to have to sublet my condo to make the mortgage payment. It didn't make sense to stay here."

"But what about Harry?" the woman named Trudy asked, finally leaning in a bit. "Wouldn't he have been reason enough to stay?"

Alicia wanted to say something pithy about setting the women's movement back another fifty years but bit her cheek. She wasn't there to sermonize; she was supposed to be making friends.

She tried for a sort of downcast, dejected pose, but wasn't sure she quite got it right. So she did the next best thing. She threw Harrison Hayes under the bus.

"He didn't ask me to."

The statement earned her another chorus of awws and more than a few disgruntled mutters about men in general. Pleased, she decided she could pull off magnanimous as well as Marlee Masters could.

"To be fair, we had barely started seeing each other," she said in a rush, hoping they would appreciate how quickly she rose to defend poor Harry's honor. "We both did the whole no harm, no foul, let's keep in touch, play-it-casual thing," she said, offering a self-deprecating smile.

"And how long did you last?" Lori prodded.

Alicia ducked her head again. When she peeked at Susie Troutman from under her eyelashes, she saw she had the woman eating out of her palm. "Three days," she replied quietly. "He lasted three days."

All the women in the room sighed with pleasure, and *voila!* The egg was cracked.

Alicia spent the next hour and a half sitting on the love seat, soaking up every tidbit of information she could like a sponge.

By the time Harry appeared in the doorway holding her coat, her head was spinning and her bladder near to bursting. Anxious to talk over her newly gleaned information with Harry, she wriggled her way off the love seat, making all the right noises about how she hated to leave her new friends, but she couldn't keep her man waiting.

When she reached him, she took her coat from his arm and leaned in close. "I need the powder room before we try to walk home from here."

He nodded to a door at the end of the hallway. "There's one there, but if it's occupied, I'm sure Simon wouldn't mind you heading down to the bedroom to use the master."

Alicia chuckled at his use of the term. "Hang tight. I'll be right back."

Before she could step away, he plucked her coat out of her hand once more. "I'll be right here."

Five minutes later, they'd said their goodbyes and thanked Lori and Simon for a nice evening. Alicia found herself laughing as they made their way down the shallow porch steps. "That was interesting."

He smiled down at her. "Good interesting?"

"Mostly, I'd say," she assured him.

Their breaths floated away in clouds of vapor. Alicia tucked her hands into her jacket pockets and scanned the street as they turned onto the sidewalk. Most every house boasted some kind of Christmas decor, some more understated than others. "People around here seriously start Christmas the minute Thanksgiving is over, don't they?"

Harry paused to take in the scene as if noticing for the first time. "What? Oh, well, it's no different from anywhere else. Retail-driven holiday spirit. Seems like we skip right over Thanksgiving anymore."

"True." She walked beside him, noticing how nicely the length of their strides matched. "I heard a couple of interesting things tonight."

He slid her a sidelong glance. "Oh?"

She nodded. "Do you know someone named Rinker?"

Harry made a sound of assent. "Yeah. Chet Rinker owns the pharmacy. Why?"

"Hmm." She filed the information away to be examined more closely later. "I guess he's developed an interest in motorcycles. Been running with a bunch of hoodlums, according to Susie Troutman." He stopped dead in his tracks. When she turned back, she found him scowling fiercely. "What?"

"Chet Rinker?" he demanded.

She let one shoulder rise and fall. "She called him *That Rinker boy.*"

Some of the confusion clouding his face cleared. "She must have meant Matt Rinker, Chet's son."

"Okay."

Alicia raised an eyebrow. She couldn't care less whether the person in question was father or son. She was focused solely on the notion of someone local keeping company with people the townsfolk obviously disapproved of. Add in the pharmacy angle, the rise of oxy addicts and heroin usage in the area, and suddenly her curiosity was more than piqued.

Harry started walking again, and she had to jog two steps to catch up when he passed her, his gaze fixed somewhere beyond the end of the block.

"Do you know him?" she asked, falling back into step beside him.

"He was younger than me in school, so not well."

Alicia didn't need to prod more to know whether they were good friends or not; Harry was affronted by the idea of this Matt Rinker coming after him. More so than he had been about the Smithson guy who had been in the same year.

Fascinated by what appeared to be another wrinkle in the small-town dynamic, she pushed. "But you're upset it might be him."

"Well, of course I am," he retorted. He slowed when they approached the corner.

"Why? You said you didn't know him well," she prodded. "Why is it worse for this guy to be in on it than the Smithson guy?"

"Because it is," Harry said, his tone brusque.

They stepped off the curb and were about three strides across the street when the squeal of tires alerted them to the approach of a vehicle. Alicia's head swiveled in time to see a dark sedan with no headlights bearing down on them, the acrid scent of burnt rubber blooming in the crisp night air.

"Harry!" she barked, catching his arm and propelling him forward.

They were aligned with the center of the hood, and Alicia knew they stood a better chance with momentum on their side. He twisted his arm around until it encircled her waist and all but shoved her up onto the opposite curb. Together, they dived into a neatly trimmed hedge strung with white Christmas lights.

Harry turned his head in time to see the car run up on the curb they'd hopped a split second ago, but before he could right himself enough to get a good look at the vehicle, the driver had hooked a sharp left onto the next

Chapter Twelve

Harry turned his head in time to see the car run up on the curb they'd hopped a split second ago, but before he could right himself enough to get a good look at the vehicle, the driver had hooked a sharp left onto the next street and floored it.

"Sedan, older model, no plates," Alicia panted. She wriggled out of Harry's tight hold and rolled off his chest. Grasping a handful of shrubbery, she leveraged herself out of the hedge, then turned to offer him a hand.

"How'd you get all that?" Harry gained his feet, then bent forward, bracing his hands on wobbly knees.

"I saw there was no front tag when it was coming at us. Caught sight of the back before he turned."

"I can't believe you had the presence of mind to do either," he grumbled. "All I could think about was getting out of the way."

She slid down to sit cross-legged on the grass. The corner of her mouth was twisted into a frustrated smirk. "Now, if I'd have been able to catch a tag and memorize it, that would've been impressive."

"Oh, well, yeah. You're right. Way to put forth mediocre effort, Agent Simmons," he said, dropping into a sitting position next to her.

"I'll try to do better next time." With a groan, Alicia rolled onto her hip and rummaged in her pocket.

"Are you okay?" he demanded, panic rising inside him. Of course she wasn't okay. She was pregnant and they were diving into bushes to keep from being run over by cars. "Are you hurt?"

She extracted her cell phone from her jacket pocket. "Oh, thank God I didn't break another one."

"Excuse me?"

She held her phone up and waved it at him. "I didn't break the screen. I'm not exactly easy on phones. I didn't want to have to replace another screen."

He stared at her openmouthed, trying to reconcile his concern for her well-being and the health of their unborn child with her relief at finding her mobile phone intact. "You're worried about your phone?"

Her head popped up. He hadn't been able to check the disapproval in his tone, and Alicia found she had to tamp down her impatience his judgement stirred. "I find cellular devices handy when one has narrowly avoided being mowed down. I need to call Ben and report this."

Harry didn't think; he simply reacted. Reaching out, he grasped her wrist and kept her from completing the call. "Don't."

She gaped at him, surprised. "Don't? This needs to go on the record."

He reached over and gently removed her phone from her hand and placed it on her leg. He sandwiched her cool fingers between his hands and expelled a long plume of breath. "It doesn't need to be called in right now. We have no make or model, no license plate. I'm not even sure what color it was." He shrugged and chafed her hand to warm it. "Ben's at the party. He's out with his girlfriend having a nice Saturday night. This can keep until tomorrow."

Alicia held his gaze for a beat before nodding. When he didn't let go of her, she dropped her eyes to their joined hands.

"People were asking how we, uh, got together..." She trailed off. "I had to tell them some story about how we got together in exchange for them telling me their stories."

He gave her a half-hearted smile. "The currency of small towns."

She met his eyes again. "The funny thing was, other than Marlee and Lori insinuating I came here with an eye toward stealing their men, I didn't have much to say. It was...there wasn't anybody here who interests me as much as you do," she said with a small lift of her shoulders.

"I'm going to take your interest as a compliment," he warned.

"It was meant as one." Alicia offered him a tremulous smile. "I thought you were interesting, but now I find you downright fascinating."

He let go of her hand. "Fascinating? Hardly."

"But you are. You've got this kind of center of calm and cool I don't often see in people who aren't cops."

He ducked his head, pleased and embarrassed. Anxious to escape her scrutiny, Harry planted a hand on the cool damp grass and pressed up. Once he'd regained his feet, he offered her both of his hands and she placed her fingers in his. "I'm adding *cool* to the pile of compliments."

She shot up and bumped right into his chest. Again. Harry felt a sizzle of excitement. And familiarity. A flashback to the night they'd spent together. He tamped it down. His life was complicated enough right now, and things between him and Alicia were only going to get more complicated as her pregnancy advanced.

"Harry," she prompted, drawing his attention up from where their bodies pressed together to where her eyes bored into his.

He had a flashback to the night they'd been together. The joy and uninhibited pleasure they'd taken in one another. Now they were running on adrenaline and fear, and Harry decided if he were to kiss this woman again, he didn't want it to be because they survived some ordeal together. He wanted to revel in genuine jubilation with her again. He lifted his hands to hers, wrapped them firmly around her fingers and gave them a gentle squeeze before removing them from his chest.

"Come on. Let's go home."

Home. He'd said the word so casually. Thoughtlessly, probably, but Alicia couldn't stop thinking about it. Thinking about him. Or about the people who were trying to make him feel uncomfortable in the town he considered his home. Alicia stared up at the ceiling long into the night. Harry's guest room was comfortable, though the decor was somewhat on the masculine, minimalist side, but lived-in. Truth be told, she liked it this way. Her own condo in Atlanta was more like a room at one of those extended-stay hotels. Probably one of the reasons why she didn't consider it home.

Home.

She tossed and turned, trying to parse out why it sounded so right when Harry said *Let's go home.* Given her background, she didn't need an advanced degree to make sense of it. He was home. Pine Bluff was his home; this house was his home. One of the women at the party had told her it had once been his parents' house, so it may even have been the home he grew up in.

Alicia tried to imagine living in any of the myriad houses her parents had either purchased or rented depending on how long her father's post was expected to last. She wondered if it was weird for him, living as an adult in the house where he'd been a boy. Had this been his room at one time? She'd seen another bedroom converted into a home office. Had it been strange for him to move into the larger master bedroom at the end of the hall? Maybe not. The redhead who told her the house once belonged to his parents also said Harry had put a lot of work into making the place his own.

Why hadn't she thought about inspecting his place in the hours he was gone? Why had she stuck so close to the public rooms of the house and not poked her nose in at least a couple of his drawers? Frankly, it was unlike her. She was a cop. Sure, they put the title Special Agent in front of her name, but when it came down to it, she was no different from any other member of the law enforcement community. Her lack of curiosity in this case would have been considered appalling by some of her colleagues.

But she didn't want to cross any lines with Harry.

He was obviously a man who liked structure and boundaries. She was a guest in his home and had no desire to pry into the private life of her host. Okay, she had the desire, but she had more willpower. She knew enough about him as it was. Probably more than he'd want her to know if she hadn't borne witness to the attacks on him.

Restless, she flung back the covers, swung her legs from the bed and padded to the dresser where she'd left her laptop. She might not be willing to go through his bathroom cabinet, but she wasn't at all above poking in some dark corners to determine exactly how real these threats were. Up until this point, the bumbling attempts to intimidate him could be considered scare tactics, some more extreme than others, but tonight…

Tonight, someone meant to cause them bodily harm.

Some ancient maternal instinct had her covering her still-flat abdomen with her hand. As if she could somehow reassure herself the child she was carrying was nevertheless safe and secure.

Ridiculous, she thought, snatching the laptop from the dresser and hurrying back to the warmth of her bed. With the duvet pulled up over her bare legs, she flipped open the top and booted the computer.

It opened to her email application automatically, but Alicia shut it down after ingesting the gist of Bronson's email. He'd put his order in writing. An email from his agency address made his order more official than the text massage. He expected to see her Monday morning, or else.

The ultimatum meant she had less than twenty-four hours to make a decision that would likely affect the rest of her career.

Instead, with a few quick keystrokes, she logged in to a message board. It appeared to be a chat room like any other, but this was a site most people would never stumble across on their own. One of the tech guys at work clued her in to it when she asked about how to search out hate groups. She only had to try two different variations of search terms before she found some hits. The name

Samuel Coulter spawned more than one thread. Only two had regular interchanges, so she zeroed in on them.

Drawing a deep breath, she clicked on the one titled "Samuel Coulter was framed" and scrolled back through the messages until she found the post at the head of the thread. Her stomach churned while she absorbed conspiracy theory after conspiracy theory. Her gorge rose when she read each justification for Coulter's acquittal.

Most of these posters had absolutely no idea who or what they were dealing with. They simply thought a man who dealt in exotic snakes had been framed by the federal government as a drug trafficker to stop them from pursuing their hobby.

They were wrong.

The evidence she'd uncovered before coming to Pine Bluff showed Coulter had a long history of involvement with some of South Florida's most infamous traffickers. He had ongoing connections with various gangs in both the Miami and Jacksonville areas. It had been absolutely no surprise to her to discover he was connected with the product moving through Atlanta. Some of the convoluted ideas people posted were plain creepy.

Gnawing her bottom lip, she reached over and switched on the bedside lamp. As Simon Wingate pointed out, she wasn't a woman who scared easily, but she was also human. If she was going to trawl through the dregs of internet society, she could do so with the light on.

She was a half hour in before she found her first direct hit. The person who posted actually typed the name Ivan Jones.

A chill ran down her spine when she scanned the subthreads connected to the entry. She was so absorbed in

her research, she barely registered the soft knock on her
door. Lowering the top of her laptop, she stared at the
door in confusion before whispering a tentative "Come
in?" She didn't want to speak too loudly in case she'd
only imagined the knock.

The door opened and Harry poked his head in. "Can't
sleep?"

Alicia closed the lid on the laptop, not wanting him
to know exactly what she was piecing together until it
was fully formed in her head. "Restless night."

He opened the door farther, propped his forearm on
the jamb and ran his other hand through his already rumpled hair. Alicia took in the view. She was only human,
after all. He wore a washed-thin T-shirt and flannel pajama pants. The angle of the arm braced against the door
only highlighted the contour of his biceps. The last time
she'd seen his hair in such disarray, it had been her fingers doing the mussing.

"Do you think you can eat something?" he asked.

Startled by the offer of food rather than warm milk,
cocoa or whatever else people thought they should drink
in the middle of the night, she let out a laugh.

It took only a second for the thought to find a foot-
hold, and her stomach growled its affirmative response.
"Actually, I think I can."

"Come to the kitchen. I'll make us some oatmeal."

He was gone before she could question his choice of
late-night snack. She swung her legs over the edge of
the bed and yanked on the yoga pants she'd discarded
before climbing between the sheets. She stuffed her bare
toes into a pair of fluffy slippers she'd bought on a whim
the previous winter. When she scuffed into the kitchen,
Harry's gaze trailed to her feet and his eyebrows jumped.

"Never pegged you for the leopard-print type," he commented. "Those are totally something my sister would pick out."

"Every woman is a leopard-print type, under the right circumstances." she asserted with more confidence than she felt. Frankly, she was embarrassed to be caught in the slippers. For some reason, she was afraid he'd find them frivolous, perhaps think less of her as a cop because her choices in footwear weren't always tactical. "But these were an impulse buy. They were on sale, so I grabbed them off the rack."

Lie. She'd seen them online and ordered them specifically because she wanted something pretty.

There were times when being a woman in a male-dominated world wore on her. Times when she wanted to let down her guard and indulge in something simply because it was pretty or fun. These were the sorts of things she had to keep to herself. She indulged by purchasing things no one else would ever see. Of course, she hadn't been living in someone else's house at the time.

Anxious to change the subject, she wrinkled her nose. "Are you actually offering me oatmeal?"

He shrugged. "I can't offer you a brandy or coffee, not that the latter would do anything to make you sleepy." He stretched to reach up onto the top shelf and pull down the familiar round container of oats. "I always found the notion of warm milk kind of gross. Like you're drinking it straight out of the cow, you know?" When she nodded, he gestured to the container. "My mom used to make me oatmeal when I couldn't sleep. It's surprisingly effective. It's warm, filling and, with a splash of milk and a sprinkle of brown sugar, pretty comforting."

Alicia stepped over to the counter. "Okay, you've convinced me."

He smiled. "Good. If you would—"

Alicia didn't know what he was going to ask her to do. It probably wasn't kiss him. But kiss him she did. When he turned toward her, his smile brightening his too serious features, and his hair sticking up in all directions, there wasn't much else she could do.

If it came right down to it, she could blame it on the adrenaline. Somebody had tried to kill them tonight. Somebody had been taking shots at him. There, in his semidark kitchen, Alicia hadn't been able to stand the thought of going another minute without kissing him again.

In case.

His lips were warm and soft, parted in surprise. It took only a heartbeat, but he quickly caught on. Their lips clung when she pulled back. She hated to end the kiss, but she wanted to be clear whether the movement of his mouth against hers had been one of acquiescence or objection. She needed to get a tighter rein on herself until she knew whether he even wanted to be kissed.

"Sorry," she whispered. "Kinda like the slippers—poor impulse control."

Lips still parted, he gave his head a slight shake. "You have to try another excuse because I'm never going to buy impulse control."

"We almost died tonight."

"I'm not sure I'm going to go with near death either," he said. "People been taking shots at us for a while now. You haven't felt compelled to kiss me after any of them."

"How do you know?" she shot back. "Maybe I did, and I held back."

"Completely blowing your story about the poor impulse control," he said, bringing the argument full circle. "Admit you wanted to kiss me."

They stood toe to toe, their eyes locked on one another. "I wanted to kiss you."

"I'm glad. I've been wanting to kiss you since you first showed up on my doorstep."

"Liar," she said with a sly smile. "You never would've called me if I hadn't shown up on your doorstep."

"Never is a pretty firm stance to take," he said. "If I'd had any indication you would've been receptive to a call, I would have, but all markers pointed to you wanting to make a clean escape."

A laugh bubbled out of her, and she patted her stomach. "So much for my plan."

He reached down and covered her hand with his. "I'm glad it didn't work out."

His fingers splayed over hers. She was carrying their child. It seemed absurd to get butterflies in her stomach when she'd already been with this man. Would be connected to this man for the rest of her life. But still, she felt as edgy and excited as she'd been the night he'd driven her home from Simon Wingate's party back in the fall.

But she had to be clear. If they were going to blur the line, she had to know they were on the same page.

"So, you want to kiss me?"

"Yes," he answered simply.

She smiled, loving how he instinctively knew he needed to take the most direct routes with her. "Okay, so kissing is on the table," she said, speaking slowly.

When she didn't go on, he quirked an eyebrow. "On the table? Doesn't sound sanitary."

She laughed again and reached up to smooth his hair into place. "I like you, Harry. I've always liked you," she said with a helpless shrug. "If I didn't like you, I never would've slept with you."

"I like you too," he said, his face settling back into its usual sober expression. "And I like kissing you."

She nodded. "Okay. Good. But things are pretty complicated right now, so maybe we should leave it for tonight."

"Makes sense. For the record, I hate making sense right now," he clarified.

She knew in that moment there was no way she was leaving for Atlanta the following morning. Bronson could reprimand her if he wanted, but she was sticking. For now. Maybe for a while. She'd have to see.

Aware she was getting way ahead of herself, needing a diversion, she nudged him with her elbow and nodded to the container of oats in front of him. "Are we going to stand here talking all night, or are you gonna make me some mush?"

Chapter Thirteen

They passed Sunday in the haze of exhaustion and hyperawareness. Alicia hadn't kissed him again, and he hadn't made a move in her direction either. It didn't feel right. Not because he wasn't attracted to her, but because there was too much going on for him to open up another line of worry.

His reasoning was lame, and he knew it.

She was already in his life. Would be for at least the next nineteen years, if not for a lifetime. And though he hadn't completely wrapped his mind around the thought of being a father, he found himself thinking about being with Alicia way too often. Which called up the question of motivation. He didn't want her to be with him because of the baby, and he didn't want to not be with her because of the baby.

Harry heaved a sigh and flipped on the buzzing overhead lights, trudging toward his office. It was only six thirty in the morning, and barely light outside, but after a day of dancing around her in his house, Harry needed an escape. Work seemed the perfect place to go.

He tossed his briefcase on the chair inside his office and made his way to the break room. The broken window had a piece of plywood covering the hole. As far as Harry could see, there had been no additional damage over the weekend. He pulled a bottle of water from the fridge and an orange from the bowl of fruit on the counter. He'd need to make a run to the Piggly Wiggly this week to restock it. He dug his thumbnail into the rind and made his way back to his office.

Yesterday, Alicia had remarked on his eating habits, asking if he was some kind of a monk or if self-deprivation was his particular brand of kink. He frowned at the orange in his hand. He tried to explain he wasn't a foodie. He saw food as fuel, and if he was going to put fuel in his tank, he tried to go for the premium. But he was no health nut. He loved pizza and pasta and a giant plate of tamales as much as the next guy.

She'd laughed at him, and the throaty sound of it made him want to kiss her again. Despite her skill in teasing, she was not a woman who laughed often. He liked the surprise of it. He wasn't anyone's idea of a class cutup either. But he didn't care if he was the butt of the joke or not; he was happy to be the guy who made her laugh. Dropping into his chair, he pulled his trash can out from under the desk and quickly and efficiently peeled the orange. The scent of citrus filled the air while he broke segments from the fruit and bit into its juicy pulp.

Between her morning, noon and night sickness, and his naturally not-voracious appetite, they'd managed to make it through a day with a container of soup and a couple of sandwiches. After she had disappeared into her room the night before, he'd made up for her lack of supper by hoovering an entire bag of tortilla chips.

Now his stomach was growling, demanding more fuel before he could start his day. He tipped the bottle of water to his mouth and chugged three-quarters of it down in long gulps. Being in the office was a relief. The quiet closed around him like a warm blanket. He'd become accustomed to a solitary life, and while Alicia was anything but intrusive, she was definitely distracting.

He rocked back in his chair, methodically working his way through the orange. Allowing his mind to drift. She'd seemed edgy the previous day. Like something was weighing on her. But she didn't offer any reason, and he didn't ask. Truthfully, he was scared she regretted kissing him.

So he stuck to chatting about Simon's party, explaining the backstory behind some of the tales she'd heard. When the conversation turned to the person who'd tried to run them down, Alicia had insisted on lining out a timeline detailing every single threat or bit of damage done to his property or places associated with him. Seeing it all laid out, one sheet of printer paper per incident, nearly blanketed the dining table he rarely used. She'd made a list of all the names she'd noted from the previous evening and pressed him for more. When they finished, she'd nodded decisively and said something about narrowing down some of the searches she was doing in internet chat rooms.

Harry hadn't been surprised to discover she was working the case from her own angles. While he'd never been one for social media or general internet browsing, he appreciated how much data people either willingly or unwittingly gave away.

His own digital footprint was small, but not nonexistent. He had a business profile, and his photo was on the county website. He'd never given it much thought. He was of the opinion the most useful thing the web provided was instant access to sports scores. Any research related to the cases he was working was usually performed by either Danielle or Layla, and the pertinent information sent to him in an email if it needed his immediate attention or added to the client's folder.

Either way, he'd never ventured onto any kind of forum or chat room. The opinions of strangers didn't mean much to him. Truthfully, he found opinions in general worthless. He was a man who dealt in facts. Evidence. Sworn testimony. Anything posted online could be easily fabricated, so he didn't bother with it much. If the rest of the world wanted to get their facts from user-curated sources, he wasn't going to stop them, nor was he going to put his faith in them.

But he knew someone who did.

Drawing his phone from his jacket pocket, he chewed another segment of orange and scrolled through his contacts. One of his roommates in college had been heavy into computers. Mostly, it seemed he liked the mischief he could make with them, but eventually they gave him a degree, and the degree coupled with his superprocessor brain led him into some high-clearance work in both the public and private sectors.

Randy was the most unlikely computer whiz Harry had ever encountered. Rather than the antisocial hermit holed up in a dark room pecking code into a keyboard, Randy had been a young man determined to live up to his name. He happened to have a skill set that lent itself well to poking around in places where he didn't necessarily belong. Harry suspected this was how the guy ended up on the dean's list every semester even though Harry had hardly ever witnessed Randy hitting the books. A guy with a computer brain probably didn't need to study as hard as mere mortals.

He smirked and tapped the screen to call up his old friend's number, but realized it was still probably too early to call. Switching to a text message, he typed with one thumb.

Hey. Been a long time, but I need to talk to you. Will you call when you get a minute?

Satisfied, Harry set the phone on his desk and turned his attention to finishing his fruit. A few seconds later the screen lit up, and his ringtone echoed through the empty offices. Harry shot forward in his seat and, seeing Randy's name on the screen, quickly swiped to accept the call.

"Hey, man, I know it's early. I didn't mean for you to have to call me right away," Harry said by way of greeting.

"I'm up. There I was, mountain biking in the Andes, and my old friend Harry calls. Bam! Out of the blue," Randy replied jovially. "Isn't modern technology fantastic?"

"You're where?"

Randy chuckled. "I'm in my apartment in DC, but on a virtual trail ride."

His friend did sound winded. "I don't want to interrupt your virtual whatever."

"It's cool. You should try it."

Harry snorted. "You know me. Probably never gonna happen."

The other man laughed, as well. "I do know you, and

you're right. You're probably calling me asking me how you can reset your email password."

"I'm not that bad," he demurred. "I've got the basic tasks covered, and I don't need much else."

"You remember Cindy? The girl you dated sophomore year? She's married and has three kids, and she's still too pretty for you," Randy informed him.

"Good old Cindy," Harry replied.

"Aren't you the least bit curious as to what people are doing?" Randy asked.

"Not curious enough to get on whatever platform you're pushing." Harry picked up the water bottle and drained the rest of its contents. "Besides, Cindy sends me a Christmas card every year with one of those newsletters keeping the world up to date on what all the kids are doing."

"Still rocking it old-school." Randy snickered. "It's cool. Of course, I think it's funny you send Christmas cards to your exes, but you won't even get on PicturSpam. Even my grandma had a PicturSpam account."

"I don't send her Christmas cards—she sends Christmas cards to me," Harry corrected.

"Oh, my mistake, Mr. Cool," Randy teased. "What can I do for you bright and early this Monday morning? Are you calling to tell me I'm not getting a Christmas card from you either?"

He sighed. For a guy who could follow the logic of code, Randy remained bafflingly lost when it came to the logic of people. "If I don't send any Christmas cards to anyone, you can assume you are also on my list of non-Christmas-card recipients."

"Cold," Randy replied good-naturedly.

Enjoying the chitchat, but needing to get down to

the business of the call, Harry launched himself from his chair and carried his empty water bottle back into the break room. He sandwiched the phone between his ear and a shoulder and held the bottle under the water-cooler spigot to refill it. He didn't want another one of Layla's lectures on landfills and the evils of single-use containers.

"Listen, I need to talk to you about how I find one of those forums where people spout off about all sorts of stuff."

This time Randy's laugh was more of a guffaw. "Could you be more specific, dude?"

"You know, like if I had a case and some nutjobs were going to spew a bunch of nonsense on a forum about it, where would they go?"

"Only about a bazillion different places," Randy shot back. "Man, you really have no clue about the internet, do you?"

"I know what I want to know about it," Harry retorted.

"Apparently not, or you wouldn't be calling me asking me how to find, and I quote, 'one of those forums.' Unquote." He added the last word as punctuation.

After carrying his water back to his desk, Harry sat down with a heavy sigh. "Listen, Rand, someone's been making some threats, okay? They're related to a case I'm involved in. I want to see what's being said in hopes of figuring out who's doing these things."

His friend sobered instantly. "Wait. Doing things or saying things? What kind of things?"

Harry didn't want to give him the nitty-gritty on the more serious stuff, so he dismissed the destruction of his business and personal property with a shrug. "Malicious mischief type stuff. Tire slashing, broken windows, a couple of threatening notes."

"So it's somebody there. Somebody local," Randy answered, suddenly keying in on the people logic.

"The general consensus," Harry said cautiously. "But we think there may be something bigger behind it. Someone fueling some of the fires around here. Prosecutors aren't always the most popular people in town. I want to see what's being said online."

Randy let out a low whistle. "No better place to fan the fires," he commented, all traces of humor gone. "The problem is, most people use screen names or aliases online. You'd have to key in on an IP address and..." He paused as if remembering Harry was still on the call. "You'll never be able to do this. Give me the particulars on the case and who it involves. I'm going to run some searches. I'll get back to you."

"I appreciate you, man," he said gruffly. "The case involves a guy named Samuel Coulter. He's a day trader turned exotic-snake enthusiast."

"Are you kidding me?" Randy asked, chuckling.

"I wish. He was arrested two months ago in a DEA bust involving the trafficking of heroin."

"Whoa," Randy breathed. "No kidding."

This time, Harry smiled. "Nope. Not kidding." He might be naive when it came to the cyberworld, but he had no illusions about what happened right here in real life. "I'm going to give you another name. He's a local guy, and I'm wondering if we can find some kind of connection between the two of them."

"Fire away," Randy prompted.

"The name is Matthew Rinker. Spelled *R-I-N-K-E-R*," he said, wondering if his friend was taking this information down. He figured if he spelled it out, the information may embed itself in Randy's steel trap of a memory. Still… "Are you writing this down?"

A snicker came through the phone. "No need. Hang on." Randy fumbled with the phone. A second later, Harry heard him say, "New note. Samuel Coulter. Snakes. Trafficking. Heroin. Matthew Rinker. *R-I-N-K-E-R*. Pine Bluff, Georgia. Save note."

"I should've known you couldn't use a pen and paper like any normal person," Harry teased.

"Most normal people never pick up a pen these days," Randy pointed out.

"Thanks, man. I appreciate you doing whatever you can."

"Anytime. I'll try to get back to you today with whatever I can find."

Before he ended the call, Harry asked, "Hey, I never asked—how's the new business coming? Do people actually pay you to hack into things for them?"

Randy chortled. "No, they pay me to make sure other people can't hack into their things. It's called cybersecurity. Plug that into your next internet search."

Harry smiled. "Okay. I will."

"Okay. I'm going to go finish my ride. Then I'll get on this. Talk soon."

Harry pulled the phone away from his ear and checked the screen to be sure the call had ended. If Randy couldn't dig up any dirt on these message boards, no one could.

Satisfied he'd set something in motion, Harry turned his attention to the odd bits of paperwork and scribbled sticky notes he'd left for himself on Friday afternoon. It seemed like months ago. Normally, his weekends were

quiet. He spent them working, either on cases or around
the house. For relaxation, he watched whatever sport
was in season, and occasionally hung out with Ben or
Simon. But like so many of his contemporaries, Ben
and Simon had found ways to pair off, leaving Harry
mostly to his own devices unless he chose to become a
fifth wheel in the group.

He peeled the sticky note reminding him to pick up
wine for Simon's party off his desk and studied it, his
thoughts drifting back to Alicia and how well she'd fitted
in with his friends. How well she seemed to fit into his
life. Postkiss awkwardness aside, she slipped seamlessly
into the rhythm of his household. Granted, the rhythm
was more a slow, steady beat than a driving bass line,
but something told him Alicia didn't mind the quiet. It
wasn't much of a stretch to deduce she was as solitary a
creature as him. But was it by choice or happenstance?

Slumping in his chair, he crumpled the square of
paper, pondering the question. He'd always assumed
he'd meet the right woman one day and get married. He'd
never given his continued single status a lot of thought.
Not even when ex-girlfriends sent perfectly posed photos of their angelic children. Was it possible he'd met
the right woman already and failed to notice? Pursing
his lips, Harry tossed the balled-up reminder into the
trash. Sure. Anything was possible. And truthfully, he'd
thought he'd have more of a chance with Alicia when
she was in Pine Bluff in the fall. Her abrupt departure
had stung, but he'd chalked his feelings up to a bruised
ego rather than a hopeful heart.

Maybe he'd been too quick to dismiss them.

Sure, they'd only had the one night together, but they
had worked closely with one another for the short time

she had been in town. He'd liked her. Not only as an attractive, compelling woman, but as a person. He'd liked her direct manner and linear thinking. They had slotted together the chunks of information Alicia had on Coulter's activities prior to planting himself in Pine Bluff and the bits and pieces Harry had gathered—thanks to Lori Cabrera's dogged determination.

And he'd been pretty sure whatever feelings he had for her at the time were mutual. Maybe even after she left. She'd been the one who'd called the US attorney and convinced him to let Harry ride shotgun on the case. Bolstered by the thought, Harry checked the time on his phone. Deciding he'd whittled away enough of the morning to make the timing of his next call not unreasonable, he pulled up Marcus Zeller's contact information. If he was doing some additional investigation adjacent to the Coulter case, professional courtesy demanded he give the federal prosecutor a heads-up.

"Zeller," Marcus said when the call connected. "How're you doing, Harry?"

"Hey, Marcus. I'm well." His breath caught as the memory of a car bearing down on them flashed in his mind. He forced it from his lungs on a hard laugh. "For the time being."

"Well, you sound ominous, even for a Monday morning. Fill me in. What's happening?"

Harry blew out another breath and scrubbed a hand over his face. "Grab a cup of coffee—this might take a minute."

Chapter Fourteen

Alicia couldn't believe the things she'd heard over lunch at Brewster's Bakery. When Marlee texted the previous afternoon to invite her, she didn't hold out much hope for pertinent information, but figured making another appearance among the women of Pine Bluff couldn't hurt. Boy, had she underestimated the power of the ladies who lunch.

Quick-stepping it down the sidewalk, she set her sights on the municipal building, anxious to tell Harry what all she'd learned. In truth, she was relieved to have something easy to talk to him about. The previous day had been an exercise in uncomfortable restraint. Topics they didn't want to talk about far outnumbered those on the table, and the gaping holes made for an awful lot of stilted conversation. It was exhausting.

She hadn't gone back to Atlanta, obviously. She hadn't emailed Bronson or responded to his messages. Instead, she contacted Human Resources and informed them she required personal leave effective immediately. Alicia knew it was a dangerous game she was playing, but she needed time, and she needed to be involved in something other than sorting through the wreckage of what was once a stellar career. She was scared to face the possibility of finding nothing worth salvaging.

The kicker of it was, like Ben Kinsella, she had done nothing wrong. As a matter of fact, like Ben, she'd excelled at her job. But winning didn't always mean you got the prize, she reminded herself.

She checked for traffic before crossing the street, trying to keep her mind focused. But it was hard. There were so many variables. Too many pieces in play.

Her circumstances had changed radically. She needed time to think long and hard about what she wanted to do next. This pregnancy and the changes in lifestyle it would require would make it next to impossible for her to do the fieldwork she loved, even if she could get Bronson to cut her loose from her desk. And if she couldn't... If her superiors decided sitting at a desk listening to hours of unedited audio and video clips was where she would best be utilized, she wasn't sure the agency was the right place for her anymore.

Shoving her worry aside, she hopped onto the curb and hurried to the front door of the municipal building. She was excited to see Harry again, which was disturbing enough. They'd only been apart a few hours. Memories of their late-night encounter hung heavy over them. She kissed him, and he kissed her back. Then he told her things were too complicated.

And she got it. Things were complicated. Her gut told her he wasn't rejecting her outright, but it sure didn't feel good. There was something between them. It was the same sizzle she felt when they first met, but now it burned inside her steady as a flame.

Alicia tried to reason with herself. Whatever feelings she might be having toward Harry could simply be an extension of her emotional attachment to the baby she carried. No doubt he was worried about the same thing. If she were in his shoes, she would be too. Another reason she was glad to be a woman. Glad to have complete control over her relationship with her unborn child. Plus, she didn't feel overly sorry for men in general. After all, they seemed to think they should rule about everywhere else.

A rush of warm air greeted her when she stepped into the glass atrium separating the sheriff's office and jail from the district attorney's and judiciary suites. Law and justice. *Together, as they should be*, she thought, not for the first time. She started toward the door to the justice side of things. Matthew Rinker. The talk about him at the bakery may have turned into an honest-to-goodness lead, and she couldn't wait to flesh it out with Harry.

She was reaching for the door handle when the door swung open, causing her to stumble back. Catching her breath, she found herself face-to-face with the man she'd been searching for.

"Harry, I was coming to see you," she said, beaming a smile at him.

"And I was coming to find you," he replied, but his expression was anything but welcoming.

Her smile faltered, and her brow knit. "What's wrong?" She reached out and touched his arm, searching for any sign of injury. "Are you hurt? Did something happen?"

"No. I'm fine," he insisted.

"You're upset," she pointed out.

"Am I? Huh. Maybe because I spoke with Marcus Zeller from the US Attorney's Office and he tells me he heard through the grapevine you might not be assigned to this case any longer."

Alicia sucked in a breath. "Oh?"

He crossed his arms over his chest and rocked back on his heels, his steady gaze locked on her. "Yeah," he said succinctly. "He tells me one of his friends at the DEA told him you'd been put on leave. The rumors are you got crossways with your boss and you're not even supposed to be here."

"The rumors are false." She grimaced. "Or mostly false." He raised both eyebrows and she sighed. "I've taken a leave. My choice," she asserted. "Put in for a personal leave, though it's not any business of theirs."

"Personal leave?"

Alicia knew she wasn't playing fair, but she also wasn't above using every tool in her arsenal. Closing a hand over her stomach, she stared down at it meaningfully, lifted her head to meet his eyes. "Yes. I have weeks of accumulated time I never use, and I thought now would be the perfect time to take a few days to think."

"So, you aren't on the case?"

She heard his quick intake of breath and felt a pang of guilt. This was Harry. They'd always shot straight with one another, and she had no reason to fudge the truth now.

"Technically, I haven't been since I returned to Atlanta. We have a new section chief, and he's assigned me to other things. Special Agent Morrisey is officially the contact, but Marcus Zeller and I have been friends for a long time and…" She trailed off. "As for the leave, I didn't plan to take one, but it's working out, so here we are."

"What do you mean it's working out?" he demanded.

"Bronson wanted me back in the office today. He's got no reason to want me there other than to prove he can order me to do whatever he wants me to do." She crossed her arms over her chest and mimicked his wide stance. "I don't think he's making the best use of my time or talent, so I informed Human Resources this morning I would be taking a leave of absence due to personal reasons."

"Why didn't you tell me any of this?" he asked, and the sincere hurt in his tone tore a big gaping hole in her indignation. But rather than let it show, she arched a brow at him.

"I wasn't aware I needed to consult you about my career decisions."

"You don't."

His response came so quickly, Alicia knew she'd hit a sore spot. She immediately regretted going on the offensive. Hoping to make amends, she reached out and touched his arm again, this time letting her hand close around his biceps and drawing him away from the office door. "Come on. Let's talk."

The center of the atrium was dominated by a large mosaic-tile fountain. Long drained and inactive, it still defined the lobby area. She led him to the edge of the fountain and pulled him down beside her.

"Harry, everything in the world is a mess right now for you and for me." She gave him a half smile. "But there's only one thing I'm truly happy about, and the rest I'm gonna have to let play out a bit before I make any big decisions."

His Adam's apple bobbed when he swallowed, but Harry nodded. "I get you."

"I know you do," she said, gentling her tone. "There

are a lot of things hanging between us, but for right now, can we set all the other stuff aside? I have some things I want to tell you. Information I picked up, but I need to get your take on how valid you think the information may be."

"Information on what?"

"Matt Rinker," she said, holding his gaze.

Harry sat up straighter. "What about him?"

"I went to a lunch today at the bakery. Something Marlee called the Ladies Guild?" she said, wrinkling her nose at the name.

Harry smirked. "Ah. The Ladies Guild."

"I take it you're familiar with them?" she prompted.

"My mother used to be the president."

"Okay, well, you probably have a pretty good idea of what goes on at their meetings."

"I know there's a lot of talk," he replied, a note of disdain tingeing his voice.

"Well, some of the talk today was about how nice it was to see poor Marjorie Rinker happier these days. She's telling everyone her boy—" she emphasized the word and pulled up air quotes to make it clear this was not the terminology she might have chosen "—Matthew is doing so much better since he's found the Lord."

Harry shot her a blasé stare. "This would be the point where one of us should insert a joke about how we didn't know the Lord was missing and blah, blah, blah," he said, circling his hand. "Let's take it as a given and get to the good stuff."

"She thinks his salvation will save him from the clutches of addiction."

Harry's lips parted in surprise. "Addiction? Addiction to what?"

Alicia couldn't help but feel smug about what she had to share next. "Pills. Apparently, young Matthew got himself hooked on pills. Painkillers, to be exact. To hear some of the ladies of the guild talk, there have been some unreported thefts at the pharmacy. Carolee Masters says Mr. Rinker has been trying to get his son into a rehab center for months, but Matt wasn't having anything to do with them."

"I hate this for the Rinkers," Harry said quietly. "My heart goes out to Chet and Marjorie that they have to deal with this kind of anguish for their only child. And Matt was a good guy...at one time."

"From what I heard, it sounded like Mr. and Mrs. Rinker believe their son has found the path to the straight and narrow after attending a tent revival over in Prescott County."

Harry pulled a face but shrugged. "Whatever works."

But she wasn't done driving home the point of her story. "Supposedly, Matt became enthralled by a preacher who liked to use serpents as a part of his sermonizing."

Harry's attention had drifted, but when she said the word *serpents*, his gaze snapped back to hers. "Are you serious?"

Alicia was unable to contain the twitch of excitement tugging at the corners of her mouth. "They say he became friends with some of the gentlemen who provided the animals for these exhibitions. He was training to become a handler himself. At the Reptile Rendezvous."

She had the pleasure of watching Harry's normally impassive expression cycle through a full range of emotions. "Well, I'll be damned," he murmured.

He came around to gazing at her with something she

could only label as shock and awe. "You're trying to tell me Chet and Marjorie Rinker's son is an oxy addict who found Jesus at the tent revival with a bunch of snake handlers?"

"Exactly." She risked a small smile. "He also has a direct connection to Samuel Coulter."

"At least to Coulter's business. We don't know about the man himself," Harry corrected.

She inclined her head in acknowledgment, pressing on. "Listening to some of the ladies talk, or rather, how they didn't talk when Mrs. Rinker was around, I get the feeling people around here know more about Matt's activities than his parents."

Harry exhaled long and loud. "I feel so bad for them," he said gruffly. "I know it's ridiculous given what's been happening to me, but I've known the Rinkers all my life."

"I can understand how you'd feel...conflicted," Alicia said, though she wasn't entirely certain the statement was true.

She had never had the kind of connections with people that Harry had with the residents of this town. She couldn't quite wrap her head around how he might be feeling generous or forgiving toward any of them, but this duality between the no-nonsense prosecutor and the empathetic man was what made him so attractive to her.

Reaching over, she clasped his hand. "I'm hoping we can set things right for you with a few well-placed questions."

The door to the sheriff's department swung open and Julianne Shields burst into the atrium with Ben and Deputy Mike Schaeffer pushing past her none too gently.

"Get out," Ben snapped, dashing past them to the staircase leading to the second level, where the county offices were housed.

"Evacuate now," Mike Schaeffer yelled as he bolted into the justice side of the building.

Harry grasped Alicia's hand tightly and rose, turning his attention back to Julianne. "What's going on?" he asked, his head whipping around and his eyes following Mike and Ben.

"Bomb threat," Julianne answered, her face panic-stricken. "We need to evacuate right now," she insisted, shooing them toward the exit doors.

"Bomb threat?" Alicia repeated, moving toward the doors and dragging Harry in her wake. "Are you kidding me?"

"I wish I was kidding. Come on," she said, pushing the outer door open wide and holding it for them.

Alicia turned back to see Ben had gathered the clerical staff who worked on the second floor and was herding them down the steps. She was dragging Harry through the door when they spotted Danielle, Layla and Judge Nichols trailing Mike Schaeffer from the building.

They moved across the street onto the lawn surrounding the historic courthouse. Every one of the municipal building's employees turned and stared at the squat brick building in shock as Ben counted heads.

"Lori's off duty?" Alicia asked Mike.

He nodded. Pulling out his cell phone, he drew up the other deputy's contact information and dialed. "She is, but I'd better let her know what's happening."

Once Ben had finished his head count, Alicia turned

to him. "Do you even have people qualified to deal with a bomb threat here?"

He nodded. "Sort of. No bomb squad or anything, but one of the guys on fire and rescue got a qualification."

Alicia stared at him, openmouthed. "Has this person ever actually worked on a live bomb?"

Ben merely shrugged. "No cause to, as far as I can tell. We don't get a lot of bomb threats around here." His expression grim, he stared at the front of the building. "This is all getting way out of hand."

Alicia snorted. "It got way out of hand a while back."

Beside her, the sheriff nodded, but didn't take his eyes off the building. Alicia peeked over her shoulder to find Harry speaking quietly with the judge and the two women who worked in his office. Layla was visibly shaken. Alicia wondered if the young woman would stick with the DA's office after all this madness or seek a safer position with a white-shoe firm in Atlanta. There, she'd only have to deal with the terrorists within while she found ways for their wealthy clients to become even more wealthy, rather than fighting the injustices of the world.

The wail of a siren cranked up and alerted them to movement from the fire-and-rescue team. A bright red fire truck pulled from its bay and turned right onto Main Street. It roared and growled the full block and a half to the municipal building. Alicia smirked as they pulled to a halt directly in front of the doors.

"They could've run down the street," she commented dryly.

Ben proved he was still a city slicker at heart with the smile he wore when he turned to look at her. "Where's the fun in that?"

"Any ideas on who your tipster might've been?" Alicia asked while they watched a handful of firemen jump from the rig in full turnout gear.

Beside her, Ben shrugged. "Julianne says it was a woman. Said she thought she knew the voice but couldn't quite place it. Maybe once the excitement calms down and she has a minute to think," he replied laconically.

Alicia gave him an assessing stare. "For a guy who doesn't field bomb threats often, you sure are taking this in stride."

Ben met her gaze directly. "After the past couple weeks, nothing is going to surprise me." He took her elbow and pulled her along with him, moving farther down the block to get a better view around the front of the fire truck. "The sooner this damn trial starts and finishes, the happier we'll all be."

"Amen," she murmured. "But we also have to hope it ends in a conviction."

"True," he grunted. He nodded to the single man wearing full body armor who jumped down from the truck holding his helmet in his hand. "Betting Toby Bates wishes he hadn't thought it would be so cool to sign up for an explosives course," he said dryly.

"Is it me, or does he look to be no older than twelve?"

"He looks young because he is young. Joined the department straight out of high school, from what he tells me," Ben replied.

She watched as the younger man hefted a metal box she assumed contained whatever tools he might need for the task. Glancing at Ben, she asked, "You know him?"

Ben nodded. "His dad's one of the managers at Timber Masters. I've met them through Marlee, but he made a point of seeking me out not long after I got to town."

Curiosity piqued, she studied the sheriff. "Why?"

He shrugged. "Toby's parents weren't happy about him not going to college. They weren't happy about him joining the fire service either. They weren't thrilled about a lot of things I thought should make a parent proud." His jaw tightened. "Since when did protecting and serving one's community become a career choice parents discourage?"

An involuntary snort escaped her before she could stop it. Ben turned to her, startled. "What?"

She turned to face him, her expression solemn. "My relationship with my parents summed up in a single question."

He opened his mouth to speak, but the blast of an explosion ripped through the air.

Cracks appeared in the building's glass doors. In a flash, Harry was by her side, his strong arms wrapping around her. They grappled as his weight drove her to the ground. She shifted her weight to land on top of him, but soon found herself flat on her back staring up at the cloudless winter sky.

Panting, she shoved against his shoulder. "Let me up."

"No way," he huffed.

"Harry, damn it, that bomb wasn't meant for me. It was meant for you," she said, hoping to jolt some sense into him. He needed to let her protect him.

No such luck. "There's no way I'm going to let you be hurt on my account. If you won't take care of yourself for the sake of taking care of yourself, think about the baby," he said, his voice rising on the last word.

Their eyes locked and held, and in the middle of all

the pandemonium, there was a beat of shocked silence. It closed around them like a bubble.

And it popped the instant Julianne Shields asked, "What baby?"

Chapter Fifteen

Harry allowed himself to be ushered along with the rest of the spectators to Brewster's Bakery, where they would wait while the law enforcement professionals combed through what evidence they could recover from the scene. No one had been injured in the blast. Toby Bates had yet to go inside, thank goodness. All around them people hovered and buzzed. Alicia had been seated at a table in the center of the room and quickly surrounded by a bevy of clucking mother hens. She sent him imploring glares, but Harry was having a hard enough time keeping his mind wrapped around the fact that somebody had literally built a bomb and left it in his place of business.

The fountain. He'd heard one of the firefighters say it blew up the fountain. For some inexplicable reason, the news made him terribly sad. Sure, it hadn't functioned in years and had become sort of a depressing eyesore, but he remembered it from when he was young. Back in the day, it had bubbled and gushed, making the spacious atrium come to life with the sound of rushing water. His dad used to give him pennies to toss into it. For the life of him, he couldn't recall a single wish he'd made with those coins, but he knew what he'd wish for now.

He wished this would all go away.

Matt Rinker. Could he have done this? Up till now, he'd been able to disassociate the notion these attacks were being perpetrated by someone he knew, but now they had a name…

"Mike, we need to take the rest of the statement in a more private setting," he said in a low voice. "Alicia and I have been putting some things together and we have some theories, but no proof. I don't want to talk about it here."

To his credit, Deputy Schaeffer simply nodded and made a note on the order pad he'd borrowed from Camille Brewster's back counter. "Absolutely," Mike replied, his tone brusque and businesslike. "I can't believe somebody put a bomb in our building."

Harry smiled at the young deputy, both in sympathy and with a wistful longing for the days when he was so certain his world was safe. "It seems like the world is getting stranger and stranger," Harry commiserated.

"I don't think the internet helps these matters," Mike said. "People get fired up over things that aren't even real. I watched a whole documentary on it on Cineflix the other night. Everyone is spouting off, and they stop seeing one another as people. The next thing you know, they're doing a damn search on how to build an incendiary device out of household goods."

Or throwing flaming bottles of kerosene through living-room windows. Harry tapped the tabletop with two fingers, then rose from his chair. "I don't want to sound like an old fogy, because I'm not one, but I agree. It seems like this is all ramping up."

Mike nodded solemnly. "My dad keeps telling me people need to remember the good old days weren't always good. A lot of bad stuff went on before. We didn't hear about it the second it happened."

Harry inclined his head, deferring to the younger man's wisdom. "You're right. And not everything you hear is true. Or needs some sort of response."

Mike's gaze traveled to the counter, a sly smile curving his lips. "Only one thing remains the same."

Harry was intrigued enough to bite. "What's that?"

"Camille Brewster makes the best darn doughnuts in all of Georgia."

Harry laughed and cast a glance at the counter himself. "A truth universally acknowledged, my friend." He raised a hand in farewell to the younger man. "I'm going to grab a couple hits of sugar, then see if I can't smuggle Alicia out of here until some of the commotion cools down. Would y'all mind coming by the house to take the rest of our statements?"

"Not at all," Mike replied affably.

Harry nodded. "Are you a jelly or cream-filled man?"

"Personally, I tend to go with a chocolate-glazed twist," Mike admitted.

"One chocolate-glazed twist coming right up."

Harry stepped to the counter where Camille was busy resetting the coffee maker. He wasn't sure if it was the excitement or the sudden rush of midafternoon customers adding the rosy glow to her cheeks. After all, one man's bomb was another woman's boom, he thought to himself wryly.

When the older woman turned, she gasped as if surprised to find him there. She pressed her hand to her heart and fluttered it a bit. "Oh, Harry, I didn't hear you come up."

"Hey, Mrs. B," he said by way of greeting. Adult or

not, there were some folks in town he never could address by their given names. "Can I get a chocolate-glazed twist and two cream-filled to go, please?"

The older woman plucked a sheet of bakery tissue from the box and snapped open a bag with a practiced flick of her wrist. "Honest to goodness, Harry, I have no idea what this world is coming to."

"Seems to be the sentiment of the day," he replied tiredly. "Would you mind putting the twist in a separate bag?"

She dropped the two cream-filled doughnuts into the open sack and rolled the top down. "Not a problem." She opened a second bag, and he pulled a five-dollar bill from his wallet. Harry held it at the ready, but when she reached the register, she waved his money away. "Absolutely not. Not today." He opened his mouth to protest, and she held up a hand. "Besides, these doughnuts are hours old, and they're probably going to give you a stomachache."

She shoved the bags across the counter. Leaning in, she pitched her voice low. "Your lady friend appears to be done in. I suggest you get her out of here as soon as you can."

Harry smiled at the notion of Alicia being described as anybody's lady friend and knew instinctively she'd be insulted by the implication she was "done in." He chanced a glance over his shoulder and found the woman in question glaring daggers at him. Unable to suppress a mischievous smile, he turned back to Mrs. Brewster.

"Exactly my plan, ma'am." He nodded to the bag. "Thank you for these."

"It's my pleasure, hon. You go on now. I'll handle these lookie-loos," she assured him.

Harry dropped the five in her tip jar.

She only nodded and turned to switch out a full coffeepot for an empty one.

Harry snatched up the bags, dropped one on the table
in front of Mike. Elbowing his way to the table where
Alicia sat surrounded, he cast a tired smile at the crowd.

"Excuse me, folks. I need to steal Alicia, if I may."
The people seated around her gazed at him blankly, and
it was all Harry could do to keep from snapping at them
to back off. Nodding to Alicia, he gave what he hoped
was an encouraging smile. "Come on. I got something
for you."

Out on the sidewalk, Harry unrolled the bag. "Mike
said he and Ben would come over to the house to take
our statements." He reached into the sack and used the
bakery sheet Mrs. Brewster had left in there to extract
one of the cream-filled doughnuts. "Here. You need to
keep your strength up."

She smirked and took the pastry from him. "There
you go, treating me like a cop again." She exhaled long
and loud. "Thank you for the save. And for this," she
said, toasting him with the doughnut.

"How well do you know Marcus Zeller?" Harry asked
as they turned the corner and headed toward his house.

Alicia's brows shot up in surprise. "Zeller? From the
US Attorney's Office? He's a good guy. One of the best.
Why?"

"He seems oddly unperturbed by all of this," Harry
said, gesturing to the street around them. "And untouched."

"You think he's in on things?"

"Not necessarily. But I worry maybe someone has
gotten to someone. Or something."

Alicia stared straight ahead, her doughnut still clutched in her hand untouched. "Part of Coulter's strategy for asking for a bench trial was he didn't want a jury, right? He didn't want to be tried in the court of public opinion."

He inclined his head. "Always part of it, but people also opt for a bench trial when they think they can beat the evidence presented. The odds are stacked against the defense. The prosecution only has to convince one man—Judge Schneider. I don't know the man, but judges are notoriously harder to convince than juries. We can only sway them with evidence and the testimony of key witnesses."

"The chain of custody on the evidence is in agency hands," Alicia reminded him.

"It is."

"Are you starting to think he has the judge or someone at the DEA in his pocket?" she asked.

Harry sighed. "I don't know what to think. Someone detonated a homemade bomb in the building where I work. My house has been shot up, and my car has suffered more abuse than any vehicle deserves," he said with a wry smile. "All I know is, for some reason I'm bearing the brunt of this. None of the others involved in bringing Samuel Coulter to justice are seeing the same kind of backlash."

"Has anyone tried to bribe you?" she asked bluntly.

"No. Of course, I wasn't on their radar at first. I'm only along for the ride on this case. It's Zeller's show. I figure they thought I was a nuisance they could scare off."

"I see." Alicia nodded, taking a large bite of the doughnut. White cream oozed from the pastry. She had a smear of it on her upper lip. Harry was tempted to stop and kiss it away. The events of the day, compounded by the kiss they'd shared Saturday night, made him wonder what he was waiting for.

"We need to find a way to get to Matt Rinker. I think if we can flush him out, maybe get him cornered, he'll let us know exactly how deep this goes."

Alicia nodded, still chewing. She swallowed the bite and peeled back the paper in preparation to take more. "Agreed." They walked in silence for a few seconds. As they approached his house, she popped the last bit of her doughnut into her mouth and chewed. Pulling her phone from her pocket, she said, "I think I have an idea of who can help us."

A SHORT TIME LATER, Harry opened his front door to find Deputy Schaeffer, Sheriff Kinsella and Marlee Masters standing on his porch. He waved Mike and Ben in, but frowned at Marlee when she passed. "I wasn't expecting to see you here."

Marlee barked a laugh. "Way to make a girl feel welcome. I'm gonna have a word with your mama about your manners the next time your parents come to visit."

Harry wagged his head and shut the door. When he turned back to find her still standing in his space, he leaned forward to brush an apologetic kiss across her cheek. "Of course you're welcome. I simply was not aware you'd be joining in the fun. I thought we were giving a statement."

Marlee straightened. "You are, but Alicia texted me and asked me to come over. It seems we have a plot to hatch."

He let the notion of a plot roll around in his head while

he and Alicia quickly and dispassionately recounted everything they'd noticed about the city municipal center atrium in the brief minutes they'd sat on the edge of the mosaic fountain.

Once they were finished, Ben nodded to Deputy Schaeffer and clapped him on the shoulder. "See, this is where rank pays off. Type all this up for us, will you, Mike?" he asked with a good-natured chuckle.

Schaeffer rose from his seat. "No one was going to wait for you to type it up, Sheriff. We'd all have gray hair."

Marlee snorted, turning to Alicia. "He's a two-finger typist."

When Mike left, Ben turned back to the rest of them. "Actually, I'm a good typist, but I don't want them to know. I hate writing up reports."

Marlee reached over and gave his hand a pat. "Sure you are, sugar," she cooed. Her expression turned all business. "Okay, so you need to lure Matt Rinker out into the open," she said, getting down to brass tacks. "I have an idea, but I don't know if you'll like it or not."

"Oh," Harry murmured. "This doesn't sound good."

Marlee gave a mirthless laugh. "I know you won't like it, Harry, but you'll go along with it because I'm pretty sure Alicia will see the wisdom of my plan."

He smiled. It was hard not to appreciate how much Marlee Masters had come into her own in the months since she'd taken over running her father's business. "All right, shoot."

"Well, as you may know, but Alicia may not, the live nativity starts this weekend," Marlee began.

"Live nativity?" Alicia asked, bewildered.

"We set up a stable and manger scene on the lawn

outside the old courthouse and cast real people to portray different roles in the nativity."

"At the courthouse? Can you even have one on public property?"

Marlee snickered. "The courthouse has been decommissioned and is now a privately funded museum, therefore not technically government property."

Alicia processed the information. When she peeked at Harry for verification, he could only nod.

"I see. And this live nativity would involve…what, exactly?"

"Well, all the churches in town are involved. It's a devotional sort of thing. We have a Mary and a Joseph, a bunch of shepherds, an angel and, of course, a baby Jesus."

"Of course you do," Alicia murmured, her eyes wide with what Harry could only assume was shock. "People really do these things?"

"It's an old tradition. We put it on for a couple of hours on the weekend evenings leading up to Christmas. We start this weekend."

Harry narrowed his eyes at Marlee. "What are you suggesting?"

"My mama is in charge of arranging scheduling for those participating," Marlee responded with an overbright smile. "I'm sure I can convince her to let you all participate. We'll let it be known you're in, and hopefully, Matt Rinker will show himself."

It was Ben's turn to snort. "I know I must be missing something, but why would something like a live nativity lure a man out of the shadows?"

Alicia sat up straighter. "Because he's been saved," she said without thinking.

Marlee flashed her a beauty-queen smile. "Bingo!" Turning to Ben, she softened the smile but didn't dim the wattage. "Matt Rinker has found religion. And he found it at a revival where some of Samuel Coulter's snakes were being handled," she said, rolling her eyes. "Either way, he considers himself a devout Christian these days."

"Apparently, he missed the whole bit about loving thy brother as thyself," Harry said dryly.

"Or the thou shalt not kill part," Alicia grumbled.

Marlee waved a hand. "Anyhow, the Rinkers participate every year. Matt plays one of the Magi."

Harry fixed his gaze on Alicia. "When did you fill Marlee in on all of this?" he asked her.

Alicia shrugged. "She's the one I texted."

"You got it all into one text message?" he asked, incredulous.

She smirked. "Maybe I'm as good a typist as Ben is."

Marlee laughed. "I was at the Ladies Guild meeting when Marjorie was talking about Matt."

"Ladies Guild?" Ben asked.

Marlee covered his hand with hers. "I'll tell you about it later."

Alicia swallowed a laugh. "Trying to lure him out isn't a horrible idea. But we can't be certain he isn't trying to do more than scare you. My gut feeling is he's not. If he really wanted to hurt you, it wouldn't have been hard to do so in a more direct way."

"Don't forget Saturday night," he reminded her grimly.

A faint flush colored her cheeks. "Except for Saturday night."

"What happened Saturday night?" Ben asked.

Harry sat up straighter. "There was one incident we

didn't report," he admitted. "The night of Simon Wingate's party, when we were walking home, a dark sedan
with no headlights came at us in the street."

Ben stiffened. He slid his hand out from under Marlee's to reach for the notebook in his breast pocket. "Why
didn't you report it?"

Alicia sighed tiredly. "We had no description of the
vehicle, no license plate number—we had nothing to
go on other than we saw a dark car coming at us. We
had to make a dive for some bushes on the other side
of the road."

"You're sure they were aiming for you?" Ben pressed.

"One hundred percent," Alicia answered.

"The driver hopped the curb," Harry said, taking up
the story. "When he realized he wasn't going to be able
to get us without mowing down half the yard, whoever
it was wheeled around and took off. Neither of us was in
a position to get an ID on the car or the driver."

"Matt Rinker drives a black Camry," Marlee said almost to herself.

"What?" Ben said, swiveling toward his girlfriend.

Marlee pursed her lips. "I saw him at the Daisy driving Marjorie's car. I asked her about it, and she said they
sold it to Matt so he could have reliable transportation
to get a job. It's newish, but not brand-new."

Alicia fell back against the cushion of her chair and
tipped her head to the ceiling. "Ding, ding, ding! Folks,
we may have a winner."

"Are Marjorie and Chet in contact with Matt?" Harry
asked Marlee.

She shrugged and wobbled her hand. "Sporadic. They
had a big falling-out when things started to go missing from the pharmacy, and I think he used to turn up

now and again trying to hit his mom up for money. But to hear Marjorie, he's completely turned things around since the tent revival. She's saying it was his salvation from addiction."

Alicia leaned forward again. "So, what are you proposing? How can we be sure this Rinker guy will show up if I put on a robe and play shepherdess?"

"Oh, Alicia." Marlee sighed. "Have you learned nothing about this town? All we have to do is let it be known you and Harry will be taking part in the nativity, and the gossip mill will take care of the rest. Never underestimate the power of word of mouth." She eyed Alicia with a raised eyebrow. "Anyway, I wasn't suggesting you dress up as a shepherdess."

"You weren't?"

The surprise in Alicia's tone reflected Harry's own. He frowned at Marlee, wary of the sparkle in her bright blue eyes. "What did you have in mind?"

"Why, I was gonna ask Mama to cast Alicia as Mary. After all, it seems we've had our own miraculous conception right here in Pine Bluff, haven't we?" she said, dividing a Cheshire-cat grin between the two. "Now spill. What's this I hear about you having a baby?"

Chapter Sixteen

"I feel ridiculous," Alicia groused.

Harry adjusted the flowing piece of fleece he wore on his head. "This was your brilliant idea."

Drawing the draped blue fabric closer around her, Alicia shivered as they walked toward the town center. "I hope somebody remembers to bring a space heater."

"I don't believe they had those in Bethlehem," Harry commented mildly. "You sure you're okay with this?"

Her jaw set resolutely, she nodded. "I am ready to draw this guy out. And take him out, if necessary."

"Let's hope it doesn't come to that," Harry said briskly. They covered another half block in silence before he spoke again. "Alicia, we have a lot of ground to cover."

She nodded. "We're almost there."

"I'm not talking about the walk."

"I know. Let's get past this. We'll talk about…everything."

"Okay. But I have a few things to state for the record before we walk into this," he said firmly.

She eyed him, wary. "Okay."

"I need you to try to lie low. No one knows who or what you are other than a handful of people. No one will expect any heroics from you. There's going to be a crowd there, and I know your first impulse is to throw yourself in front of any danger. I'm asking you to think before you act."

Alicia swallowed the surge of indignation rising inside her. The implication she was a hothead who acted before thinking was completely unfair. But she and Harry had been doing the who's-protecting-who polka since she'd arrived, so maybe he had some right to ask her to rein it in. And maybe it was time they drew some firm lines.

"I promise I won't do anything foolish," she said, speaking slowly and deliberately. "But I also take exception to the notion of me thoughtlessly endangering myself or anyone around me. I am a trained professional, Harry."

"You're also a pregnant woman who may be carrying her one and only chance to have a child," he reminded her. "Likely my one and only chance too." She opened her mouth, but he raised a hand and drew to a halt. "I care about you, and I want to have the chance to see how things unfold between us."

She stared at him. How was she supposed to respond to such direct honesty? Was this what he was implying by saying this child might be his only chance at being a parent, as well?

Drawing a deep breath, she gave him a dose of her own truth. "Harry, I care for you too. I'm attracted to you, as I showed the other night. I believe there might be something more between us, and I'd be open to exploring those feelings, but I don't want this to be only because of the baby."

He inclined his head. "Fair enough. And I need you to believe me when I tell you it isn't only about the baby."

Unable to resist touching him, she reached for his hand and his fingers closed warmly around hers. "Okay, so let's catch this guy and see if we can't get on with the rest of our lives."

"Sounds like a plan," he answered.

The area set up for the live nativity was small, which Alicia figured was a good thing since there was a distinct lack of heaters available. They crowded into the open stable constructed from two-by-fours and a slanting plywood roof, and stood where Carolee Masters directed. A wooden crate with spindly crisscrossed legs attached served as a manger.

"Kneel beside it, dear," Carolee said, placing an implacable hand on Alicia's shoulder and applying a surprising amount of pressure. "And try to look adoring. You've given birth to our Lord and Savior."

Alicia stifled the urge to laugh, but a startled gasp escaped when she realized the baby doll she expected to see nested in the hay was a live infant swaddled tightly against the chill. "That's a real baby," she blurted.

Carolee Masters let out a tinkling laugh, pressing harder on Alicia's shoulder. She allowed her knees to buckle and she sank down beside the makeshift manger.

"Of course it is, darlin'. We strive to be authentic," Carolee said, waving her clipboard at a wandering shepherd to shoo him back into place.

Alicia stared up at her, stunned anyone would allow a small baby to lie exposed to the cold like this. "But they were in the desert. It's only forty degrees out here. It's too cold to keep a baby out here for hours at a time."

"Oh, we swap them out," one of the other women called to her. "Don't you fret none."

Alicia's eyes widened. She returned her attention to the contented baby sleeping through all the hubbub. "Swap them out? How many babies do you have?"

"Well, this has been a good year," Susie Troutman informed her. "We have three Jesuses all between the ages of six and nine months. We don't let them participate until they're over three months old." She wrinkled her nose. "I know he's supposed to be a newborn and all, but anything under six months is too young for the night air, you know?"

All around her, people nodded in agreement as if this reasoning were perfectly sound. Alicia saw Harry stationed near the front of the manger scene. Other people in various homemade costumes arrived.

"Oh, good," Carolee Masters cried, clapping her hands with excitement. "Our angel has arrived, and so has our Joseph."

Alicia spotted a beautiful preteen girl with strawberry blond hair dressed in a white robe and sporting a gold tinsel halo. As Carolee fussed over the man who would play her biblical spouse, Alicia surveyed the assembly. She'd memorized the photographs Marjorie Rinker had provided and was convinced she'd recognize Matthew Rinker if he was nearby. But the only familiar face, aside from Harry's, knelt down at the other side of the manger and flashed a devastatingly potent smile.

"Hello, wife," Simon Wingate said jovially.

Alicia could not hold back her snort. "Are you kidding me?"

"We couldn't let Mary have any old husband," he said with a retaliatory sniff. "Only the best." Kneeling over the makeshift manger, he whispered, "Don't worry. I took years of tae kwon do as a child. Don't forget—I'm the one who broke Samuel Coulter's wrist."

"I remember. You're Pine Bluff's answer to Bruce Lee."

He gave her a sober nod. "Damn straight." He pulled a face when he spotted the sleeping baby. "Sorry, Jesus," he apologized completely straight-faced.

Carolee Masters directed the rest of the cast to their places, and a small group of people assembled a few feet away from the makeshift stable. The chatter died down as the woman standing in front of the group raised her arms. They opened their mouths and began to sing "Away in a Manger."

Alicia wanted to speak to Simon but found him gazing adoringly at one of the women in the choir. She turned and squinted at the assembled singers. Deputy Lori Cabrera stood in the second row, her usually neatly coiled hair flowing like a dark river over one shoulder. Shaking her head in disbelief, she muttered under her breath, "This town."

She saw Harry's lips tilt into a smirk as his gaze locked with hers. Sometimes it seemed the man could read her every thought. In case he could, she marshaled all of her powers of concentration and sent one right back at him.

This place is too much.

His smirk grew into a full-fledged smile and she knew he'd read her loud and clear.

They sat for thirty minutes, Alicia doing her best to maintain the guise of the adoring new mother. The more she watched the child sleeping in the hay, the easier it became. She had no idea if the baby wrapped in the wool blanket was a boy or a girl, but it didn't matter. The baby was pink-cheeked and healthy, and the sight of the child tugged at something deep inside her.

She was scrolling through a mental list of all the things she would and would not allow her baby to do when someone jostled her from her thoughts. A woman stepped forward with another baby in her arms.

"It's time to switch them out," she said with a friendly smile. Nodding to the baby in the manger, she asked, "Would you mind?"

"Oh."

Alicia stared down at the still-sleeping child and her heart rate kicked up. She'd never held a baby before. She didn't have siblings or nieces or nephews. She didn't have close friends whose kids called her auntie. Never in her life had someone thrust a baby into her arms, desperate for a brief respite from motherhood. She met the woman's expectant expression, then studied the way she was holding the next child slated to portray the infant Savior.

"Yes. I can get him. Or her."

The words were out of her mouth before the reality of what she was being asked set in. Alicia hoped someone else would step forward to volunteer for the task. Perhaps this child's mother? But no one came to her rescue. Drawing a deep breath, she reached into the manger and slid her hands under the sleeping child, pulling up handfuls of straw with the baby. She cradled the child's back and head like she'd seen on television.

"How dare you lay hands on the Christ child?" a voice boomed from the back.

Shocked, the assembled residents turned toward a tall man holding a box spray-painted gold. He wore a

hooded cape of deep purple velvet, but his face was thin
and gaunt. Alicia recognized him in an instant. This
Matthew Rinker didn't resemble the confident young
man captured in his mother's photos.

The people surrounding him parted. His eyes blazed
as he stepped toward her. "How dare you lay hands upon
our Lord? You, a woman who lies with a man who is
not her husband," he said in a voice both slurring and
tremulous. He swung around to speak to the group at
large, and almost as one, they took a step back in the
tiny, confined space. The choir's version of "O Holy
Night" drifted away.

He rounded on Carolee Masters.

"How dare you bring this whore of Babylon into our
sacred adoration? Do you not know what she is?" he
demanded.

To her left, Marjorie Rinker stepped forward from
the crowd. "Matthew—" his mother began in a calm-
ing tone.

"And you shall cast out these demons! Listen to those
who speak in new tongues," he cried.

Rinker turned his gaze on Alicia, and she could see
his pupils had contracted to mere pinpricks in his eerie
light blue eyes. Heroin. The man hadn't found salvation from his addiction. He'd simply found somebody
who would feed both of his hungers. Samuel Coulter
had done this to him, and she would make sure Samuel
Coulter paid.

Moving slowly, she pulled the child closer to her,
opening her fingers to let the straw fall to the ground at
her knees. She hugged the baby close and turned to place
her body between the infant and the shouting man. Fran-
tically, she scanned the stunned faces around her, trying

to make eye contact with one of them so she could make a subtle handoff. But they were all watching Matthew Rinker. Surely, he wouldn't try to harm her while she held the child he believed to be the son of God.

"Rinker—" Harry began, stepping closer to her. The man knocked back the hood he wore, and Alicia was dazzled by the glint of the floodlights catching the gold metallic emblems sewn into his robe. He was dressed as one of the Magi, she assumed. A king who would come to worship before an infant.

"And you," the man spit. "Don't you know the disgrace you've become? Don't you understand the work we do is holy?"

Harry took another step closer, but Alicia motioned for him to stop. "Holy in what way?"

She was on her knees holding an infant, not a doll. Certainly not the best position to take somebody out, but she could stall him long enough to mitigate the scene unfolding around them.

Out of the corner of her eye, she saw Lori Cabrera peel away from the choir and circle to the back of the stable set. Her gaze automatically sought Marlee Masters, for where the blonde was, Sheriff Ben Kinsella was sure to be nearby. Sure enough, there was an empty spot beside her new friend.

Alicia was assessing her next move when Rinker tossed back the side of his robe and lifted his arm fully extended. He held a gun and the business end of it was trained on Harry. Her Harry.

"In my name they will cast out demons. They will speak in new tongues. They will pick up serpents, and they will drink any deadly thing. It will not hurt them.

They will lay their hands on the sick and they will re-cover," Rinker cried, his voice rising to a fever pitch.

Alicia didn't care if Harry thought she was a reck-less hothead; someone had to act. Turning to the per-son beside her, she thrust the now squirming child into their arms and swung back to the manger. Grasping it by the spindly legs, she swung the wooden crate upward. Straw flew everywhere, raining down on her as the side of the wooden manger made contact with Rinker's out-stretched arm.

A gunshot rang out, and a chorus of wails and cries quickly followed. She swung the manger again as she rose, and this time it made a satisfying clunk when it connected with the side of Matthew Rinker's head.

Suddenly they were swarmed.

She gained her feet in time to see Ben Kinsella tackle Rinker to the ground. The assembled group closed in on them, every person desperate to see the outcome of the commotion. Everyone except Alicia. Pushing toward the front of the set, she cried his name.

"Harry! Harrison Hayes!"

She pushed her way past body after body. Where had all these people come from? Before she could open her mouth to yell again, he appeared in front of her. His hands closed around her upper arms and he gripped her slightly harder than was absolutely necessary, but she couldn't blame him, given the circumstances.

"You said you wouldn't do anything reckless. You promised you'd think of the baby," he ground out from between clenched teeth. His lips grazed her temple. She was sinking into his embrace when he thrust his arms out, pushing her away again. "Damn it, Alicia, you promised to think of our baby."

Our. Not *the* or *your*, but *our* baby. Who knew a simple pronoun could mean so much?

"I was thinking of the baby," she whispered against the fleece fashioned into his shepherd's robe. "All I could think of was how much our baby needs a father."

HIS HOUSE WAS CRAWLING with people. Not only were Ben, Lori and Mike taking statements for the sheriff's department records, but also a guy named Alan Campbell, from Alicia's department at the DEA, had been dispatched to gather information on what was happening. At first, he thought her boss sent someone to check up on her. The man's presence got Harry's hackles up, but he seemed to be an ally. He'd driven down to Pine Bluff on his own time to pass on some information. Harry was relieved when Alicia seemed happy to see the guy. From what Ben had told him, her current section chief wasn't the easiest person in the world to work for.

Thankfully, Marlee Masters had arrived on his doorstep and taken dealing with the extraneous pieces of this circus out of their hands. She'd swooped in with a coffee maker under one arm and bags of snack food dangling from her fingers. With the brisk efficiency of the CEO she was, she shooed any nonessential hangers-on out the door, put Simon Wingate on refreshments duty and graciously offered the use of a Timber Masters rental home to Special Agent Campbell, effectively dismissing him, as well.

Harry thought things were wrapping up when the doorbell rang one more time. Excusing himself, he checked through the newly replaced sidelight, and a tangle of disbelieving laughter caught in his throat. US

Attorney Marcus Zeller was standing on his doorstep at nearly nine o'clock on a Saturday night.

"News sure travels fast," he said by way of greeting. He stepped back and ushered the other man in. "Come on in. I have a new coffee maker and they're cranking it out in there. No one will be sleeping tonight."

Zeller smiled and stepped past Harry into the foyer. "I don't mean to intrude, but I heard what happened and I thought it might be better if I came here in person so we could speak face-to-face."

Harry ushered him into the deserted living room. As usual, everyone had congregated in the kitchen. He couldn't blame them for avoiding this room. The stench of kerosene still lingered in the air, and they'd had to order glass to replace the broken window, so the view was mostly plywood.

Zeller took it all in, before taking a seat on the sofa. Harry couldn't help but think of how Alicia had perched on the same seat the night she'd shown up at his house out of the blue. She'd sat there with her chin tipped up in defiance, but her voice carefully controlled. She came here to tell him she was pregnant with his child. Until now, Harry hadn't truly realized how what had seemed like a shocking disruption in his life had grounded him rather than turned his world upside down. Rinker brought the chaos. Alicia brought the calm.

"Harry, I hate to do this after all you've been through in the past few weeks," Zeller began.

Harry held up his hand to stop the other man. "I'll be asking to be removed from the case."

Zeller blew out a breath. "Man, I hate this. You have every right to be sitting on this case, but…"

Harry shrugged. "But," he said, as if the conjunction had magically transformed into punctuation.

"I want to assure you the chain of custody on the evidence is solid. We have more than enough to convict Coulter."

Harry wanted to believe the other man's assertion wholeheartedly, but he couldn't help but wonder why Coulter would forfeit his chance to sway more than one person. The judge alone...

"I also wanted to inform you Judge Schneider has asked to be recused from hearing the case."

Harry blinked in surprise. "He has? Why?"

"It turns out the judge isn't wholly unconnected to what has been happening here." He tipped his head toward the rise of voices coming from the other room and pitched his lower. Harry had to lean in to hear. "The judge is Matthew Rinker's uncle."

Harry's eyes opened wide. "Excuse me?"

Zeller nodded. "Marjorie Rinker's brother. Her maiden name was Schneider," he explained. "The judge claims he had no knowledge of what was happening here with you and his nephew, but given the circumstances, we all agreed it was best he removed himself from the case."

"Holy—" Harry scrubbed a hand over his face, staring at Marcus again in disbelief. "Are you serious?"

"I wish I weren't. But you know how it is around here, Harry. It's not unusual to have relations spread all over the county and beyond. Folks generally don't stray too far from home."

"True," Harry said. He took in the living room where he'd watched television with his parents and sister growing up. Sure, the place looked completely different since he'd renovated, but it was still the home he'd always known. Shaking himself from his reverie, he tried to focus on the practicalities. "What does this mean for the trial?"

"The trial will go on as planned. We've asked for a change of venue. We'll try him before Judge McIntosh in Macon. He's made room on the docket so there will be no need to postpone. I'll be taking a second chair on from within my own department."

"Wow. Okay. You sure can get a lot done fast."

"Harry, I want to assure you I'm going to do everything in my power to convict Samuel Coulter on the evidence and put him away. We'll be charging Matthew Rinker in federal court, as well."

Harry's head jerked back. "You will?"

"The cases are tied together. One of the guys over at the DEA uncovered some proof Coulter's been in communication with Matthew Rinker."

"Alan Campbell." Harry let his eyes drift up to the ceiling. "I can't believe all this was going on right under our noses."

Zeller snorted. "Well, you've been distracted. We all thought this was the usual petty stuff surrounding a high profile case. We didn't see something bigger happening here, and I apologize. We should have dug deeper the first time you called and told me you were getting vandalized. But you know how it is. This stuff comes with the territory."

Harry's lips thinned into a grim line, but he bobbed his head in agreement. "Yeah, it does."

A sudden burst of laughter came from the kitchen, and Harry wished he was in on the joke, whatever it was. He hated not being in there. Hated being separated from Alicia even for a brief time. They had far too much to iron out.

Slapping his knees, he rose and offered his hand to Zeller. "Thank you for coming to tell me in person. I hate you had to drive all this way at this time of night to do it, but I appreciate the effort."

"It was the least I could do." Zeller clasped his hand. "And don't think I won't be calling you, you know, in case I need to get some particulars once the case starts rolling."

"It would be my pleasure. Nine days and counting," he said.

"Nine days and counting," Zeller repeated. Then he cracked his first smile. "We've got him, Harry. We've got him, and we won't let him get away."

"All I need to hear."

Chapter Seventeen

Alicia sensed Harry's approach. When he appeared, he stood in the doorway, staring at them each in turn as if trying to get a sense of what he'd missed. Alicia tried to see things through his eyes. She, Ben, Lori and Marlee sat in the chairs surrounding his kitchen table. Mike Schaeffer stood hunched over the counter, scribbling notes and shoveling a steady stream of chips and salsa into his mouth. Simon Wingate leaned against the counter, a bottle of beer in his hand and his trademark smirky smile lifting the corner of his mouth. He stared at the back of Lori's head, clearly smitten.

Alicia envied Mike his ability to eat. For once, her queasiness had nothing to do with the baby and everything to do with the echo of a gunshot in her mind. Her stomach had been tied in knots since the second she realized she couldn't see Harry at the front of the set.

She hadn't been kidding when she said she wanted their baby to have its father. What was more, *she* wanted their baby's father.

"Guys?" she said, interrupting some playful bickering between Marlee and Ben. The room fell instantly silent. "If you don't mind, Harry and I have some things to talk over, and it's getting late."

Almost as one, they rose or straightened, murmuring about their own need to get home. Lori and Marlee extracted a promise she'd meet them for breakfast at the bakery the following morning. Knowing she couldn't put their interrogation off entirely, she agreed.

She stayed put at the table as Harry showed them out. Snippets of conversation drifted back to her, but she was too tired to piece them together. Closing her eyes, she tipped her head back and forced herself to take three slow breaths. The edge of panic in Harry's tone jerked her from her meditation.

"Are you okay?"

She exhaled, lifting her head, and met his concerned gaze squarely. "I'm fine. It's only… If there's going to be any more talking tonight, I think it needs to be you and me."

He tipped his head to the side slightly, as if needing to translate her words. Then he moved so fast he became a blur. He stood beside her, but rather than taking the seat Lori had vacated, he reached for her hand and pulled her up. Alicia was half-afraid he was going to go all protective but distant on her again. Peck a gentle kiss to her forehead and lead her to the guest-room door with promises to talk more when they were thinking clearer. But she didn't want promises or protection. She wanted—

His mouth.

He pressed his mouth to hers in a kiss so ardent it almost hurt. Before she could catch on, he broke away and pulled her hard against his lean body. "Damn, I was so scared," he murmured into her ear. "I couldn't see you, and I was so scared."

"I couldn't see *you*. I was scared for *you*," she corrected, turning her face into his neck. If she was settling for a hug, she was going to take a big hit of his scent while she could. "For us," she added.

"I know." He ran a soothing hand over her hair. "If anything had happened to you and the baby—"

She cut him off right there. "I wasn't scared for the baby." When he pulled back slightly, she winced. "I mean, yeah, I was scared for the baby. Of course I was. But it's not *the* baby, it's *our* baby, and I needed you to be okay so I can ask you…" She trailed off, heat rising inside her.

Before she could stuff her embarrassment back down, he spoke. "Ask me anything."

"Do you want to take a chance on seeing if there can be an *our*— An *us*, I guess," she corrected.

"Yes," he answered with gratifying swiftness. "Yes. Definitely."

She tipped her face toward him. "You'd better kiss me again. Like you mean it. And if you try to tell me this is too complica—"

His lips were on hers before she could finish the word. When they parted, breathless, he peered into her eyes. "I'll go to Atlanta if you want."

Taken aback, she peeled away to search his eyes. "What?"

"I can get a job with the DA's office up there, or maybe even see what they have going at the Department of Justice. Aside from Zeller down here, I know one of the US attorneys working out of the northern district offices—"

She pressed her fingertip to his lips to stanch the flow. "Do you want to leave Pine Bluff?" she asked, genuinely dubious.

He shrugged. "I'll go anywhere."

Alicia stared at him in amazement, wondering what had happened to the cautious, skeptical man she'd encountered a few weeks before. "I wouldn't ask you to move."

"But your career—"

"But *your* career," she countered. "Besides, mine has not been going the way I'd like it to," she admitted. At his puzzled frown, she sighed. "Harry, what you saw here in the fall was a fluke. I had an opportunity under a chief who wasn't threatened by a woman who is too good at her job, and I took it."

"How can someone be too good at their job?" he asked, genuinely perplexed.

"By standing out. By showing up the other people on her team, rather than playact at being one of the guys." She scowled. "I won't apologize for being the best they had, but I won't be punished for it any longer."

"Punished for it?"

"Relegated to research or scouring through hours of surveillance. The only reason I caught the Coulter case was because I was the one who traced and tracked him. I was the only one who thought he was the one. They thought I was on a wild-goose chase, but I proved I wasn't. How did the agency reward me? They promoted the guy who gave me the chance and brought in another guy determined to keep me tied to a desk so I don't dare show up anyone else."

"That's ridiculous."

"That's bureaucracy," she countered. "If the agency can't appreciate excellence, I will find a place where people do. Maybe someplace like Pine Bluff."

"Alicia." Her name came out in a tortured whisper. "I can't ask you to move here."

"You aren't asking—I am," she said, lifting her brows to drive home the point.

"But Ben's department... There's no budget for anyone else, and you're grossly overqualified to be a deputy."

"But I'm an excellent investigator. Surely I can cobble together some sort of career."

"Sure, but is this what you want? You've worked so hard—"

"And it's gotten me nowhere," she concluded. "But the leave of absence buys me some time to think. What if I wanted something different? What if I don't want to be chained to a desk or married to my job? What if my parents were wrong, and life is about more than the constant pursuit of excellence? Excellence has gotten me a set of credentials I rarely get to use. Some meaningless commendations, an empty apartment and no friends to speak of."

She paused, her finger tracing the grain of the table where she'd sat surrounded by people she'd come to think of as friends. "I don't want to be perfect. I want to make magnificent mistakes," she said, pulling his hand around to press it to her belly. "There has to be more. I want more."

"There is," he assured her, his hand pressed to the slight curve of her stomach. "There already is."

"I want a place to call home. Someone I can count on. Friends who come running with coffee makers, chips and salsa."

"They're your friends too."

"I want you," she said simply. "Who knew I'd discover so much when I came to Pine Bluff to arrest Samuel Coulter?"

Harry's smile was slow to unfurl, but when it stretched fully across his face, the effect was astounding. "Special Agent Simmons, you had me at *I have a warrant.*"

* * * * *

COLTON 911: FORGED IN FIRE

LINDA WARREN

A special thanks to the gracious and super nice Patience Bloom for including me in this series. And to the wonderful Kathleen Scheibling for her steadfast guidance. Thank you, ladies!

Chapter One

The sweet feeling of success was empowering. Lila Colton's tummy bubbled and fizzed as if she'd downed a bottle of champagne. She wanted to dance, sing or run across the street and kiss that good-looking guy who'd winked at her this morning. That would put a smile on his face. Maybe hers, too.

She tapped a key on her laptop and the printer responded with a soft clicking sound. It belched out the financial report without a problem and she held it in her hands for a moment. She'd made it. All her life she'd wanted something of her own. A dream in her silly head, but she'd made it happen. The gallery was finally making a profit. She folded the report neatly and tucked it into her purse.

It had been six months since she'd opened the Weston Street Gallery in North Center, and the first two months were lean and hard as she had to chase down artists and beg them to show their work in her gallery. It had been a monumental task since no one knew her.

Tomorrow she had a show featuring the work of Homer Tinsley, a modern artist who was popular.

When she'd first seen a Tinsley, it looked as if someone had thrown paint at a canvas. She'd hovered around
it to get a better view; all the colors flowed and meshed
together in a way she couldn't explain. She just wanted
to step into the painting and experience the feeling it
had generated in her. She had three paintings in the
show, and usually every Tinsley sold quickly and would
bring in added capital.

Now she was going to go see her mother and celebrate. Her mother had been her biggest supporter and
Lila would never forget that. She might pick up a bottle
of wine and they'd dance around her mom's kitchen.
Her father didn't care what she did and that hurt at
times, but she tried not to let it show.

She reached for her purse as she heard the bell jin-
gle at the front door. Who could that be? They were
closed for the day. She stepped into the hallway that
went to the front door to see who it was. A man stood
there in a two-piece suit, looking around. By the cut
and the way it fit him, she'd guess it was a name brand.
He had an air of confidence and self-assurance. His
dark brown hair was cut short like an executive. She
couldn't see his eyes from where she was standing,
but from his broad shoulders to his lean body encased
to the max in the suit, she knew she could really go
for this guy. What was she doing? She wasn't used to
falling for guys at first sight, but there was something
about this one.

She cleared her throat. "May I help you?"

He swung around. "Yes. I'm looking for Lila Colton."

"Why?" She didn't understand why she was being

defensive. He wasn't a threat to her. Or maybe he was. Once she looked into his gray eyes, she was mesmerized. They were light with hidden nuances that suggested he could laugh in an instant. Or they could turn as dark as a thundercloud if the occasion arose. The man was very striking.

"Oh, I'm sorry. I forgot to introduce myself." He reached inside his suit pocket and pulled out identification. "I'm Carter Finch, an art insurance investigator."

"You mean like fraud?" Why did the good ones come with baggage?

"Yes. I hear you're showing some of Tinsley's work tomorrow."

"We show Tinsley's work a lot lately. His agent is very forthcoming with pieces."

"I'd like to meet the agent and Mr. Tinsley. Do you think you can arrange that?"

Lila thought about it for a minute, and that sweet feeling she'd experienced earlier disappeared like foam on a beer. That meant the Tinsley paintings in her gallery could be fakes and worthless. And that made her bottom line a little shaky.

"Do you think I have forgeries in the gallery?"

With one easy movement, he slipped his ID back into his pocket, as if he was taking time to answer the question. "I haven't looked at the paintings, but that's what I'm here to investigate. Namely, the Tinsley paintings you're showing. Do you think you can arrange a meeting tomorrow?"

"Walter Fox, the agent, will be here. I haven't even met Tinsley. I've asked Fox several times for Mr. Tinsley to show up for the viewing, but he tends to ignore me. I'll introduce you to Fox and you can take it from there."

"That should work. I'd like to see the paintings."

"Now? Everything is locked up and I have plans. Can we do this in the morning?"

"What time do you open?"

"At ten."

"What time is the viewing?"

"Two."

"I'll see you at ten."

"Are you going to seize the paintings?"

"No. I told you, I'm here to authenticate, and if they are forgeries, you'll probably have to give the buyers their money back."

"Oh, lovely. Do you know what that means for me?"

"I'm sorry. That's just the way it is." He strolled out the front door and she released a long breath. One minute she was floating on a cloud and the next a whole lot of bad had been dumped on her. What if Tinsley's paintings were fakes? It would bankrupt her. Good heavens, how was she going to survive this?

CARTER WAS AT the gallery at ten o'clock as promised. Ms. Colton was busy in the gallery with another woman as they were checking to make sure every piece, every painting, was perfectly hung and displayed. While she was busy, he took a moment to look around. The gallery looked freshly painted and bigger than he'd expected. Gorgeous hardwood floors and the walls were a delicate ecru. Intricate carved dark mahogany trim highlighted the room but didn't take anything away from what the room was displaying. There was a case for jewelry from foreign countries. He wasn't aware she sold jewelry.

He watched her as she talked to the woman with her back to him. Her dark hair was up in a twist and two decorative combs held it in place. Several strands had come loose and dangled by her face, giving her a soft feminine appeal. From out of nowhere he had the urge to remove the combs and let her hair flow free. She really was a beautiful woman and he hated what he had to do. In other circumstances he might have even asked her out.

She finally spotted him. "Oh, Mr. Finch, I didn't realize you were here."

"Do you mind if I look at the paintings, and please call me Carter."

"Mr. Finch, I don't think we'll be close enough to call each other by our first names. Let's leave it business."

"Yes, ma'am."

The Tinsley paintings were displayed on one wall and he stared at them for a long time. The bright colors always seemed to jump out and send a message that he could never figure out. Tinsley was a genius, but these paintings were not. Carter knew without checking further that they were forgeries. But somehow he just couldn't tell her. He'd notify Neil Dunning in the office and he would be here tomorrow. They would make a decision on the paintings for authentication, and if they agreed, the forgeries would be seized. That would take time. So he saw no reason not to let her have her show. She was aware of the risks.

"Thank you," he said as he walked away from the paintings.

"That's it?"

"No, it's just the beginning. I have another expert coming to look at them. It's a long, twisted road and a lot of paperwork, but I hope we can put the forger out of business."

He could almost read those beautiful green eyes. *And me, too.*

"I'll be back later," he said and then paused. "Wait. I need to get your phone number in case Fox or Tinsley shows up early." They exchanged phone numbers and he left feeling as if he was getting all wrapped up in Ms. Colton's affairs. He had made it his motto to never get involved with anyone he investigated, and he planned to keep that record clean.

The rest of the morning Carter went over information trying to piece together Fox, Tinsley and Ms. Colton's connection. Why was Fox offering the paintings to a small gallery in Chicago? His paintings used to show in Paris, New York and Washington. But now all of Tinsley's work was in small galleries and sold quickly.

Carter had hired a PI to see if he could find Tinsley. A little over a year ago, Tinsley's wife had passed away, and he'd become a recluse and no one had seen him since. That was puzzling since his paintings kept popping up everywhere. There was no connection between Fox and Ms. Colton. The only interaction they had was at the gallery.

He called for room service and then talked to Neil in the office. It was after three when he headed back to the gallery, and the showing was in full swing. She had a good crowd. People were looking at paintings, drinking champagne and talking. Ms. Colton was in the middle of a group of people asking questions about a sculpture.

A waiter offered him champagne and he took a glass while watching Ms. Colton. She was styling for the night with a below-the-knees black skirt and a white silk blouse. The short jacket had a beaded collar and beads down the front. Her high heels were adorned with tiny beaded straps around the ankles and over the toes. He had to blink to make himself look away.

When he found her alone, he walked over. "Has Fox or Tinsley been here?" He had to be all business.

"No, or I would've called you."

"Is that different? Doesn't Fox usually show up?"

"Yes. I called Mr. Fox when the paintings sold and he answered, but when I called him with some questions the buyer had, he didn't respond. And he still hasn't. I don't know what's going on."

People started to leave, and Ms. Colton went to the entry to say goodbye and to thank everyone for coming and supporting her gallery. Something very suspicious was going on and Carter's first guess would be Fox was alerted that he and Tinsley were being investigated for fraud. That was the only reason he wouldn't show, but Carter was betting he'd show up for that money.

A blonde with blue eyes walked over to him and shook his hand. It was the same woman Ms. Colton had been talking to earlier.

"My name is Savon. I'm Lila's assistant."

"Nice to meet you. Seems as if the showing went well."

"Yes, it did. I'm happy for Lila. She's worked very hard to make this gallery succeed, and then a con artist like Fox comes in, and you..."

"Savon, please," Lila said as she walked up to them. "I was very naive."

"Do you want to clean up tonight or wait until tomorrow?"

"You can go ahead and go. I know you have a date. I'm going to package the items that were sold and have them ready to go on Monday morning."

"I'll stay," Carter offered. "I need to ask more questions, if you don't mind."

"I don't think I have a choice." She hugged Savon. "Have a good time."

Carter followed her to a back room full of shipping materials. She sat in an old chair, undid the straps and kicked off her heels. "Aw, that feels so much better."

"Why wear them if they hurt your feet?" He took a seat on a bench that was against the wall.

"Said like a man." She lifted a dark eyebrow at him.

"What?"

"I don't see you kicking off your shoes."

"They don't hurt my feet."

"Aha." She pointed a finger at him. "Exactly. Do you know men's shoes are made for comfort and women's are made for style and to accent the feet and legs?"

He leaned forward, resting his forearms on his thighs. "This is an interesting conversation."

"Sorry. Sometimes I get carried away, but it bugs me that it's a man's world."

"I don't know about that. All you have to do is put on those heels and you can be in control of every man on this planet."

She laughed out loud, a soft, melodious sound that warmed his heart, and whatever tension there had been between them disappeared. "I believe you're a charmer, but I have to warn you I'm very good with charmers."

"I bet." He smiled and knew beyond a doubt she could charm him out of anything. They worked for the next hour together. He held things when she asked him to. He took paintings down to be shipped. And he carried things to the large safe to be stored for the night. She also sold two sculptures and she had a big bag with Weston Street Gallery emblazoned on it. It was like a big clothes bag. It would keep the sculptures clean during shipping. She placed tags with names and addresses on the items sold. They sat on the floor in the storeroom as she went over everything she had to do. He had come out of his jacket a long time ago, as she had hers.

She fanned herself. "It's getting hot in here. Do you mind if I take off my blouse?"

He leaned against a box, one arm over his raised knee. "I don't think anyone would say no to that."

She made a face at him and undid the pearl buttons on the blouse. Beneath was a white tank top. His disappointment was similar to an eighteen-year-old whom he thought he'd left behind a long time ago. But beauty was beauty even if you were eighteen or thirty-four. It was to be admired just like a painting.

"You said you had more questions. Fire away."

"Huh…" He was lost and hadn't heard a word she'd said. That was the first time that had ever happened to him.

"Okay, I'll ask some questions. Where are you from?"

He recovered quickly. "I was born and raised in New York. My dad worked on Wall Street and my mom worked at the Metropolitan Museum."

"That must've been an interesting life."

He moved uncomfortably against the box. He never liked to talk about his life. "Not as interesting as you'd think."

"What do you mean? You could go to the Metropolitan anytime you wanted."

"It wasn't like that. When I was small, Mom would take me to school and someone would drop me off at the museum. And I had to sit in my mom's office and do my homework. It was boring. It wasn't until I got older that I started to roam around and I found the nudes. They became my favorite paintings, but my mom became concerned and wanted my dad to find a psychiatrist because she thought it was unseemly that a boy my age would enjoy looking at naked women. My friends and I laughed about that a lot. And there was an influx of teenage boys to the museum."

"That's funny."

He brushed dust from his pants. He wished most of the stories had been like that, but they hadn't. "Ever since I was ten years old, all I ever wanted was freedom from the small space of the apartment. It was confining living in New York, but like all things, you get used to it."

"But it didn't keep you from still wanting freedom?"

"You bet it didn't."

"How did you get into the art business?"

"Due to my dad's insistence, I attended Columbia University because he went there. I was eighteen and could go where I wanted, but I didn't want to disappoint him. I stuck it out and was thinking about leaving when I met an art professor, Neil Dunning. He taught a class once a week and I was lucky enough to get into his class. He knows everything about art—the good, the bad and the forged. I learned so much from him. When I graduated, he asked me to work on his team and I've been with him ever since. I've traveled all over the world, and my home is now out of a suitcase, and that's just fine with me," Carter said.

"Do your parents still live in New York?"

He shook his head. "When my dad was turning sixty, he started talking about retiring, and my mom insisted that they weren't. They were too young. I don't know what happened. I was doing my own thing by then. When I came home for a visit, they said they had something to tell me. They were retiring and moving to Southern California. And that was it."

"Do you see them often?"

"No. I usually spend the holidays with Neil and his family."

Her face creased into a frown.

"Why are you frowning?"

"I think it's so sad when a child loses touch with their parents. That's a bond that shouldn't be broken.

My dad is dysfunctional, but I still talk to him and check on him every now and then because he's my father."

"I knew you would be like that."

"How?"

"Soft and kind." He shifted again. "You know, it is getting hot in here."

Lila sniffed. "What's that smell?"

Both jumped up and ran into the gallery. In the right corner, flames licked toward the ceiling and smoke billowed toward them.

"Oh, my God! My gallery's on fire!"

Chapter Two

"We have to get out of here," Carter shouted. "Where's the exit?"

Lila pointed to the left. Smoke covered the back entrance and they couldn't see. The fire alarm screeched in their ears. Carter grabbed her jacket and blouse and his jacket and then took her hand and ran into the hallway. "Maybe we can get out the front door."

Flames clawed at the front entrance like an angry monster, roaring and destroying what it touched. Carter, still holding her hand, rushed into her office. He looked around. "No windows."

There was one long window at the top, but it wasn't a potential exit. The gallery was fully secured. Without a key, there was no way to get in or out.

"Wrap the blouse around your face to protect it and put your jacket on to protect your skin," Carter said as he wrapped his jacket around his head and covered his mouth. "Try not to breathe too much of the smoke. I called 911, so someone should be here quickly. Just stay calm."

"Yeah, right." Her hands shook and she tried to do

as he'd asked, but that was impossible. The fire was all around them and no help was in sight.

"What's on the other side of this wall?"

"It's the exit that goes out into an alley."

Carter tapped on the wall. "It's drywall." He picked up a stapler from her desk and started hitting the wall with blunt-force blows. The drywall splintered and he pulled away big pieces with his hands.

She reached in to help him until they had a big hole. He kicked the two-by-four out with his foot, taking most of the outside office wall. "Be careful of the wires."

"You first," he said. "Fast! The smoke is building in here."

With the blouse wrapped around her head and over her face, he pushed her through the hole and she tried not to breathe. He tumbled through after her and they faced the big exit door, which was locked. Carter reached up and hit the security pad, and the door opened. They fell out into the alley into a fireman's arms.

Other firefighters charged into the building. "Anyone else in here?" one of them asked.

"No," Carter shouted.

An ambulance backed into the alley, and within seconds, she was lying on a stretcher, thanking God for her life and Carter's.

She looked at him sitting on a bench beside her. He removed the jacket from his head, and a paramedic checked him over and put an oxygen mask on him. She had one, too, and was trying to breathe normally, which was difficult since her heart was pounding in her chest.

"Are you okay?" she asked.

"Yeah. Now that we're out of there. How about you?"

"I'm good now that I can breathe." She wanted to say she was sorry and so many other things, but she didn't know what for. It was all tangled up with the fear inside her.

To make sure they were out of danger, they spent the next two hours in the ER as they underwent tests and X-rays. In the end, the doctor said she was okay, but he wanted her on oxygen for thirty more minutes.

She hadn't seen Carter and she wondered how he was doing. She'd ask the nurse when she came back. The curtain moved aside, but the woman who came in wasn't a nurse. It was her mother, Vita. Her brown hair was in a short bob, and the expression on her face was one of those take-charge-mother moods.

"Mom, I told you I'm okay."

Her mother hugged her and pushed back her damp hair. "Your hair's wet."

"I've had a shower to get the soot off of me."

She laid a small carryall on the bed. "I brought you some clothes, so get changed and you can come home with me. I'll take care of you."

Lila sighed. "Mom, as soon as I'm released, I'm going back to the gallery. I have tons of things to do, like deal with the insurance companies."

"It will all be there tomorrow."

Just as Lila was about to prepare her best comeback, a gray-haired man with a goatee and a big smile walked in. Her stepfather, Rick Yates, kissed her cheek. "How's my girl?"

"I'm good. I'm just trying to convince my mother of that."

"Well, she worries, you know."

"And I love her for that, but I really need my space right now. Please."

"Well, Vita, I guess we go home and do our thing and let our grown-up daughter do hers. What do you say?"

Her mother straightened the sheets as if they needed it. "You'll call first thing in the morning?"

"Promise, but I'll be out late, so don't expect it too early."

Her mother rolled her eyes. "There are always conditions with children. Let's go home, Rick. Love you, baby."

"Love you, too, Mom."

She jumped out of bed and hurriedly dressed in the jeans and stretch knit top her mother had brought. As she slipped into sneakers, the nurse came in with discharge papers and she quickly signed them. "Do you know if Mr. Finch has been discharged?"

"Yes, I believe he's already left."

No! She wanted to talk to him, but she wouldn't worry. She was sure he would come back. She'd just take a cab to the gallery and get her car. Then she realized she had no money and her purse was in the gallery, probably burned to a crisp. What could she do? She could call her mother, but she'd just made a big deal about needing her space. Her brother, Myles, was probably still working in his law firm. She could call him and wiggle cab fare out of him.

On the way to the nurses' station, she stopped short.

Carter was there in scrubs and leaning on the counter, talking to a nurse. She should have known women liked him. She thought of her dad for a brief moment. He cheated on her mother constantly and had several children outside the marriage. She probably would never marry because of the scars from her childhood. How could she really trust a man?

"Hey, I was just looking for you. Do you need a ride back to the gallery?"

"Yes. Thank you."

"I called a cab. It should be here any minute."

As they walked out the door to the yellow cab, she said, "Love the outfit."

"It's better than soot-covered clothes. I'm thankful the doctor was so generous."

Carter opened the door, and she slid into the back seat and made no effort to move over. Carter sat right next to her, almost together, as one. She didn't want to move away. She needed this closeness. She needed someone. The fear was still very real, and she needed to be with someone who didn't know her well enough to know that she was about to fall apart.

They didn't speak all the way to the gallery, but he gently touched her hands, which were gripped together in her lap. "Are you okay?"

"No." She was as honest as she could be. "But I have to see what's left of the gallery and all the months of work I put into it."

"From the insurance, you'll be able to recoup and start over. You can hold my hand if you want."

She wasn't afraid to grab it quickly for support. The cab stopped in front of the gallery and they got out. All she could do was stare at the blackened rubble that once was her beautiful gallery. The roof had caved in, and the whole place was just a charred mess. Somewhere amid all the ashes were treasured pieces of art. Her eyes strayed from the building to her car parked in front. She gasped. Part of the roof had fallen through her windshield into her car and the tires had been burned off. It was totaled. She was totaled. She had to get away from here.

By the expression on Lila's face, Carter could see she had reached her limit. He had to take her home. Before he could offer, a man walked over to them and held out his hand. "Frank Richards, chief arson inspector." The man was tall and his slacks and shirt were wrinkled, as if he hadn't been out of them in a couple of days.

"Do you think it was arson?" Carter asked.

The man shrugged. "We're not sure, but we have to check everything. We'll let you know when we've finished the investigation."

"Thank you," Lila replied. "Do you think you can see what's left of my purse? My identification is in it and I'll need it if it's still usable."

The man thought about it and Carter knew he didn't want anyone to disturb the scene, as most firemen would.

"What would it hurt to let her have her identification?" he appealed to the investigator. "Just her ID."

The man sighed and hollered at one of the firemen to do as she'd asked.

"It's on a chair in my office," she said.

In a few minutes, the man came out with her wallet and handed it to her. "It's kind of warm, so be careful, but everything is intact."

"Thank you."

A Lincoln Navigator swung into the parking lot. A bald guy with a little extra around the middle got out. "What the hell happened here?"

"Somehow the gallery caught fire," Lila told him.

"I told you about all that wiring. Every month it's something about the wiring. The electrician put new lights in this week and probably overloaded the breaker, which caught fire," the man said.

The arson investigator shook his hand. "We've already checked the breaker and that wasn't it. I'm assuming you're the owner of the building."

"Yes. Lou Rossini." He pointed to Lila. "She's responsible for this and she's going to pay for everything."

"Hey, you don't know that." Carter stepped in. "You don't know what started the fire, and until they do, I'd advise you to keep your mouth shut."

The man's eyes narrowed. "And who are you?"

"Carter Finch, insurance investigator. The insurance companies are involved now and will make a decision on who pays for what."

"I'm sorry, Mr. Rossini. I don't know how the fire started."

When Lila spoke, the man seemed to calm down. "The insurance people will sort it out. I'll talk to you later."

Lila wrapped her arms around her waist and Carter realized she was trembling. He touched her arm.

"Come on. I'm taking you home. Do you want to go to your mother's?"

She blinked. "How do you know my mother?"

"I heard her in the ER."

She brushed her no-doubt messy hair behind her ears.

"Oh. You know that saying about always listening to your mother because she knows what's best for you? I should've listened, but right now all I want to do is go home to my apartment and let the wounds heal. My mother would smother me with love and kindness, and I don't need that right now. I need to be strong to get through this. It's my problem, not hers."

He admired her courage, but she really shouldn't be alone. "Do you have a sister or brother who I could call for you?"

She linked her arm through his. "Wait until you hear about my convoluted family and then you'll understand when I say no. I'll do just fine by myself. I could call my sister-in-law, Faith. We've always been close, but she has her own problems right now. I could call Savon, but she's having the time of her life and I won't bother her."

He helped her into the car, which he didn't have to do, but she didn't say anything, just clutched the wallet to her chest. "Where to?" he asked as he slid into the driver's seat of his rental. She gave him her address in Lincoln Park. It was a town house and not too far away.

"Why don't you come in," she said as he stopped in the parking lot. "There's no need to go back to your hotel."

He was thirty-four years old and he was pretty good

at reading women, but this one flew right over his head. He didn't know what she was thinking, but he knew what he was thinking.

"Why?" he asked. "We barely know each other."

"I feel like I've known you for a very long time and—" she rubbed the leather on the wallet "—I don't want to be alone tonight. And, yes, I'm fine," she added quickly. "Don't read more into this than there is."

"I wouldn't dream of it." He grabbed his briefcase and suitcase and followed her into the town house. It was a two-story with a living/kitchen area downstairs and the bedrooms upstairs.

With her foot on the bottom step of the stairs, she said, "There's a small bedroom to the right and a small bathroom that you can use. I have a lot of paintings and artifacts in there, but you can get to the bed and the bathroom."

"Thanks." If he had any wild notion how this night was going to go, she had just disillusioned him. She really didn't want to be alone and he understood that. He settled into the room and stared at all the paintings stacked against the wall. They were all by the same person and she was probably going to have a show for that person. There were several small sculptures and vases in a corner. On the desk were hand-drawn pictures with an old Wild West flavor. He pushed them toward the back and laid his laptop there. On the bed he opened his suitcase and put away his clothes in the chest of drawers and closet. There were also paintings in the closet, but he had enough room for his clothes. He sat on the bed and took a moment. What was he doing here?

He liked her. He liked her a lot, and if she needed someone, he was willing to be that person. Truth was, no one had ever really needed him. As a child, he'd spent more time with the lady across the hall than he had with his own parents. They were social people and went out several nights a week, and he was left to be entertained by the neighbor.

He stretched. The day had been a killer. He smelled like smoke and his muscles ached. Escaping a fire was not in his job description. He had to get all this information to Neil, but first, he needed to shower and change clothes. Then maybe he would feel better.

Nothing could change the outcome of the fire. There would be some rough days for Lila and he would stay as long as he could. His work was on the road and he would have to leave as soon as he sorted through the Tinsley debacle.

LILA FELT MUCH better after she had a shower, and she smelled better, too. She heard the water running and knew Carter had decided to take one, too. She went downstairs. Why had she asked him to stay? The answer was very simple: because she wanted him here and, yes, maybe she was a little afraid, but not of the darkness or the fire, but of being alone. She'd had that fear most of her life, and today she really couldn't shake it and she couldn't explain it.

Carter came into the kitchen in pajama bottoms and a T-shirt. Her heart accelerated at the sight of him. His wet dark hair clung to his scalp and a five-o'clock shadow enhanced his sexy masculine look. There was another reason she wanted him to stay. She was thirty years old and attracted to him, and she was old enough to act on that attraction.

"You seem better," he said, eyeing her from head to toe in the short bathrobe. Her senses spun with an almost forgotten delight of being with a man.

She swallowed hard. "You look better, too."

He walked toward the refrigerator. "You have anything in here to eat? I'm starving."

"I ordered pizza."

"Great. Just what the doctor would suggest." The doorbell rang. He went to get the pizza, and they sat at the island in the kitchen.

"You can't stay in Chicago and not eat a deep-pan pizza."

"It's delicious, but you're not eating very much."

"Nothing seems real." She laid her pizza piece in the box. "I think I'm going up to bed. I want to be at the gallery early in the morning."

"I'll clean up down here and probably go to bed, too."

She paused on the stairway, wanting to say something to explain her strange actions. "Have you ever been afraid to be alone?"

He took a sip of wine. "Everyone has. Even big old guys, so don't beat yourself up about being afraid. It's a normal reaction."

"Nothing stays the same. Everything gets shattered and broken, and I don't know how to put my life back together without crying my eyes out."

"Then cry your eyes out. Do whatever it takes, and I promise you tomorrow everything will look better."

"You're no help." She ran up the stairs. How could

she expect him to understand? He didn't even really know her or about her childhood of broken dreams and broken promises. Everything changed on a regular basis, and maybe this time it was just too much.

Chapter Three

He'd said the wrong thing, but he wasn't a kiss-and-make-better type of guy. She was hurting, so he should've done something more mature, more comforting, even though she'd said she didn't want that from her own mother. He put the rest of the pizza in the refrigerator and finished off his glass of wine. Tomorrow they would talk and he'd apologize for being so crass.

As he passed her doorway, he could see from the light in the hall that she was sitting on the floor at the foot of the bed with her knees drawn up and her face resting on them. Was she crying? He started to go in, but changed his mind. She needed this time alone.

He brushed his teeth, turned out the lights and sat on the bed. For some reason, he couldn't force himself to crawl beneath the sheets. He couldn't sleep when she was going through such a traumatic upheaval.

Her door was slightly ajar, and he tapped on it. She didn't respond and his first reaction was to go back to his room and leave her alone. Instead, he walked in and sat beside her with his back against the bed.

"I'm sorry I was so crass. I should have been more understanding of what you're going through. You lost your place of work and your car and survived the fire. That's a lot for one day."

She raised her head. "It's not about that. Those are material things that can be replaced, though I would have rather not have lost them. It's just…just… Have you heard of the Colton families in Chicago?"

"Can't say that I have."

She leaned forward, snagged a newspaper from the dresser and placed it in his lap. The lamp was on, but still he could barely read *Colton vs Colton*. She'd said something about her convoluted family, and maybe she would tell him about them.

"Are you one of these Coltons?"

"Yes. So many weird things have been happening lately that it's hard to take it all in."

"What happened?"

"I never met my grandfather Dean. He had a wife named Alice and a mistress named Carin Pederson. I'm told the marriage was a happy one until Alice couldn't conceive. There was a lot of tension in the marriage, and then Carin got pregnant and my grandfather decided to leave Alice for Carin to be with his children. Before he could break this news to Alice, she told him she was finally pregnant and he made a decision to stay with his wife and raise his proper family. This made Carin very angry and she's been that way to this day. Carin blackmailed my grandfather many times using her sons as leverage. He bought Carin a house on the outskirts of Chicago and paid her a huge monthly salary." She took a deep breath. "Carin is my grandmother."

"The mistress?"

"Yes. And to up the tension, so to speak, Alice had twin boys, Ernest and Alfred, and my grandmother gave birth to Erik and Axel. The two families lived here in Chicago never knowing about the other until Ernest and Alfred were murdered outside their office. They caught the murderers and then found out there was a codicil to Dean Colton's original will. It named my father, Axel, and Uncle Erik as heirs. Of course, this was a shock to all of us, on both sides. How could we have been duped for this long?"

"It's easy to be deceived. I deal with it every day in art and in the real world. Everybody wants their fair share and more."

"That's my grandmother. When she heard there was a codicil to the will, she hired a lawyer and forced my dad and my uncle to side with her so they could get their fair share."

"Is there a lot of money involved?"

"Have you heard of Colton Connections?"

"Sure. It's a big company."

"That's the business Alfred and Ernest created, and now my grandmother wants half of it, which comes to about thirty million. If the judge rules in my grandmother's favor, it will bankrupt the other Coltons. That's what makes me sad. It's not our money."

"But if the will says so, you're entitled to it…"

"They asked to meet us."

"The other Coltons?"

"Yes. We met at Farrah's home and talked. She's the widow of Ernest and was very gracious to have us in her lovely home. You know, you could tell they are very wealthy and yet they all hold down jobs. My father and Uncle Erik have been get-rich schemers all their lives and have accomplished nothing. They live off of my grandmother. And now she wants her sons to have what they deserve because Dean denied them all of their lives."

"And you don't feel that way?"

"It was hard to hate these people who seem to have everything. They were very nice to us and they didn't have to be. We've been trying to get along these past few months and trying to get to know each other and exactly what we want for the future. Myles—he's my brother—and I feel that the money isn't ours, and so do my cousins Aaron, Damon and Nash, Erik's sons. But we don't have a say in the matter. It's up to our fathers and they are controlled by our grandmother. I don't look for anything to change until my grandmother gets her way. She wants revenge for the way Dean treated her, and she's not going to stop until she gets it."

"It's clear you have issues with your grandmother."

"Oh, you bet I do. She manipulates my dad to the point where he is still like a little boy asking favors from her. He will never go against her."

"You weren't raised by your father?"

"No. My mom and Nicole, Erik's wife, got out as soon as they found out their husbands were cheating on them and had children by other women. I was raised by my mother, and it was hard for her that first year as we moved around a lot. There was no place to call home. And then my mom met Rick and our lives settled down. He became the father we never had. He and my mom own Yates' Yards plant nursery. It's in the sub-urb of Wheaton and a lovely place if you like plants of all kinds, trees, blooming flowers, shrubs and fruit trees." She flexed her arm. "That's where I got these muscles, working in the nursery."

He touched her bicep. "You don't have any muscles."

"You better watch out," she singsonged in a happy voice, "or I might show you these muscles."

He pushed her hair away from her face. "You're the most beautiful and captivating woman I've ever met."

"And you're a handsome charmer who saved my life."

"The authorities would've been there to save you."

She shook her head. "I keep thinking what if I had been in the gallery alone..."

"Shh." He gathered her close in his arms. "You weren't, so no more *what-ifs*. Now, do you think you can get some sleep?"

She blinked at him. "I don't know. I might need company..."

"Lila..."

"How long have we known each other?" She sat up to look at his face, and even though it was almost dark, she saw a lot of questions and a lot of answers there. But she couldn't decipher any of them.

"Maybe forty-eight hours."

She placed her hand over his heart and it raced like a stallion waiting at the gate. "From the first moment I saw you standing in the doorway, I thought you could be someone I could really go for. I didn't know anything else about you, but somehow our hearts connected."

"Lila, you've been through a lot today and I don't

want to take advantage. I think it's best if I go back to my room and we'll talk about this tomorrow."

At his words, rejection filled her. Even though she tried to hide it, she could feel the tightness of her face scrunching into a frown. She sat back on her heels, trying to wiggle out of an embarrassing situation.

He quickly cupped her face. "Hey, hey, I didn't mean it that way. I don't want you to regret it in the morning."

"Do you know how old I am?"

"No, and I would never ask."

She patted his chest. "Good. I'm old enough to know what I want. I'm not in college, fooling around for the fun of it." She made a face. "Although, I've never been that girl, either."

"Well, then stop talking." He brought his lips to hers and the room tilted as a storm of emotions exploded in her, emotions too long denied and emotions that she needed to feel. His lips took her on a journey of pure heat as hot as the fire in the gallery. He trailed his lips to her cheeks, over her jawbone and down her long neck to her breasts. Just when she thought she couldn't get enough, he lifted her into his arms and fell backward onto the bed. They laughed like teenagers and quickly discarded their clothes. But unlike teenagers, they made love in a slow, satisfying way. It was unlike anything she'd ever experienced. His hands and lips made a thorough investigation of her body, and she could very well say he had the touch to drive her crazy. Her breasts swelled and her body ached for more. She heard moans and cries and realized it was her enjoying the pleasure of a man who knew what he was doing.

He trailed a finger down the length of her body. She shivered.

"You have such smooth skin."

"And your hands are lethal tantalizing weapons."

She pulled his head down to hers, and nothing else was said for some time as they soothed each other's aches, pains and worries in a way that satisfied both of them. The world with its gigantic headache floated away. As she drifted into sleep, she thought she could be falling in love for the first time in her life. Or making the biggest mistake of her life.

THE SOUND OF the phone woke Carter at six. He looked down at the woman beside him curled into him like a soft and warm kitten and wanted to stay there forever. His phone sounded again, and he scrambled looking for his pants and then realized they were in the other bedroom. He lightly kissed Lila and she stirred.

"I'll be right back."

"Carter…"

He found his pants and his phone. It was Neil, his boss. He'd forgotten about him. "Neil."

"I'm at the hotel and you're not here. Where are you?"

"Uh…" He looked around at the very feminine decor and the many paintings and thought he was in heaven…with an angel. "Give me a few minutes."

"Okay. I'm eating breakfast in the restaurant, so that's where I'll be."

Carter went back to Lila's bedroom and crawled in beside her. He kissed the curve of her neck. "I have to go."

"Oh." She stretched, and his eyes strayed to her flawless white body and all his engines roared to life. "Is it morning?"

"It's after six."

She sat up straight. "Oh, heavens. I've got to go, too. I'm meeting the car insurance guy at the gallery and hopefully I can get a rental, but you'll have to drop me off on your way to wherever." She tried to crawl from the bed, but he caught her and pulled her back.

"Carter," she screeched.

"You can't just run away."

He stared into her green eyes, which were full of laughter and fun, and that was the way he always wanted to see her.

She raised an eyebrow. "What do you have in mind? You've got five minutes."

He chuckled. "I'll only be getting started."

Laughter filled the room, and once again everything faded away except their attraction for each other.

Afterward they were in a rush to get out the front door. Lila called her mother with Carter's phone to let her know she was okay. As they drove up to the gallery, Carter watched Lila's face. It was much worse in the daylight, a large pile of charred rubble, smoke still emanating from some of the destruction. The right wall and the front of the building were completely gone. All that was left was Lila's office and safe.

"Oh," erupted from Lila's throat. "It's all gone. Somewhere in that pile are the Tinsley paintings. Now you won't be able to validate them."

He reached over and took her hand. "You don't have to try to be brave. If you want to cry, cry."

She linked her fingers through his. "I've already had my cry, and thank you for being there for my melt-down."

"My pleasure." Then he reached over and engaged her in a long kiss that he would remember for the rest of the day.

A car drove up to Lila's burnt one. "That's the insurance agent. I sent him pictures yesterday, so it should be quick."

"Do you want me to wait?"

"No. The insurance guy will help me get a rental. I'll call you later."

"You don't have a phone."

She sighed. "Okay. I will get a phone after I get a rental and I will call you, but I don't remember your number."

He reached for his wallet, pulled out a business card and handed it to her. "You can usually reach me at those numbers, but my cell is the one I usually answer."

"Thank you." She tucked it into the wallet she was carrying.

She gave him a quick kiss and he drove away. He looked in his rearview mirror and saw her just stand-ing there staring at the destruction of the fire. Was she okay? Did he need to stay?

The insurance guy walked over to her, they shook hands, and he knew she was fine. She'd gotten it all out of her system last night. She was strong and resil-ient, and he was lucky enough to have been there when she'd needed someone. He never had a problem leaving town, but today he was feeling a pull to stay in Chicago for a while. That had never happened to him before.

He'd fly into a new city, do his job and get on a plane and go to another city. That was his life and he enjoyed it. Since the Tinsley paintings were ruined and they couldn't validate them, they'd probably be leaving as soon as tonight. How could he tell her he was leaving?

Chapter Four

Lila was in a rush mode all morning. Before she could talk to the insurance agent, Inspector Richards drove up and wanted to talk to her. She made arrangements to meet the agent later.

They stood near Richards's black Ford car with a Chicago Fire Department logo on it. Since it was August and summer in Chicago, it was a nice sixty-two degrees this morning. There was a slight chill in the air, though. She felt it all the way to her bones. If Richards was seeking her out, there had to be a reason.

"Mr. Rossini seems to think you had something to do with the fire and is being very vocal about it, so I'd like to ask you some questions."

Her nerves tingled. "Oh, sure. So it was arson?"

"It's kind of leaning that way, but we're not finished yet. Mr. Rossini said that you were in debt and had a very good reason to set the fire."

"The gallery is steadily making progress. I've only been open about six months. Why in the world would I choose to destroy what I created? I expect the profits will be more next month, but now…" She took a long breath. "I did not set the fire."

"What was the name of the electrician who put in the new wiring?" He pulled a small notebook from his pocket and began to write in it.

"Philip Boyd."

"Does Mr. Rossini know the electrician?"

"He hired him—that's all I know. When I paid my rent last month, I asked about the wiring because he had promised to get it done. He told me he would get things fixed up like I wanted. A few days later, the electrician showed up and did the work."

"Who else works in the gallery with you?"

"Savon Elam. Oh, no! I forgot to call her. May I borrow your phone?"

"Uh… I guess so, but don't be too long. That's my work phone."

"Thank you."

She told her friend everything that had happened and what she was doing now with the insurance people.

"Are you okay?" Savon asked.

"Yes. I have my own personal hero."

"You mean handsome Mr. Finch?"

"Yes. I don't know what I would have done if he hadn't been there. I'll talk to you later. The arson inspector is glaring at me because I'm using his phone. I'll let you know when I get a phone."

Lila clicked off and put on her best smile. "Inspector Richards, do you think it would be possible to get my phone back?"

"Let me check and see if they're through with it." He talked on the phone for a minute and then shoved his cell in his pocket. "You can pick it up at the station on Central."

She wanted to hug him. Instead, she said, "Thank you." Her excitement didn't last long as she realized she didn't have a way to get there. She would have to call a cab, but again, she didn't have a phone. She shouldn't have let the agent leave.

Men in red cars that had the fire department logo on them parked in the parking lot.

"That's my team," the inspector said. "We'll be working here most of the day."

"Uh…may I use your phone again?"

"What for?" His eyebrows knotted together.

"I have to call a cab."

He looked around. "How did you get here?"

"A friend dropped me off."

He reached for the phone in his pocket. "Remember…"

"Don't stay on it too long," she finished for him. "Got it."

Within minutes, she was in a cab headed for the car dealership to get a rental. It took longer than she'd expected, but she had a nice Toyota to drive. Then she went to the fire station and it was a nightmare. It took over an hour to get her phone, but it still worked. The first person she thought about calling was Carter. He said he had a meeting this morning and she didn't want to disturb him. Instead, she sent him a text to let him know she had her phone.

Last night was a moment out of time. She never dreamed she would fall for someone so quickly, but there was something about Carter that appealed to her. Maybe it was the way his eyes were so clear and honest and made her feel attractive and wanted. She never slept with guys on a first date, and for the last six months her focus had been on building the gallery into a successful business.

Carter was gentle and easy to talk to and she'd shared more of her life than she should have, but she'd needed someone. Her skin grew warm as she thought of his touch. She bit her lip and warned herself that she couldn't get too serious. Carter would be leaving soon. She had to be prepared for that, but how did she prepare herself for a broken heart? With everything she had on her plate, she would be lucky to survive the week, and she didn't want to endure it alone. She could only hope that he would stay a little while longer.

CARTER SLID INTO a chair across from Neil Dunning in the hotel restaurant. "Sorry I'm late."

Neil closed his laptop and reached for his cup of coffee. He was a man in his fifties, very suave, very sophisticated and very knowledgeable about art. He always dressed impeccably in a suit and a tie, as he was today, and always had a handkerchief handy.

"Have you had breakfast?"

"No. I didn't have time for breakfast."

Neil signaled for the waitress and Carter ordered food. As the waitress poured Carter a cup of coffee, Neil tapped his fingers on the table, a habit that Carter hated. That meant the wheels in his head were spinning and a lot of questions would follow.

"You weren't at the hotel, so where were you?"

Carter took a sip of coffee. He didn't have to tell Neil where he was. It was none of his business, but they were good friends and Carter respected him. And he knew Neil. He didn't mean anything by it.

"I met someone and I spent the night at her place."

"That quick?" One eyebrow shot up.

The waitress brought Carter's food and ended the conversation, which Carter thought was a good thing. "Have you looked at the paper this morning or the Chicago news on TV?"

"No, I haven't. I slept on the plane and arrived here about five this morning. Luckily, you put my name on the hotel room, too, and I was able to get in and take a shower. Hurry so we can get over to the gallery."

"The gallery burned down last night."

Neil's eyes opened wide. "What?"

"It burned to the ground. The large safe is left and part of the office space, but otherwise it's a total write-off."

"You're kidding."

"No."

"What about the Tinsley paintings?"

"They're in the rubble, ruined. The arson inspector wouldn't let us in yesterday, but he might today."

"Arson?" Neil tapped a finger against his chin. "That's interesting. Why would they call in the arson expert?"

"To determine the cause of the fire. I'm sure it's procedural."

"Yeah. Let's get over there and see what's left."

As Carter followed Neil out of the restaurant, his phone beeped. He looked at the caller ID. Lila. Then there was a text. I got my phone back. See you later.

Yes, he would see her later. Definitely.

Chief inspector Frank Richards and his team were on the site when they arrived. They shook hands. "How's it going?" Carter asked.

"We're about through. I'll have my findings in a couple of days."

The fire department vehicles drove away. "Well, I guess our work here is done. There's no way to validate the paintings. They're gone, basically. That means the forger gets away with it. And he's still doing it."

"Yeah, and I didn't get to look at them really good because Ms. Colton was having a showing, but I'd stake my reputation on the fact that they are forgeries."

"Too bad we didn't get to them sooner, but don't worry—we'll catch him or her. It will just take some time. Now on to Milan."

"Milan?"

"Yes. I got a call from a man who operates a gallery there. He's being offered an Ila Chay painting, but he has a feeling it's a forgery and is willing to pay a lot of money to prove that it is. He wants to hang it in his gallery, but he's waiting until he knows for sure if it's a real work of art by Chay."

"She died many years ago and dealt mostly in abstracts. I'd be very surprised if it was real, unless a family member owns it and wants the money."

"That's what I want you to find out. Get your ticket and call me when you get there." Neil was already getting into the rental.

For the first time, Carter didn't want to leave. He

had vacations, but this wasn't a vacation. He wanted to be here for Lila if she needed someone.

He slid into the driver's seat. "I'd rather not go to Milan."

"Why not?"

He told him how they were trapped in the building and how upset Lila had been and he just wanted to stay here for a while to make sure she was okay.

"So you like this girl?"

"Yes. Just give me a few days." The thought crossed his mind if he would be ready to go in a few days. Only time would tell.

"Okay. I'll see if Marla would like to go on a trip to Milan. She loves visiting her home country."

His wife had a temper that could peel the wallpaper off the walls, so Neil did all he could to please her. But she had the warmest heart of anyone he knew. She was always trying to feed him and find him a wife. Carter didn't need any help in that department.

At the hotel, they said goodbye. "Call me when you're ready to come back to work."

"Thanks, Neil. I appreciate the time off."

Neil patted him on the shoulder. "Have a good time, but not so good that you don't come back to work. Not many men enjoy being away from home that much and I don't know what I'd do without you."

Carter waved as he drove away. His tense muscles relaxed. He would get to know Lila better and explore these feelings he had for her or whatever they were. After a few days the newness would wear off and he would be ready to go. That was the way it usually went with him. Staying wasn't in his nature. That wouldn't be fair to Lila, though, if her feelings got involved. The best thing for him was to leave now while they both understood there was nothing serious between them. That was just hogwash. His nerves tensed again and he really didn't know what he was doing. He just wanted to be with Lila, and that was so telling. They were both adults and they would work it out. He pulled into a parking lot and called her.

"Where are you?"

"At home digging through some stuff Inspector Richards brought over."

"What kind of stuff?"

"Everything that was salvageable. It's not much."

"That was very nice of him."

"Yeah. I thought he was a grouch, but he's really nice, especially after almost accusing me of burning down the gallery."

"He did that?"

"Earlier this morning when I talked to him, but I think he knows I didn't do it. It still makes me nervous, though."

"I'll be there in a few minutes."

He found her sitting on a big plastic sheet in the middle of her living room. On the plastic were charred items. He sat beside her with one knee raised and his forearm resting on it. She smiled at him, and everything looked a little brighter and his fear of hurting her disappeared.

"Find anything?"

"The hard drives off the computer might still be good. They took the security cameras to the lab hoping they could get something off them. I'll check on everything tomorrow. My purse is a gooey mess." She opened it for him to look inside. He made a face. "Makeup does not stand up well to heat. The rest is trash. Inspector Richards said that tomorrow they would let me in the safe to get the items out, and my insurance agent will be there, too. I have to make a list of everything that was in the fire, and that's going to take a while." She tapped his leg with her forefinger. "But luckily, and you should know this, I'm very organized due to my mother's insistence that everything has a place, and clothes do not belong on the floor, and drawers do not need to be rattraps. My mother had rules. She would say, 'When you're on your own, you can live like you want, but while you're in my house, you will be neat and organized, just to please me.'"

"Sounds like a very smart lady."

"Yeah, my mom is the best. My dad was… Forget it. I'd rather not talk about it." She fiddled with a picture frame she was trying to wipe the soot off of.

He scooted to rest his back against the couch. He heeded her wishes because he knew her father was not a topic she liked. Another topic was on his mind and they needed to talk about it.

"About last night…"

She laid the frame beside another batch of things she was saving. "What about it?"

"I don't want you to think it was a one-night stand. It was more to me."

She turned to face him. "Me, too. I'm well aware you will only be here a few days, and like I told you, we're adults and make our own choices. I chose to sleep with you and I don't regret it. And whatever happens next is up to us. I know you're leaving and I'll be fine with that." She raised an eyebrow. "But I think we should curb the sex for now because I don't want to be clinging to you and begging you to stay. I needed you last night in ways I never imagined. It was nice and...now..."

"That sounds rehearsed," he interrupted.

"Maybe it is." She got to her feet. "Look, Carter, I've never been in a relationship like this before, so I'd prefer to take it slow." She glanced at the mess at her feet. "I have to throw all of this stuff away."

He helped her wrap up the plastic and carry it to the garage to put in a big receptacle. The things she wanted to keep she put in a box. His mind was buzzing as they worked. Could she be that perfect? Could she be that understanding? Lila was a mystery that he was slowly unraveling, and before he left here, he might be the one begging and clinging.

LILA TOOK A shower to get the soot off her. She never knew she was such a good liar. She gave him points for being so open. When he left, she would be strong in her hope that one day he would return. She had to let go of the most wonderful man she'd ever met. Until that time, she would enjoy every minute.

She slipped on sneakers and jogging pants and hurried into the living room. Carter was looking through an art book. "Let's go jogging and get a Chicago hot dog. You have to have one before you leave."

"Great. I'll change my clothes."

In a few minutes, they were outside her town

house, jogging toward a business section of restaurants. "There used to be people on the street selling hot dogs like they do in New York, but now they've all moved indoors and have their own place."

"I've heard of the Chicago hot dog."

"You're in for a treat." She turned to look at him. "I forgot to tell you the hot dog place is almost two miles away. Do you think you can handle it?" His laughter followed her and she jogged away.

They stopped at an intersection to take a breath. She pointed. "We're going to Portilli's. They have the best." She put her hands on her knees and took several deep breaths.

He patted her on the back. "Are you sure you're up for this?"

She made a face at him. "You work out, don't you?"

"All the time." He gave her a quick smile and linked his arm through hers, and they slowly walked down the street to the hot dog place. They ordered the original and Carter also ordered fries and a beer. She did, too. They sat at a blue gingham-covered table near windows.

"This is nice," Carter said. "Very home-style and very busy." People milled around them. Two little boys looked in the window at them. People started a line outside, eager to get in.

Carter stared at the hot dog the waitress placed in front of him. "Are you kidding? What's on here? It looks like a little bit of everything."

"It is, from the poppy seed bun, the beef hot dog, to the mustard, tomatoes, slice of dill pickle, sport pickle, green relish and onions. It's a great combination for your taste buds."

They ate in amicable silence and it was comforting to be out with a man. She'd put so much of her time and energy into the gallery that she forgot how to enjoy herself. And now she didn't know what she was going to do. First, she would enjoy this evening with him.

"How about chocolate cake?" Carter asked. He glanced at the table next to them. "They're having chocolate cake and it looks delicious."

"I'm game for anything chocolate."

Later, they caught the transit back to her town house. They had an easy, comfortable relationship that she loved. She'd said no sex, but she was slowly changing her mind. If he was leaving...

He pulled off his T-shirt and sat on the sofa in an effortless movement of strength and muscles. Oh, yeah. He had muscles. She turned her eyes away and sat beside him, taking off her sneakers and wondering how she should handle the night.

Before words formed in her head, the doorbell rang. She jumped up to answer. A young man stood there and asked, "Miss Lila Colton?"

"Yes."

He handed her a large manila envelope. "This is for you." He then walked away.

Lila didn't get a chance to say thank you or much of anything. She stared at the envelope and saw it was from a lawyer. Her insides tightened with a foreboding. Thoughts of throwing the envelope on her desk and looking at it tomorrow crossed her mind. But she was more adult than that. She hoped. She ripped it open with more force than necessary.

Anger built in her as she quickly scanned the document. "That sorry SOB!"

"What is it?" Carter came over to her.

"Fox and the Tinsley estate have filed a claim against me for the ruined Tinsley paintings."

Chapter Five

She handed him the document. "He wants more money than the buyers paid for them. What's he trying to pull?" She sat on the sofa and curled her feet beneath her. "I don't have that kind of money."

"Fox must be desperate for money to go this far. He's not waiting for them to rule the fire arson. He's pointing the finger at you in hopes that he can get money out of you. He's hiding something and I'm almost positive he had something to do with the fire, but I'll have to prove it."

He looked up and saw her sitting there with her head on her knees, curled up, defeated and alone. He sat beside her and pulled her into his arms. "Cheer up. We're not done yet."

She tilted her head to look at him. "What do you mean?"

"I know a lot of people who are arson investigators and I'll contact a couple to see if I can get some information. People are always destroying stuff to get the insurance. It's very common and they look for that."

"And how is that going to help now?"

He kissed her forehead to ease the worry lines. "Inspector Richards said he's going to have his ruling in a couple of days. I hope by then I can get someone else to look at it."

She sat up. "Richards will never allow a stranger interfering with his team's case."

"We'll see."

A smile crossed her face. "You're devious, but brilliant."

He pulled out his phone. "I'm going to be on the phone for a while. Do you mind if I use your extra bedroom tonight?" She hesitated with her answer. What she said now she had to be able to handle. "I can go back to the hotel."

"Oh, no. You're welcome to the room." She got to her feet. "I'm going to bed. I'll see you in the morning."

He stared after her as she walked upstairs to her bedroom. What had he done now? He hated it when he got different vibes from women. Maybe that was why he was still single. He needed to adjust.

Putting his thoughts aside, he called his friend David Dreyer. He'd worked with him several times on cases and he was an expert arson investigator. "Hey, David. It's Carter. Do you have a minute to talk?"

"Sure. We just got the kids down for the night. What's up?"

"How are the kids?"

"Growing like weeds. They are three and five now and hard to keep up with, but you didn't call about my kids. What's going on?"

He told him about the fire at the gallery and his suspicions. "I'm afraid they're going to try to pin this on the gallery owner, noting that she's the only one who had a motive."

"Is there any evidence that points to her?"

"The investigator, Frank Richards, is closemouthed and I haven't seen the file, but he keeps coming back to Ms. Colton, the renter. And Tinsley's agent is now trying to get as much money as he can. It's all a little fishy."

"Do you want me to look at the gallery? And if you do, you know what's going to happen. The lead investigator will put the skids on quickly."

"I know." Carter put the phone on speaker and laid it on the coffee table. "But between the two of us, I feel we have a good chance of convincing him. I just need a little help to point out certain things like the agent's eagerness for money and how the renter is not in debt like was told to the investigator."

"Is the owner of the building involved?"

"Well, he owns the building and would stand to gain a big sum of money from the insurance."

"How much?"

"I don't know yet, but it's in a very good location."

"I do owe you a favor."

"Yes, you do, but I would never call it in. Do what you feel is right."

"I can be there in the morning about nine. Have everybody at the table so we can discuss this or argue about it. But first, I'll have to look at the gallery fire. Has anyone touched anything?"

"Only the firefighters and the investigators."

"Okay. Can you pick me up at the airport?"

"Sure. No problem."

He finished his conversation with David, picked up his phone and went to his bedroom. Lila's bedroom door was closed. She was upset about everything that was coming down on her, and it was hitting her all at the same time. He would stay as long as he could to help her, but she had to be willing to let him. That might be a big stumbling block.

He took a quick shower and crawled into bed. The thought that she might be crying kept him tossing and turning. From the moonlight shining through his window, he could see a shape in his doorway.

It was Lila.

LILA DIDN'T KNOW what she was doing. She couldn't sleep alone tonight. Memories of the hot fire and the smoke filling her nostrils kept spinning in her head, keeping her awake. She just wanted to forget and get lost in something that was real.

"Lila…"

"Yes," she replied in a hoarse voice. "Are you asleep?" That was such a crazy thing to ask, but it was all she could come up with.

"No."

She walked farther into the room and sat on the bed. "I changed my mind."

"You mean…?"

"Yes."

He pulled back the comforter and she crawled in. "I'm such a ditz," she said. "But I can't get all this stuff out of my mind, and every time I try to go to sleep, I see this fire that's consuming everything…even me."

He stroked her hair and she relaxed, leaning on him.

"Stop worrying. I told you I'm going to help. I called an old friend who's going to look at the gallery." He told her about David Dreyer.

"He's coming here?"

"Yes. I hope he can bring some new knowledge to the case."

"Did you get Richards's permission?"

"Not yet, but I'm hoping he'll see the good in letting another expert take a look at the case."

"Oh, Carter, thank you." She grabbed him around the neck and kissed him. The kisses continued into the night and Lila didn't even remember falling asleep. She was too excited. Too much in love and… Too much in love? The thought stopped her. She couldn't be in love. Her emotions were high, and she was just clinging to the only lifeline she had.

THE NEXT MORNING, they were in a rush to go their separate ways. Carter was going to the airport to pick up David, and Lila had to deal with removing the artwork from the safe.

"Remember," Carter said, going out the door, "don't schedule the truck until this afternoon. We don't want anyone stomping around in the gallery until David has a chance to look inside."

"Got it."

He gave her a quick kiss and he was gone. David was right on time and they were at Richards's office before nine o'clock in the morning. Carter had called ahead for an appointment.

"He's not going to like this," David said.

"No, he's not. No one wants to hear they might have missed something. We just have to play it by ear."

David was in his early forties and had been working arson for about fifteen years, while Richards had been working arson for about thirty. It wasn't going to play that the younger guy knew more than the older guy. But Carter was hoping that reasoning would go a long way to solving this crime. And he knew it was a crime.

They walked into a sparse office: a desk, filing cabinets and pictures of fires on walls, probably fires that Richards had solved.

They shook hands and introductions were made. Carter and David took seats in metal folding chairs. Carter was glad to see that Richards had a comfortable chair. The city didn't allow for luxuries and it showed in this small office with scuffed walls and old tile floors.

"What can I do for you guys?"

Carter took a breath, gauging his words carefully. "David has been a friend of mine for a long time and I was hoping that you would allow him to access the fire records and give his opinion."

Richards leaned back in his chair. "You don't trust my opinion?"

"Not when you're pointing the finger at Ms. Colton."

Richards shook his head as if he finally figured out something. "This has to do with Ms. Colton." He pointed a finger at David. "She's hired you, hasn't she?"

"No, sir. I've never met Ms. Colton. I only came to give my opinion because my friend Carter asked me."

"You guys all stick together, don't you?"

"I hope you included yourself in the 'guys' part because all of us are in this together. We want to catch who did this. We want to make sure that it's arson and not just a wiring problem. Don't you want the same thing, Inspector Richards?"

"All right, but I'm going with you. I don't want you planting things that weren't there before."

"I resent that," David said.

Grabbing his jacket, Richards replied, "And I resent you sticking your nose into my case. I guess we'll both have to live with it."

Inspector Richards followed David around like a little puppy while he went through everything. They had put on plastic shoes, a mask and safety covering for protection from the toxins. Carter leaned against his car and watched. Every now and then, David would squat and brush something away with a small brush and take pictures.

At the back right corner of the gallery, David squatted and motioned for Richards to come over. Richards squatted, too, and they talked for a while. Carter figured they'd found something. The two men stood and made their way out of the rubble.

Richards showed him a tiny black wire that had different-colored wires inside it. The whole thing was less than an inch long. It was burned on both ends.

"You know what that is, Finch?"

"I've seen a wire like that connected to a detonator."

"Yep. You're right. Someone set this fire and I'm opening a full investigation now. We'll catch who did this. Thanks for your expertise, Mr. Dreyer."

"You're welcome. I did it for a friend. Most of the

time, the evidence is just under the ashes, and most investigators hate digging through that."

"Well, my boys are going to get a workout and a lesson."

"You know, Richards, I've seen small detonators used before. It's like a toy. You set the time and then wait for it to explode and it explodes with a burst of fire. Teenagers are known to use them and they are sold by several companies. We tried one time to shut down the sale of these detonators, but we couldn't get it through Congress. So now the investigators have to deal with them."

"Thanks for the information. I have to go and call Ms. Colton before she gets here to remove items out of the safe. I don't want anything touched until this investigation is over, and that's going to take a while."

Carter and David shook hands. "Thanks, pal. That was one lucky break."

"You won't believe how much evidence is under the ashes. What's underneath was there before the fire started. It takes a lot of training to figure this out."

"I'm so glad you decided to come."

"It seemed important to you."

Carter shoved his hands into his pockets and thought about that for a minute. Yes, it was important to him. Lila was important to him. "How about if I buy you lunch?"

"Deal. I want to try a Chicago deep-dish pizza."

"You got it."

On the way to the nearest pizza place, Carter called Lila. Before he could say anything, her cheery voice came on. "Have you heard?"

"If you're talking about the full investigation, yes, I heard."

"Your friend must have found something."

"Yes, he did. I'll tell you about it tonight. I just want to make sure you don't move any art out of the safe."

"Oh, yes. Richards has already made it clear to me."

"There will be many eyes looking at the scene and they will find something to connect someone to that fire."

"But not me."

"But not you."

"I'm on my way to see my brother about Fox's claim and see what he can do. I'll see you later. Give David a hug for me and tell him thanks."

"I already have." It was good to hear her so happy and to be a part of it. How long could he stay here?

LILA TOOK THE elevator up to the third floor, where Myles's office was located. He had his own clients, his own space, and that wasn't enough. He wanted to make partner, to make more money, and he said it was all for his wife, Faith, and four-year-old son, Jackson. He worked all the time to impress his bosses, but he didn't impress the woman he loved. She'd taken all she could take and left him. Faith had said what good was marriage when you never saw your husband. Lila tried not to get entangled in their problems, but she loved them and it was hard to keep her mouth shut.

She opened the door that had her brother's name on it. Inside was Ellen, his secretary and receptionist, sitting at a desk wearing an unwavering smile.

"I'd like to see my brother for a minute," she said to Ellen.

She pushed her tortoiseshell glasses up the bridge of her nose. "Faith is in there now."

Oh, great. They were talking. She'd wait and come back a little later. As she turned, Myles's door opened and Faith backed out, waving to someone inside. "Mommy will be back. Bye."

Myles and Faith had been in love since high school. She was the beautiful redhead every boy wanted, but she'd wanted only Myles. How could such a good marriage go so wrong?

"Oh, Lila." Faith held a hand to her chest. "You startled me."

They hugged. "It's good to see you," Lila said. "We need to stay more in touch."

"Yeah, but that's hard when Myles is being a jerk."

"You'll work this out," Lila told her. "You love each other."

Faith looked away. "Sometimes I wonder. Myles hardly ever sees Jackson, and when he does have him, he takes him to your mother's and she takes care of him. So what's the point of Myles having days with Jackson?"

"Oh, Faith, I'm sorry."

"I have a dental appointment in fifteen minutes, and my mom has a migraine and there was nowhere else to leave Jackson, so I brought him here. Myles threw a fit, but I had no choice. I really have to go." She gave Lila another hug. "Let's do lunch sometime and you can listen to me gripe some more."

Faith rushed out the door and Lila took a deep

breath. She had no qualms about just walking in on Myles. She had a few things to say to him and he was going to listen.

Myles was at his desk on his laptop and Jackson was throwing a red ball. When Jackson saw her, he ran into her. "Li." He hadn't put her name together yet and she was fine being Li.

She picked him up and kissed his cheek. "You're getting so big."

He raised his hands above his head. "Tall."

She kissed his cheek again. "Yes."

"Wanna play ball?" He still had the ball in his hand and he threw it. The ball hit Myles's desk and knocked the framed picture of Faith and Jackson to the hardwood floor. The glass broke.

"Jackson!" Myles shouted.

Jackson buried his face into Lila's neck and Lila wagged a finger at Myles. The wagging finger said more than words to stop.

Myles quickly backpedaled. "It's okay, Jackson. Daddy is just a little upset." He tried to take the boy, but he wouldn't go.

"Li," he said.

The door burst open and Faith came through it and took Jackson from her while looking directly at Myles. "If you can't keep your son with a loving heart, then you don't need to keep him at all." With those scathing words, she headed out the door.

"Faith…" Myles shouted after her.

She stopped for a moment.

"You know the office is no place for a child. He's already broken something."

"Oh, horror of horrors." She turned on her heel and left.

Lila placed her hands on her hips. "That was lovely to witness. I sincerely hope that you two do not do this all the time in front of Jackson."

Myles ran his hands over his face. "I do not need you to come down on me today." He sat at his desk. "Did you come by for a reason?"

She pulled the document out of her purse and placed it in front of him. "I got this by courier and I thought you might be able to help me. I know you're busy. I know you have family problems, but you're the only one I know who has this kind of expertise."

"Mr. Fox, who represents Mr. Tinsley, wants his money fast, but it doesn't work that way. Have they ruled on what started the fire?"

"No. Due to new information, they're starting a full investigation and it's not going to be a right-now type thing. It's going to take some time and I don't have that kind of money to pay Mr. Fox and the estate."

"I'll draft a letter and get Ellen to send it over to—" He glanced at the top of the paper. "Look at the names on that letterhead." He paused and she could see the envy in his eyes. His dream was always to be head of a law firm, but it was coming at a cost to his family. One day he would see that.

"I'll inform them that until there's a ruling on the fire, no money will be changing hands. If not, I will take it before a judge, and no judge is going to rule on a case when there hasn't been a ruling on the cause of the fire. That should keep Mr. Fox off your back until you get your money from the insurance."

"Thank you." She threw her arms around his neck and kissed his cheek much as she had Jackson. "That gives me some breathing room. I love you, but I have to run." At the door, she stopped. "Have you heard anything on the Colton case?"

Myles shook his head. "I had lunch with Heath Colton the other day and he was wondering the same thing. The lawsuit has really put a strain on the family, and I told him as far as myself and my sister were concerned, we didn't want the money, but no one can change our grandmother's mind or our father's. Heath said he understood and I hope he does. I might try talking to Dad again. Hopefully some sort of compromise can be worked out."

"With our grandmother involved?"

"Yeah. She's not going to settle for anything less than she thinks she deserves."

"You know, it's very hard to imagine our grandfather adding Erik's and Axel's names as the heirs since he avoided them all of his life. Carter—that's the guy who was with me in the gallery when it caught fire— is an expert in forgery and I was just wondering if the will might have been forged."

"That's a good thought, but I'm sure the other Coltons have checked into that angle and have done everything possible to prove it a fake."

"I guess so. I'll talk to you later. Bye."

Myles grabbed his jacket and headed for the door, too. "I have to find Faith and get my son. I won't be able to get any work done otherwise."

He stopped long enough to tell Ellen about the broken glass in his office and to get someone to clean it up. They walked together to the elevator.

"By the way, how are you?"

"Nervous about the future. In one blow, my whole life was destroyed. I'm having a hard time dealing with that. But on the other hand, it's opening up new possibilities for me that I never expected."

"Does this have anything to do with Carter?" He pushed the elevator button.

She lifted an eyebrow. "It just might." A soft laugh erupted from her throat, but it didn't last long. Carter was leaving in a couple of days, and she would find out just how strong she really was.

Chapter Six

After dropping David at the airport, Carter went grocery shopping. He noticed there wasn't much food at Lila's house. He ate out so much that sometimes he enjoyed a meal at home or wherever home was. He got everything he needed and headed back to her town house to surprise her. She'd given him an extra key this morning, and that might mean a little more than he wanted it to. But he wasn't ready to walk away from her just yet.

Lila came charging through the door, threw her purse at the couch and grabbed him in a fierce bear hug, which ended up in a long, sweet kiss. She stepped back and glanced at the apron around his waist.

"What are you doing?"

He kissed the tip of her nose. "Fixing supper for us—spaghetti and meatballs, salad and garlic bread and a good Merlot."

"You know how to cook?"

"Sure. I eat so much in hotels and restaurants that sometimes I like to eat in."

"You should've said something. I can cook, you know."

He slanted a smile in her direction. "Your refrigerator gives a different message—yogurt, water, butter, something dried up in a bowl that's unrecognizable."

She slapped at his chest. "Don't be critical. I work long hours, and most of the time I just pick something up on the way home."

He bowed from the waist. "Tonight you're eating a home-cooked meal and all you have to do is enjoy it." He glanced toward the dining table. It was set with a linen tablecloth and napkins, and in the center was a beautiful bouquet of flowers.

"You bought flowers. You're such a sweetheart." She kissed him slowly and he eventually pushed her away.

"Hold on. Hold on. I cooked the food and we're going to eat it while it's nice and hot."

"You're hot." She chuckled, but obediently took her seat at the table.

"We're celebrating a victory today." While he put food on the table, he told her the whole story about finding the detonator wire. They conversed all through dinner and he marveled at how easy it was to talk to her. They did the dishes and took their wine to the living room.

"I have some good news, too. Myles said that I don't have to pay Fox anything until the arson investigator rules on the cause of the fire. He's making the law firm that Fox hired aware of the situation. At least, I get a breather. The last couple of days my stomach is spinning like clothes in the dryer, going round and round."

He cupped her face. "Try not to worry. That little wire gives them a very big clue the fire was set."

"That's not going to tell them who set the fire, and I'm afraid they're still going to point the finger at me."

He gathered her into his arms. "Lila, please don't torture yourself. They'll have to have evidence that you set it, like where you bought the detonator, as I'm sure Richards is checking stores right now."

"What kind of stores?"

"Stores that sell that type of device. David says it's more used by teenagers who are trying to make a statement. It's small with a timer on it and shoots out a blast of fire. David said they tried to get them off the market but failed. They're causing too many fires because they are so easy to use. And there's no way they can connect you to a detonator."

She raised her face to look at his. "You have a lot of trust in me."

"I can read people, and you, my lady, are as innocent and honest as they come."

She gave a comforting laugh and nestled into him, and it felt so good and right at that moment that he couldn't see himself ever leaving her or the comfort of her arms. He glanced around the room to get his mind on something else.

"What are you going to do with all these paintings?"

She sat up. "I don't know. At this point, I don't even know if Rossini is planning on rebuilding the gallery or if he'll rent it to me again. I have paintings and art stacked everywhere, even in the hall closet and the entry closet. I guess I could have a…" She jumped up. "Oh… Oh…"

Carter got to his feet, too. Clearly, she was excited about something. "What?"

"With everything that's going on, I forgot I had them."

"Had what?"

"You're going to be so surprised." She took their wineglasses to the kitchen and walked to the entry closet door. She pulled out several small paintings wrapped in heavy plastic and laid them on the coffee table. "Fox offered me these about a month ago, and a man shopping in the gallery said he would be interested, but it would have to wait until he got back from Europe. I promised him a private showing and stored the paintings in the closet until then."

He stared at the paintings, two on the coffee table and one on the sofa. He couldn't believe his eyes. They were all signed by Homer Tinsley or supposedly by the man.

"Do you know what this means?"

"I... I..."

"This could help us find the forger. I thought everything was lost in the fire, but now..."

"Do you think they're forgeries?"

He held up a painting to the light. "I don't know yet. They're very good if they are."

"But how can you really tell?"

"By sniffing it, for one thing. Oil changes smell over time." He sniffed one of the paintings. "The oil is probably a little over a year old. It's been painted recently. Next is to examine with the naked eye to see any imperfections. Then we check the back of the canvas, and this is painted on canvas and secured with tiny nails. If we feel it's a forgery, we take it to our lab in New York and go over it thoroughly with ultraviolet lights, X-rays and a microscopic view, and a lot of other things that will tell us the age of everything on the canvas and what colors were used to paint it. It's an involved process, but it will tell us if these Tinsleys are really Tinsleys. And hopefully give us a clue as to where these paintings are coming from." He went to his room and got his high-powered camera and the things that he needed.

Lila sat on the arm of the sofa and watched him as he got down on his knees and took close-ups of the paintings and then transferred them to his laptop. He then took his laptop to the table. Lila followed.

"Look," he said as he brought up the paintings on the screen.

"The ones on the left are true Tinsleys and the ones on the right are the ones I just took pictures of. I have to blow them up to get a better view."

Lila pulled a chair close to his and he had trouble thinking for a moment with the scent of lavender all around him. He quickly brought his thoughts back to the painting. "This guy or woman is good, but he failed on the signature. Take a look and see if you can see it."

She stared at the screen. "They look the same to me."

"Look closer. Tinsley makes a fancy loop before he makes the slant for the *H* and the end of the slant comes out slightly. On the other three paintings, the slant stops and doesn't come out. It's minor, but if you look at Tinsley's real paintings, you'll see that the slant is on every one of them."

"I would never notice that and I see a lot of paintings."

He got to his feet. "I have to call Neil and get a flight out as soon as I can. Do you mind if I take the paintings?"

"Uh... I guess not."

"Thanks, Lila. You just helped us catch a forger."

Lila sat on the sofa, staring at the paintings. And then she got up and packaged them together again, but at the back of her mind she was screeching, "He's leaving and doesn't seem to mind."

He came out of the bedroom with his carryall, briefcase and laptop and took them out to his rental. He came back in for the paintings. Standing in the doorway, he said, "I hate to leave like this, but duty calls and I will call you about the paintings."

What did she say at a moment like this? *Thank you for saving my life. Thank you for being there for me. Thank you for everything.*

She was saved from saying anything because he was already in his rental backing out, leaving her alone once again. But she'd known this would happen. She just hadn't known it would hurt this much.

She slammed the door with more force than necessary and went into the kitchen to wash the wineglasses. As she worked, she realized she knew very little about Carter Finch. She had no idea where he was going. She just assumed it would be New York, but she didn't know where the lab was or where Neil lived. All she had was Carter's phone number, and that would bring very little comfort in the days ahead.

CARTER MADE IT to New York and the flight was uneventful. Neil was waiting for him and he climbed into the town car and headed toward Manhattan. He and his wife had a big Upper East Side apartment, which had been in Neil's family for a long time. The lab was in the building's basement, so they would be working at his home.

Marla was asleep and the kids were in college, so they went right to work. At six the next morning, Carter woke up on the sofa in the lab and wondered where he was. He reached for Lila and found nothing but a brown tweed sofa. Oh, man, what had he done? He sat up and ran his hands through his hair, trying to remember what he'd said when he left. He hadn't said much of anything. Oh, man. He buried his face in his hands.

"Go take a shower," Neil said. "And we'll go over the data."

"I need coffee first."

Neil pointed to a coffee maker on a table. "Just made a fresh pot. These paintings are forgeries and I don't have a problem validating them as such. The guy is getting sloppy. Even the elements and pigments don't match. The signature is the telling point. Tinsley would never sign his name like that. He was very meticulous."

"Yeah," Carter said, pouring a cup of coffee. "My eye caught it right away."

"Did you notice anything else?"

"Yes. I was going to talk to you about it when Marla called you upstairs, so I decided to take a thirty-minute nap instead."

"You were out for two hours."

"Really?" He glanced at his watch. "I guess I was."

"It's understandable since you'd been up all night, but let's get back to these paintings. What did you notice?"

"Some artists are left-handed and some are right-handed. We put away a guy a few years ago who was left-handed, but he could paint with any hand. He was doing so many forgeries that he forgot and used his left hand on a couple of paintings, and it showed up when we examined it. I think he got five years and is still in prison. But—" he pointed to several spots on the computer screen "—that was done left-handed and the rest of the painting is right-handed."

"Smart man. I taught you well. Now, can you remember who that guy is?"

"Tony Martell, and as far as I know, he's still in prison."

"Let's find out." Neil turned to his laptop.

"While you're doing that, I'm going to take a shower."

"Okay."

Carter quickly showered and shaved and sat on the bed he used while he was at Neil's working. Lila was getting up about now and he should call her and try to explain what had come over him. But he wanted to do that in person and he didn't know when he could get away from Neil to do that. He had to come up with a plan to see her.

He went back to the basement and Neil was getting off the phone. "Martell is out. He's been out for about a year now, and that's exactly about the time the Tinsley paintings started showing up in small galleries."

Carter reached for his phone in his pocket. "I'll call the detective we hired to get information on Tinsley and see if he can locate Martell."

Carter sat on the sofa as he talked. "Hey, we haven't touched base in a while and I was wondering if you had any information for me."

"It's your lucky day, man."

Carter sat up straight. "What do you mean?"

"Tinsley's wife died fourteen months ago and the people in the village where he lived in France said Tinsley grieved himself to death two months later. He is buried in a small cemetery there and hardly anyone knows this. It's a best-kept secret."

"Tinsley is dead?" Carter was trying to take this in and what it meant.

"Yep. You got it. I finally located a great-nephew of Tinsley's. He's the only living relative and he inherited Tinsley's fortune. Or I should say he inherited eighty percent of Tinsley's wealth."

"And Fox, his agent, inherited the rest."

"You got it."

"This is great work, Jim. Send us an invoice."

"You bet I will. Just be sitting down when you open it." Jim always had a weird sense of humor. Carter had known him for a long time. He came from the South and was down-home country all the way, but he was one of those guys who could find a needle in a hay-stack and his skill was invaluable.

"Try not to be too hard on us." Neil was doing sign language at him, and Carter realized he'd forgotten to mention Martell. "Wait a minute. I have another case, if you're interested."

"Sure, but then I'm taking a vacation for two weeks."

"We need information on Tony Martell, an address, phone number or anything you can find on him. He's an ex-con and he's probably going to be hard to find, but I have no doubt you can. I need it ASAP."

"On it." Jim chuckled and clicked off.

Carter told Neil about the new revelations.

"Damn, he's dead? That should've jumped out at us like a two-headed demon months ago. Why didn't it occur to us?"

"Because that's not our job. Our job is to determine if the paintings circulating are forgeries, and now we pretty well know that they are. There's no doubt in my mind that Fox is behind all this. That twenty percent of Tinsley's estate must've been a slap in the face. He's done everything for the old man for the past twenty years. I guess Fox found a way to continue to make money off Tinsley. Now we have to prove it."

"Marla and I are leaving for Milan tomorrow, so you're in charge of the Martell forgeries. Keep me posted."

For the first time in his career, Carter wasn't eager to leave and move on to another city. He was still stuck in Chicago. As soon as he got the phone call from Jim, he would leave for another city or wherever Martell called home. But first, he needed to see Lila one more time.

LILA WOKE UP early the next morning eager for a new day. She wasn't going to wallow in hurt feelings and disappointments. She'd known Carter was going to leave. She just hadn't expected him to leave at the drop of a hat. But she was sure he had his reasons. She knew one of his reasons: he loved his job in tracking down criminals. She'd heard it in his voice when he talked about his work and she'd heard it when he was showing her the forgeries on his laptop. She hurriedly showered and dressed and was out the door before her mind could wander anymore.

As she slid into her car, her phone buzzed and her thoughts zoomed right back to Carter. It wasn't Carter. It was Tatum, her cousin from the other branch of the Coltons.

"Hi, Lila. It's Tatum."

"Hi, Tatum. It's nice to hear from you."

"I was hoping you would say that. I'd like to invite you for lunch today, if you have time."

"That sounds lovely." What else could she say? She liked the other Coltons, and giving them the cold shoulder wasn't in her nature.

"What time?"

"About one."

"I'll see you then." Lila slipped her phone into her purse and wondered what that was about. Tatum owned True restaurant. It was a new farm-to-table restaurant and very popular. The place was known to be packed every day. She backed out of the parking lot with a smile on her face. She would enjoy spending some time with her cousin. Tatum was getting married soon and Lila would love to hear all the details. That made her think of Carter, the man who didn't have a home and a man who didn't even want a home. In her heart, she knew he would come back, and she couldn't tell herself otherwise. She'd been told that as men aged they started thinking about home and family, and she was hoping Carter was no different. She didn't want to force him into a relationship. She just wanted them to be happy like they were supposed to be. Oh, good heavens, her mother had read her too many fairy tales.

She had a meeting with her car insurance agent to discuss her getting a car since hers was totaled. She was told that since the car was destroyed by the fire, they couldn't pay until they had a decision if it was arson or not. If it was arson, Rossini, who owned the building, would have the insurance to pay for the car. They just had to wait. The only good news he had to say was that the rental would continue to be paid with her insurance and she could use it as long as she needed. Everything in her life hinged on Richards's ruling of the fire.

Tatum's restaurant was in the updated North Center area. When they had the get-together at Farrah's house, Tatum said she'd renovated an old warehouse there for her restaurant, True. Lila had no problem finding it as she saw people sitting on benches waiting to get in. She was sure there was a waiting area inside, too. Now what did she do? She didn't want to get in front of people who had been waiting for a while.

She got out of her car and walked toward the entrance. As she was pondering her problem, the guy at the door motioned to her. "Ms. Colton?"

"Yes."

"Come this way, please."

She followed him into the restaurant, pausing a moment to look around. The inside was a rich green, and dropdown lighting reminded her of European restaurants. The windows were tall and the ceiling high, letting in lots of light and causing the crystal behind the bar to sparkle off the marble bar. Green plants were everywhere, adding a homey touch to the place. Everything was open, airy and nice.

Suddenly Tatum appeared out of nowhere and

linked her arm through Lila's. "I have a place in the dining room, just for us, where it's not so noisy."

Tatum was a blue-eyed blonde bubbling with excitement. She could imagine it would have been fun having her for a cousin when Lila was growing up. It was the same way with the other Coltons. There had been a little awkwardness at first, but once they started talking, there was a connection that couldn't be denied.

They sat in an out-of-the-way table facing huge windows offering them a view of Chicago. "This is nice," Lila said.

"And lots of work. Some days I wonder why I took on so much, but then, I can't sponge off my family. I have to have a job to support myself and to feel good about myself."

"I know how you feel."

Something must have changed on Lila's face as she reached over and touched Lila's arm. "I'm so sorry about the gallery. How are you doing?"

"Taking it a day at a time and dealing with a lot of insurance people."

A waitress in a black-and-white uniform stepped over. "Ms. Colton, would you like to order now?" Her eyes were on Tatum, and Lila assumed she was talking to Tatum.

"Give Lila a menu," she told the girl. "I really don't need one."

Lila took the menu and said, "You choose. You know what's delicious."

Tatum leaned over and whispered, "It all is."

Lila smiled. "I'd still like you to choose."

"Do you like salmon?"

"Yes, I love it."

"We got some fresh in this morning and I made a new buttery wine sauce for it, so you and I will be tasting it for the first time."

"That sounds delicious."

"It comes with couscous, chayote squash and fresh spinach salad. It's all fresh from the garden. My suppliers come in early and that means I have to be here early. Don't be surprised if I fall asleep at the table."

The waitress brought water and took their drink orders. Tatum handed her the menu and said, "I'll send Apollo our order." She sent a message over her phone.

The girl didn't move. She shifted from one foot to the other, obviously nervous. "I know you said not to bother you for anything, but Eddie didn't show up for work and the dishes are piling up."

Tatum took a long breath and then looked at the girl. "I'm sure that you, Heather, Bob or Vincent can figure out how to work a dishwasher."

"Yes, ma'am." The girl scurried back to the kitchen.

"If you need to check on something, it's okay," Lila felt she needed to say.

"No, that's fine. They'll figure it out."

They munched on appetizers and talked about any and everything until the meal was served. It was as delicious as Lila had expected. And then they were served a baked Alaska that was better than anything she'd ever eaten.

She laid her napkin on the table. "That was absolutely delicious and I can see why you're so busy. Thank you for inviting me."

"You're welcome, but I had a reason."

Lila clasped her hands in her lap, hoping it wasn't about the lawsuit. "Oh."

"I wanted to invite you to our wedding."

"Oh, Tatum, that's so nice, but with our families battling each other in court, I don't think it's a good idea."

"I think it's a great idea," Tatum said, her blue eyes bright with energy.

"There would be too much tension and it would ruin your wedding."

The waitress finished removing the rest of the plates and it gave Lila a minute to gather her thoughts. She never dreamed Tatum would invite her to her wedding. Her mother wouldn't mind, but her dad... She wasn't sure what he would say. And did she care?

"Listen to me." Tatum began her appeal again. "You and your brother and your cousins have made it known how you feel about this lawsuit, and we as a family appreciate your support and would love for all of you to attend the wedding."

"There are so many *ifs* here that I'm not sure what to say."

"Then say yes."

"And if the judge rules in my grandmother's favor, will you be able to even look at us? It would bankrupt Colton Connections and would destroy your family."

Tatum put a hand to her forehead. "Oh, Lila, you think too much. Let's just enjoy the moment that we have, and I'm getting married soon and I want you to be there to celebrate with me. Who cares what happens? We'll still survive. We all work every day and can work our way through this, build another business, because if there's one thing we are not, it's quitters. So, cheer up. I'm getting married soon and I'm dying to tell you all about it."

Lila loved her attitude. For the next thirty minutes, they talked wedding details, and Lila got caught up in Tatum's excitement. Her eyes glittered as bright as a neon light. "I kid you not, my mother calls me at least three times a day asking me questions—what to do about this or what to do about that. She's an interior designer and I trust her instincts. I told her I'm busy and just make a decision. She said, 'Young lady, you're getting married and you need to pay attention to the details.' So I'm paying attention."

They laughed and sat back and stared at each other.

"This has been fun," Lila said, losing some of her nervousness.

"Then you'll come to the wedding?"

"You're so persuasive I'll think about it."

They got up and hugged, and Tatum really did feel like a cousin. Lila hoped it stayed that way through the months ahead.

Chapter Seven

Lila drove by the gallery to see if anyone was working there. Yellow tape was wrapped around it with Do Not Enter signs. For the past eight years, she'd worked steadily on building a clientele and buying more quality works, and now it was all ashes. She wanted to cry that life had been so cruel, but she was stronger than that. She'd done her crying and now she had to rebuild and look to the future. Every time the thought crossed her mind, she could see Carter's face. She wondered where he was and if he had caught the forger. She couldn't think about him anymore.

Since her talk with Tatum, she decided to pay her dad a visit. Axel Colton lived in Naperville and was nearly an hour's drive away. But she had nothing else to do and she hadn't talked to him in months. She didn't call until she was almost there because he usually would say he was busy or playing racquetball.

"I'm going out for a little while," her dad said, trying to put her off.

She'd heard that line before and she wasn't budging. "I'll be there in five minutes." And then she clicked off. He lived in a nice house, but she had never been invited there and neither had Myles. He answered the door immediately, no kiss, no hug. Like strangers who shared DNA. She went through a foyer into a large living area with stark furniture. It wasn't a place to relax, but there were nice paintings on the walls. No family pictures, though. And the paintings he didn't buy from her, which caused her temperature to rise to the danger level. She banked it down.

On the ornate coffee table were a bottle of expensive bourbon and two glasses. "Are you expecting someone?"

"Later. Don't worry about it. What's so important that you had to come all the way out here?"

"I'm your daughter and I haven't seen you in a long time."

"That never seemed to matter before." He took a seat in a Queen Anne–type chair. "Your mother made sure I never got to see you and Myles."

Lila shook her head. "No, that's not true. When it was your turn to pick us up to stay with you, you would never show up. We would sit on the front steps and wait and wait and wait. Do you know how bad that is for a child?"

"Yeah, it was all my fault." Axel Colton stood up suddenly and shoved his hands into his dress pants. At almost sixty, with gray hair dusting his dark hair at the temples, he was still a very strikingly handsome man, just like Myles. Except Myles didn't have the pouch around his middle.

"I'm not going to argue that. It's over and done with. I'm more concerned about the future."

He sat in the chair again. "What about it?"

She took a deep breath. "It's unfair what Carin, Uncle Erik and you are doing to the other Coltons. It's their business. Their life, and we had nothing to do with it."

He jumped up again. One of the things she would always remember about her father was his restlessness. He couldn't sit still for a minute. "Nothing to do with it? Our father pushed us aside while he raised his proper family. We were forgotten while they lived a life of luxury."

"He's paid for everything you've ever gotten. Your home, your clothes, your fancy cars, your schooling. Everything. The money kept coming in to Carin and she never turned it down. Now she wants revenge because she never could get Dean's attention again. She wants to flaunt that relationship in front of the other Coltons. I don't like that and I wish you could see that it's not right."

"I can't go against my mother. She would be furious."

"And the money would make it all better?"

"Do you know what it's like to be forgotten by your father?"

Lila stood to her full height and replied, "Yes, I do, every day of my life. I came to say what I had to say and now I'm going." She glanced at the bourbon. "Have a good evening."

"Lila… I've been thinking a lot about Wyatt."

The statement was like a fly ball right over her head. Wyatt was the child he had with his mistress Regina. Lila had never met the boy or his mother. It was a best-kept secret until Wyatt drowned in the swimming pool while her dad was supposed to have been watching him. He had been just a toddler and Regina wanted to bring charges against Axel, but Carin had put a stop to that with threats. Regina moved away after that and her mother divorced Axel. That was when their lives fell apart.

"Why are you thinking about him?"

Axel reached for the bourbon and poured a glass. "I don't know. Maybe because I lied. Mother told me to and I didn't feel I did anything wrong. It was Regina's job to take care of the kid. She asked me to watch him. How was I supposed to know the kid would walk into the pool?"

She swallowed something that tasted like acid. "What were you doing when he fell in the pool?"

"I was asleep on the sofa. When I heard the splash, I jumped in to get him, but it was too late."

She had no words. They were all snuffed out with his callousness and insensitivity. Years ago, he had been questioned over and over about the incident, and he'd said over and over that Regina was there and she was supposed to be watching the boy. Secret after secret, lie after lie. It seemed it never stopped in the Colton family. She headed for the front door.

"I'm not good with kids, okay?" he hollered after her. "You were lucky I was never there."

With her hand on the doorknob, she replied, "I'll look at it as a blessing. My advice is to call Regina and apologize for all the pain you caused her. My number one advice is to stop listening to Carin. She's going to take you down with her."

In the car, she rested her head against the steering

wheel and took a moment. Why did she think talking to her father would make things better? It never had.

A gloomy dusk settled in as she arrived home. Raindrops peppered her head and she ran into the town house. She kicked off her shoes, sat on the sofa and called Savon. She had to talk to someone to ease the ache in her heart. They talked about the gallery and the future, and she put thoughts of her dad aside.

"Do you know if Rossini is going to rebuild?" Savon asked.

"I haven't talked to him since he accused me of burning it down on purpose, and the police are listening to him. That's what has me scared."

"Surely they don't think you did it?"

"Yes, Richards believes I had something to do with it."

"He's an idiot."

Lila laughed.

"We can open somewhere else," Savon assured her. "We don't need his building."

"There's a lot to happen before I make that decision. The first and most important thing is the ruling on the fire. It's taking forever, it seems."

"Call me when you're ready to move things out of the vault. I'll help you."

"Thank you."

She stretched out on the sofa. Tears gathered in her throat and she tried to control her emotions. Her dad had hurt so many people, yet he felt no remorse. He didn't even mention the gallery fire and neither did she. It wouldn't have made a difference. He wasn't the cry-on-your-shoulder type of father. She finally realized her father didn't have deep feelings for anyone. Carin had a sick hold over him and Erik. She brushed away an errant tear and sat up.

She reached for the TV control to see if there was any news about the fire. Just then, her doorbell rang. She wasn't expecting anyone. It could be more legal papers, like Fox demanding a quart of her blood. She made her way to the door and looked through the peephole. Her heart pounded against her ribs. Carter!

She leaned her forehead against the door. What should she do? She followed her heart and opened the door, but only halfway. "You're back," she said in a bland voice.

"I'm sorry." He was dressed in slacks and a blue pinstriped shirt, impeccable as always. "May I come in?"

She wasn't going to be one of those women who let "I'm sorry" cover a multitude of sins.

"I didn't mean to leave so quickly, but with the paintings in my hands, I wanted to get the information to Neil as soon as I could. We've been after this guy for almost a year and the excitement clouded my judgment."

She opened the door wider. Guess she was one of those women. And he apologized so nicely.

"Were you able to validate the paintings as forgeries?" she asked as she walked into her living room and took a seat on the sofa.

He sat beside her and told her what had happened since he'd left. His excitement was evident in his voice and in his eyes. She wondered if he would ever talk about her with that note of excitement, joy and deep emotions. It was clear he loved his work and he was one of those guys who would never settle down. She told herself so many times that it didn't matter and that she would enjoy her time with him. That wasn't true. Love didn't work that way, as she had learned.

She brought her thoughts back to what he was saying. "So you're supposed to be in New York?"

"Yes. We have a PI looking for Tony Martell, the forger, we believe. As soon as he calls, I'll be leaving again, but I couldn't do that without seeing you."

"Aw." She stroked his face and his gray eyes darkened. She got lost in the beauty she saw there. Nothing mattered anymore, not her hurt feelings, not his love for his job. It was just the two of them right here, right now, and what happened next was their choice. Tracing his lips, she added, "If you don't kiss me soon, my heart is going to pop out of my chest."

He cupped her face and touched his lips to hers in a long, sweet kiss that lasted all the way to the bedroom. Clothes were discarded along the way. She giggled as she fell backward onto the bed and he quickly followed, covering her with his hard body. Their lovemaking reached a crescendo equaled by the thunder. The rain pounded the roof and water dripped onto the drain outside, making a *tap-tap* soothing sound. Lila felt only the rhythm in her body and the joy in her heart.

A long time later, she lay in the comfort of his arms and told him about her day.

He rubbed her shoulder. "I'm sorry you had to go through that with your dad."

"I talk to him mostly on the phone and I rarely see him. After having lunch with Tatum and seeing what a nice person she is, I thought I would talk to my dad and maybe get him to see reason. But reason isn't in his makeup. Carin manipulates him and Erik."

"You call your grandmother by her given name?"

"That's what we were told to call her when we were small. She hated the word *grandmother* or *grandma*."

"I guess I didn't miss anything by not having grandparents. My parents were older when they had me and my grandparents had already passed away."

"When I was smaller, I used to wish for a grandmother who baked cookies." Lila laughed. "I have no idea why I would wish that because my mom made really good cookies. It's just that other kids had grandmothers who were fabulous, and we all want what everybody else has."

"I wanted a dog." He smiled. "I can't even imagine a dog in my mother's perfectly decorated apartment. Everything was in its place and everything had a place."

She sat up. "I'm hungry. How about you?"

"We're not going to make cookies, are we?"

She chuckled as she slipped a T-shirt over her head. "Leftover spaghetti."

They sat at the bar eating spaghetti and drinking wine. Later, curled up in the bed, Lila listened to the beat of his heart mingling with the patter of the rain. It was perfect. How she wished it could stay that way.

THE NEXT MORNING, they were slow to get dressed. Carter was in the guest bath shaving. Lila stood in the doorway watching him, already dressed in slacks and a pullover sweater. She was beautiful in whatever she wore, tall, regal and absolutely gorgeous. Her hair was pinned up again and he just wanted to take it down. He wouldn't mind waking up with her every morning.

"When will your PI call?" she asked.

"Soon, I think."

"And you'll leave again?"

He wiped his face with a towel. "Yes. That's the way my life is and has been for years. I know you were upset…"

"I wasn't upset."

"When you opened your front door, your green eyes were flashing daggers at me."

"Okay, maybe I was. I've just never met anyone like you who doesn't have the need for a home."

He kissed the tip of her nose. "Lila, I've never really had a home, so I don't feel the need for one. I know you must have this vision in your head of a house, the picket fence, the dog and happy-ever-after."

"I've never had that vision. My vision is a man who would love me and support me and be there for me always and we could live anywhere we wanted just so we were there for each other."

"Oh, Lila—"

Her phone jangled and she reached for it in her pocket. She talked for a minute and clicked off. "That was Richards. He wants to see me in an hour in his office."

Carter grabbed his shirt. "Then let's go."

"He must've made a ruling on the fire," Lila said as they made their way out the door.

In the vehicle, she clasped her hands in her lap and he knew she was nervous. He placed a hand on her arm. "Try not to be nervous. I'll be there with you."

She tentatively smiled at him. "Thank you."

They didn't say anything else as they rushed into the building. Once they reached Richards's office, they were directed to another room and it was full of people. Rossini was there, along with several men Carter didn't know. But they were most likely fire investigators. Richards had a stack of photos and files in front of him.

He motioned for them to come in. "Have a seat."

Introductions were made, and they sat to the right of Richards's desk.

"As most of you know, the department has done an intense investigation of the fire in the Weston Gallery. We even brought in experts to confirm our findings. The fire was started with a device." He picked up a small plastic bag. "This is a wire that goes to a detonator." He pointed to more bags. "And there's more of the same wiring we found when we dug deeper." He held up a small object with the wiring attached. "This is what set the fire. Looks like a toy, but you plug it into a socket and set it and you have a fire. Simple, but deadly."

He held up pictures. "This is a photo of where the device was placed. The plate covering the wall socket was taken off and one of these—" he held up the object again "—was inserted into the electrical socket and set to go off after the showing. It was intentional. It was arson."

Silence filled the room and no one made a move.

Carter was the first to speak. "It seems really strange that no one would have noticed that. The plate was taken off and the detonator would stick out."

Richards nodded to a guy. "Greg Holder is an explosives expert. He'll explain how it was done."

The man had an electrical socket and detonator in his hand. "The plate was taken off so the device could be plugged in and pushed deep inside." He demonstrated as he talked. "When it went off, the blast would go between the walls, igniting the wiring and the insulation."

"No one would have seen it." Lila finally spoke up. "There was a sculpture in front of it. The last time I checked the gallery before the showing was at one to make sure nothing was out of place, and I checked that corner and there was no detonator there at that time."

"So someone had to come in after that," Richards replied. "Did you notice anyone, Ms. Colton?"

"No. I was busy talking to people and I didn't see anything out of the ordinary."

Richards folded his hands on the desk. "Well, it comes down to this. We have two suspects who would benefit from the fire—Ms. Colton and Mr. Rossini. We showed your pictures to stores that sell these devices and no one could identify either one of you. That's where we stand now. We're still contacting stores out of our area and contacting other fire stations who might be familiar with this MO. We'll catch this person sooner or later. Ms. Colton and Mr. Rossini, please don't leave town."

Lila stood. "May I get my artwork out of the vault?"

Richards leaned back in his chair. "Yes, I think that's possible. Our investigation now goes beyond the scene."

Lila walked out and Carter followed. She was upset,

so he didn't say anything. She had to be alone with her thoughts. They spent the morning renting a van, loading the artwork and taking it to a storage facility. Savon helped. It was a busy morning and Lila said very little. When they got back to her town house, she was restless.

"I need to do something. Would you like to walk the Magnificent Mile or the Riverwalk?"

"The Magnificent Mile is shopping, isn't it?"

"Yes. Anything you can imagine."

"I'll take the Riverwalk."

She chuckled as she put on her sneakers. He grabbed his, willing to do anything she wanted. They parked his rental and walked along the Chicago River, and there were many restaurants and sites to see. The rain last night made everything seem fresh and invigorating. When they reached the Navy Pier, they were exhausted and stopped at a small pub to eat and get a beer. They caught a water taxi back to the car and Lila seemed in a better mood.

Once they reached the town house, Lila went straight to the bedroom and stripped out of her clothes. He squatted and took off her tennis shoes and handed her her T-shirt. Within seconds, she crawled beneath the comforter and he soon joined her. Lightning blasted outside and a boom of thunder followed.

"Another rainy night," she murmured into his shoulder.

"Just go to sleep."

She kissed his shoulder. "I'm glad you're here with me."

"Have you thought of calling your mother? I'll be leaving soon and you don't need to be alone."

"I'll think about it."

"I can feel your restlessness."

"I must inherit that from my father. He was always moving. I don't want to think about him."

He pushed her long hair away from her face. "Listen to me. They said you had motive—that's it. They can't arrest you on motive. They have to have evidence and they have none. If they had, you would be in a jail cell. They have nothing and they won't find anything, so please relax and kiss me."

She laughed and did as he asked. "I'm so glad you came into my life," she whispered against his lips.

"Me, too."

He held her a little tighter as he was almost certain he would be leaving tomorrow to probably some ungodly place. Tony was going to hide deep and he wasn't quite sure where that was, somewhere where he could paint in quiet.

His mind came back to the woman in his arms, and the negative thoughts of leaving surprised him. She deserved a home and family and a man who would love her deeply and be there for her always, just like she'd said. Could he give her that? Could he be a nine-to-five guy who mowed the grass on Saturdays? With her, he was beginning to believe that anything was possible.

Chapter Eight

The next morning, they didn't have any plans, and she just wanted to spend time absorbing everything about Carter: his warm smile, the intensity in his eyes when he talked about something he loved and the soothing caress of his touch. After seeing her dad and dealing with Richards, Carter was her rainbow after the storm, even though the thought of him leaving made her sad. But if she was anything, she was resilient, and today she was ready to face whatever she had to.

Carter went out to get breakfast tacos and coffee while she finished dressing. It was a casual day in jeans and a T-shirt. Carter was soon back with breakfast and they sat at the bar eating and discussing what they would do today. Her phone rang and she grabbed it on the bar. It was her mother.

"How are you? You haven't called."

"I'm fine, Mom. I've just been busy dealing with everything."

"I know, but I worry. Guess who I have today?"

Lila didn't have to think hard to know that answer. "Jackson."

"Yes. He is such a sweetie. Faith had to have a root

canal today and Myles is working as usual, so I'm entertaining. Faith's mother is driving her back and forth and I have Jackson. He's going to help me plant. He loves digging in the dirt."

"Have fun, Mom."

"You could come out and visit."

"Not today. I have other things to do." She glanced at Carter and realized just how important he was becoming in her life. "Bye. I love you."

"Your mother?" Carter finished off his coffee.

"Yes. She's babysitting my nephew today."

"It's nice to have family to help out."

"Sometimes." She didn't want to get into the separation of Myles and Faith. She firmly believed that one day they would get back together.

"Was that tall building we saw last night the Sears building?"

"Yes, but it is now called the Willis Tower."

"I'd like to go over there today if we have time."

She spread her arms. "We have nothing but time and, remember, it's one hundred and ten floors. You think you're up to all one hundred and ten?"

"After yesterday, probably not."

Carter's phone buzzed and he walked into the living room, talking. He turned around. "This is it. The PI has located Martell and you'll never guess where he is."

Her heart sank. "Some faraway place like Bangladesh."

"No. Chicago. He lives in South Deering. There are rows of older two-story apartments and he lives on the end with his girlfriend and her mother. It's the girl's mother's apartment."

"Do you have an address?"

"Ninety-Seventh Street."

"There are a lot of big blocks of apartments around there."

"So you know where it is?"

"I can find it."

He went upstairs to his room and came back with a gun on his belt.

She was startled. "You carry a gun?"

"Yes, when I have to deal with criminals. Tony has never been violent, but I have to be prepared."

He slipped handcuffs into his pocket. "Tell me how to get to South Deering."

She grabbed her purse. "I'm going with you." If there was any chance of him getting hurt, she wanted to be there.

"No way. It could be dangerous and I'm not putting you in harm's way."

"If I stay here, I'll just be worried. I'll sit in the car and be very good."

She marched toward the door, hoping he wouldn't stop her. She didn't think she could sit here and wait for him to come back or not come back. That would be too hard on her nerves.

"Okay, let's get this straight," he said as he slid into the driver's seat. "You will sit in the car. It shouldn't take long. I don't want you even close to danger. Understood?"

"Understood," she said in a stern voice that surprised even her. She gave him directions and they zipped through traffic at times and others they stalled due to heavy traffic.

Once they reached Ninety-Seventh Street, Carter called the police. He explained his situation. "I will need backup." He talked for a minute more, and then he put his phone back in his pocket.

"The police will be here, so everything should go smoothly."

She pointed to where she saw the older two-story apartments. "There they are. If he lives on the end, it would be the first one."

"That's the number," Carter said. "I'm going to check and see if anyone is home, and you stay put." He parked the car on the other side of the street near more apartments.

Lila watched as he crossed the street and went up the steps to the front door. The car was parked three apartments down and she had to twist her head to see. A wooden railing enclosed the small porch, plus a metal fence circled the apartments. Most of them had screen doors, but this one didn't, just a white entry door peeling from age. Carter stood to the side and knocked on the door. The person inside wouldn't be able to see Carter because he wasn't standing in front of the peephole. Smart.

She put down her window so she could hear. She worried about Carter's safety. A short man with a graying ponytail opened the door. His jeans and T-shirt were covered in blotches of paint. The moment he saw Carter, he tried to slam the door shut. Carter put his foot in the door and pushed it open. He reached for the man's T-shirt and pulled him onto the porch.

"We meet again, Tony," Carter said.

"Come on, Finch. I did my time. Why are you always picking on me?"

"Because you're back to your old ways painting forgeries."

"I need to make a living and it's not hurting anyone."

"You can think about that statement while you spend a few more years in prison."

"I'm not going back to prison."

"That's exactly…"

The man shoved Carter, who stumbled back against the railing as the man leaped over it to the yard and sailed over the metal fence. Carter quickly followed, but the man had a head start. Before a sane thought could enter her head, she jumped from the car and collided with the man. They both went flying into the neighbor's yard. Carter was there and he jerked the guy's arms behind his back and cuffed him.

"That was a big mistake, Tony. Resisting arrest is just going to make it worse."

Carter helped Lila to her feet with a frown. "Are you okay?"

She let out a long breath. "Yes."

"You don't look okay." He glanced to the front of her shirt and jeans, which were stained with grass and dirt. Her right hand throbbed where she'd tried to catch herself, but she kept it at her side, not wanting Carter to see. It was just a little thing.

A police car drove up. Carter talked to the officer exiting the vehicle and they put Tony in the back seat. "I'd really like to look inside the house," Carter said.

"You have to get a search warrant for that and it takes time," the officer replied. "Or the owner's approval. All of these apartments are rentals owned by Sapp Realty, and the main man would be Donald Sapp. I'll see if I can get a number for you."

Carter turned to Lila, took her by the elbow and led her across the street to the car. "Can I trust you to stay put?"

"Yeah." Her body ached in places and her hand was on fire. She didn't plan on going anywhere or doing any more heroics.

"What were you thinking?"

She brushed grass and dirt from her clothes and slid into the car. "That's the point—I wasn't. I just didn't want him to get away. And—" she held up a finger on her left hand "—I do not need a lecture."

He reached in the car and kissed her lips. "We'll talk about it later. The officer is motioning for me. I'll be back."

She leaned her head against the back of the car seat. She'd landed on her shoulder and right hand as she'd tried to keep from sliding into the fence, and they both ached. Taking a deep breath, she forced herself to open her hand. *Oh, no!* Dirt and grass were embedded in the meaty part of her palm, and it was red, throbbing and bleeding in spots.

Carter ran back to the car and jumped into the driver's seat. "I'm taking you to the town house and then I'm coming back. Mr. Sapp is on the way, and you don't need to sit in the car all the time."

She smiled at him. He always did the right thing. He was such a nice man and she just wanted to hold him and never let him go. Her thoughts were zigzagging all over the place, but she wanted to go home and deal with her hand.

"Thank you. I appreciate that."

He started the car. "No argument?"

"No. I plan to be a very good girl for the rest of the day."

He touched her face with the back of his hand and her tummy fluttered with excitement. "That was very brave what you did today, but don't ever do it again. My heart wouldn't survive it."

"Mine, either." She held her hand where he couldn't see it until she had a better look at it. In the few days she'd known him, she knew he was going to be upset if she was hurt. So she would be as quiet as a mouse until she cleaned the dirt and grass from her hand. Carter was eager to get back and didn't notice her awkward movements. She kissed him goodbye and ran into the town house before he could notice anything. She went straight to the bathroom to look under her makeup lights so she could get a better view.

She found tweezers and tried to remove the grass, but found it impossible without a lot of pain. She ran cool water over her hand and jumped. It stung.

The doorbell rang. She dabbed at her hand with a towel and went to the front door. Who could it be? It wasn't Carter because he wanted to be there when the owner arrived so he could find incriminating evidence against Tony whatever-his-name-was. She glanced through the peephole. Savon. Oh, no. She'd forgotten their lunch date. She had intended to cancel since Carter was here, but she'd forgotten that, too.

She yanked open the door. "I'm sorry. I forgot."

Savon walked in. "The hunk is back, huh?" She looked around. "No big deal. I'll talk to you later."

"Come with me."

"What?"

Lila dragged her into the bathroom and opened her palm. Handing her the tweezers, she said, "Can you pick the grass out?"

A look of horror crossed Savon's face. "Are you kidding me? I faint at the sight of blood. What happened to you?"

Lila told her the whole story.

"You tackled the guy? Are you insane?"

"I'm beginning to wonder that myself."

"Come on. I'm taking you to the emergency room."

"Savon, no. I don't want Carter to know."

"Why?"

"He didn't want me to go, and I promised to sit in the car and be good and... Well, the guy was coming right toward me and I couldn't let him get away. I wasn't even thinking."

"You got that right."

"Savon—"

Her friend handed her the tweezers. "If you can pluck the grass from your palm, we won't go."

"You're evil."

Savon laughed as they headed out the door and over to the hospital. As they sat in the waiting room, she tried not to look at her hand, but it was swelling and hurting more. When she was called back, things happened quickly. The doctor asked what had happened and she told him. She thought he would ask more questions, but he didn't. He was more concerned about her hand.

"I'll have to clean and remove debris from your palm. There's grass and dirt under the skin, and I'll have to remove it or your hand will get infected. It will be painful, but I'll deaden it first. It should take about an hour. Is someone with you?"

"She's in the waiting room and she's kind of squeamish."

The doctor looked at the nurse. "Tell her friend that Ms. Colton is going to be a while and get her a gown and into the bed. We'll need the attachment for an arm."

The nurse handed her a hospital gown with a slit up the back. Oh, yes, it was fashionable. She crawled beneath the cool sheets and wondered how things were going with Carter. She had no choice now but to tell him. It was silly to keep it a secret anyway, but she didn't want him to feel guilty.

The nurse came in with a long, padded board and attached it to the right side of the bed. The doctor stood behind her with a needle. She turned her head away. Maybe she was squeamish, too.

"Ms. Colton, stretch your right arm out on the board and I'm going to deaden it. Just be very still."

She closed her eyes and gritted her teeth. The sting made her grit her teeth a little harder, and then she couldn't feel anything. The nurse gave her an injection in her left arm. "That should help you to relax."

She dozed off a couple of times while the doctor worked. He was meticulous with a small scalpel and tweezers, and the nurse flushed it with a sterile saline solution several times. When they finished, the nurse rubbed antibiotic ointment on it and wrapped it. She brought Lila a sling to go over her shoulder so she could rest her arm in it. Then she was ready to go home.

In the town house, she rested her head on the back of the sofa and laid her arm across her stomach. It wasn't painful, but the doctor said it would be later. He'd given her a prescription for some pain pills and they'd stopped and picked them up. She had thought that Carter would be here, but he must still be at the apartments or at the police station. Maybe by the time he came she would feel better. At the moment she felt queasy.

Savon made herbal tea for Lila's nausea and ordered soup and sandwiches for dinner. Lila could eat very little. The vegetable soup tasted bland and she went back to lie on the sofa. Where was Carter? If Carter was here, she'd feel better. He was her rock and... She had to stop depending on him.

WHEN DONALD SAPP finally showed up, Carter was relieved. He was worried about Lila. She was acting very strange after her tumble with Martell. He wanted to make sure she was okay, but things here were holding them up.

Sapp allowed him to look inside the house and he signed a piece of paper that the officer had brought in case he changed his mind later. Inside was a messy apartment. Clothes and empty cartons of takeout seemed to be everywhere, even dishes in the sink and food on the stove. Sapp started cursing at the conditions inside. They didn't find any paints or painting materials in the downstairs or upstairs. That surprised Carter. If Tony lived here, he was painting here.

"Is there an attic?" he asked Sapp.

"It's very tiny and I don't allow my renters to keep stuff up there. It's just a fire hazard."

"I guess that's it, Mr. Finch," the officer said.

No, he wouldn't believe that. He kept searching. He walked out the back door to a small porch, but there was nothing out there, either. In the kitchen was a small door he'd taken to be a broom closet earlier.

"Where does this door go?"

"To the basement."

Basement! Why hadn't Sapp mentioned that? Carter opened the door, and the scent of turpentine and oils hit them in the face.

"What the hell?" Sapp yelled. They went down the narrow stairs and Sapp continued his tirade. "What's all this stuff? It stinks."

Across the room were easels with paintings half-finished on them and they were all Homer Tinsleys. Old wood was stacked in a corner from which Tony was making frames. Boxes of tubes of paint were stacked everywhere with gallons of turpentine.

"What does he do with all this stuff?" Sapp asked.

"He paints, Mr. Sapp." Carter waved his hand toward the paintings on easels. "And then he sells them, but they're not really his creation." He pointed to the first painting, which was complete and ready to go. "See the signature? Your tenant is a forger."

Carter took pictures of everything, and he went through the small desk against the wall and didn't find anything. No name. No address. Nothing to incriminate anyone else. But he had Martell against the wall and he was going down for a long time.

They walked out of the house and onto the porch for fresh air. Sapp was on the phone, talking to the lady who rented the apartment. "I should just kick her out," Sapp said as he clicked off. "She's rented from me for many years and I know this is not her doing. I told her she's got to get rid of that stuff in the basement, and if I find anybody else in the apartment, I will kick them out."

"It's very nice of you," Carter said. Sapp was a hell-and-brimstone kind of guy and Carter felt sure he would bring his full wrath upon the old lady, but he seemed to have a fondness for the woman. That just proved there was a little good in everyone.

At the police station, he hit a waiting wall. Tony was still being processed and he couldn't interview him until that was over. He sat in one of the interview rooms when an assistant district attorney walked in. She introduced herself and asked about Tony. He told her everything he knew.

"I'd need your file and everything you have on him." She pushed her card across the table and she had written in hand her private number.

"I'll get everything to you."

"It sounds like an open-and-shut case. Maybe we can make a deal."

"A deal? He's been out of prison a little over a year and almost immediately he's back doing what he did before, making money off the talents of others."

"He's not a violent guy. We have a jail full of violent

characters who we have to prosecute. If we can get this one off the table, I'm going to do it."

Carter stood. "It's your choice, but I'll be in there fighting all the way. I've been tracking the forger for almost a year, and for him to get a light sentence because your docket is full is unacceptable to me."

The lady picked up her briefcase and walked out the door. Carter fiddled with the business card she'd given him. He would send her a boatload of information on Tony Martell, and then they would talk deal again.

The man himself walked into the room in handcuffs and jail clothes. The officer behind him unlocked the handcuffs and Tony took a seat across from him.

"Sorry I hit you, man, but you don't know what it's like in prison."

"Did you lose your memory when you got out?"

"No." He shuffled around in the chair.

"Then why go back to doing the same thing?"

"People won't leave me alone. They keep telling me how much money I can make and how I won't get caught this time. I guess I'm weak."

Something in Carter eased in his feelings toward Tony. He wasn't a violent guy, like the ADA had said. He was just weak and criminals often preyed on the weak. Money was always the bait. In that moment, Carter knew he would agree with the ADA and try to make a deal in hopes that Tony could be rehabilitated. First, Carter wanted something from him, and until he got it, Tony wasn't getting anything.

He placed his forearms on the table. "We have tons of evidence against you this time. There's no question you've been painting fakes and someone is paying you to do it. If you want a lighter sentence, you're going to have to talk to me. I want the name of the man who's paying you."

"Ah, Finch, I can't do that. He'll have me killed."

"Why do you think that?"

"I don't know. Just get the feeling that nobody crosses him."

Carter leaned back in his chair and stared at him. "Well, it comes down to this. If you don't give up his name, you're probably going to get five more years tacked onto your original sentence, and this time you won't be getting out for good behavior. It's your decision."

"It's not much of a decision."

Carter leaned forward. "I already know the man's name." He pushed the tablet that was on the table toward Tony. "Write down his name. That's all you have to do and I'll take it from there."

"Ah, man, you're killing me."

"The name, Tony."

Tony picked up the pen and scribbled a name and then shoved it toward Carter. Walter Fox was on the tablet. Carter pushed it back to him. "Sign it. Tell me how he got you involved in this."

"He came to the house."

"Where you're living with your girlfriend?"

"Yeah."

"How did he know you were here? Did he call you? How did he find you so quickly?"

"I don't know, man. He showed up one day at our door and says I have a talent he wanted to utilize and he was willing to pay for it."

"Like an angel from heaven, huh?"

"I told him I wasn't into that anymore. I was going to stay clean. Three days later he came back and offered me more money. I turned him down again. But he came back again and offered me more money and I couldn't turn it down. The rent was overdue and bills needed to be paid and I had to help my girlfriend out."

The story was a little far-fetched and Carter had a hard time believing it. There had to be a connection between Fox and Tony, or how else would Fox know where to find him?

"If you're lying to me, I'll make sure you get more years than you ever dreamed about."

"Come on, man."

Carter pointed to the tablet. "Write down everything you just told me and then sign it."

As he wrote, Carter kept thinking about a connection. There had to be one. It usually involved someone who knew both parties. "Where does your girlfriend work?"

"At a bar on Weston Avenue. Her mother works there, too."

Her mother works at the bar, too. That didn't make sense.

"Is the mother the cleaning lady?"

"Man, look, I don't know what she does in there and I don't ask."

The bar was on the same street as the gallery. What were the odds? Could Tony be involved in setting the fire? He immediately shook that from his head. Tony was too weak for that kind of work. Carter stood and gathered the papers on the table. Putting them in his briefcase, he said, "Either the ADA or I will be in touch with you."

"Thanks, man."

Carter stretched his shoulders and was ready to go home to Lila. *Home.* Did he just think that? He'd said he didn't need a home. He was happy traveling around the world, but something about Lila was making him think about home.

Chapter Nine

Carter entered the front door and yelled, "I'll put my gun up and be right down. I have so much to tell you." He removed his jacket and his gun and then stored the gun away in his bag. Lila hadn't answered him. The TV was on. Maybe she didn't hear him. He ran down the stairs and stopped short in the living room. She lay on the sofa with her right arm in a sling and resting on her stomach. Her hand was bandaged. Why was her hand bandaged?

He picked up the remote control and clicked off the TV. Lila stirred and sat up, her dark hair all around her. She pushed it away with her left hand. "Oh, you're back. Did everything go okay?"

He eased down beside her. "What happened to your hand?"

"Oh, well...now don't freak out."

"I'm not freaking out. What happened?"

She told him a story that had him close to freaking out. "Why didn't you tell me?"

"I didn't know it was that bad. Not until I tried to remove the grass with tweezers. That didn't work. It hurt. Savon came by and made me go to the ER. The doctor deadened my arm and I don't feel much pain right now, but he gave me a prescription, which I had filled for later. In a few days I'll be as good as new. So it's nothing to worry about and no reason to give me a lecture."

He rested his head against hers. "I'm just glad you're okay."

"Yes, I am, but right now I need to go to bed. The nurse gave me something to relax and I'm feeling very relaxed."

He helped her up the stairs and into bed. "Do you need anything?"

"No, just for you to get that guilty look off your face." She held up her hand. "This is my fault, not yours." She snuggled beneath the comforter. "There's a sandwich in the fridge if you want it."

"Thanks." He looked closely at her pale face. "Are you sure you're okay?"

She didn't respond. He pushed her hair away from her cheeks and saw she was sound asleep. "Sleep tight." He kissed her cheek and cursed himself all the way to the bathroom. Even though she'd said it wasn't his fault, it was. He should have never taken her with him.

He took a quick shower and put on pajama bottoms and a T-shirt. When he'd seen her open the car door and run into Tony, he'd screamed, "Lila, no!" She just kept running and his heart jolted like it never had before. He feared Tony might hurt her. And the last thing he wanted was for her to get hurt, and she had. Tonight and tomorrow she'd probably be in a lot of pain because of him. He would be right here to help her with whatever she needed.

He grabbed his laptop and checked on her one more time. She was out and he hoped she would be for the rest of the night. Taking the stairs two at a time, he went to the living room to work on the file for the ADA. At least he would have that ready to send in the morning. Then he realized he was hungry and went to the kitchen to find the sandwich and something to drink. All the while, his ears were tuned to the upstairs in case Lila needed him. An hour later, he made his way back up the stairs to find Lila still sleeping.

He flipped off all the lights and crawled into bed. Just as he got comfortable, Lila crawled out of bed. "Where are you going?"

"My hand is throbbing and I'm going to get a pain pill."

"No, no, no!" He jumped out of bed. "I'll get it. I saw them on the counter in the kitchen. Go back to bed."

Once again he ran downstairs, grabbed the pills and a glass of water and went back up. She was sitting on the side of the bed. He gave her a pill and a glass of water. Dutifully she swallowed it and he helped her back in bed.

"Anything else you need?"

"Maybe another pillow."

"And that would be where?"

"In the closet."

He found the pillow and stuffed it behind her head. "How's that?"

"Better." Her voice was groggy and he quickly turned off the light and crawled in beside her, hoping she would go back to sleep. He was almost asleep when she stirred.

"What's wrong?"

"I don't feel good."

"What do you—" Before the last word could leave his mouth, she leaped out of bed and ran to the bathroom. A moment later, he heard her vomiting. Oh, man! He got out of bed and walked toward the bathroom, not knowing what to do. He'd never been in this situation before, but he couldn't lie there while she was sick.

He peeked around the corner and saw her sitting on the floor with her head over the toilet, making gut-wrenching sounds. Finally, she flushed it and leaned back against the wall, noticing him.

"Go away, Carter. I don't want you to see me like this."

"That's not going to happen." He stepped into the bathroom and opened the cabinet for a washcloth. Putting it under the water faucet, he got it wet and squatted on the floor beside her. He held her hair and wiped her face.

"Carter—" she protested.

"Shh."

"I stink. It's on my hair, my clothes and the floor. Just go back to bed, and when I feel strong enough, I'll get cleaned up."

"No way." He scooted closer. "Now let's get your clothes off and get you in the shower. That's the only way to get it off of you so you can sleep and rest."

She held up her right hand to indicate she couldn't get in the shower.

"I'll fix that." He ran downstairs again looking for a plastic bag and a rubber band. When he had the goodies, he went back upstairs and she was still sitting there looking disgusted with herself.

"Get that look off your face," he said. "I've seen you naked before, so what's the big deal?"

"I didn't have vomit all over me," she shot back.

"Doesn't make a difference," he told her as he removed her T-shirt. At the sight of her breasts, his thoughts went in a completely different direction and he curbed them quickly. He adjusted the shower's water temperature while she removed her panties with her left hand and stepped into the shower.

"Hold your right hand up so water can't get in it."

"I'm not a bronc rider." She laughed under her breath. "Do I get eight seconds?"

"You're getting giddy." He poured shampoo into her wet left palm.

"Smells like lavender," he said.

She made a face at him as she attempted to lather her hair. She wasn't doing a very good job, so he helped her. Standing under the spray, she tried to get rid of the soap and the smell. He grabbed a couple of towels out of the cabinet and reached in and turned off the water. One towel he wrapped around her head and the other he wrapped around her body.

"Better?"

"Yes. Thank you."

She got out and sat in the chair at her makeup table, drawing her fingers through the thick wet strands. "I'll have to dry it some before I go back to bed." She opened the bottom drawer and he helped her to get the dryer out and plugged it in.

"While you're doing that, I'll get cleaning supplies. Utility room, right?"

"Right." She stood up.

"Where are you going?"

"To get a clean T-shirt."

"I'll get it."

"Second drawer of my dresser." He helped her get it through one arm and over her head. She stiffened. Obviously, the hand hurt.

"I'll take these clothes down and put them in the washing machine and bring back cleaning supplies."

The smell gagged him a few times, but he powered through until the bathroom smelled like bleach.

"Thank you," she said in a sleepy voice as she crawled into bed.

"You're welcome. Now I'm going to get out of these wet clothes and join you." When he came back, she was asleep. He slipped in beside her and tried not to move the mattress too much. Time and rest would help her. He lay there looking into the darkness and saw a new side to himself. He never thought of himself as a loving, nurturing person. He felt sure the young Carter would have run from the bedroom until she had everything under control. But with Lila it was different. He cared about her and you didn't run from people you cared about.

He looked at her beautiful sleeping face. *What have you done to me?*

LILA WOKE UP to pain. Wincing, she slid out of bed as quietly as possible. She didn't want to wake Carter. She grabbed the pill bottle, picked up her bathrobe from the floor and made her way to the kitchen. Taking the pill was her top priority. Once that was done, she made coffee, and it wasn't easy with her left hand, but she was sure Carter would want a cup when he woke up. After what he did last night, she would do anything for him.

She sat on the sofa wrapped in the bathrobe, waiting for the pill to do its thing. Last night she was so embarrassed and just wanted him to go away. The fact that he'd stayed shocked her since he didn't have a sense of family values. Mr. Finch had a lot of family values he didn't know about. Most men would have left, but he'd stayed right with her. She wondered how he felt this morning.

"There you are." Carter stood there in his pajamas and T-shirt, looking as handsome as ever. "When I woke up and you weren't there, I got worried."

"I woke up to pain and needed a pill, so I came down very quietly so as not to wake you."

"Is the pain better?"

"Yes, it is."

Carter looked around. "I smell coffee."

"I made it."

"With your left hand?"

"Yes, just for you."

He leaned his face against hers and her left hand stroked his stubble, and new, deeper emotions surged through her. She loved him and she knew he would leave one day and that would be sooner than later, probably as soon as tonight. Every second she had with him, she was preparing herself for the inevitable. She wouldn't beg. She wouldn't cry. She would be grateful for the man who'd held her hair while she puked.

"I'll get us a cup of coffee." In a minute, he was back with a mug of coffee for her. "Can you handle it?"

"Yes."

He headed for the stairs with a mug in his hand. "I'm going to shower and shave while you're resting, and then I have to go get groceries and food for us to eat."

"Okay."

"What would you like to eat today?"

"My mom's chicken noodle soup," she mumbled, realizing she was falling off to sleep. She sat up straighter. "And if you call her, I would have to kill you. Understand?"

He laughed. "I understand." He went to her desk and got a piece of paper and a pen. "What would I need to make chicken noodle soup?"

"A chicken, of course, but that's too much for the two of us. Just get a split breast and a couple of thighs with the skin on and the bone in. Celery, onions, carrots, chicken broth and those little squares that Mom drops in."

He smiled at her. "You're going to have to be more specific."

"It's little squares of flavor. Bouillon. That's what it's called. They're wrapped individually in a small jar and it just gives the soup a little more flavor. That's what my mom says."

"I will find them." He finished his way up the stairs and Lila tried to get comfortable, but the pain was bad. She went to the kitchen for another cup of coffee and just walked around the living room trying to ease the pain.

Carter came back all dressed, and he looked so nice

and handsome with his dark hair combed neatly. She just wanted to hug him. He handed her her laptop. "I thought you might need these." He put a pillow on the couch.

"Did you see my phone in your car? I can't find it."

He went outside and came back with her phone in his hand. "It fell between the seats."

"Thank you."

"I'm going to the grocery store and you rest."

"I want to take a shower and wash my hair. I think it still has shampoo in it."

"No." He shook his head. "You'll have to wait until I get back."

"I'm not helpless." For some reason, he ignited her temper. She didn't want to feel helpless. She wanted to go out with him and enjoy their time together instead of being stuck at home with a throbbing hand.

He lifted a sharp eyebrow.

"Okay, go, go."

He walked to her. "You're not helpless. You hurt your hand and it will take a couple of days for you to feel better. Just rest, please. Can I trust you to do that?"

She took a long breath. "Yes. Being stupid once is enough."

He gently kissed her. "I'll be back as soon as I can."

Lila put her coffee cup in the sink and went to the sofa to call Savon, but then realized Savon wasn't up yet. Instead, she called her mother. Sooner or later she would find out about Lila's injured hand and would be upset that Lila hadn't told her.

"Hey, Mom, how's everything?"

"Where have you been?" There was a lot of worry and concern mixed in her mother's voice.

"I'm at home."

"Myles has been calling and calling you. He's on his way over. We worry when we can't get you. Are you okay?"

She bit her lip. "Actually, I'm not."

"What happened?"

She hesitated, but only for a second. "I fell and hurt my hand."

"How bad?"

"I tried to catch myself with my right hand as I slid through some dirt and grass. I scraped my palm and got some dirt and grass in it. I had to go to the ER and the doctor cleaned it up very nicely. Just a little accident and I'll be okay tomorrow, but I'm resting today."

"Are you in pain?"

She bit her lip a little harder and gauged her words. "A little, but the doctor gave me some pain pills. I'm okay, Mom. Really."

"I'm coming to get you. You can stay here until your hand heals."

"Absolutely not. I'm thirty years old and you don't have to baby me. I can really take care of myself."

"Then why aren't you answering your phone?"

"I lost it and found it this morning." That was about as good a lie as she had ever told. But it was to protect her mother, she told herself. She changed the subject quickly. "Why is Myles calling me?"

"Carin has been calling him and your cousins."

"Why?"

"She's upset that her grandchildren are interfering

in the lawsuit. She's been calling you, too, but since you lost your phone, she hasn't been able to get you. So be prepared."

Her doorbell rang. "Mom, Myles is here." Or she hoped it was Myles. "I'll talk to you later."

She let Myles in and he stopped short. "What happened to you?"

"I fell."

Myles burst out laughing. "I believe that. You've always been a little clumsy."

"I have not."

"Remember that time you fell into the big cactus Mom had? She picked stickers out of your butt for a whole afternoon."

"That's because you, Aaron, Damon and Nash were ganging up on me and I lost my footing."

"You were always interfering in what we were doing."

"I had no one to play with and you guys were mean."

He took a seat on the sofa. "We were not. Sometimes we let you play."

She stuck her tongue out at him.

He pointed a finger at her. "That's what you were doing that day. You were sticking your tongue out at us and we tried to make you stop and you fell into the cactus."

She laughed and sat beside him.

"We let you play, remember?"

"Yeah. I'm so grateful." And then she laughed again. They did have good times as kids and most of the time they let her play. But as she got older, things changed. They wanted to meet her friends and she would stick her tongue out and prance away. She found ways to get even.

"Does the hand hurt?" Myles asked.

"Yes."

He put an arm around her shoulders. "I'm sorry, sis. I'm happy to say my clumsy sister has turned into a beautiful young woman."

"Aw. That's so sweet."

"That's me." He grinned.

"Why aren't you at work? Isn't it crucial that you spend almost every moment there?"

"Carin is a pain in my backside. Since I'm a lawyer, she wants me to talk to the judge to see if I can get the case moved up. I told her I have no authority to get the case moved up and the judge wouldn't listen to me anyway. I told her, too, that I didn't want anything to do with the case. She got angry and hung up. Then she started calling our cousins and I'm sure she called you, too. I'm not interested in getting the case moved up."

Lila picked up her phone. "Neither am I. I have seven calls from her."

"That should be a nice conversation when she does get you," Myles said tongue in cheek.

"Yeah, but I'm not having anything to do with the lawsuit."

Myles got to his feet. "Since you're okay, I've got to go to the office. Good luck with Carin."

"She's maniacal about this."

"Unrequited love, I think it's called."

"She can't hurt Dean, but she's putting a big old hurt on his grandchildren and she will be one happy woman if she brings down the other Coltons."

As soon as she closed the door on Myles, her phone rang. She picked it up from the coffee table and stared at the caller ID: Carin Pederson. Showtime. She clicked on.

"Lila, is that you?" Carin asked.

"Yes, it's me."

"Why haven't you answered your phone?"

"I lost it."

"Lost it! You're a grown woman and you should have enough sense to take care of your phone."

Lila took a long breath. "Did you call for a reason?"

"Yes. I want you to stop filling your dad's head with nonsense about the lawsuit."

"I only told him the truth."

"Truth? You don't have a clue about the truth."

"I know that Alfred and Ernest created the patents that are still making money for the family and Heath has taken up the legacy. We have no right to anything they have earned."

"You silly girl. Your grandfather ditched me and my sons for his proper family. He should pay for that. We were discarded like trash."

"But he made sure you lived in luxury, and Dad and Erik never had to work. This is all about revenge and I don't want any part of it."

"I'll remember that when I'm awarded a large sum of money."

Lila laughed. She couldn't help herself. "When have you ever given Myles or me anything?"

"You don't teach children by handing them money every day."

"It wasn't just the money. When Mom finally got the

courage to leave Dad, she needed help for the rent and other things for us. But you refused to help."

"She should have stayed where she was and she wouldn't have had any worries. Men cheat. That's a fact."

"Is that what you did? Stayed where you were so Dean could fund your lavish lifestyle? Blackmail was a good way to keep Dean in line. It worked and…"

The phone went dead in her hand.

She carefully laid her phone on the coffee table. Her nerves were stretched to the max and her hand was throbbing again. Carin had the power to raise her blood pressure and made her view the world a little differently. Through all the bitterness and resentment they'd endured because of their grandmother, Lila, Myles, Aaron, Damon and Nash turned out to be good human beings. And they all believed in love, home and family. Myles, Aaron and Damon had found their special person to spend the rest of their lives with. Lila had, too, but it was only temporary.

Chapter Ten

Carter saw an SUV drive away from Lila's town house. He didn't recognize the man. Maybe it was someone from her family. He hadn't met anyone in her family, and she hadn't met anyone in his. Of course, he had only his mother and father. He had no idea why he was thinking that, but it had been nice the last couple of days spending time with Lila and being in one place. He'd never really thought about it before because he liked being on the road. Now the idea was waning.

He carried grocery bags into the house and saw Lila sitting on the sofa, her face creased into a frown.

She quickly stood. "Now that you're back, I'm going upstairs to take a shower and get dressed."

He followed her upstairs to see if she needed anything. She shrugged out of her bathrobe and he hurried to help. The plastic bag lay on the vanity and he reached for it, securing it to her right hand with a rubber band. "How's that?"

"Should I raise my right hand?" she asked with a twinkle in her eye.

"Yes." He tried not to smile and failed. "You're not going to let me forget that, are you?"

"No, because you blush so nicely."

He changed the subject. "I saw someone leaving when I drove up and you looked a little upset."

"It was Myles, but he didn't upset me. My grandmother called and told me to stop talking to my dad and to stop interfering in the lawsuit. She knows how to push my buttons."

"I can see." Her left hand was gripped into a tight fist and the beautiful lines of her face were clenched into a one-size-fits-all frown. He took her into his arms. "Have a nice shower and I'm going down to start lunch. Do you need anything?"

"For you to stop worrying and hovering over me. That's my mother's job."

He held up his hands and backed away. He hurried downstairs to start lunch. Lila was in a cantankerous mood. Most people were when they didn't feel good. When Neil had prostate cancer, no one could get along with him, not even Marla. He seemed to take his bad moods out on her. Once he found out he was going to be okay, his moods changed drastically. He was back to being his old self. It was mind changing when you were perfectly healthy one day and the next you needed help.

Since the two Colton families were at odds, he knew Lila was worried about that, too. She was probably still worried about the arson charge and how to replace everything that had been destroyed. He hadn't even had a chance to talk to her about Walter Fox. That would cheer her up, and he intended to talk to her just as soon as he could.

He went to the internet to see if he could find a chicken noodle soup recipe. Wow! There were so many places to get recipes. He chose a simple one and washed and dried the chicken and then found a big pot to put it in. It surprised him that she would have a big pot. He put in the designated amount of water and then washed the vegetables and cut them up. As he dumped everything into the pot, he heard her coming downstairs. He wiped his hands on a towel and just stared. She was completely different from earlier. Her hand was still bandaged, but the bad mood was gone and her eyes lit up with a happy-to-be-alive gleam.

"What a transformation."

Her hair was up and held in place with colorful combs. In skinny jeans and a white long-sleeved knit top, she looked fresh and happy.

"I feel better, too. I had to put all the gloom and doom behind me."

He frowned.

"What?"

"You put up your hair."

"It keeps it out of my face and it's been annoying me." She walked into the kitchen to see what was in the pot. "You put it all together."

"Yeah. Is that wrong?"

"The chicken is supposed to cook longer."

"No problem." He scooped the veggies into a bowl. "When do I put these in?" He held up the jar of tiny squares of bouillon.

"Not yet."

He put the lid on the chicken. "Good. I need to talk to you."

"About what?"

He took her arm and led her to the sofa. "It's nothing bad. With everything that was going on, I forgot to tell you what happened with Tony yesterday."

She got comfortable and laid the lower part of her arm on a pillow. He told her everything that had transpired with Tony. "The ADA is going to make a deal with him."

"A deal?"

"By the tone of your voice, I can see you don't like that. I didn't at first, either, but the ADA pointed out that he's only been arrested once and he's not a violent man. So I talked to Tony and we made a deal. He gave me the name of the man who was paying him to paint the forgeries. And I'll work with the ADA to get him a lower sentence."

Her eyes grew big. "He gave you the name?"

Carter nodded. "It wasn't a big surprise."

Her eyebrows drew together. "You knew?"

"I didn't really know, but I had a feeling Walter Fox was involved."

"Walter Fox is paying Tony to paint the forgeries?" She shook her head. "That doesn't make sense. Why would he destroy the Tinsley paintings?"

"I don't have an answer for that. All I can think of is that he got wind that he was being investigated and he wanted to destroy everything that my company could get their hands on. I don't have anything else, but I intend to. I will talk to Richards after lunch while you're resting."

She shook her finger at him. "Oh, no! I'm going with you."

"Lila—"

"He destroyed more than the Tinsley paintings.

He destroyed my whole gallery and I have a right to face him."

"You're going to be stubborn about this, aren't you?"

She leaned over and whispered, "Yes, and I want to know why he did it."

"Money," Carter told her. "Everything is about money. Getting the short end of the stick on the Tinsley estate meant he had to cut back on his lifestyle. I'm going to do some more checking into his background. There has to be a connection between Fox and Rossini. I'm only guessing here. That's why I want to talk to Richards. He may have more background information."

"But will he give it to you? Richards is not my number one fan."

"Well, he hasn't come up with anything and he might be looking for a little help. I'm sure the insurance companies are pushing for answers, too."

A bubbling sound came from the kitchen and Carter got out. "I better check on the chicken."

"I have to change the bandage on my hand this morning. Are you willing to help?"

"I have to do it if we're going to catch criminals together," he said with a big grin. "Do you have the supplies or do I need to go get them?"

"A white pharmacy bag is on the counter."

"Got it. Where are the scissors?"

"First drawer near the pantry."

"Got it." He gathered all the goodies and went back into the living room. "Do you need a pain pill for this?"

"Probably." She looked at the clock on the wall. "It's not even nine yet."

"No. We got up early. Does that make a difference?"

"Yes. I took the pill at six and I have to wait four hours."

"Okay, we'll wait until ten."

In the meantime, they talked about Fox and his involvement with Tinsley and maybe the fire. Her eyes lit up with hope that they might connect Fox to the fire as well as the forgery.

"Tony seems scared of Fox and that got me to thinking. What has Fox done that Tony knows about that scares him? There has to be some answers out there and we're going to find them."

"How much time do you have? I mean, you usually leave after an investigation."

He reached over and kissed her cheek. "I'm not quite through investigating yet." Leaving was constantly on his mind and it wasn't like before. He wasn't anxious to see the next city. He wanted to stay in Chicago with Lila. It would work out in time, he told himself. Right now, finding answers was the main goal.

He got to his feet. "I'll check the soup and then we'll get started on your hand. It's almost ten." He gave her a pill and sat beside her, removing the gauze. When he got down to the palm, he didn't want to jerk it off, so he left a piece. "I'm afraid that might be stuck and really hurt when I pull it off."

"There's a lot of stuff in the bag. Check and see if he gave us anything for that."

He pulled out the contents. "Numbing cream, a box of gloves, sterile water, gauze, tape, antibiotic cream and instructions. We have to pour about a cup of sterile water over your hand to clean it and then add antibiotic cream and numbing cream."

He looked into her eyes. "Ready?"

She nodded and they walked to the sink and did as the instructions had said. She gritted her teeth and leaned on him until it was finished.

"Oh, the numbing cream is wonderful. The doctor said to leave the bandage off for about thirty minutes and to flex my fingers and to move my shoulder."

While she walked around flexing her fingers and moving her arm, he finished working on the soup. The chicken was almost done. He held up the bouillon cubes.

"Ready?"

She gave a thumbs-up and he dropped the cubes in and stirred. "Taste test."

"Oh, that's good." She licked the spoon. "Noodle time."

It wasn't long before he had it on the table. Lila had a hard time eating with her left hand, but it didn't take her long to get the hang of it. Afterward, she sat on the sofa and he cleaned up the kitchen. They had plenty of soup left for later. He turned around and saw she was asleep. It gave him time to call Richards.

"What can I do for you, Mr. Finch?"

"I'd like to talk to you for a few minutes."

"I'm very busy at this time. Unless this is urgent, I'd prefer to do it later."

"It's urgent. I have new information that you could use."

There was a pause. "I can see you in about thirty minutes. That's all the time I can spare."

"I'll be there."

"Where?" Lila stood behind him, pinning up her hair that had come down. Elegant movements with her left hand and arm drew his attention. Everything about her was elegant.

He cleared his throat. "Richards's office." He didn't even try to stop her. That would just bring on another argument, and he was learning that arguing with Lila wasn't something he enjoyed.

"Oh. I'll grab my purse, freshen up and be right with you."

He removed the towel he had tucked into his jeans while he'd cooked. The interview could prove vital to the investigation. Richards had to be ready to listen and Carter wasn't sure he was ready yet. It was Richards's investigation and Carter had stuck his nose in once. Would he be willing to listen a second time?

THANKS FOR NOT making a fuss." Lila had intended to come whether he did or not, but it was nice not to have to fight the battle beforehand.

"Could you let me do the talking?"

She rested her hand on his shoulder. "If you're a good boy."

He laughed and it filled the car with a happy mood, and that was what she wanted to feel right now. A little happiness. A little calm. And a whole lot of love.

Her arm was tucked neatly into the sling and her hand wasn't throbbing as much. She was ready to talk to Inspector Richards. Or at least let Carter do most of the talking. He knew more about the situation than she did. It was nice to lean on someone.

He took her hand as they walked up to the big door that housed the arson experts and held it open for her. They walked to Richards's office and he got to his feet.

"Ms. Colton, I didn't know you were coming." The sarcastic tone triggered her anger. She wanted to slap that sly grin off his face, but she maintained her composure. "Have a seat."

"I tend to show up every now and then." She responded with a wisecrack, but he didn't seem to notice.

But he noticed her arm. "Were you in an accident?"

"That's part of what we wanted to talk about." Carter pulled up a chair.

A frown stretched all the way to his eyes. "If you got hurt moving stuff out of the gallery, there's nothing the fire department can do money-wise and little else."

"She's not saying that." Carter jumped in. "You asked and she told you, and she's not asking for anything."

Richards leaned back in his chair. "Then why are you here with Ms. Colton?"

"You know that I was here checking the Tinsley paintings to see if they were forgeries."

"Yes. I know all of that."

"Well, they are. Tony Martell was arrested for the forgeries and he's in a jail cell here in Chicago. He had some interesting things to say."

"Like what?"

"He wanted a deal, but before he could get one, he had to tell me who had paid him to paint the forgeries. He wasn't eager to do that. I had to apply pressure. In the end, he gave it up, and I thought you might be interested in who it was."

"What has this got to do with the gallery fire?"

"That's what I'm trying to figure out and I thought you might be able to help."

Richards leaned forward. "You want information, don't you?"

Carter stood, his back ramrod straight. "I don't need to put up with your attitude, Richards. I can go over your head and give someone else the credit for solving the arson. That's what I believe this information will do." He turned to leave the room and Lila was immediately on her feet.

"No, wait a minute." Richards was on his feet, too. "I didn't know you had a hair-trigger temper. I didn't say I wouldn't help you."

"Then lose the attitude, and you were disrespectful to Ms. Colton. She doesn't deserve that."

"My apologies, Ms. Colton."

Lila eased back into her chair. "Thank you." She didn't say what was rolling around in her head because her mother had raised her to be polite.

Taking his seat, Carter told him about the arrest of Martell. "That's how Lila hurt her hand. I'm going to visit him later today and try to get more information out of him. I asked about the fire and he said he didn't know anything about it. He's not into that and I believed him."

"But you believe he knows who is?"

"I'm hoping he can point me in the right direction."

"So what do you need from me?" Richards resumed his seat.

"Information on Rossini. Is he in debt? And a little

about his background, like where he spends his time. His hobbies."

Richards picked up a pencil and scribbled something on a pad. "But first, you tell me who was paying the forger."

"Walter Fox."

Richards threw the pencil on the desk. "Come on— Fox? Tinsley's agent? Why would he set fire to paintings that he would profit from?"

"Think, Richards."

"They were forgeries?"

"Yes. And he must have found out that my company was investigating him and that he could go to prison. He'd do anything to stop that, and destroying the paintings was a way no one would ever know."

"And you think Rossini is in on this?"

"Yes. I just have to connect them in some way."

Richards scooted back in his chair, leaning on one arm as he thought things over. "Good luck with that. I don't have anything that ties Rossini to Fox. Rossini is a rich man. He took the real-estate business over from his father-in-law. He owns several strip malls, hotels, apartments and houses all over Chicago. If he gets in trouble financially, he just sells something and he's back doing business again. He knows how the system works and I don't think you'll be able to get anything on him. He also knows how to cover his tracks. The only thing we had on him was that he liked to party and gamble and has a mistress living in one of his hotel suites, but we got nowhere with that."

"Gamble? Poker?"

"Yes. There's a group of rich gentlemen in Chicago who have a high-stakes get-together about twice a month, and Vice has been trying to catch them for years. I'm sure Rossini is one of those gentlemen."

Carter leaned over and pushed the tablet closer to Richards. "Write down any others who might be a member of that group and I'll take it from there."

Richards picked up the pencil. "This is just a guess. You won't be able to use it in court."

"I'm just fishing right now. Something has to connect Rossini with Fox."

Richards began to write. "As I told you, good luck. I've been on this case since the fire happened, and I've come up with nothing and neither has my team. We're all trained professionals."

"The problem is, Richards, you keep looking at the same old thing and this arson goes beyond that. It has to do with money. I know, you said Rossini is loaded, but everyone has a weakness. And somehow that gallery was a weak spot for Rossini." Carter stood and ripped the page off the pad. "I'll be in touch." At the door, Carter turned back. "Would it be possible to get a listing of all the properties Rossini owns in Chicago?"

"You're asking for a lot, Mr. Finch, and something better pop from all of this or your name will be mud in Chicago."

"I'm well aware I'm putting my name on the line here, but..."

"Where do you want me to send the file?"

Carter wrote his email address on the pad. "Thank you, Richards."

"Now I have a question for you."

"Shoot."

"What's the deal with Fox? Has he been arrested?"

"I have a tail on him right now, waiting to see what he does. If he tries to leave Chicago, he'll be arrested."

"It's probably best to get more than Martell's word."

"That's what I was thinking. Talk to you later."

"Hope your hand gets better," Richards called to Lila.

Lila didn't respond as they walked out of the office and through the big doors. All the while, Carter was reading the gamblers' list.

"Anything interesting?"

"Yeah. I figured out how Fox found Tony."

She looked over his arm at the list. "How?"

"Donald Sapp's name is on here and I'm guessing that he told Fox at a poker game about his tenant in the basement. That was all it took. Of course, I have no way to prove it. I think I'll just have to talk to Mr. Sapp to see what he has to say. But first, I have to get over to the jail." He folded the list and stuffed it in his pocket.

"Wait. I didn't get to read all the names. I'm from Chicago, so I should know most of them."

"There's no need for you to look at the list. I got this."

She grabbed it out of his pocket. "What are you hiding from me?"

"Lila, I'm just trying to protect you."

"Well, don't. I can do that all by myself." Her eyes quickly scanned the names and froze on one near the bottom. Axel Colton. She stopped walking and just stared at the name. Where would her father get money for high-stakes poker games? Carin, of course. If he begged enough, she would give in.

She crammed the list into his pocket. "Stop keeping secrets from me, even when it includes my family."

"I wasn't going to keep it a secret. I was just trying to figure out how to tell you."

"Don't treat me as if I'm fragile." She opened the passenger door and got in, slamming the door so hard it jarred her arm.

Carter crawled in beside her, trying to straighten out the list she'd managed to wrinkle. With the list on his thigh, he painstakingly stroked out the wrinkles. As she watched, laughter bubbled up inside her. She was feeling anything but humor. It was his calm demeanor. Nothing ever seemed to shake him.

"Do you ever get angry?"

"I try not to." He placed the list on the console. "I learned that as a kid. If I got angry about something, I was always punished by having to stay in my room. And I hated that. Learning to control your emotions is not an easy thing."

"You'll have to teach me. I can be wide-eyed and crazy sometimes, and I'm almost positive I get that from my grandmother's side."

He smiled. "I like you wild-eyed and crazy. It makes me realize what I'm missing in life."

"What? Someone to light your fire?"

"Exactly." He glanced at her. "Do you want to talk about your father?"

"I don't know what to say. I had no idea he had money to gamble. I know he did when I was younger, but Carin pulled the money strings on him and he had to cut back. Now he's playing in the high-stakes games.

You know, I'm wondering why Richards didn't mention his name. Surely he knows Axel is my father."

"I was thinking that, too."

"Do you think Richards is playing us?"

"I doubt it, but anything is possible."

He pulled into a parking garage of a stark-looking building. The sign read Cook County Jail. "Sorry, you can't go in, but I'll only be a few minutes. Keep the doors locked."

Lila watched as he walked away to a door farther down. She hadn't been inside a jail cell before and she didn't want to start now. She leaned her head back against the car seat and thought about everything that was happening, especially with her father. She was tired of agonizing over their father-daughter relationship. The truth was, they didn't have one. To get the answers she needed, she had to talk to him. She pulled her phone out of her purse.

"Lila, you again? This is very unusual."

"I have a few questions I hope you'll answer."

"I'm not talking about the lawsuit. Mom had a hissy fit when I told her what you'd said. I'm going along with what she wants and that's it."

"It's not about the lawsuit. Do you know Walter Fox or Lou Rossini?"

"Where did that question come from?"

"Are you gambling again? Does Carin know?"

"This is none of your business."

"Do you know them? I already know that you do, so don't try to lie."

"All right, I know them and have attended a few games when Mom supplies the money. Fox even got some original artwork for Mom and she was happy about that."

"Carin bought artwork from Fox?"

"Yeah. That's what he does. Mom liked him, so she didn't complain about giving me money to gamble."

"Does she know that Fox sells forgeries?"

"No, he doesn't. Why are you making up all this stuff?"

Lila closed her eyes and wondered just how insane her family was.

"You do know the fire is being investigated and they've called it arson. Are you aware of that? Are you aware the police and the arson teams are involved? Someone is going to get arrested for the crime. If you know anything, please tell me."

"My life is none of your business. Stay out of it, just like Mom told you."

Her father clicked off before she could say another word, and she sat there with the phone in her hand, not knowing what to do.

Could her father be involved in the arson?

Would he set fire to her place of business for money?

Chapter Eleven

Carter signed in after they checked his credentials. An officer showed him to an interview room. The place had the bare essentials: a table, two chairs and a legal pad on the table. The floor was bare concrete. No frills here.

Tony was brought in dressed in jail attire and handcuffed. "Mr. Finch, have you gotten me a deal?" He slid into a chair.

Tony had a one-track mind. "The ADA will be contacting your lawyer appointed by the court, and then you'll meet and she will lay out the deal for you. You will agree to it or not, but I'd advise you to take it."

"I intend to. Why are you here?"

"I have more questions."

His shoulders sank. "Oh, man. I don't know anything else."

Tony wasn't in a cooperative mood, so Carter had to give him a little incentive. "I know how Fox found you."

"How?" Tony sat up straight in his chair. Carter had his attention.

"Did Sapp know you had a record and was convicted of forgery?"

Tony hung his head. "Wendy told him and talked him into letting me stay at the apartment until I could find a job."

"Who's Wendy?"

"She's my girlfriend's mother."

"Is she the elderly lady who rents the apartment?"

Tony laughed. "Hell, no. She's not even fifty. She had my girlfriend when she was seventeen."

That was interesting. Why would Sapp lie about something like that? Why was he afraid of the truth? And what was the truth?

"So Sapp and Wendy are seeing each other?"

"If you want to call it that. She works in a bar, serving drinks. That's how she and Sapp met. She was looking for a place to stay and Sapp had one. I'm not sure she even pays rent, but I'm not asking as long as she lets me stay there."

This had nothing to do with the information Carter was looking for. It just proved that everyone had dirty little secrets.

"Sapp was one of Fox's gambling buddies. That's how they know each other. And when Fox was looking for a forger, Sapp found him one."

"That son of a…"

"I have another question."

"Man, you're full of questions and I don't even know what kind of deal I'm getting."

"I don't know what it is, either, but trust me, it will be better than going to trial. As soon as I find out, I'll let you know. Just be patient."

"Yeah." Tony was anything but patient. With the

ADA's caseload, Carter figured she'd get it off her plate real soon, so Tony had to hang in there.

"When I first talked to you about a deal, you were afraid of Fox. Is he violent?"

"I don't guess it matters now."

"No. You're both going to jail." Carter waited for a second and then asked, "Did he ever threaten you?"

"He always comes to pick up a painting when no one is at home. One day he asked if I would carry the painting to the rental. I noticed there was a fresh scar on his neck, which I could barely see 'cause he's always dressed in a three-piece suit with a bow tie and a fedora. I casually asked if he hurt himself and he replied that a guy owed him money and thought he could convince Fox otherwise. He then gave a funny laugh and said that man is now in the Chicago River, and if I ever went to the cops, I would join him. He had this evil look in his eyes and I knew he meant it."

Carter doubted if Fox had ever killed anyone. It was just a way to keep Tony in line. He got to his feet. "If you think of anything else, have someone call me."

The clanging of metal doors followed him out of the building. He slid into the driver's seat and placed his briefcase in the back. With a look at Lila's face, he knew she was upset about something.

"What's up?"

"I talked to my father."

"Why do you put yourself through that?"

"I had to know about his part in the gambling."

"Did you find out anything?"

"Not really. He admitted to the gambling and told me it was none of my business. He also said that my grandmother supplies him the money to gamble. And, get this, Fox has sold my grandmother paintings for her home."

"Let's see if we can put this puzzle together. It's getting very muddled every time we check something. And yet no one has a clear motive. Sapp's involvement is only that he found Tony for Fox. Other than that, I don't think he has anything to do with the fire."

"Does my father?"

Her eyes begged for an honest answer and he didn't have one, so he went with his gut feeling. "From what you've told me about him, I don't think he has the guts for something like this. And what would he gain? If Rossini offered to pay him, I still think he couldn't do it. He just doesn't have the guts to face much of anything in his life, especially his own children."

It was after five when they walked through the front door of the town house. "I'll put the soup on the burner while you check your laptop for Richards's files. We'll look at them after dinner."

"Okay. They're here." Carter loved the way they worked together so well. It wasn't long before they had the soup on the table. Lila made coffee and it was a peaceful time before they started sorting through all the information Richards had sent. At least he was cooperating.

Lila took a pain pill and he didn't say anything. Since they had a lot of work to do, he wanted her to be as pain-free as possible. He really wanted her to rest for a while, but he knew without asking that wasn't going to fly.

Carter brought his laptop to the table and sent all

the files to Lila's computer. They started to go through them. "Richards was right. Rossini owns a lot of real estate."

"My gallery was just a drop in his pocket."

They were deep in when the doorbell rang. Lila jumped up to get it. "Faith," she exclaimed, and Carter got up and made his way to the door. He knew Faith was her sister-in-law.

A beautiful redhead stood in the doorway with a dark-haired little boy standing in front of her. "I'm sorry. I didn't know you had company."

"Don't be silly," Lila told her. "This is Carter and we're sorting through some papers about the fire."

"It's nice to meet you," she said, and he shook her hand. She bent down to her son. "And this is Jackson. We heard Lila hurt her hand and we came by to bring her some goodies to make her feel better."

The little boy held up a bag in one hand; a toy truck was in the other. He handed the bag to Lila. "For you. You got a boo-boo."

Lila leaned down and kissed his cheek. "Thank you, Jackson."

"They're chocolate chip just like you like and I do, too."

Lila took the bag. "Come in and have a cup of coffee."

"No, we better go."

"I want a cookie," Jackson muttered.

Carter knew the hesitation was about him. "Please, come in and have a cup of coffee. I'll get it while you visit." He took the bag from Lila.

He didn't realize the little boy had followed him until he almost tripped over him.

"What's your name?" Jackson asked.

"Carter." He found a decorative plate for the cookies.

"My name is Jackson and I'm four years old."

Carter had never been around children and he had no idea what to say to the boy. Luckily, he didn't have to. The little boy kept talking.

"Can you throw a ball? My daddy can, but he's not home too much."

Carter handed him the plate of cookies. "Can you carry this into the living room?"

"Sure. I'm a big boy."

"Yes, you are." Carter followed with the coffee.

"Thank you," Lila said with a smile. It was clear she liked Faith and enjoyed talking to her.

He handed both women a cup. "Lila was just telling me what you do for a living," Faith said. "That sounds interesting and fun to be able to travel the world."

"Can I please have something to drink?" Jackson asked.

"How about milk or a soda?"

"Milk," Faith answered for him.

"Mommy—"

"Soda has caffeine and it will keep you up all night, so the answer is still no."

Jackson followed him into the kitchen to get the milk. He drank about half of the glass and set it on the counter. "Want to play with my truck? It's real neat."

"Uh…" He really didn't want to play with the truck, but he couldn't tell the little boy that. From the few minutes he had talked to him, he could see his father's absence was hard on the boy. At least Carter's parents had always gotten along. His parents argued like all parents, but he'd never feared that one day they might get a divorce and he might have to go live with one of them. That had to be hard for a four-year-old.

"Carter, where are you?"

He looked around and saw the boy was at the top of the stairs. "Let's play. The truck's coming to you. Don't let it have an accident."

Carter was totally confused, but he was sure Jackson would show him the way. The boy gave the truck a push and it came flying down the stairs and landed in about eight pieces at Carter's feet.

Jackson hurried down the stairs and sat on the bottom step. "Oh, no, we had an accident. Now we have to fix the truck."

Carter sat beside him on the step and started putting the wheels back on the truck, then a hood, then a tailgate, then a motor...

"Jackson, let's go," Faith said.

"We're working on the truck."

"We have to go. Lila has to rest."

Carter handed Jackson the truck all back together. "That is a really neat truck."

"Yeah. Can I come play sometimes?"

"Jackson! Do not invite yourself."

"Mom—"

"Jackson."

"Okay. Okay." He ran into the kitchen and finished drinking his milk. Then he ran into the living room for another cookie and met his mother and Lila at the door.

Jackson probably knew his way around his mother, and that last "Jackson" must have been it. The kid was fun to be around. Since he'd never been around kids, he didn't see them in his future. Nor did he see a wife or a home. That was just the way he'd thought since graduating high school. He would be the bachelor who had gotten away and that suited him fine. Back then.

Lila squatted and hugged Jackson. "Thank you for the cookies. That was so sweet of you."

Jackson then ran to him, stuffing the cookie in his mouth before Faith could notice. "Bye, Carter," he mumbled around a mouthful of cookie.

Did he shake his hand or just say bye? Good heavens! It couldn't be that hard.

He reached down and picked up Jackson. "It was nice to meet you and your mother, and I hope you can come by again."

"See, Mommy?" Jackson glanced at his mother and then he kissed Carter's cheek. "Bye."

Carter cleared his throat. "B-ye," he managed.

Lila closed the door after them and patted Carter's chest. "You look a little shell-shocked."

"I've never been around children and it was nice."

"Didn't you say Neil had two daughters?"

He picked up coffee cups from the table and Lila took cookies to the kitchen. "Yes, but the only time I really spent with them was on holidays. And they're in college now." As Carter put cups in the dishwasher, the doorbell rang again.

"Jackson must've forgotten something." Lila headed for the door.

"Mom!"

Carter almost dropped a cup. He juggled it for a second and then caught it in time. Her mother and stepfather were here. He wasn't usually a nervous person, but today his nerves were taking a hit for stability. Lila was grown and so was he. What was the nervousness about?

A woman of medium height with graying brown hair and a big smile walked into the kitchen carrying a big pot. "Oh, Lila, why didn't you tell me you had company?"

"Mom and Rick, this is Carter, the man who was in the fire with me. We're working on some information that might help catch the arsonist."

Her mom set the pot on the stove. "Nice to meet you, Carter. When my baby is sick, all she wants to eat is chicken noodle soup, so I made her some." She turned to Lila. "How are you, baby?"

"I'm fine." She held up her hand. "It's not throbbing as bad as it was before."

Rick walked up to Carter and shook his hand. "Are they close to solving this thing?"

"Lila and I are searching for something that might help the arson investigators. It just takes one little thing to point us in the right direction."

"Well, hon, let's go and let these two get back to work."

Lila hugged her parents at the door and Rick shook his hand again. Lila's mother hugged him until he thought he was going to pass out from lack of air. Her mother was a hugger.

"Call if you need anything." Rick shouted as Lila closed the door.

"You didn't tell them."

"I didn't want to hurt their feelings. Besides, I love chicken noodle soup and I'll be eating it for about a week."

They laughed and sat at the table, getting back to work. Before Carter could open a folder, the doorbell rang again.

"How many family members do you have?"

"Too many right now," she called over her shoulder. "Nash. Come in."

"No, no. I just saw your parents leaving and I was out this way and wanted to stop and see how you were doing. I told the brothers I would check in. Oh…" He noticed Carter in the kitchen doorway.

"This is Carter, the guy who saved our butts from the fire. And this is my cousin Nash, the architect."

They shook hands. The guy was well over six feet tall with dark blond hair and hazel eyes. He and Lila looked about the same age and they must have played together as kids. It had to be nice to have those kinds of memories.

"I really can't stay. I'm looking at an old house out this way to see if it can be restored, and I told Aaron and Damon that I would look in to see if you were okay or needed cheering up."

"I just fell and I'm fine, but thanks for thinking of me."

"It's hard to imagine sometimes that someone who is so beautiful and graceful can be a klutz."

"Don't start…"

He put an arm around her waist and kissed her forehead. "Love you. Gotta run. I'll spread the news that you're okay. Nice to meet you, Carter." In a flash, he was out the door.

Carter stared at her serene face. She loved her family and she loved that they thought of her. That was what life was about, he'd heard. Love, family and home. He could see in her eyes why it meant so much to have someone there for you. If he got sick, he would be on his own with no one to make him chicken soup. Part of him had always known that and he was comfortable in that skin. Why was he now having doubts and second thoughts and insecurities? That wasn't him.

"Want to chance it?" She walked toward the table. "I think that's the last of my loving family."

Before Carter could sit, his phone buzzed. "My turn." He pulled his cell out of his pocket. "Neil," he mouthed and walked into the living room to talk.

"The painting in Milan was a forgery," Neil said. "The police were waiting for the man when he came in to get his money. Marla wants to spend a little more time here, so I won't be coming home for about a week. I got a call about a painting in London that is suspected to be a forgery. I haven't had time to go over all the details, but when I do, you'll be going to London."

"Oh, London, okay."

"Did everything go smoothly with Martell?" Neil asked.

"Yes. They're working out the details and he'll go straight to prison."

"Have the authorities arrested Fox?"

"No, but the police are keeping a tail on him in case he's involved with the fire. We thought that since Tony was in jail, Fox would bolt. So far he's staying quiet. He may not even know Tony has been arrested."

"Carter, the fire doesn't concern us. Arrest Fox and get it over with."

"It concerns me." His voice grew rigid.

"How are things with the Colton woman?"

This was what Carter hated: the questioning. Neil was an expert at it. "Listen, Neil, I have to go. Just let me know when you're coming home or when you get details about the London painting."

He turned to see Lila's eyes on him. "Are you leaving?"

"Not just yet." He tried to take the hurt from her eyes but failed. They both knew his time was almost up.

"You're going to London?"

"In about a week." He didn't lie, but honesty came with the price of hurting her. He tapped his laptop on the table, wanting to think about something else. "There's so much information here that it will take forever to get through it. I think our best bet would be to talk to the main players."

"Like?"

"Fox, Rossini, Sapp or any name that is on a file. I have this gut feeling that something was missed."

Lila went through the titles of files on her screen. "Looks like Richards sent us everything he has."

Carter had the same thing on his laptop. "Yeah, everything. Even Savon is on here."

"She said they interviewed her and that they even checked out her story with the boyfriend. They even confirmed it with security cameras at the restaurant.

Richards and his team did a thorough job. I just don't know what they could have missed." She got up and went to the counter for a pain pill.

What was he thinking, keeping her up this late? He gently put his arm around her waist. "Bedtime. We're not going to argue about this. You need some rest and we'll start over tomorrow."

She leaned against him. "I'm not going to argue. I am feeling a little tired."

They went up the stairs and Lila was more than ready to go to bed. He tucked her in. "Need anything?"

She shook her head and went to sleep.

Carter wasn't ready for bed, so he went back downstairs to go through the files again, hoping something would catch his eye. He kept coming back to the same file. Tanya Wilcox, Rossini's mistress. She lived in a suite at a hotel that Rossini owned near downtown. She'd been there for about two years, and what stood out to him was Tanya and Wendy worked at the same bar. If they had millionaire boyfriends, why did they have to work?

He ran his hands up his face and stretched. Every time he kept digging, he found information that didn't make sense. Like the Wendy/Tanya situation. He scrolled down the information, looking for the owner of the club. And there it was in black and white. Lou Rossini. Once again, the thought visited his mind: Rossini had no motive to burn down the gallery for money. The bar was very profitable.

He went to bed to give his eyes a rest, hoping something would come together in his head. But all he was accomplishing was pointing the finger more and more at Lila.

Chapter Twelve

When Lila woke up, the room was dark and quiet. He wouldn't leave without telling her. Then she heard running water and felt a moment of relief. She sat up and saw it: a glass of water and a pain pill. He was the sweetest guy. She quickly took the pill and headed for the shower.

As she was drying herself, she noticed she had a message on her phone. Darn! She had a doctor's appointment this morning with her primary care doctor. She told Carter that as she poured a cup of coffee.

"Okay." He gave her a once-over. "You're looking perky this morning."

"I am perky." She gave him a long, lingering kiss. "But I'm mad, too, because you didn't wake me up last night when you came to bed."

"You needed the rest."

She glanced at the bar. "Eggs? Where did we get eggs?"

"I bought them yesterday when I went grocery shopping. Eggs, toast and coffee." He pulled out a bar stool. "Have a seat."

"I don't have long. My appointment's at nine. I

didn't notice it until this morning, and Savon wants me to meet her for lunch to view new locations for my business."

"I'll go with you."

"No. You'll be bored sitting in a doctor's office, and viewing vacant buildings."

"Lila…"

"I'm fine, Carter."

"Okay. I have some things I want to do this morning." He told her about Rossini's and Sapp's mistresses.

"That's odd. It could be very simple, though. If Rossini owns the club, he probably gets to choose the girls who work in there and probably shared some comments with Sapp."

"It's probably not that simple."

She carried her plate and cup to the sink. "I've got to go and I'll call you when I'm free."

"Okay. Go ahead. I've got the dishes."

She wanted to shout "I love you" but refrained from doing so. There was so much she wanted to say to him, but she had to choose her words wisely. Within the week, he would be leaving, and as she'd said so many times to herself, she had to be prepared and she had to be ready to handle the gallery fire. Carter was working very hard to solve it and she had faith in him.

At exactly nine o'clock, she walked into the doctor's office and then waited forty-five minutes for him to see her. He cleaned her palm again and said everything looked great. He put very little gauze back on and mostly for protection. In a couple of days, she could take it off completely. She hurried to meet Savon. A Realtor showed them three places. The first two were lacking in size and the third one was very expensive. It once had been a jewelry store that had gone bankrupt. It had a big safe, which was on the plus side, and it would need very little renovation. It was in the updated North Center and Lila liked it, but she couldn't afford it, especially since the insurance people were dragging their feet.

"What do you think?" Savon asked.

"It's nice, but unaffordable for us."

"I knew you would say that. I was hoping Carter could find the arsonist and put us back in business."

"Keep dreaming. He's working on it, but there doesn't seem to be any luck coming our way. Carter says there's something that will connect everything. We just have to find it. I keep waiting and hoping. The insurance money will make a difference in what I decide."

Savon hugged her. "How about margaritas for lunch?"

"Oh, do you mind if Carter joins us?"

She shook her head. "I don't do well as a third party, especially when I'm number three. Have a good time. I'll keep going over the numbers and the Realtor will call if anything else comes up."

"Thank you."

In the car, she called Carter, but there was no answer. She left a quick text. I'm going home. Call me.

Home was such a nice word, big, inclusive and happy. It filled every part of her, and she had only a few days to enjoy that feeling of home.

Carter made it to Wendy Olson's apartment by nine. Sapp's Cadillac was parked outside at the curb. As if by magic, Sapp and Wendy came out. She had long blond hair, and a satin robe was wrapped around her curvy body. She definitely was not elderly. They kissed at the car and Sapp drove away. Carter followed him to a large real-estate office in northeast Chicago. The two-story brick structure looked more like a house than an office.

He watched the clock on the dashboard, and after a few minutes, he went inside and asked to see Mr. Sapp. His assistant said he needed an appointment.

"Thank you," he replied and walked straight into Sapp's office.

"Hey, you can't…" The assistant's high heels made *tap-tap* sounds on the hardwood floors as she followed him. They were met by Sapp.

"I've got it," he said to the woman and closed the door.

Carter sat in a leather chair across from Sapp's desk. "I don't like it when people lie to me."

"Lie? I haven't lied to you. You got Tony, didn't you?"

"Wendy Olson was harboring a criminal and you knew about it and you encouraged him to continue his criminal activity after his release from prison. The ADA will have a few more charges to tack onto the indictment, which would include you and Ms. Olson. You know, the elderly woman who rents from you."

"Okay. I upped her age because my wife takes care of the books. If she suspected Wendy was pretty and younger, she'd be on my case. We've been through that before." Sapp got to his feet in a nervous gesture. "I had nothing to do with the fire. I allowed Tony to stay at the apartment because he was dating Wendy's daughter. How was I to know about his past?"

Carter stood. "Walter Fox. Does the name sound familiar?" He held up a hand. "And before you lie, I already know the truth."

"Listen—"

"I'd advise you to get a lawyer. You pointed Walter Fox in the right direction when he was looking for a forger. You didn't care that it was illegal. You just wanted him to start making money so he and his girlfriend could move out."

"You're just making this up. You can't prove that I know Walter Fox."

"Poker games." Carter swung toward the door. "Get a lawyer, Sapp. You're going to need one."

From there he went to the hotel where Rossini's mistress, Tanya Wilcox, lived. The place wasn't far from downtown and had a lively business. He found a parking space in the garage and made his way to the entrance. A valet tried to take his briefcase, but he declined.

The foyer was huge with glass and stainless steel and lighting that made visitors stop and stare. It was a swanky place. There were people at the checkout and the check-in counter. He chose the check-in one because the guy was young and he might be a little more agreeable.

"Good morning." He gave him his best smile.

"What can I do for you?"

"I'm looking for Tanya Wilcox. She said she lived here."

The guy looked to the other employees who were

busy working. "I'm sorry. I can't give you any information. You have to contact her yourself."

Damn! He got a smart one. Carter leaned in closer. "Can you at least tell me what floor she's on? I would like to surprise her."

"I'm sorry. I can't help you." He typed something into the computer and whispered, "All our suites are on the top floor."

Carter took the unexpected gift and headed for the elevators. A cleaning crew was at the end of a long hallway. They were starting their day by arguing across their cleaning cars. Their angry tones carried to him and he quickly made his way there.

"Good morning, ladies."

"How can we help you?" one woman asked.

"I'm looking for a friend."

"Well, unless you've got a key, we can't let you in." The other woman made to push the cart away.

He ignored the snide comments. "Tanya Wilcox. Do you know her?"

The two women looked at each other, and now Carter became their number one enemy. They weren't talking about Tanya Wilcox.

A third woman with long dark hair and a bathrobe stepped into the hallway behind the cleanup crew. "What's going on out here?"

"Nothing, ma'am," one of the cleaning ladies replied. "This gentleman is looking for someone and we told him we don't know her."

"Go," the woman in the robe said. "You're not paid to gossip in the hallways."

As the cleaning crew got on the elevator, the woman

asked, "What's your deal?" She folded her arms across her ample breasts and leaned against the doorjamb.

"I'm afraid I was being rather sneaky. I'd heard there were poker games here and I wanted to get in on one."

She laughed. "Mister, you're looking in the wrong place."

"I don't think so. Someone told me the games were here and the payout was big."

She moved a little closer to him and he got a strong whiff of delicate perfume. "Take it from me. There's no game here. Go home and play cards with your neighbor or something."

"My money is as good as anyone else's."

"Who did you hear this from?"

"A guy in a bar."

"Oh, sweetie, every guy in a bar is tipsy, so I wouldn't take everything at face value. There is no poker game going on here."

"If you're sure, Tanya Wilcox..." He threw out her name to shake her up, and it did.

She threw back her long hair. "How did you get my name? Did those insipid maids tell you?"

"No. They weren't willing to give out any information."

"You sound like a cop."

"You never know." He saluted, turned his back on her and headed for the elevators. He didn't have to sneak a glance to know that Tanya was back in the suite, calling Rossini. His visit should shake things up, and that was what he wanted. Someone had to get nervous and offer up information. He hoped that day was soon.

LILA STOPPED AT a bakery to get éclairs for dessert. They would need something to make the chicken soup more appetizing. Newspapers were outside the door and Lila noticed the headline: Colton Fighting Back.

She bought a newspaper and went inside to purchase the éclairs. She didn't open the newspaper until she was back in her car. Her grandmother was up to her old tricks. She'd hired a new lawyer to get the lawsuit moved to an earlier date. The attorney obviously had had a press conference this morning and had said that Erik and Axel had been ignored for so many years by their father and it was time to recognize them and their rights. And he would make sure that the other Coltons paid.

Lila threw the newspaper on the passenger side of the car and went home. She hated that everywhere she went she would see the Colton name again, strewn all over the newspapers. People whispering behind her back, pointing fingers. Carin craved all the attention and Lila did her best to avoid it and her grandmother. If she could survive the fire, she could survive this. But could she survive Carter's leaving?

Carter's car was at the town house and it meant he was here, too. Her spirits lifted. She opened the door and smelled soup.

"Mmm." She kissed him. "Just what I wanted for lunch—you and soup." She held up the newspaper. "And reading material. A judge is going to rule on it by the end of the week."

"Your grandmother doesn't miss a beat."

"No. Now everyone will be talking about it again."

"That bothers you?" He put his arms around her and

held her close against his chest, and that was what she needed. His comfort.

"A little. I wish it didn't, but my family is involved."

"Let's not talk about it."

She drew back. "Why not?"

"Because it upsets you."

"So? I'm not a weak woman who's going to crumble at your feet when something goes wrong."

"I didn't say that."

"And in five days you'll be leaving and won't have to deal with it at all."

Silence filled the room. "Yes, I'll be leaving in five days," he replied in a low voice. "We talked about this."

At that point she realized she was making a fool of herself. "I'm just overwhelmed by everything and taking it out on you. I'm fine, though. Really."

"Lila—" his voice softened "—a judge will have the final say in the Colton case, and there's nothing you can do to change that."

"I know," she mumbled.

"How did the doctor's appointment go? And why aren't you eating lunch with Savon?"

"I wanted to call and ask you for lunch, but Savon would rather not be a threesome. Besides, she had some other things to do." She wiggled her right hand. "It's great. He said I can take the bandage off tomorrow if it feels okay. I didn't put the sling on this morning. How did your morning go?" She reached for bowls in the cabinet as he told her about the mistresses.

"You certainly got their attention. I'm sure Rossini and Sapp do not want their mistresses involved."

"Probably the last thing they wanted. It's frustrating that nothing is popping up like a target ready for us to hit the bull's-eye."

"Wouldn't that be lovely?"

Carter put the soup on the table. "What's in the white box you brought in?"

"éclairs. I thought we needed something decadent."

"You're decadent. You're my éclair."

He grabbed her around the waist and swung her round and round until her laughter filled the room and her heart. She was happy in his arms and she wouldn't think beyond that. After all, she had five days. That was a lifetime to her.

After they finished eating, Inspector Richards called and wanted to know if Carter had come up with anything. He put it on speakerphone so Lila could hear.

"Why aren't you finding anything?"

"There are a lot of files to go through."

"Then go through them instead of antagonizing Rossini and Sapp. They both are filing restraining orders against you."

"They'll have to come up with a good reason to get one, and I only visited Sapp's office and a hotel that Rossini owns. They can't prove that I was there for any other reason than real estate and poker."

"You asked about the poker games?"

"Yes, I did. And that's what has everyone in a frenzy. The poker game is supposed to be a secret in law enforcement. Why is that, Richards?"

"I don't know. Just find something so we can close this case."

"Did you tell Rossini I talked to you?" Carter asked.

"Of course not. I'm on the side of justice, Finch, whether you believe that or not."

Carter turned off the phone and looked at Lila. "Ready to work all afternoon?"

As long as he was beside her, she could get through this. She'd never needed anyone before. She wasn't a needy person, but she needed him in ways she couldn't even explain to herself. "I'm ready."

They spent the next few hours going through the files, looking for something that was out of place, something that would grab their attention, but there wasn't anything. In fact, there was too much stuff, too much information on Rossini and the others. No one had a motive except Rossini and Lila, and that was beginning to make her nervous.

At six o'clock they warmed up the soup and laughed until they couldn't breathe. "We can order in, you know."

Carter grabbed his chest. "And let this good food go to waste? Never!"

"I'm ordering a pizza."

"You're weak."

"So I'll order just for one."

"You better not." His eyes gleamed with a lot of feelings, and the one she wanted to recognize the most was love. It was there, but would he ever recognize it? Or admit it? They were so good together. Why couldn't he see that? Yet he was set on leaving and breaking her heart.

Soon they went to their laptops, searching and hoping for answers, but the happy-in-between moments kept her going.

"I keep coming back to Tanya Wilcox. I saw another Tanya somewhere. Could they be the same person?" Carter scrolled through the file doing a search-and-find on his laptop.

"Wait. I have her page up on the screen. As a teenager she married Ken Wilcox. The marriage lasted about a year and they divorced. She then started working at the club and got involved with Rossini. She's twenty-four years old and Rossini has to be over fifty. What an age difference!"

"She has olive-toned skin, brown eyes, brown hair. What's her maiden name?"

"Boyd."

"Wait, wait. That name is familiar. Who else do we have named Boyd?"

Lila shook her head. "I don't remember any, but again, there are so many names."

"Think, because I've heard that name before."

"Wait a minute. Wait a minute." Lila jumped out of her chair as the name fully hit her. "I can't believe it. I can't believe I didn't remember it."

"What?"

"Philip Boyd was the electrician who put in the new lights at the gallery."

"What? This is the connection we've been looking for." Carter leaned back in his chair. "And how is Tanya Wilcox related to Philip Boyd? Husband? Brother? Cousin? There has to be a connection."

Lila went back to her laptop. "She doesn't have another marriage license on record, but that doesn't mean anything. Let's see what else we can find."

"I'm already on it. I have three Philip Boyds in the

Chicago area. And one of them lives in South Deering on the same street as Wendy Olson. What are the odds of that happening? Continue looking," Carter said. "Let's make sure it's him."

Lila went back to Philip Boyd's file. "He works for Sapp Electric and has been for about two years. He's lived in the apartment a little over a year. This doesn't tell us much."

Carter didn't respond and she looked up. "Carter..."

"Sorry, I got involved in this report."

"From where?"

"Police report. Boyd was arrested four years ago on a drug charge and spent one year in prison. When he was released, he went to electrical school and got the job with Sapp. We won't get anything beyond this until we question Sapp and Boyd." Carter closed his laptop. "Someone had to pay for him to go to school and my guess is Rossini. Tanya is at the center of all of this, pulling Rossini's strings the way she wants."

"I don't even know them. Why would they burn down my gallery?"

"We'll be closer to an answer tomorrow. I'm just wondering why the police report wasn't in the file."

"This makes the second misstep," Lila said. "Richards didn't mention my father's gambling, either."

Carter put an arm around her waist. "You need to go upstairs and go to bed. Tomorrow is going to be a long day and you'll need your rest."

She raised her hand. "It's fine. And I'm not going to bed unless you go, too. I don't like sleeping by myself when I can have a strong, broad-shouldered guy beside me."

Arm in arm, they went upstairs and took a shower...
together. It had to have been one of the most sensual
experiences of her life. He didn't touch a place on her
body that didn't beg for more. They managed to push
the Colton lawsuit and the fire out of their minds and
enjoy each other's company.

Time with him was too valuable to miss and his
touch gave her strength to face tomorrow. He didn't
seem to realize that these special moments were coming to an end. But she was very aware of each day passing and her time with Carter.

Chapter Thirteen

They were up and out of the apartment early. Electricians were on the job early to avoid the heat of the afternoon, but in Chicago the heat would probably reach eighty-two degrees. It was a nice fifty-seven degrees this morning and rain was in the forecast.

"We have to go into this with our eyes wide open," Carter said. "Since Boyd is working for Sapp, we have to assume Sapp and Rossini are connected, too."

"This isn't getting us any closer to solving the fire."

"It will. It just takes time."

"You're a very patient man."

He winked at her and he was in that kind of mood. Something had to pop today because he didn't have a lot of time left. Sapp had inherited a lot of property and businesses when his father had died. Sapp Electric was one of them. The business was near West Town with a storefront and a warehouse in back. It was in an older area. Carter figured the electrical business was the best place to find Sapp this early in the morning. They went inside a little after seven and the receptionist wasn't in yet. Everything was quiet, but someone must've opened the door.

"Anyone here?"

A man from the back shouted, "I'll be right with you. It's early."

"No hurry."

"Oh, Finch," Sapp mumbled as he saw Carter. "Would you like a cup of coffee?" He was startled at first but recovered nicely.

Carter glanced at Lila and she shook her head. "No, we're good."

"What can I help you with?"

"I'd like to talk to Philip Boyd."

"It's about the fire, isn't it?"

"Yes, it is. Philip is the electrician who put in the new wiring and lights."

Sapp glanced around Carter to Lila. "That's the lady whose gallery burned down."

Lila took a step forward. "Yes, I'm Lila Colton. We'd like to talk to Philip just for a minute."

"Why? The police cleared him and the only suspect they have for the fire is you, Ms. Colton. I see no reason for you to talk to Philip."

A young man with dark hair and eyes walked in. "The truck's ready to go…" Philip looked from his boss to Carter and Lila. "What's going on?"

"He's an insurance investigator and he's investigating the fire and wants to talk to you."

Even though Philip's demeanor was calm, his complexion changed a shade. "I don't mind talking to them again. I've done nothing wrong."

"I'm calling a lawyer," Sapp said and walked into his office.

"I don't need a lawyer," Philip shouted after him

and pointed to some chairs in the lobby. "Have a seat. Nice seeing you again, Ms. Colton."

"Thank you."

Philip continued to stand. "The arson investigator didn't find anything wrong with my work. Did you find something?"

Carter decided to go honest on this all the way. "One little tidbit jumped out at us when we were going over the files."

"What was it?"

"That Tanya Wilcox is your sister."

He shoved his hands into the pockets of his jeans, the second sign of nervousness. "Yes, she is."

"Did she get you this job?"

Philip thought it over for a second. "Yeah. Mr. Sapp is a friend of Lou's."

"Rossini?"

"Yeah."

"Did Mr. Rossini get you an apartment?"

"I'm not going to lie because I know you already have the answers. Tanya found it for me and asked Lou to rent it from Mr. Sapp. The man owed Lou money and it was a way to get his money back. I would pay Lou until the debt was paid off."

"That's why you didn't rent from Rossini?"

"Yeah. And he didn't want to get involved with Tanya's family. Because of my record, I wasn't able to rent anything, so Tanya helped me out. You see, I have a girlfriend and she was pregnant and I wanted a home for us."

"You're being very honest, Philip," Lila told him.

"That's about all I have left. I didn't set the fire.

I had no reason to do anything like that. Everything was going good in my life and I wouldn't do anything to change that."

"Not even if you were paid a lot of money?" Carter watched the emotions as they flickered across the man's face. He was actually thinking about it—if someone approached him, would he take it? At that moment he knew Philip had nothing to do with the fire. He was trying to make a life, not destroy it.

"No. I wouldn't take the money. My girlfriend would leave me and we have a three-month-old baby girl that I would never see again. No, I wouldn't do it."

"Would you testify to everything you've just told us?"

"Aw, man." He sank into his chair. "This is never going to go away, is it?"

"Not until we get to the reason why someone wanted the gallery gone."

Philip twisted his hands in his lap and didn't speak.

"You know something about the fire, don't you? If you do, it's time to tell us and get it off your shoulders."

"I know. I just wish I didn't have to say anything."

"Saying it now would be best for you."

"Or it could be worse."

Carter frowned. "What do you mean?"

"When I went over to do the wiring for Ms. Colton, I noticed it was outdated and it needed to be replaced. Some of it was just bare wires. All the brittle insulation needed to be replaced, as does the plumbing. I told Lou the whole place could go up any day with that kind of wiring. He told me to forget it. The place was built in the 1930s and is a fire hazard. I guess Lou and his father-in-law must have been able to pay people off and do nothing about it. I did not set the fire, but it wasn't a surprise when I heard about it. Now I'll probably lose my job and my apartment."

Carter got to his feet. "I believe you. You just got caught up in a terrible mess. Just don't tell anyone what you and I talked about, not even your boss. Don't do anything until I do more investigating."

"What?" Clearly, Philip was confused.

"Just keep quiet for now. If you do tell your boss, Rossini will find out within minutes and your job and your apartment will be gone. Trust me on this one."

"Sure."

"Not even your sister. I know she helped you, but her number one loyalty is to Rossini, and the man is up to his neck in this. When your boss asks you what we talked about, just tell him I had a few more questions about the fire. And be sure to mention to your sister that I was here asking questions. That way it won't be a secret."

"What kind of questions?"

"Like the type of wiring Ms. Colton requested. Did she ask for any changes? Was she satisfied with your work or did she complain? Did she say anything about Mr. Rossini? Things like that."

"Okay. I hope you catch the person who did it."

Carter shook Philip's hand, as did Lila. "I'm sorry you lost your business, Ms. Colton. I didn't have anything to do with it."

"Thank you, Philip."

The man nodded and walked back into the building.

"What do you think?" Lila asked as they got into the car.

"I think Philip just gave us a real good motive."

"What motive?" Lila turned in the seat to face him.

"I'm guessing that pulling out all that insulation, putting in new wiring and plumbing would amount to a lot of money. Money Rossini is not willing to pay. But burning down the place would've been a big profit for him."

"I love the way your mind works."

"Devious, huh?"

"You got it. Now let's go visit Richards and yank his chain for a while. I'd just like to know why he didn't mention my father."

"I love the way your mind works," Carter said back to her.

They smiled at each other with remembered kisses and last night's passion.

THEY GOT OUT of the car and went through the double doors of Richards's office building. In the foyer were newspaper stands and vending machines. Lila walked over to the newspaper stands. She reached in her purse for money and bought a paper.

"You need the torture, huh?"

"I guess. Just don't bug me about the craziness of my family."

Carter held up his hands. "Never! I would never do that."

They were smiling as they went down the hall to Richards's office. There must've been a meeting, because men were coming out. They walked in and took seats.

"Since you're here, I'm guessing you have something." Richards leaned back in his chair and waited.

Lila glanced at Carter and he nodded for her to go ahead. She had something on her mind and he let her go with it.

"Why didn't you mention my father's name was on the list?"

Richards raised his hands in a defensive gesture. "Finch asked for wealthy gamblers in Chicago and I gave them to him."

"My father is not a wealthy gambler," Lila said.

"I beg to differ on that. You have to have at least ten thousand dollars to get in the game, and Mr. Colton has gotten in the game several times."

"How would you know this?"

"The police do manage to raid these poker games every now and then, and of course, being the people who they are, like city council members, elected officials and big-time businessmen, they are given a warning and let go. A big fine comes with that. Your grandmother has gotten your father out three times. That's how I know."

"I think you enjoyed writing his name on that piece of paper. And I also think you're hoping I'm the one who set the fire. You're wrong, Inspector Richards. And there's nothing you can tell me about my father that would shock me."

"You think I enjoyed that?" He slapped his hand on the arm of the chair. "I wrote it on the list to spare you any embarrassment with Mr. Finch. I didn't know if he knew. That way you could tell him about it in private. I thought you would appreciate that, not be insulted by it."

"I'm sorry if I misjudged you." She was awesome in battle and defeat, and if Carter wasn't wrong, he thought Richards might have a crush on her. He was trying to impress her and that had misfired.

"You may be unaware of it, Ms. Colton, but your grandmother is a very wealthy woman, and your father has access to that money. Not to mention the lawsuit with the other family of Coltons. If your grandmother gets her wish, she will be much wealthier, as will you and your father."

"If you believe that, you have not investigated thoroughly. My grandmother hasn't given my brother or me anything, and we are not expecting, nor do we want, anything from the lawsuit."

"That's very big of you, but talking to your father, I got the feeling that he feels differently."

"Yes, he does, as does my grandmother. But I don't believe my father had anything to do with the fire. Someone pointed out to me that he doesn't have the guts and I believed them. My father is after money, Inspector Richards, and he would receive nothing from the fire. And getting money out of me would not be an easy task for him. Thank you for being honest about it, though."

Inspector Richards leaned forward, his eyes totally on Lila. "I'm sorry if your father's name on the list insulted you. I did not mean it that way."

"Could we please get back to the fire?" Carter asked in a voice he didn't recognize. That jealous voice was his and he had no right to be jealous. Lila could talk to anyone she wanted. He didn't have any hold over her.

"Tanya Wilcox," Carter said slowly and waited for Richards to take his eyes off Lila.

Richards turned to Carter. "She's Rossini's mistress and lives a very high-dollar lifestyle. We double-checked her and couldn't find anything that connected her to the fire. We had tons on her and Rossini, but not the fire."

"Philip Boyd."

"He's the electrician who did the work in the gallery for Ms. Colton?"

"Yes."

"What about him?"

Carter was getting to Richards. He pulled out his laptop from his bag and clicked it on.

"He's Tanya Wilcox's brother."

Richards shook his head. "I'm sure we would have caught that."

"You didn't, and you didn't catch that he has a record."

"No, that can't be correct." Richards tapped a few keys on his computer. "There's nothing on Philip Boyd."

"Try Daniel Philip Boyd."

"Dammit!" Richards hit the table with his fist. "How did this slip by us? Are you sure these names are correct?"

"You can continue to investigate if you want to make sure, but I talked to him a little while ago and I believe we have the correct man. Although everything is pointing to him right now, I don't believe he's our guy. He's trying to turn his life around and I don't think Tanya Wilcox would allow Rossini to put the screws to her brother. The first thing would be to check his banking account to see if any money was deposited besides his weekly check."

"We did that. Nothing else showed up. We couldn't find motive on Boyd unless he was paid in cash and has it hidden somewhere."

"It's not Boyd," Carter said. "I was told this in confidence, and you might check it out. It's part of my conversation with Philip. I made some notes and I'm sending them to you."

Carter glanced at Lila and she was reading the headlines of the newspaper. How agonizing it must be to have her family's affairs splashed all over the newspaper for the public to read.

"Damn! Now we have motive."

"What do you think it would cost Rossini to replace the wiring, the insulation and the plumbing in the building?" Carter asked. "And why wasn't the defunct wiring noticed by building inspectors and electricians?"

"The gallery is in a good location and it would cost Rossini a bundle to put in all those repairs. Money is the answer to the second part of that question. I think you mentioned that a time or two."

Carter packed up his laptop and got to his feet. "We have work to do."

"And I hope by the end of this week we'll know who set fire to the gallery, First, I'm going to talk to Rossini about Philip Boyd and get his response. I know he's not going to come out and admit to hiring Boyd to set the fire. I just want to make him nervous. And then I'm going to talk to Boyd, and don't worry—I'm not arresting anybody."

"You might interview Sapp. When Philip told him about the defunct wiring, he was told to forget it, that it was a Rossini building. And today he was real defensive on Philip's behalf for some reason. Instead of telling him to cooperate, he told him to do just the opposite. I thought that was odd for a man not to step up and guide this young man to keep him out of trouble."

"I asked him some questions before and he bragged about Boyd. Said he was one of the best workers he'd ever had. Call if anything pops up."

"See you later," Carter said, and Lila tucked the newspaper under her arm.

Richards noticed the paper. "Sorry about that, Ms. Colton. Your grandmother is determined to bring the other Colton family to their knees to pay for what has been done to her and her sons. Everyone is interested in the outcome."

"Yeah," she replied as they walked toward the door.

"Maybe when this is all over, you and I could go out for a drink. It would be my way of apologizing for my big gaffe."

"Uh…maybe."

"Hope your arm is better."

"Yes, it is. Thank you."

Carter watched her as they walked to the car. Was she serious? She would actually go out for a drink with the man? Had he misjudged her?

"You seem a little down."

"Why wouldn't I be down? I have to read that crap

almost every day, and Carin is... Oh, she makes me so angry in how she thinks we should all march in line to her step."

"You have a new fan. That should cheer you up."

"You mean Richards?"

"Yes. I think he's interested in you."

"Carter, you're giving me a headache," she said with a frown as she slid into the passenger side of the car. "Isn't he married?"

"I don't know. The people I've talked to since I've been here have said that his work is his life."

"He's a lot older than me."

"What? You're thinking about him?"

"You brought him up."

"I did, and I don't have any right to judge you or make comments about the men you date. I'll be leaving in a few days anyway."

His stomach clenched as he said the words and he wanted to yank them back. How could she be interested in Richards? How could she think of anyone else? That was when the lightning rod of reality struck him. She would be dating other guys, and the thought made him feel ill. Could he be falling in love?

LILA GOT A call from Savon, and Carter dropped her at the town house to get her car. Her friend had three more listings for Lila to look at and the Realtor had given her the keys. Savon wanted them desperately to rent something, but they were all too expensive. And she hated to make big decisions when she didn't have any idea of what her future would be. Her whole life hung in the balance. They had made progress, thanks to Carter, but they still didn't have a suspect in jail.

They stopped at Colectivo Coffee Shop on Clark Street, not far from where she lived, and went over their options. The patio under the brown awning was fresh and inviting, so they sat there and ordered their favorite coffee.

"You're not even trying, Lila. You've vetoed everything before we've even had a chance to really look at the property."

"I know and that's not fair to you, but my future is very insecure."

"You were very positive about what Carter was doing and you felt sure the arsonist would be caught soon."

"Yes. It was all positive, but the deeper Carter dug, more suspects kept popping up. It's very frustrating."

"This is about something else. You're not usually like this. It has to be Carter. Did you have an argument?"

"He thinks he has the right to tell me who I can date." The words came spewing out before she could stop them.

Savon's eyes grew big. "What? Aren't you dating Carter?"

"He's leaving on Friday and I don't know if I'll ever see him again." She might never see him again. Tears stung the backs of her eyes.

"You knew that before, though."

"I knew he would be leaving, but I had no idea he would have an opinion on who I can date."

"This sounds too complicated for me. One guy at

a time is all I can handle." When Savon realized how that sounded, she burst out laughing, and Lila joined in. They ordered a specialty beer and Lila got into a better mood. They talked on and on and then ordered nachos. She'd known all along that Carter was leaving. She didn't understand why he was jealous. That was what it all boiled down to—his jealousy. He had no right to be jealous if he was leaving.

"Is there ever a perfect relationship?" she asked, sipping the beer.

"No. Remember that jerk you dated in college?"

"Don't go there." Lila popped a nacho in her mouth and thought how different Carter was from the other men she'd dated, not that there were a lot. But he'd touched a part of her that had been waiting for someone to love. She loved him. There was no way to explain the obsession of her heart. She had to let go.

The neon sign blinked the time. It had to be wrong. "Is it really six o'clock?"

"Yes, it is, and I have a date at nine."

"I had no idea it was this late and that we had been talking this long. I have to go." Carter was probably worried about her, but he didn't call. That bugged her even more.

Savon leaned in close and whispered, "I don't know if you've noticed, but we're a little tipsy."

"I'll call a cab."

They ordered coffee to go. During her cab ride home, she wanted to think reasonably instead of getting clogged up with happy-ever-after. When she entered the town house, the lights were on and Carter was at the kitchen table on his laptop.

"Sorry, I'm a little late."

"You don't owe me an explanation."

The tension was so thick that she'd need a snow-plow to get through it. She carefully placed her purse on the sofa. He wasn't going to do this and make her feel guilty. She walked to the table.

"Are you upset that Richards asked me out for a drink?"

"Of course not. That's your decision, not mine."

"Even though we've only known each other a small period of time, I feel like we could talk about anything. And that we can be honest. I'm aware your plans are to leave on Friday, and that will hurt. I've gotten used to you being here and it's been nice. But I also understand your reasons and I hope you would understand mine and realize I have no desire to go out with Richards. We've gotten to know each other so well. This jealousy is out of place."

"I'm sorry." He closed the laptop. "You're right. It's totally out of place, but I never expected to feel this way and I'm not good at dealing with it or saying goodbye to someone I care about."

"Then why get mad at me?"

"Because I just want to smash my fist into Richards's face at the way he looked at you."

"And that makes you mad at me?"

"Lila," he sighed. "I don't know what to say."

"How about 'I love you' or 'I want to spend forever with you'? Anything like that would work."

He ran a hand through his hair. "It's not that simple."

"To me, it is." She waited for more, but it seemed there wasn't anything he had left to say. "I think you better sleep in your room tonight and until you leave."

Chapter Fourteen

The next morning, Carter had breakfast ready when Lila came into the kitchen. She held a hand to her head. "I don't usually drink that much. I need coffee."

"Are you still upset with me?" he asked as he handed her a cup. "I was out of line."

"Yes, you were. Your jealousy threw me."

He carried their plates to the table. "I don't have a response for that. It threw me, too."

"Let's forget about it and enjoy the time we have left together." She stared at the plate in front of her. "I'm going to miss this. It was nice having you around, but I've finally accepted that you'll be leaving on Friday." That sounded natural and not like her heart was breaking.

"I talked to Neil last night and I definitely will be leaving. I have an eleven o'clock flight out of O'Hare. I don't want our relationship to end on a sour note."

She took a sip of coffee. "I hope one day you take an honest look at what it really meant."

"Lila—"

"It's okay, Carter. I won't press you for anything, but I will say I have enjoyed this time with you, and I don't regret a minute. If you say it's over, it's over. I'm not the clinging kind."

"I don't regret a minute, either, just that I might have hurt you."

Lila thought it best to skip the topic. It wasn't getting them anywhere. "Do you have any more information on the fire?"

"I'm totally committed to that until my plane leaves. I'm waiting on a call from Richards to see how his interviews turned out yesterday."

"And I'm going to get dressed and meet Savon. She's really pushing me to rent a new place."

"Then do it. Go forward. I believe it's clear to everyone that you're not the arsonist and you can make plans for the future."

Lila went upstairs and Carter sat for a long time thinking about their relationship. They had a perfect relationship. How long did perfect last? She was easy to talk to and to share his life with. And again, how long did that last? Why was he so afraid it would end? That was his problem. He couldn't put a finger on what scared him so much. People got divorced every day and moved on. He had nothing to move on from except...

He picked up his phone and called his parents for the first time in three months.

"Hi, Mom. It's Carter."

"Oh, my goodness, George," she shouted to his father. "It's our son. Come talk to him."

"How are you guys doing?"

"It's so lovely here. I wish you could see it. We spent the whole day on the yacht yesterday and everybody says I look so much younger and tanned. I think it's getting away from the crowds and the noise, and out here we have time to just be quiet and enjoy the sunshine in an easygoing lifestyle. It was certainly the right decision for us. We're not so edgy all the time."

"Let me talk," his father said.

"I'm talking. You can talk when I'm through."

"Then why did you call me?"

"Okay. Here he is."

"Hey, son. How you doing?"

Carter smiled. It was reminiscent of so many days of his childhood, the two of them trying to talk over each other.

"I'm doing good. I caught a forger in Chicago and I'm getting ready to move on to London."

"You lead an exciting life. I'm proud of you, son," his father said.

"Yeah, but sometimes it gets frustrating. I met this girl…"

"Dorian, he's met a girl."

"A real live girl, not a criminal or anyone like that?" his mother asked.

Carter closed his eyes and groaned. Why had he thought he could have a normal conversation with his parents? Their thoughts always went off in a different direction and it wasn't his direction.

"Yes, she's a live girl. What did you think she was?"

"Someone who can have babies?" His mom was back on the phone.

"Babies? You never mentioned babies before."

"Our friends here just had a new grandbaby and

she's so sweet. I told your father we'd probably never have one because Carter is never settling down."

"Is this Dorian Finch?" His mother had thrown him for a loop, because she never talked about having grandchildren. At times, she didn't even seem to want the son she had. Had he been looking back and seeing a fake life?

"Don't be silly. I like babies, just like everyone else. When you were small, I had to work so we could make a living. It's expensive to live in New York, but it was close to my job and your father's, and it was near the school we wanted you to go to."

"Then why leave me so much with Mrs. Kinkoski? I loved her, but I would've liked to spend more time with my parents."

"Now, Carter, don't bring all that up. We were in a social circle and we had to keep up and we were young and enjoyed it. You were well taken care of and Mrs. Kinkoski taught you to play chess. Remember all the walks you took her on because she was afraid to walk alone?"

"She was like my grandmother."

"Exactly. Now tell me about this girl."

"It's nothing, really. I was going to tell Dad she owns a gallery and we worked together to catch the forger. She's a very nice lady."

"But nothing serious?"

"No, Mom, nothing serious."

A long sigh filled his ear. "Talk to him, George."

"You had to bring up babies and scare him away."

"I'm here, Dad." He had to get his dad's attention,

and the only way to do that was to shout into the phone as his parents argued with each other.

"Hey, son, how about coming home for Thanksgiving?"

Now he knew he had the wrong number. His mother did not cook or celebrate holidays with food. What was up?

"Mom's cooking?"

"She has been taking cooking lessons and plans on making a big Thanksgiving dinner, and it would be nice to have you home. It would be even better to see you."

He swallowed. "It will be great to see you, too. I'll plan to be there. Who else have you invited?" As he'd gotten older, strange women tended to show up at his parents' and it didn't take long to figure it out. His parents were playing matchmakers.

"Just our neighbors. Your mother doesn't want to invite too many people in her first attempt at Thanksgiving dinner. She wants them to meet our handsome son."

"Dad, I met them when I came for Christmas two years ago."

"Yeah, but don't tell your mother," he whispered into the phone. "They're bringing their niece."

"How does that concern me?"

"Never mind. Here's your mother."

They talked a few minutes longer and Carter was left holding the phone and wondering if he would ever understand his parents. That was probably true for all kids. There was no doubt his parents loved him, but he never felt their love because his parents had been so busy, and he'd wanted their full attention. As an only child, he'd wanted it even more. Wow! The mist on his rearview mirror cleared.

Lila came back in skinny jeans and a colorful blouse tucked in at the waist and wearing low ankle boots. Her hair, as usual, was twisted at her nape and she looked as beautiful as he'd ever seen her. It was no wonder Richards couldn't take his eyes off her.

"That was my parents," he said, slipping the phone into his pocket.

"You were talking to your parents?" She didn't disguise the shock in her voice.

"Yes. They want me to come home for Thanksgiving."

"That's nice and I hope you go."

"I told them I would."

"If I can manage a relationship with my father, you can manage one with your parents. It just takes a lot of gritting your teeth," Lila said.

He smiled at her and dreaded the days ahead. He would miss her.

"Do you have time to drop me at the coffee shop to get my car?"

"Sure, no problem. Just let me put these dishes in the dishwasher."

"You know, you can leave dishes in the sink sometimes. I do it when I'm in a rush, but I think you have a 'perfect' problem. Everything has to be perfect. And no one is and no one will ever be."

"It's just… You let me stay here and I appreciate it and want to keep things tidy," Carter said.

"You can sing that song to someone else, Mr. Perfect. Let's go. It's going to take most of the day to wake up Savon. She has appointments for us to see more buildings."

Carter dropped her off in the parking lot and there were only two cars there. She waved as she ran to her car and he watched her fluid movements. *Perfect.* She had said he was perfect. Maybe he tried to be just a little too much. He always wanted his parents' apartment in New York to be neat when his parents came home so they wouldn't yell at him. Not that they yelled that much, but he always wanted their approval, their attention. *Oh, man, you might need a therapist.* The woman walking away might be the only person who saw him as he was, a man with faults and dreams and a heart that may never be the same again.

She asked him to be honest. Why was he jealous of Richards? Carter didn't want her to be with anyone else. There it was. Honesty. It burned like Tennessee bourbon going down strong.

He entered the offices of the arson investigators of the fire department and noticed by the big clock on the wall that it wasn't even nine o'clock. Richards was hard at work, his head bent over a laptop, his tie hanging loose and his grayish hair tousled as if it hadn't been combed in a while.

"Do you ever go home?" He had nothing against Richards. He just wanted to see this case through to the end for Lila. Carter's problems were within and he was the only one who could fix them.

"Now, that's a good question." Richards stood for another cup of coffee and handed Carter one. "When I was with my wife, I thought I had a home, but my wife informed me that since I was never there, I could move out. I moved in with my mom so I could pay for my kid's college. So to answer your question, I don't know where home is anymore."

Home was a place Carter shouldn't have brought up. It weighed heavily upon him. "Have you found out anything?"

Richards touched a big file on his left. "Enough to put Rossini away for a long time."

"Who was the arsonist?"

"I haven't tied that one down yet. I'm trying to tie up all the loose ends and there are a lot of loose ends. Rossini packed an attitude at the interview and Philip wouldn't say much about his sister's boyfriend except to say that the wiring needed attention. I can't arrest a man for that. I have Sapp coming in at nine thirty. Thanks for that tip. It's proving very lucrative. My guess is that it's someone who works for Rossini. I don't believe Sapp would personally place the device for Rossini. But then again, I don't know how much money was involved. I'm waiting on Sapp's financial records and I should have them sometime this morning."

"So Rossini wanted the gallery torched? Why? Have you answered that yet?"

Richards flipped through the folder. "The insurance payout on that building would be one-point-two million, a little over what it's worth. I'm leaning heavily on that answer."

A knock at the door interrupted him and a woman poked her head around. "Sorry, sir, but Sapp is in the interview room."

"Thanks." Richards got to his feet. "Let's shake

some answers loose. Look at your laptop. I just sent you some information on Sapp."

While Carter went over the information, Richards took a moment to go to the bathroom to freshen up. As they walked into the interview room, Sapp got to his feet. "What's this bull about? I had nothing to do with the fire."

"Sit down, Mr. Sapp, and take a deep breath," Richards told him as they took seats around a metal table. "Mr. Finch and I would just like to ask you some questions." He glanced from Finch to Sapp. "You do know Mr. Finch?"

"Yes, I know him. I don't understand what's his involvement in this case. He works in a different field. And, yes, I looked him up."

"Not that I owe you an answer, but Mr. Finch has worked very closely with the fire department since the fire happened. We have now caught the forger and Mr. Finch is staying on the case until we catch the arsonist. But we can end this meeting quickly if you'll answer one question."

"What?"

"Tell me and Mr. Finch who set the fire at the Weston Street Gallery."

"How am I supposed to know that?"

Carter glanced at his laptop. "You do a lot of work for Mr. Rossini?"

"Yes. He's a good customer."

"You've actually been working for him for over twenty years."

"I guess. I haven't added it up."

"Mr. Rossini has been paying invoices from Sapp Electric for twenty-one years. Is that correct?"

"I guess it is."

"In all the years Rossini has owned the building and your company has done work at that site, which had previously been a bank, an investment company and a gallery, no one who works for you has written up a report for the defunct wiring? Or the bad insulation?"

"It wasn't reported to my office?"

A tap sounded at the door and Richards bellowed, "Come in."

An assistant came in and handed Richards some papers. Richards studied them for a second and glanced at Sapp. "Do you want to do this the easy way or the hard way, as they say?"

Richards laid one of the papers on the table and turned it around so Sapp could see it. "Does that look familiar?"

Sapp glanced at it and turned away. "No."

Carter could see clearly what it was: burned parts of a device, probably from a very tiny pipe bomb.

"Pieces of this device were found in your work area in your electrical business. Someone bought it and put it together in your building. Do you want to tell me anything?"

"I want a lawyer."

"Stand up, Mr. Sapp. You're under arrest for arson. You have the right to remain silent. Anything you say can and will be held against you…"

As Richards continued to read Sapp his Miranda rights, an officer came in and put cuffs on him.

"I didn't do this," Sapp said, his face red and deviant. "You won't find my fingerprints anywhere on the device. I didn't do it."

"Think about it, Sapp. Rossini's going to let you take the fall." Carter pointed out the obvious, but Sapp didn't take the bait.

As they walked back to Richards's office, Carter said, "It was too easy. I expected a lot more indignation from Sapp. What's his motive?"

Richards ran his hands through his hair. "That one has me and I'm going to need a good one to take this to court. Sapp stood to gain nothing from the fire. Rossini is the only one who profits." He handed Carter the rest of the papers in his hand.

"Interesting. Ten thousand cash was deposited into Sapp's account the day before the fire and no way to trace it. This kind of sets him up."

Richards reached for his jacket behind him. "I got a lot more legwork on this one. Just when you think all the answers are clear, they're not. If you have any suggestions, just let me know. I won't be going home tonight, either."

Shuffling into the jacket, Richards asked, "Where's Ms. Colton today?"

Carter kept his emotions in check. "She's looking for a new place of business."

"That's probably a wise idea."

"It might be an even wiser idea to let the insurance company know Ms. Colton is not involved in any way in starting the fire."

Richards nodded.

At least when Carter left he would know that Lila would not be prosecuted. But he was hoping before that time came that the suspect would be arrested and in jail.

WHEN LILA MADE it to Savon's apartment, she was surprised to find her up and drinking coffee.

Savon winced. "Who had the idea to try the beer?"

"You."

"And I also made appointments at ten and eleven, so we better hurry," Savon said.

For the next two hours, they looked around properties that were priced out of their range and would need a lot of renovations. She tried not to get too down, but depression was one big wave washing over her.

This time they went to a coffee shop to get a sandwich for lunch and go over their options once more. She hesitated in telling Savon that she wasn't all that crazy about spending so much money and not having anything to back it up. First, they would have to be able to pay the rent. Second, they would need to renovate as quickly as possible. Construction workers were known to be late, late, late.

"Our best option is still the jewelry store," Savon pointed out.

"Yeah, but first, please try to understand where I'm coming from. Carter feels that the arsonist will soon be caught, and I'd like to get that behind me before I jump into something else."

"When is Carter leaving?"

"On Friday. His plane leaves at eleven."

"That's going to be a rough day for you. We'll have a margarita night. No more beer."

"It's going to take more than a few margaritas."

"I'm sorry, Lila." Savon reached across the table and touched Lila's hand. They'd always been good friends and Lila hoped that would never change, but she couldn't just come out and tell her that her interest wasn't in the gallery anymore. She would soon, though.

Savon fiddled with her napkin, folding it over and over. "Do you mind if I continue looking for work?"

"No, no. Go ahead. You have to find a way to make a living."

"You're talking like it's over."

Lila tried not to fidget. "I'm just not into it right now. Maybe I need a little more time. I don't know." That was what best friends were: they made life easier. And that was what Savon had just done.

"It's a heartache, that's what it is, and it will take more than time," Savon pointed out.

"Please don't say that. I told myself going into this relationship that I could just walk away. Be tough like a man. That's laughable. Women can't just turn off their feelings. It's all or nothing. Why didn't I realize that sooner?"

"You aren't the only one involved in the relationship. It's not going to be easy for him, either."

"I don't want him to be forced to stay here because of me."

"Why not? Grab him while you can."

Lila chuckled. How she wished it was that easy.

Savon leaned over. "There's a man staring at you."

Lila lifted an eyebrow. "Is he handsome?"

"Very. Tall. Dark blond hair that curls into his collar."

She turned to look and saw it was Heath Colton, the oldest son of Ernest Colton and president of Colton Connections. "I'll be back." She placed her napkin on the table and walked over to him. "It's nice to see you." They shook hands.

"Our offices are not far from here and I stopped in for coffee. I'll be working late tonight." He grimaced.

"Is that a regular thing?"

"No, but your grandmother is putting pressure on us now. She's got the media's attention and they won't leave us alone. She's hoping we'll cave and give in to an earlier court date."

"Don't do that." The words came out before she could stop them, but then, she didn't know why she would want to. Maybe family loyalty should mean something. The family had never meant anything to her grandmother.

"That's nice of you to say. We don't plan on giving up anytime soon."

"Should I be indignant?" she asked with a laugh in her voice, and it must've gotten to him.

He smiled. "I wish we had the time to get to know each other as a family."

"We are family, just a little different from most."

"Thank you, Lila. I needed to hear that today. Take care."

All the way home, she thought about the other Coltons, and it took her mind off Carter. At least for a moment. She saw his car was back at the town house and her heart leaped at the thought that she had a little more time with him.

Carter was on his laptop at the table, engrossed in whatever was on the screen. Probably studying the painting he was asked to authenticate in London. In a polo shirt and jeans, he looked right at home. In her home. Would he never want a family and a home?

"Hey, you're home. Did you find anything?"

She dropped her purse into a chair. "No, and I finally had to admit that my heart's not in it right now. I need capital before I can do anything else. I'm trying to be wise." She kicked off her shoes and found a comfy spot on the sofa.

"You're deep in thought."

"I was thinking about the other Coltons. Savon and I had lunch at a small coffee shop and Heath Colton walked in to get coffee. He's the head of the family and I could see the role is taking a toll on him, but they are a close-knit family. I just wish my grandmother..." She got up and paced. "There is something about that will. Why hasn't it shown up before? If my grandmother knew about it, what took her so long to confront the other Coltons? There's no one greedier than her. She would have no problem taking the money and using it for her own purpose. I just don't understand how this will was somewhere and no one knew about it."

"Are you thinking forgery?"

"Forgery! That's it."

"Who has a copy of the will?"

"It was in the safe at Ernest and Alfred's offices, and now I guess it's in Heath's."

"Would he have the original?"

Lila looked at him and a light bulb finally went off in her head. Could Carter tell them if it was a fake? She could ask him. He was getting ready to leave. It...

"I'm not in the signature field, but I know a couple of experts who might be able to help you or, more specifically, the other Coltons. Probably the most important thing they could do would be to test the ink. It would have to be the same age as Dean Colton's signature. Everyone puts different pressure on the pen when they write, and that can be tested, too. An expert will run several tests to validate that it is the original will of Dean Colton. Of course, after looking at it, sometimes, if you know what you're looking for, it's obvious to the eye."

"I'm probably stepping out of my bounds, but would you recommend someone to Heath?"

"Sure, if he's interested." He looked directly at her. "Are you sure about this? It will go against your family."

"Yeah, that." She paced again, that thought going around in her head. "If it's a fake, everyone on both sides of the Colton family needs to know."

"Sounds reasonable."

"Then you'll do it?"

"For you, I will talk to Heath and offer my advice."

"You would do that?"

"For you, I would do just about anything." Except stay. Their eyes collided as if they were thinking the same thing; she held on to him with all her strength and he kept pulling away. They couldn't continue the push and pull. Their relationship wasn't about that. It was about their hearts. Carter had to decide what he wanted and he couldn't do that while she was hanging on. She had to let go, and she'd known that for some time. And she had to do it with a smile, which might prove the hardest thing she would ever have to do.

Chapter Fifteen

Before doing anything, Lila called her brother and cousins to tell them what she had in mind. They thought it was a great idea. Everyone needed to know if it was a forgery. She then called Heath. He was startled at first but listened to what she had to say. He then talked to Carter and Carter gave him a name and a phone number and told him to use his name, if needed.

The next morning, Carter went over to Heath's office because he had asked him to. Carter looked at the original will and spoke to his expert friend on Zoom. Heath was afraid he wouldn't be able to give the expert enough detail to take the case. The expert said parts of the document looked doctored and agreed to delve further into it and ask some of his colleagues to participate. It was a win-win all around. It would give everyone time, except her grandmother. Lila expected a call at any minute.

She and Carter were worlds apart and acted more like friends than lovers. Last night they'd talked and talked about Sapp's involvement with the fire. It didn't make sense and they couldn't figure it out. Like always, it was nice to have someone to share her life with. They shied away from a personal level. He slept in the guest room and she slept in hers, just as if their nights together had never happened. In two days he would be gone and she wondered if she would ever get used to that.

THAT MORNING, LILA had an appointment with the insurance agent about her car. It wouldn't take long. Her cell rang as she reached for another cup of coffee. Rossini Realty? Why would they be calling her? The only way to find out was to answer.

"Hello, Ms. Colton. I'm Mona Tibbs, Mr. Rossini's secretary, and I would like to go over some things with you."

"Like what?"

"We have a list of the items that were taken out of the safe and we need your signature to say that everything is correct so Mr. Rossini couldn't be held liable if items come up missing."

"You need me to sign a piece of paper?"

"Yes. They are tearing down the big safe tomorrow and I'm trying to get all these papers in order."

It sounded strange to Lila, but she agreed to meet in Rossini's office in thirty minutes. She should call Carter, but she knew he was busy with Heath. He was meeting her later at Richards's office to see if they could get a confession out of Sapp. He had no reason to burn down her gallery. He profited nothing.

As she was going out the door, her phone rang again. "Hey, you okay?" Savon asked.

"Yes, I'm fine. You don't have to worry about me."

"I have two job interviews today."

"Good for you."

"But if you change your mind, please let me know."

"Rossini's secretary called and I'm headed there to sign some papers."

"For what?"

"About the inventory in the safe. He wants to make sure that I can't come back and sue him for a missing item."

"He's covering his butt."

"I'll talk to you later and it's great about the job interviews. Let me know how they go."

Rossini Realty was in a large two-story sparkling and bright building with many office spaces. The glass and steel made it stand out. Rossini occupied the upstairs, which she'd heard through the grapevine, but she wasn't sure where to go. He'd always come to the gallery for the rent, and when she'd signed the lease, they'd done it at the gallery.

A huge chandelier hung over her head. In front of her was a desk with pamphlets on it. She glanced at a few, then noticed a map on the wall of all the offices. She studied it and found Rossini's office was right above her head.

She went up the stairs to double doors leading to his office. It said so in gold letters. Opening the door, she found a big foyer and a receptionist's desk, but no receptionist. She looked around and took a seat in a plush chair, hoping the receptionist would return.

At the sound of heels tapping against the wood flooring, Lila got to her feet. A blonde with long hair and dark eyes came into the room and offered her hand. The woman was the opposite of what Lila had been expecting.

"Mona Tibbs. Come this way."

She led her into a large office, and Lila noticed some of the artwork had been bought from her gallery. Maybe he wasn't such a scumbag.

"Have a seat," Ms. Tibbs said and handed her a document. "Mr. Rossini just needs to know if this is correct."

Lila sat and pulled a file out of her purse. She compared the two documents and noted they were the same.

"If they're the same and you're satisfied with it, please sign at the bottom."

She scribbled her name and said, "I would like a copy."

"Yes, of course. My printer is broken. I'll go down the hall to make a copy."

The woman disappeared out the door and Lila had an uneasy feeling. She got up and looked at the paintings she'd bought in France. It had been a good deal. What was taking so long? She walked into the receptionist's office. No one was there, either.

She opened the door to the landing and saw Walter Fox coming through the big double-door entrance below. There was no mistaking him. He always walked with quick steps as if he was in a hurry. His vests on his suits were an eye catcher, the fabric interwoven with different colors of threads and ribbons. It was topped off with a bow tie and a fedora. He was a colorful character.

She quickly jumped back so he couldn't see her. Mona had a private bathroom and Lila hurried there.

After several minutes, she went back to the secretary's office to get her copy. Pulling out her phone, she started to call Carter, but then she heard voices and clicked off.

"What the hell are you doing here?" That was Rossini's voice.

The door was slightly ajar, and Lila took a peek to see if she could see them.

"I want my money." Fox's beady eyes narrowed in anger.

"Haven't you heard Sapp's been arrested?"

"Everything is clear now for you to get the insurance money, just like we planned, and I want my share. I need to get out of town."

"I'm not giving you anything until the police are off my back."

"You can pay me ten thousand now and pay me the rest later. No one knows what really happened that night and it will stay that way if I get my money. Do you know what I'm talking about, Lou?"

"You sorry—" Lou stopped and then started talking again. "They're going to arrest you anyway. The forger gave you up, Walter. Money is not going to save you now."

"It was a stupid idea. I don't know why I let you talk me into it."

"You kept selling those fakes and were afraid of getting caught. Finch was on your trail and it was just a matter of time. When you get greedy, bad things happen. Now get out of my office."

"I'm not going anywhere until you give me the money." Walter pulled out a small gun from his jacket pocket.

Lila gasped before she knew it. She covered her

mouth, but it was too late. Rossini yanked open the door. "Walter, we have company, the lovely Ms. Colton." He grabbed her arm and almost flung her into the room. Catching Walter off guard, Rossini swiftly took the gun from him.

"What are you doing?"

"Shut up, Walter. The better question is, why is Ms. Colton eavesdropping?"

Lila tried to swallow and then she tried to speak, but fear had a death grip on her throat. She managed to sputter out, "You…set…the fire. You burned down your own building and everything I own for no reason but money. You are scum, Rossini!"

"Shut up." The gun wavered in Rossini's hand. "What are you doing in my secretary's office?"

"She…called me."

"Why?"

"You told her to."

"What?"

"To sign a document that stated I took all of my belongings out of the safe. She went to make a copy and I heard you and Mr. Fox talking." She glanced at Mr. Fox. "How could you take profit from an old man who had such talent? You are more than scum."

"Ms. Colton, my secretary was supposed to call you this afternoon. Why are you here now? Who sent you? Finch? Richards?"

"I told you it was your secretary…"

"Where's the paper?"

"Your secretary has it. She went to make a copy."

"Shut up." A dark shade of red colored his face. "Get the duct tape out of the bottom drawer of my desk."

Duct tape? She'd seen all kinds of movies and TV shows where victims were duct-taped and then their bodies were disposed of, dead or alive. Chills popped out on her skin. She would not make this easy. She bolted for the front door. Rossini caught her and tumbled to the area rug in front of his desk. She saw stars for a second.

"Get the tape, Walter."

She recovered quickly, kicking out with her feet, trying to dislodge Rossini from her back. Her hand hit the gun and it went flying.

"Walter!"

She scooted toward the gun and Rossini put a knee in her back. She screamed in pain just as duct tape went around her wrists and then her ankles. She still didn't give up. She raised both arms to hit Rossini as Fox slapped duct tape across her mouth. Fear held her motionless and a scream died in her throat. What were they going to do to her?

"Now what?" Mr. Fox asked.

"Open the closet door," Rossini ordered.

No, no, no! She couldn't breathe. She would suffocate.

CARTER LEFT HEATH'S office and called Lila. She didn't answer and that puzzled him. She had a meeting with the insurance guy and then she would wait for his call. Five minutes later, he called again and still didn't get a response. Where could she be? The meeting could have lasted longer than she'd expected, but she would still answer her phone.

He tried Savon. "Have you heard from Lila?"

"Earlier this morning."

"Did she say where she was going?"

"She had to meet with the insurance agent, but Rossini's secretary called and needed her signature."

"On what?"

"Basically it was a document that said everything that was in the safe is now in her custody."

"Okay, thanks."

"Is anything wrong?"

"I don't know, but I'll call you later."

He called Richards and told him the story. "You think something's up?"

"Yes, I do. I'm going over there and I would like backup."

"I'll meet you there. Don't go in without me."

It didn't take Carter long to reach Rossini Realty. He drove into a parking spot, and Richards drove in right beside him, followed by a police car. The man had covered his bases. Carter hurried in and Richards and two police officers were behind him. People stared and stretched their necks to see what was going on.

A young girl about eighteen greeted them at the receptionist's desk. She was on her phone. They walked straight through to the secretary's office. A woman with brown hair and tortoiseshell glasses got to her feet. "May I help you?"

"We're looking for Lila Colton," Richards informed her.

"I haven't seen her."

"Are you sure? Are you Rossini's secretary?"

"Yes."

"What's your name?"

"Mona Tibbs."

"Is Rossini in?"

"No. He was supposed to be, but when I got back from my beauty shop appointment, he wasn't."

This was taking too long. Carter stepped closer. "Ms. Colton came here to sign a document. Do you know anything about it?"

"Yes. Mr. Rossini told me to call her later in the afternoon to get her signature. I left the document here on my desk and when I got back it was gone. I just assumed Mr. Rossini took it."

"Where is Rossini's office?" Carter asked.

She pointed to the door on the left. Richards opened it and they went inside. They looked around at the lavish office with mahogany furniture, hardwood floors and windows from ceiling to the floor that looked out onto Chicago. "Look at that view," Richards said.

"Concentrate, Richards. Where's Lila?"

Richards scratched his head. "She came here to meet with the secretary, but Ms. Tibbs hasn't seen her. Do you think she's lying?"

"No. She seemed more confused than lying."

Richards picked up a gold paperweight from the desk. "Twenty-four-karat gold. Nice gift." Richards cleared his throat. "If she didn't meet Ms. Tibbs, who did she meet?"

"Whoever was in the office, and that's a chilling thought. Rossini was supposed to be here, so I can only conclude that it was Rossini. Now, where did he take her? Let's check the security cameras. I noticed them on the way in." Carter hurried back to the secretary. "We'd like to look at the security cameras footage."

"You'll need a warrant for that."

Carter leaned over and said, "If you don't tell me where the security cameras footage is, I'm going to make sure your name is on the indictment. Ms. Colton told a friend she was going to a meeting with you and that's the last we've heard from her. Where do I find the footage?"

"I'm not involved in this. I'm just Rossini's secretary." She ran her hand up her arm in a nervous gesture.

"Do you know what jail is like?" Carter asked.

Her face turned a pearly white. "Down the hall, last door. Tell Steve I sent you."

"Call him."

Carter ran down the hall and into the room. A young man got to his feet. "What's this about?"

They showed him their credentials. "We need to see the footage from nine o'clock this morning."

"Sure. I guess you talked to Mr. Rossini. He gets very upset if we don't follow the rules and the rule is you need a warrant." A smug expression told its own story. He had them.

Just when Carter thought all hope was lost, the door opened and an officer came in with a piece of paper in his hand. He handed it to Richards.

He waved the warrant in front of the young man. "Is this what you need, you little piece of crap?"

"I have to follow the rules or I'll get fired."

"Sit down and start showing us pictures."

"Let's start with the camera that faces Rossini's office," Carter said. "That should take less time.

"How did you get that so fast?" Carter whispered to Richards.

"It helps when you've been around for twenty years."

The young man tapped on the keyboard, no smug expression. Carter and Richards stood, one over each shoulder of the guy, and watched as a few people entered the office. Two businessmen who the young man said had offices at Rossini Realty. A janitor and cleaning crew flashed across the screen and then...

"Stop it," Carter asked. "Back it up." The young man did as asked and Carter pointed to the screen. "That's Tanya Wilcox. I'm almost positive, but she's wearing a blond wig. What the...? Keep going."

Soon after, Ms. Tibbs came out. A minute or two later, Carter asked him to stop again. Lila was on screen. She opened the door of the office and went in. "That's it. We don't have cameras inside the offices. That would violate a person's privacy." The film kept rolling.

"Wait. There's Tanya Wilcox again in the wig, leaving alone."

After a minute, Carter said, "Stop it." He looked at Richards. "Did you see him?"

"Yeah. Fox went into the office."

"Does Mr. Rossini have a private entrance?" he asked the man.

"Of course. He has a private parking space in back and can go straight into his office."

"So we won't find him on these tapes?"

The man shook his head. "Not likely."

"Do security cameras cover the back?"

"Yes." He sighed.

"Bring them up from about nine this morning."

"I'm sure to lose my job," the young man mumbled under his breath.

It didn't take long for the photos to come up. Rossini and Fox came out of the office, hurried down the stairs and got into Rossini's car.

"Now, isn't that something?" Richards said.

"But Lila's not with them." A tremor of fear ran through him. "Where is she? She went in, but she didn't come out. She still has to be in there."

"I'll call in more officers and search every inch of this place." Richards looked at Carter. "Do you have a photo of Ms. Colton?"

"No, but I know somebody who would." He called Savon and she sent him a photo. She wanted to talk, but he told her he didn't know anything. He had to get back to searching for Lila and he couldn't let himself get involved in endless conversations.

He showed the young man the photo from his phone. "Transfer it and keep looking for this woman."

"Wow. Now I know why you're anxious to see her. She's gorgeous."

"Shut up," Carter told him with a spark of anger.

"Run off some copies for us," Richards said.

"I don't run a photography shop," the young man replied.

Richards glanced at an officer. "Arrest him for obstruction of justice."

"Wait, wait. Man, you guys have hair-trigger tempers."

"No more lip. We don't have time for it."

Carter and Richards stepped outside the room. "What's your take?" Richards asked Carter.

"She's still in there somewhere. I don't want to think about her being hurt or anything else, but I can't be naive. I have to be realistic. She was a thorn in their side and..." He had to take a breath. Thoughts of Lila made his heart ache and his nerves stretch near the breaking point. His feelings for her had happened so suddenly. The moment he saw her standing in the gallery, looking at him with those beautiful green eyes, he was lost. He was supposed to be thinking about the Tinsley paintings, but his concentration was totally on her. If he had been doing his job, he would've seized the paintings and kept them until he could prove they were fakes. Instead, he let her keep them for the showing. That should have told him something. Now he might have lost her.

"As soon as the guy gives us the photos, I'll get officers to start searching. I'm going to shut the building down until we find her. And I've got an APB out on Rossini's car. We should catch them shortly and we'll learn more about what happened in that office."

"I'm checking Rossini's office. We must've missed something."

"Sure. Just hang on, man. We'll find her."

That was his fervent prayer.

He went back into the secretary's office with a fierce determination. "We're going to go over this again, Ms. Tibbs. Who else came into this office?"

"I don't know. I get my hair done every week on the same day at the same time and I wasn't here."

"Who was?"

"The receptionist is supposed to be here answering

phones, but she's in the bathroom a lot talking to her boyfriend. Mr. Rossini was going to fire her."

"So she wasn't here earlier?"

"She was supposed to be, but when I got back, she was gone, and then later she told me she went to lunch early."

"Did she say anything about what happened while you were gone?"

"No. The less I talk to her the better."

"Someone else was here, Ms. Tibbs. Who was it?"

"I don't know what you're getting at."

"We just looked at the film and another person came into these offices. Do you still want to keep on saying you don't know?"

She frowned. "You mean Tanya?"

"Yeah, Tanya with the blond hair."

"She was here in that ridiculous wig."

Carter moved in closer, anger chewing at his insides. "Ms. Tibbs, when I said another person, that's exactly what I meant—another human being like Tanya Wilcox. Did I not make myself clear?"

"I just didn't think she was of any interest."

"Let me decide that."

"She wore a god-awful tight dress and ostentatious wig. She said she was going to surprise Mr. Rossini. A minute later, she was back in my office, complaining that he was on the phone and ignored her. She asked what I was doing and I told her I was preparing a document for Ms. Colton to sign later on this afternoon. She said she could do that and I told her no thank you. Mr. Rossini has told me several times not to let her do anything in the office. She wants to work here but he keeps refusing. His wife and his kids come in occasionally and he doesn't want her here." She let out a long breath, having used every ounce of breath she had saying what she had to.

"Wait a minute." He thought about everything she'd said and something stood out. "What time did you go to your beauty shop appointment? And remember I can check it."

"I left about ten minutes to ten. My beauty shop is just around the corner."

"Was Tanya still here?"

"Oh, yes."

"And Mr. Rossini?"

"He was in his office."

"And Ms. Colton?"

"She was never here while I was."

"Thanks." He hurried down the hall to the computer guy. "I need to know something."

"I don't work for you, Mr. Finch."

He calmly picked up the warrant on the desk. "This says you do, and if you don't comply with what I want, you'll be spending some time behind bars. Have you ever spent a night in jail?"

That line always worked and didn't take long to work this time, either.

"All right. All right. What do you want?"

He reached for a pen and paper. "I need to know the time Tanya Wilcox entered the office and the time she left. The same with Ms. Colton, Walter Fox, Ms. Tibbs and Mr. Rossini." He laid the names in front of the guy.

"You want me to do it now?"

"Like an hour ago."

"You guys don't ask for much."

Carter waited patiently until the guy handed him back the paper. "Thanks," he said and walked out. He went back into the office and studied the times. Everyone who entered the office from nine o'clock that morning until almost eleven had come out. Lila was the only one who hadn't. What stood out the most was that Lila and Tanya were in there together alone for at least fifteen minutes. What was Tanya's part in this?

"They caught Rossini and Fox, both at the airport," Richards announced as he entered the room. "They're being transported to the jail. We should be able to interview them in about an hour. Rossini had a gun on him and... It had been fired."

What?

"Now, man, don't freak out. We'll get the whole story soon enough."

Soon enough.

He clenched both hands into fists and wanted to lash out, wanted to hurt somebody. Lila didn't deserve this. He sucked air into his tight chest and tried to breathe without feeling the pain.

Chapter Sixteen

The duct tape cut into her skin and Lila could barely breathe. The darkness closed in on her and she tried to stay calm. With the tape on her mouth, a feeling of claustrophobia washed over her. She started counting and taking slow, deep breaths to ease the feeling. Carter would find her. She kept her eyes closed to avoid the real darkness. Dust and tobacco filled her stomach with a sick feeling. She couldn't throw up. She would choke to death.

Her whole weight was on her left side and she moved around to ease the pressure on her shoulder. Depression hung on her like a dead weight, but she refused to give in to it. She moved around, making noises to try to get someone's attention. There was nothing but complete silence.

She raised her head. She heard voices. Had Rossini come back? She listened closely.

"Did you hear something?" That was Carter. Her heart almost pounded out of her chest.

"No, I didn't hear a thing." That was Richards. "Let's go to the station. They'll keep searching here."

No, no, no! They couldn't leave her here. She had to do something to get their attention.

She still had her ankle boots on and scooted until she could get her feet against the door. The first kick didn't do anything but jar her body. She drew a deep breath, raised her knees toward her chest and kicked with all her strength. The door broke away from the hinges.

"What the…? It's Lila!" Carter shouted. With his hands on the door, he yanked it away and then fell down beside her. She tried to talk but couldn't.

"Shh. Shh." He kissed her forehead. "Don't try to talk. You're the best sight I've seen in a long time."

"Is she okay?" Richards asked, leaning into the closet.

"Call an ambulance. She has duct tape on her wrists, feet and mouth. They can take it off without injuring her skin. Do you have a pocketknife? And get some water."

Richards handed him a small one and he cut the tape on her ankles and wrists so she could move freely. She wanted it off her mouth and she pointed to it.

He shook his head. "The paramedics will be here any second. You've been brave so far. Just a little more time."

How long had she been in the closet? It felt like forever, but it was probably more like an hour or so. She did her best to fight claustrophobia, but she could feel it coming on again. She had to move. She had to get out of here, and there was no way to explain that to Carter.

"Mona, do you have any lotion?" he shouted.

The woman was there instantly, and Carter massaged the lotion onto the tape and around it. Bless him. He could read her mind.

"Just stay calm and I'll try to get it off."

She nodded and raised her hands to do it herself. He caught them. "No. Give the lotion a chance to soak in. Where's the damn ambulance?"

"I can hear it in the distance," Richards replied.

Carter started at the top of her lip, the narrowest part. She pushed with her tongue as he began to peel it away. She exhaled a long breath as her top lip came away from the tape. "Carter," came out hoarsely.

He picked up the knife to cut away the loose tape. "The paramedics can do the rest."

Richards handed him a bottle of water with a straw in it. He held it to her mouth and she sucked greedily on it.

"Take it easy."

"Carter."

"Shh. The ambulance will be here soon."

"Does my family know?"

"It's all over the news."

She winced. "Did you call my mom?"

"I haven't had time and I don't know her number."

Lila quickly gave it to him. Her mother must be worried sick. How could Lila let this happen?

The paramedics rushed in, pushing a gurney. Carter helped them load her onto it. "Carter…"

"Take a deep breath." He wrapped his arms around her and held her for a second. "I'll be right behind the ambulance after I call your mother."

"Thanks." That was all she needed. She didn't want

her mother to worry more than she already had. She closed her eyes, trying to forget this nightmare.

CARTER FOLLOWED THE gurney down the stairs and called Lila's mother. It was answered the moment it rang. "This is Carter Finch."

"Did you find Lila? Please tell me you found my daughter."

"We have. She's in an ambulance on the way to the hospital."

"Oh, my heavens. Thank you! Is she okay?"

"She looks fine, just a little shook up."

"We're on our way."

Richards shouted at Carter as he reached his car. "Where are you going?"

"Hospital. I won't be able to interview Rossini tonight. I'm staying with Lila until I know she's okay."

"I just got a call from the police station and we're not going to be able to interview anyone tonight. Rossini's lawyer is out of town and we have to wait until he arrives at about nine in the morning. Will that work for you?"

"Depends on Lila. When I looked at her scared face, I just wanted to hurt Rossini real bad, and I still do."

"That'll wear off by morning."

Carter didn't know how he would feel in the morning. So much was going on inside his head, but uppermost was his concern for Lila. She had to be okay or he would never be able to leave Chicago. That thought buzzed around in his head for a while and made him realize just how much she had come to mean to him.

He tried to join Lila in the exam room, but a nurse stopped him. Lila must have heard it. "Please let him in," she called.

She leaped into his arms and held on tight. "Did you catch Rossini and Fox?"

"Yes, we did. They're both in jail. Now we'll see how they like being locked up in a room."

She sat back and put her hands over her face, which had a little red around her mouth. "It was terrifying. The smell was sickening. There had to be boxes of cigars in there."

He stroked her hair away from her face and sat by her on the bed. She rested her face in his neck. There were red marks around her wrists and around her bare ankles, but it didn't seem to bother her. The hospital gown fit her loosely. He gathered it together at the back.

She smiled at him. "You don't want anyone to see my backside?"

"No." He kissed her forehead. "What made them lock you in the closet?"

"The secretary had called and said she needed my signature. I signed the document and wanted a copy. She said she had to go to another office to do that. I waited and waited, but she never came back. I went to look out into the hallway, and I saw Fox coming. I hurried back inside and went into the bathroom. When I came out, I could hear voices in Rossini's office. I eavesdropped at the door, which was open a crack. Fox wanted his money and Rossini told him he wasn't getting any money and he needed to get out of town as quick as possible. Fox pulled a gun. I was so shocked I gasped and they knew I was there. Rossini yanked me into the room and demanded to know who'd sent me. That's when I lost it and told them what scumbags they were. Rossini took the gun from Fox and then Rossini and I got into a tussle. I tried to take the gun, but that didn't work because he was much stronger. Fox helped to hold me down while they put duct tape on my hands and wrists and mouth. Now they were genuinely afraid and didn't know what to do with me. Rossini said to shove me in the closet. I was terrified." She rubbed her face against him.

"It's over and tomorrow we'll have a long talk with Mr. Rossini."

"What do you mean I can't see my daughter?" came from the hallway.

Carter got up and went to talk to the nurse. "Lila wants to see her mother and family."

"Okay, but the doctor's getting ready to see her."

"I'm sure they'll get out of his way."

The next two hours Carter sat with the family and waited while Lila underwent tests. The doctor appeared in the doorway of the waiting room. "Family of Lila Colton."

Mrs. Yates got to her feet. "I'm her mother and this is her family."

The doctor walked up to Mrs. Yates. "Your daughter is going to be fine. She has some bruises that will heal. We were most concerned about the knot on her head. She said she hit the floor, but everything looks good. I would suggest resting for the next couple of days, but Ms. Colton didn't seem to like that idea."

"I'll take care of her," Mrs. Yates said with determination. Lila had that same determination.

Mrs. Yates and her husband went back to talk to Lila. Her brother and cousins went in to say goodbye. The cousins' mother was there, too, and she hugged Lila and left. It surprised Carter that Lila was already dressed and her hair was pulled back and tied with a rubber band.

"You're going home with me and Rick for a few days so we can pamper you." Mrs. Yates started her case.

"Sorry, Mom. Right now I just want to go home and lie in my bed and wonder how my day got so screwed up. I don't need pampering. I don't need anyone to hold my hand. I got myself into a mess and now I have to deal with it." She kissed her mother's cheek. "All grown up, Mom. Sorry I worried you, though."

Mrs. Yates appealed to Carter. "Please talk sense into her."

"Mom, don't put Carter in the middle," Myles said. "You know how Lila is. She's always been stubborn."

"Shut up." Lila turned on Myles. "Look who's calling me stubborn."

"Kids." Rick held up his hands. "No bickering. After what you've been through, Lila, I suspect you're very tired."

"Yes, I am, and I just want quiet. Thank all of you for caring so much about me. I'm a mess right now and will probably ask for your forgiveness later."

"Oh, baby." Mrs. Yates hugged her daughter. "Please take care of yourself and come out to the house if you get lonely. You're always welcome. You know that."

"I love you, Mom." They hugged tightly and then Lila turned to Myles. "I'm sorry I'm so short-tempered."

He kissed her forehead. "I'm just worried about you. Anything could've happened to you today."

"I know."

"Please try to stay upright for the next few days."

She swatted at him with her fist and he laughed as he went out the door. Mrs. Yates and Rick followed without making another case for Lila to go home with them.

The nurse brought the discharge papers, and Carter and Lila walked out to his car. "You sure you don't want to go to your mother's for a day or two?"

"I'm positive." She slid into the passenger side.

"Where's my purse?" she asked when Carter got into the car.

"I never saw your purse. Where did you leave it?"

"In a chair in front of the secretary's desk."

Carter thought back. "The chairs were all empty."

"It has to be there. That's where I left it and it has my credit cards and personal info in it. The hospital had my medical info on record and I didn't need it."

"Do you feel up to swinging by there?"

"Yes, but I'm not getting out. I never want to see that place again."

Once they'd arrived at Rossini Realty, Carter hurried to the offices upstairs. Mona was getting ready to leave for the day and the receptionist was, for once, at her desk.

"I'm looking for Ms. Colton's purse," he said to Mona.

"I haven't seen a purse."

"She said she left it in one of these chairs."

Mona looked around but didn't find anything. "It's not here."

"It was. Now where is it?"

Mona looked at the receptionist and back at Carter. The girl was thin, painfully thin. Her hair was a blond-orange color from being dyed so many times and there was a purple streak on the right side. Her blue eyes were dull as she stared back at him. He'd seen that look many times. Drug addict.

"Where's the purse?"

"Why do you assume I have it?"

"Where…?"

The door opened and a woman in her fifties walked in. Her blond hair was styled in a short bob around her face. Suave and sophisticated from her high heels to her jewelry to her expensive brand-name purse, she looked like a woman in charge. She hoisted the purse strap higher on her shoulder.

"Why is everyone standing around?"

It took Carter a second to figure out that the woman was Mrs. Rossini. He stepped forward and shook her hand.

"Carter Finch."

"Oh, yes, the man who helped to arrest my husband. I'm Sharon Rossini." She glanced around the room. "Mona, what's going on here?"

"Uh…uh…" Mona stuttered. Obviously, the secretary was nervous around the woman. Mona cleared her throat and replied, "Ms. Colton was here earlier and she left her purse and now we can't find it."

Mrs. Rossini turned to the receptionist and held out her hand. "Where is it?"

The receptionist opened a drawer on her desk and pulled out the purse.

"Go to Accounting and pick up your check. You're fired."

The woman disappeared out the door without a word. Sharon Rossini handed him the purse. "I'm sorry that happened here, but it won't again. I'm taking over the business." She headed for the door to the bigger office. "Can I see you for a minute, Mr. Finch?"

She took a seat at the big leather chair and asked, "How long will my husband be in jail?"

"I don't know. That's up to a judge, but he'll probably be released on bail soon."

"Not if I can help it. I'd just as soon they kept him there. I finally reached a breaking point of the embarrassment, the affairs and the countless ways he has wasted our money. It ends today. His lawyer is on his way back from a trip, but I will speak to him before Lou can."

"Good luck with that, Mrs. Rossini. Your husband has hurt a lot of people. I hope you get your wish."

As she talked with resentment and bitterness, it came to him that she might know a lot more about the fire. "Do you know anything about Lou's activities?"

"You mean the fire?"

He nodded.

"I hired a PI and I know what Lou does every moment of the day, but if I told you, they would say it's only an angry tale of a discarded wife."

"Not if you have photos."

She leaned back in the chair and crossed her legs, and he could see she was clearly thinking like a woman with revenge on her mind. "I'll have to think about it. I have my kids to think about, too." She leaned forward and wrote something on a pad and handed it to him. "That's my private number. Call me if you know Lou is going to be released on bail and we might be able to make a deal."

"I don't have that kind of power. The DA does and that's who you should be talking to."

"I say who I talk to and what I will divulge."

She had about twenty years of pain and suffering building in her from Rossini's treatment and Carter didn't blame her for wanting revenge. He would find a way to work it out with Mrs. Rossini, but he didn't have a lot of time.

"This case hinges on revenge? We know your husband and Walter Fox hired someone to torch the gallery. Make it easy for the DA, Mrs. Rossini, and your life will be a lot easier, too. You have the upper hand and can decide the rest of Rossini's life. That would be called satisfaction."

LILA ACHED FROM head to toe, and when she got home, the first thing she did was take a shower. She would hate tobacco smell for the rest of her life. She even washed her hair to get rid of it. She dreaded the night ahead. Nightmares would plague her and there was no way to stop them.

She put on her comfy T-shirt and dried her hair. Afterward, she crawled into bed and welcomed the relief of home and safety. She never would understand why home never appealed to Carter. She couldn't expect him to feel the same way she did, though. She drew a long breath and was grateful that he was here at this point in time. After being in the closet so long, she welcomed the joy to move freely. She never wanted to be locked up again. Freedom was a wonderful blessing, and she never realized that until the darkness shut out the world. It would take a while for her to get over it, but she knew she would.

Tomorrow she wanted to face Rossini and Fox. She wanted them to say to her face why they chose such a diabolical way to hurt her. She didn't know either of them that well, but tomorrow she would have her say and then she would start to put her life back together again.

"Are you awake?" Carter asked as he walked in.

She pushed up in bed. "Yes. I probably won't be able to sleep. I'm afraid to close my eyes."

He sat on the bed as she scooted up against the headboard. "I have some news that's interesting." He told her about his talk with Sharon Rossini.

"She might have photos?" Lila couldn't believe her ears. She curled into a sitting position, needing to know more.

"I'm guessing she does. But she's not willing to show them until she knows Rossini goes away for a long time."

"That must've been a terrible marriage."

"Most of them are..." He put a finger over her lips as she made to protest. "Listen to the news. Read the newspapers. Most marriages don't last. I think it's something you have to work at like everything in life.

If you care about it, you will give it one hundred percent. Look at Myles and Faith."

"Don't you dare say anything about them." She couldn't hold her temper in check. "They love each other and eventually will get back together. They needed a break."

He didn't say anything else, just stared at her with those gray eyes that were dark and challenging.

"Okay. No one has a perfect marriage and I agree you have to work at it. Your problem is that you expect it to be perfect. There is no such thing. You have to be able to love, compromise and always be there for the other person. No two people are alike, either. Someone has to change to make a relationship work."

"I have to leave day after tomorrow," he blurted out, as if she needed to know.

"I'm aware of that."

"And you need to get some rest."

"I'm going with you tomorrow to talk to Rossini. Please don't argue." She scooted under the covers.

"I've tried that. It never works. Seems I'm the one changing."

She laughed. She couldn't help it. It gave her a lift that she needed badly.

"How are you feeling? Does your skin burn?"

"Whatever they put on at the hospital has done the job. I'm kind of hungry. What about you?"

"What would you like, my lady?"

They were so good together. Why couldn't they have a lasting relationship?

"Pizza and salad."

Later they sat on the sofa and ate from the coffee table and talked about the case. "We should know who the arsonist is by tomorrow, or if Rossini actually set the fire himself." Lila had her fingers crossed. She'd been through a terrible ordeal and tomorrow it would end.

"Rossini and his lawyer will be looking for a deal. We have too much evidence. If Mrs. Rossini will cooperate, we might have the nail to close the coffin for good. And then you can get your insurance money and plan your future."

Yeah. Future. Her future sat beside her. He was a paradox and thought he could explain everything. It was true that many marriages didn't make it. But his conclusion was unacceptable for Lila.

THAT NIGHT, LILA woke up screaming and Carter had her in his arms before the fear could take over. Her body shook and her breath came in gasps.

"Hey, hey, you're dreaming."

She clutched him. "I can't see. I can't move. Hold me."

"I have you. Relax."

They eased down into the sheets and Carter pulled the comforter over them. "Just relax."

"Don't leave me."

"I'm not going anywhere."

Oh, but he was, and she started to pull away to keep from getting in too deep. It was too late, though. She'd been all in from the get-go.

"Are you okay? I'll go back to my room."

She slid her arms around his neck, loving the feel

of his masculine skin. "I don't want you to go to your room. I want you to stay."

He pulled back to look at her face, which he could see only by the moonlight. "Are you sure?"

"Positive." She brought her lips to his and forgot about everything else. This was what she wanted...to feel like a woman and to be secure in a man's love. She wanted it all, but she would settle for now.

Chapter Seventeen

Carter woke up to an empty bed. He could hear Lila moving around downstairs. He leaned back and thought of last night. It was perfect. For him. How could he be so selfish? For Lila it would be a different story. It seemed to be that way for them from the start. Their need for each other overshadowed everything else.

He swung from the bed and took the stairs two at a time. She was at the coffeepot filling a cup; her long dark hair flowed down her back, just the way he liked it. In slacks, a multicolored blouse and flats, she looked as beautiful as ever. No evidence of trauma from yesterday. But sometimes the trauma came from within.

"You're up early," he said, watching the way her hair swayed around her hips.

"I'm excited about today. You want a cup?"

He nodded. *"Excited?"*

"Today we're going to find out who set fire to my gallery and today I'm not the one who's going to be hurt. I want to hear Rossini say why the money was so important to him that he set the fire with us in the building. That has to be a crime and I will be there every day of his trial. Then he gets locked in a room as small as a closet."

"Take a deep breath," he urged. The terror was still evident in her, but he had no doubt she could handle it.

"You take a deep breath." She poked him in the ribs, a sly grin on her face. "I'm going to fix my hair." As she passed him, she said, "If you're thinking last night was a mistake, it wasn't. I was weak and needed you. That's all I'm going to say. That's all that needs to be said."

Lila Colton would be fine, and if she needed someone, she had a big family to help her. He just wished those guilty feelings about leaving tomorrow would go away. His cell buzzed and he dashed up the stairs to get it. It was Richards.

"The ADA called and Sapp wants to talk. I'm guessing he wants to make a deal. I told her about your involvement in the case and she said it would be okay for you to sit in."

"Let's go, Lila," Carter shouted. "They're bringing Sapp over from the jail to the courthouse. He wants to talk."

She stuck her head around his doorway. "I'm dressed. You're not."

"Give me ten minutes."

"Ten minutes, Finch."

In exactly nine minutes and fifty-eight seconds, they were in the car. Carter stopped for coffee and sweet rolls, and then they made their way to the courthouse. They met Richards outside an interview room. He glanced at Lila.

"I didn't realize you were coming, Ms. Colton. I thought you would be resting for the day."

"This concerns me and I should be here to listen to what the scumbag has to say."

"Any arguments?" Carter asked Richards.

"No, but the ADA might."

A middle-aged woman with blond hair and sensible shoes came around the corner. "What might the ADA do?"

"Ms. Colton would like to sit in on the interview," Richards told her.

"Do you think that's wise, Ms. Colton? I've read every word of the file, and if I were you, I would be sitting at home waiting for a phone call. It would be better on your nerves."

"I'd rather be here. Sitting at home just doesn't work for me."

"Okay. You can't sit in, but you will have to watch through a two-way window."

"Thank you."

The ADA spoke on the phone and then said, "They're bringing him over. Ms. Colton, you can sit or stand around the corner in front of the window. Your choice. But please don't talk where Sapp can hear you. Understood?"

"Understood."

Carter gave her a brief smile and filed into the interview room with the others. Soon Sapp was brought in with handcuffs locked around his wrists as well as his ankles. An officer pushed him into a chair.

The ADA sat in the center of the table and laid a

small tape recorder on it. Carter and Richards flanked her. Sapp sat on the other side, facing the ADA.

A young man with spiked hair and a tight skinny suit rushed in. "I'm Sapp's attorney. Sorry I'm late." From his youthful appearance, Carter assumed he was court appointed. Gambling and women must have left Sapp broke.

"What's on your mind, Mr. Sapp?" the ADA asked.

"I want out. I'm about to go crazy in here."

He was a shell of the man who had been arrested. His arrogance had been tested by sleeping a few nights on a cot, having company like roaches and rats and eating substandard food. He was used to the finer things in life and a jail cell was not one of them.

"I'm innocent. I didn't plant that device."

"Who did?" Richards asked.

Sapp hunched forward. "I heard Rossini was arrested."

"Yes," Richards replied. "We don't have all day. If you know something and want to clear your conscience, start talking or you're going to spend a lot of time in this place."

"I owed Rossini money," he said. "A lot of money."

"How much?" The ADA opened her notebook and had a pen ready.

"Ten thousand. I lost it to him in a poker game and he told me not to worry, that we would work something out. He showed up in my office one day and told me he needed a favor for the money I owed him. He wanted me to torch the gallery. He said the Colton woman was always complaining about the wiring, and before she called an electrician, he wanted the gallery gone. I told him I didn't do things like that and he told me to find someone who did. Since I own an electrical business, he assumed I knew those kinds of people. He told me I didn't have any choice. Either I give him the money I owed or find someone to get the job done.

"I didn't do anything for several days and he showed up in my office again with a magazine. It had guns and bombs in it. He showed me a tiny pipe bomb that could be converted and would start any fire. And he ordered me to either purchase it or make one. I bought the parts and made it, but I didn't give it much power. It would only burst into flames with hardly a sound. If the building had blown up, it would have hurt a lot more people. After that, I told him I was out. That was all I was going to do, and as far as I was concerned, my debt to him was paid."

"You seem to know a lot about bombs." The ADA looked right at him. He didn't move a muscle or appear nervous.

"My grandparents lived on a farm and I would visit them during the summers. My grandpa had a lot of tree stumps and wanted to get rid of them so he could farm more land. His neighbor told him his grandson had instructions for a small bomb but wasn't having any luck putting one together. I helped him figure out how to make it. We dug a hole in the center of the stump and pushed the device inside. Of course, we didn't have electricity, so I couldn't use a timer. I used a fuse instead. It worked. I haven't done anything like that since."

"What's your grandfather's name?" the ADA wanted to know.

"Edward Sapp. He passed on a few years ago."

"Mr. Sapp, does your grandfather have any stumps on his property today?" Richards asked.

"No. It's all been cleared."

"So you would say that you're very familiar with making small bombs?"

He moved restlessly in the chair. "Yes. Those kinds."

"And you used the same kind for Rossini?"

"Yes, but smaller."

"Where did you make the bomb for Rossini?" the ADA jumped in.

"In the working area of my electrical business. After I finished it, I gave it to Rossini, and I don't know what he did with it afterward. I didn't ask him and stayed away from the poker games. I didn't have any money anyway. But I'm not the one who put the device in the electrical socket."

"Why did you send Boyd to put in new lighting?"

"I knew Philip had a record and I gave him a job because Rossini told me to. Rossini called me and said to send him to install a light in the gallery. The Colton woman was driving him crazy. She was going to hire an electrician on her own and he couldn't have that because they would find the faulty wiring. Rossini didn't count on Philip having scruples."

Carter glanced to the window where Lila was listening. Everything was falling into place and hopefully she would get her answer.

"May I ask a question?" Carter asked.

"If it pertains to this case," the ADA replied.

"It ties into the forgery."

"Okay, but I will stop you if I need to."

Carter turned his attention to Sapp. "Where did the discussions for the gallery and the forgeries take place?"

"The poker games. It started with Walter Fox looking for someone who could forge a painting. And Rossini was always complaining about the gallery and Ms. Colton and her fixation on getting the wiring repaired. The lights would blink when she had a show and she wanted something done."

"How many people knew about these discussions?"

"Just me, Fox and Rossini. Of course, Rossini's girlfriend was always around because the games were usually in a hotel suite. She served drinks and appetizers and Rossini called her the hostess. After a game, we were drinking one night and Fox said an insurance investigator was on his tail and he had to get rid of the paintings. But he'd already offered them to Ms. Colton, who was going to hang them for a show. He'd look stupid if he asked for them back. Rossini was a little drunk and he said we should just torch the whole place. I thought he was joking, but the next day he showed up in my office."

"Mr. Sapp." Carter scooted forward with his forearms on the table. "I know you're trying to be honest—or at least, I hope you are—but Fox recruited Tony long before the fire."

Sapp placed his hands over his face, the steel handcuffs starkly standing out. "It's hard to keep all this straight. Yes, Tony started working for Fox about a year ago. I was trying to get him out of my apartment. He was always there painting something and the smell was terrible. I told Wendy I wanted him out, and then at a poker game Fox mentioned needing a forger and it was a godsend, except Tony never moved out. But he had money to go out to restaurants and to pay rent."

The ADA picked up the tape recorder and clicked it off. "Mr. Sapp, I will have this typed up and an officer will bring it to you to sign. Once that is done, I will meet with you and your lawyer and we will go over a deal."

The whole time Sapp's attorney sat there occasionally making a note. "Are you kidding me? He needs to be set free. He's done nothing wrong except help his friends."

The ADA held up two fingers. "There were two people in the gallery when the fire started. I have attempted murder on the books. I'm willing to take that off and make as low a sentence as I possibly can once we prove Rossini set the fire. But, Mr. Sapp, if your lawyer insists on going for dismissal, you had better talk to him. That's all I have to say."

"You're fired," Sapp said to the lawyer.

The man got to his feet. "You win some, you lose some. Have a good day."

"Where do they find these public defenders?" The ADA stuffed papers into her briefcase.

"Obviously, from Disney World." Carter chuckled as they walked out.

"We have an interview with Fox at one and then Rossini," the ADA said. "It all comes down to what Rossini has to say. He had the device. Now will he admit to pushing it into the electrical socket? We'll have to wait and see."

As THEY GOT into the car, Carter said, "I think I'll pay Mrs. Rossini a visit again She might need a little more incentive to help us. She might be our last hope."

"I think everything Sapp revealed was true," Lila said.

"Me, too."

"Every time I complained about the wiring, Rossini took one step closer to burning it down. I should've left it alone."

"Now, don't get weak on me. Rossini's been breaking the law for years. He got comfortable in his no-strike zone and thought no one would ever have enough courage to challenge him. Bribes were a way of life for him and now he has to face everything that he's done."

"But will he?"

"That's why we're talking to Mrs. Rossini."

Carter turned to Lila. "Are you sure you want to go back in there?"

"That was just a moment of weakness. I don't ever plan to let it cripple me. I would love to meet the woman who married Mr. Rossini. She's probably been downtrodden all her life."

"You'll be surprised."

And she was. Sharon Rossini was not the woman she was expecting. She was impeccably dressed in a white sleeveless shirtdress. The large buttons were brown on the front and matched her heels. The bracelets on her wrist jingled as they shook hands.

"You're the woman who rents the gallery and who was locked inside during the fire?"

"Yes," Lila replied. "Carter and I were inside when the fire started. It was a scary time."

"I can imagine. Have seats, please, and you can tell me why you're here."

"To talk about your husband," Lila told her.

"Not my favorite subject." She wiggled her nose as if she smelled something bad.

"It comes down to this, Mrs. Rossini…"

"Please call me Sharon."

"Okay, thanks." Carter seemed a little rattled. "It comes down to this. For a conviction, the DA's office has to put Rossini in the gallery, and they can't. Nor can they place him with the device, even though Sapp will testify to giving it to Rossini. A jury will have to choose who to believe. And that's leaving it to something like a coin toss. If you want to keep Rossini in jail, now is the time to come forward and help the cops make this a slam-dunk case."

"Are you married?" The question was directed to Lila.

"No."

"I met Lou in college and we got married when I was twenty-two. It was the best time of my life. My dad had money, but he wanted me to learn about money and how to control it and not let it take over my life. Lou and I lived in this little one-bedroom apartment and lived off of McDonald's. My dad gave us an allowance and we had to live on it. We would save our pennies so we could go to the movies on the weekends. I wished our lives could have stayed that way. When I turned twenty-five, I received my inheritance from my parents, which was the bulk of Dunbar Realty. Lou graduated and started working for the company. A few years later, my dad became ill and Lou took over completely, renaming the company Rossini Realty. I had planned to work in the business, too, but Lou decided I needed to stay home and take care of our children. Never let a man take away your power, Ms. Colton."

The words settled on Lila's skin like flakes of ice. "Lou took everything from me, even my pride, but he's not taking anything else. I spoke with a judge yesterday and the board of directors. I've taken over ownership of the company and closed all of our banking accounts. Everything is now in my name and Lou can't get to anything. He will be furious and expect me to give over to him. That day is long past."

"If you feel this way, why won't you help us?" Lila pointed to the closet and a chill shot through her. "He put duct tape on my wrists, ankles and mouth and shoved me into that closet. I couldn't breathe. I was so scared, and my stomach churned with nausea. I thought I was going to throw up and die lying on the floor. He's an evil person and needs to be stopped. I hope you will help us."

Sharon picked up the gold paperweight. "I gave this to him for our twenty-fifth wedding anniversary, knowing he had a mistress. I was such a gullible fool, but not anymore." She glanced up. "When do you have an interview with Lou?"

"This afternoon," Carter answered.

"Do you have enough evidence to get a conviction?"

"As I told you earlier, we have evidence but not enough to be positive about the conviction. It will take more."

"Why can't you help us?" Lila asked, not understanding the woman. She wanted Rossini to be put away a long time, yet she paused at giving information that could make that happen.

"You have to be a mother to understand."

"What are you talking about?" The answer made no sense to Lila.

"I left Lou the first time I found out he was having an affair. He talked me into coming back. We had two small children and I wanted them to be raised in a family atmosphere like I was, so I went back to him and got pregnant again. The two older children know about their father and his many affairs and have no respect for him, but I kept it from the younger daughter. She's Daddy's little princess and she loves him, and I find it very hard to break her heart. She'll be devastated."

"Then why hire the investigator?" Lila asked, not pulling any punches. "If you really want out of your rotten marriage, your children have to be with you. They have to know everything, and that includes the younger child. How old is she?"

"She just turned eighteen and graduated high school."

"She knows."

Sharon frowned. "What?"

"My dad had many affairs and even as a young child I knew he was cheating on my mom. They argued a lot and children pick up things. He didn't stay home some nights and I knew he was with some other woman. Take it from someone who lived through it. Your daughter knows. She just doesn't want to admit the truth or hurt your feelings."

"How do your other children feel?" Carter asked.

"My son, who is the oldest, wanted me to kick him

out years ago. He has very little respect for his father. My older daughter is at the University of Chicago and lives in one of our apartments. She has her own life and wants nothing to do with her father. She's known for some time and tries to avoid family functions."

Sharon got up and walked to the floor-to-ceiling windows. "It's not an easy decision to make."

"You made the decision when you hired the PI," Lila said. "You wanted evidence, probably hoping deep down that there wasn't any. But I'm guessing you found more than you wanted. Use it, Sharon. You'll be grateful afterward. My mother was."

Sharon turned around to look at Lila. "Your mother left your father."

"Yes, years ago. The moment she knew for sure that he was cheating, she took me and my brother and left without much of anything. It was hard for her at first, but now my mom is happy. She found a great guy to love her and to be a father to us. Sometimes when I hear her singing or humming in the kitchen, I'm grateful for the decision she made, not only for herself, but for my brother and me, as well."

"You're part of the Colton family that has been in the news," Sharon stated as Lila's name seemed to finally click in her head.

She didn't flinch or give an inch. "Yes. I've had my fair share of gossip and media, so be warned. Luckily, there will be another news story coming along."

Sharon walked to the desk. "It's not only that. I'm afraid for my own life and what Lou might do when he finds out I've taken over the company. He knows a lot of bad people."

"Sharon, you have money and can hire round-the-clock bodyguards for you and your children." Carter got to his feet. "Give it some thought, but you don't have much time. The interview will probably start about two in the DA's offices. The ADA would love any help to put Rossini away."

"Don't expect a miracle. Lou is notorious for having the police under his thumb and probably the DA's office, too."

Lila reached for her purse, knowing that nothing they said would sway her. She had to make her own decision.

"I'm sorry for all that you've been through," Lila said. "The only thing that's going to ease your pain is to show Rossini just how strong a woman you really are. Stand strong and he can't hurt you anymore."

"That's what I'm doing in this office, Ms. Colton. My father built the business and now I'm taking it back for my own peace of mind."

They walked out of the office, down the stairs and to Carter's car. "What do you think?" Lila asked.

"We have to wait and see what decision she makes, and it is her decision."

"Yeah. That's the hard part."

"Let's eat lunch before we go back," Carter suggested.

"That sounds good, even though I'm not hungry."

"You need the strength. This'll be the first time you get to see Fox and Rossini after their arrests."

"I can't wait."

Lila's cell buzzed and she grabbed her purse, hoping Sharon had made up her mind. The caller ID gave her pause. It was her father. Should she answer or call him back? Maybe he'd heard about the so-called kidnapping and wanted to know how she was. *Gullible, thy name is Lila.* She answered anyway.

"Hey, Dad."

"What do you think you're doing?"

"Excuse me?"

"Your grandmother is livid. The other Coltons got information from a friend of yours and the judge is now pushing the court date back until experts can thoroughly examine the will. You have betrayed the family. How could you?"

"Don't you want to know if the will is a forgery?"

"Hell, no. Mom wants that money and she better get it or we'll never speak to you again."

"I have no control over that."

"Well, you seem to have control over other things."

Tears were threatening to squeeze from her eyes, but she was strong enough to hold them back. He didn't ask about her kidnapping, as the media was calling it. He didn't care about her. How many times had she told herself that, and today she believed it for the first time. It finally sank in.

"By the way, I'm fine. I didn't have to spend the night in the hospital or anything. It's amazing how strong a person can be at times."

"What are you talking about?"

"The kidnapping."

"Oh, that. Mom said you faked that to get attention."

"No, Dad. The knot on my head is very real and the fear in my heart was very real. Nice talking to you. Give my regards to your mother."

She held the phone tight in her hand. A tremor ran through her. Carter was right. There was no happiness in a marriage or home and family. There was no happiness anywhere.

Chapter Eighteen

Carter paced as they waited in a small area. The ADA was running late. Richards came in and took a seat. No one spoke. This was the end of the line for the truth and Carter prayed the truth was all dressed up and ready to be exposed.

They were called back and gathered in a large interview room. Lila had talked to her dad on the phone and she seemed upset. The excitement of the morning was gone and replaced with the seriousness and determination he knew well. Nothing would keep her from having her say.

They made room for the ADA. Richards was on one end and Lila and Carter were on the other. The ADA would sit between them, and Carter hoped they could get this over with quickly.

The ADA rushed in with an armful of files, a laptop, a briefcase and a purse slung over her shoulder. "Good afternoon, everyone." She laid everything carefully on the table and took a deep breath. "They're bringing Walter Fox in. The forgery is a done deal. My concern now is the arson charge."

"Why?" Lila asked. "Sapp says he was in on it."

"I intend to take this slow, Ms. Colton. I'm allowing you here because it was your place of business that was destroyed. I feel you have a right to face them. Just let me handle this."

"Yes, ma'am."

Lila's expression was tight. She was upset, but he had a feeling it wasn't about Fox. It was about something else.

He reached out and touched her arm. "Relax."

The door opened and Walter Fox in jail attire and handcuffs was escorted in by an officer and a lawyer. Fox was a small man, probably five feet seven inches, and always dressed as if life was an occasion. Carter thought he probably lived it that way, too, needing money and more money to fit his lifestyle. Now it had all come crumbling down and his demeanor was one of a broken man.

Today there was no hat and no bow tie and no three-piece suit to grab one's attention. He was just a man looking for forgiveness.

"Mr. Fox will plead guilty to the forgery charge, but he had nothing to do with the arson." His lawyer took up the cause.

The ADA placed the tape recorder on the table. "We have a witness who will testify that you and Rossini talked about burning down the gallery, which Rossini owns."

The lawyer whispered to Fox and nodded for him to speak. "I talked about wanting to get rid of the paintings because I knew Mr. Finch was coming to town and I would get caught selling forgeries."

"May I ask a question?" Carter asked.

"Go ahead."

"How did you know I was coming to Chicago?"

"Just a friend who works in the art industry."

"What's his name?"

The lawyer and Fox whispered again and then the lawyer spoke. "That has nothing to do with the arson case and my client has no reason to answer it."

"I agree," the ADA said. "You're a good detective, Mr. Finch, and I know you can figure it out on your own. Let's move on."

Damn! He was hoping to get a little help, but she was right. He would find it in the archives of people who wanted to get even for putting them in prison. It could wait until another day. This day was for finding the arsonist.

"Mr. Fox, our witness says that you talked with Mr. Rossini about torching the gallery. Mr. Finch could verify the paintings were fakes and the only way to save yourself was to get rid of them. Am I correct?"

"My client..."

"I'm willing to tell you my part in this—" Mr. Fox interrupted "—for a lesser sentence."

"I'm listening."

"Yes, Lou and I talked about it. He wanted to get Ms. Colton off his back before she called an electrician. We agreed to pay half if we could find someone to do it."

"What is half?"

"I paid five thousand and Lou paid five thousand."

"Who did you pay this money to?"

"I gave my share to Lou and he would give his share to the person he hired."

"Who did he hire, Mr. Fox?" Richards asked.

"I don't know. He never told me."

"So you just gave him five thousand dollars?"

"Yes. He promised to give me thirty thousand when he got the insurance money for the building."

"Thirty thousand? For what?" Carter asked.

"So I can get the full amount for my paintings."

Rossini didn't even need Fox. There was something that wasn't ringing true about the stories.

"Mr. Fox, did you ever receive any money from Mr. Rossini?" Richards wanted to know.

"No. That's why I went to his office to find out what was going on. I needed my money." He turned his gaze to Lila. "I'm so sorry for what happened to you. I didn't mean to hurt you."

"But you did hurt me to keep from getting caught. And you stole from Homer Tinsley to feed your gambling habit. He trusted you and that trust meant nothing."

"Where did you get the gun, Mr. Fox?" The ADA took control again.

"It's a small Smith & Wesson. I bought it for protection after poker games. It went off in the car when I tried to take it away from Lou. I didn't mean for anything like this to happen. I'm sorry."

The ADA clicked off the tape recorder. "Mr. Fox, I will talk to your lawyer later. I will definitely have a deal for you if you will testify against Rossini."

"Yes, yes. I would be willing to do that."

The interview ended and Fox and his attorney left the room. The ADA looked at her watch. "I have to go to my office and make a phone call. Rossini should be brought over in about fifteen minutes. The girlfriend is here and trying to bail him out, but Rossini just learned that his wife put a lock on everything he owns. He's not happy and the girlfriend is demanding to see me. Oh, what a wonderful day."

"I have to check in at the office," Richards said and walked away.

Lila and Carter made their way to the waiting area and a young girl brought them coffee. "Thank you," Lila said. "That's very nice of you."

"You're welcome."

"Are you okay?" Carter asked as they sat down.

"Why wouldn't I be okay?"

"You talked to your dad on your cell and I could see it upset you."

"He and my grandmother found out about the experts looking at the will, and the hearing has been pushed back till a judge can rule on the expert's findings. They're very upset and said it was all my fault."

"It's not. Lila—"

"I know it's not my fault. My fault is loving too much and believing that one day my father would love me the way most fathers love their children. I realize that's never going to happen, and even though I know it's true, it still hurts."

"I'm so sorry he hurt you again. I wish I had more time to—"

"You were right all along. Love hurts, and having a home and a family does not make it better. It is not the solution to everyone's problem. I can see that now. Marriage has to be a personal commitment that you're willing to make. It's a risk that you have to be willing to take. Sometimes it works out and sometimes it doesn't."

"Please don't change into a bitter person who doesn't believe in love. I know that it exists. How do I know? I see it every time I look into your eyes and I see it in the way you deal with life and your family. That's love. Don't throw it all away because of my jaded ideas."

Richards slid into a chair across from them. "They're bringing Rossini over. Showtime."

Carter pulled out his phone and sent a text to Sharon. *The interview with your husband and the ADA is about to start. Just thought you might want to know.* He slipped his phone into his pocket and hoped she showed up. If not, there was a very good chance Rossini's attorney could get him out on bail.

He turned to Lila. "Ready?"

"Ready."

They sat in the interview room once again in almost the exact same positions. Rossini was shown in with his lawyer, who was cursing and yelling at the top of his lungs.

"This is ridiculous. I demand that Mr. Rossini be released."

"Sit down, Mr. Harris, and if you don't change your attitude, I will have you removed from the interview."

"You can't do that."

"Try me. This is not a courtroom. I'm just trying to see if we have enough information to take Mr. Rossini before a judge."

"You don't." Mr. Harris set his monogrammed briefcase on the table. "Can you place him at the fire?"

"No. But his fingerprints are all over the place."

"He owns the building."

"I'm aware of that. I'm just letting you know."

"You can't put my client anywhere near that building on that night."

"No, not at this point."

"What do you have?"

"For starters, the kidnapping of Ms. Colton and being held against her will." The ADA held up two fingers. "Two witnesses who say that Rossini talked about setting the fire. One made the device for him and the other actually gave him money to destroy the paintings in the gallery. Mr. Rossini offered him thirty thousand dollars after the fire from his insurance money."

"Why would Mr. Rossini offer anyone thirty thousand dollars after the fire?"

"For his silence, Mr. Harris," Carter replied. "Silence is worth a lot of money."

"That's hogwash. You'll never get a jury to believe that. Mr. Rossini is well-known around this city and is a respected businessman. This is a witch hunt, and a jury will never believe this insane nonsense."

Voices outside distracted the meeting. The ADA motioned to Richards. "See what's going on?"

He was back in a second. "Ms. Wilcox is demanding to see Mr. Rossini and she's taking offense at your attempt to keep her out."

Carter leaned over and whispered to the ADA. Lila could hear him, as he had to speak over her. "Let her in. She was at the poker games and knows more than she's saying and she might accidentally let something slip."

The ADA gave it some thought. "Let her in."

Ms. Wilcox charged into the room like a bull into

an arena full of energy. With a twist of her head, she tossed back her long dark hair, daring anyone to question her presence here. Richards brought another chair and she sat close to Rossini, stroking his arm. "Don't worry, baby. We'll get you out of here."

"Ms. Wilcox." The ADA's voice rose. "Sit back and listen or I'll have the officer remove you."

"I'm only trying to help Lou."

Mr. Harris leaned in and spoke to Rossini. "Tell her I can handle this."

Rossini patted Tanya's hands. "Just be quiet, baby."

Tanya crossed her legs and scooted back in the chair with a smug expression.

Lila stared at the woman and something clicked in her mind. "You're the woman who called me from Rossini's office and wanted my signature on a piece of paper that concerned the safe's contents."

"Yeah, that was me." She twirled a strand of dark hair around her forefinger. "Mona's always trying to get the best of me. I offered to take it to you, but she said I didn't have enough sense to do that. I showed her."

"How many times have I told you not to come to my office?" Rossini's anger sparked.

"Don't yell at me! I heard you come into your office and had to leave quickly. I took it back later that afternoon when no one was there. I just laid it on Mona's desk with a sticky note attached. I drew a smiley face on it."

Mr. Harris cleared his throat to get the interview back on track. "You don't have enough evidence to charge Mr. Rossini with anything. I demand a bail hearing so he can be released."

"Attempted murder, kidnapping and arson are not crimes I dismiss without a lot of thought," the ADA told him.

"You can't be serious."

"Don't push me, Mr. Harris. Rossini was caught at the airport fleeing our jurisdiction. He is not going to be granted bail."

"Mr. Rossini did not set the fire and did not know two people were in the building. Mr. Rossini did not build the device to set the fire. Mr. Rossini has done nothing wrong. He is innocent and I demand that he be taken before a judge."

Lila looked down to see Carter reading his phone. She read it, too. It was from Sharon. She couldn't embarrass her children. Lila's heart sank. She'd made it to the courthouse, but then changed her mind. After all they'd been through, it came down to a wife who didn't have the courage to stand up to her abusive husband. Rossini was going to get away with it.

She glanced at Carter and she could see the same thoughts were running through his mind. Lila got to her feet. "Excuse me, please."

"Lila…"

"Is there something you'd like to share?" the ADA asked.

"No. I just have to make a quick call. It's private."

Lila left the room and expected Carter to follow her, but he didn't. She hurried to the big foyer and asked the receptionist if she'd seen anyone waiting. The girl pointed to the front doors and Lila ran for her life, trying to catch Sharon. She stopped and caught her breath as she saw Sharon standing there with her car keys in her hand and the strap of a big purse over her shoulder.

"Sharon!"

The woman turned toward Lila's voice, and in a split second, Lila thought she was going to run, but decided otherwise and walked toward Lila. "I'm sorry, Lila. I'm just not a hero."

"I bet your children think otherwise. From everything that you've told me, I'm assuming your life was miserable. Even expensive clothes and a fancy house can't disguise that. Your children know the pain you've been through—at least, the older ones." Lila touched the big bag on Sharon's arm. "You probably have enough evidence in there to put him away for a long time."

Sharon clutched the purse a little tighter.

"You don't have to use it if you don't want to. You can just walk away and your husband will, too, as well as his girlfriend. She came to his rescue and she's in there, sitting right by his side, thinking he has millions of dollars to share with her." Lila gave her a minute and then added, "Maybe he does. Maybe he knows you better than you do."

Sharon clenched her jaw but didn't say anything.

Lila went back into the building and she didn't know how she was going to handle Rossini being released. Scream. Cry. Kick the furniture. Probably none of those. She would wait patiently until they found more evidence that pointed to him. She wondered if they sold patience at the pharmacy.

She slipped back into the room and whispered to Carter, "Tell you later."

"Do you have anything to share, Ms. Colton?" the ADA asked.

"No, ma'am."

"Okay, Mr. Harris, you get your arraignment. The judge will decide bail, but I'll fight it."

Tanya jumped out of the chair and leaped onto Rossini, almost knocking him out of his. "Oh, baby. We'll be in Hawaii in no time." She held out her left hand. "And I'll be wearing a beautiful wedding ring. You said they couldn't touch you and you were right."

"Shut up, Tanya."

"It's best if we go." Mr. Harris spoke up.

The ADA's phone buzzed and she took it. "Yes, send her in." She placed her phone on the desk with a thoughtful expression. "It seems we have more information, so please keep your seats."

"What?" Rossini was on his feet, his earlier happy expression marred by a scowl. He looked at his lawyer. "We don't have to put up with this, do we?"

"Yes, you do." The ADA was quick to correct him.

"Who is this person that has information?" Mr. Harris asked.

"Mrs. Rossini."

"My wife?" They now had Mr. Rossini's full attention.

"She can't testify against him. They're married." Relief was evident on Mr. Harris's face.

The ADA picked up her phone and touched a couple of numbers. The door opened and Mrs. Rossini walked in dressed in a navy sheath with short puffed sleeves. She was every bit the businesswoman she opted to be.

"What the hell is she doing here?" Rossini wanted to know.

"Everyone take a seat," the ADA ordered. "And I will speak to Mrs. Rossini." They went into the hallway and the others sat there, not saying a word.

Carter glanced at Lila and she gave him a thumbs-up, hoping Sharon's appearance meant exactly what she wanted it to.

In a few minutes, the two women came back. The ADA folded her hands over a large folder she'd brought in with her. "Mr. Rossini, do you have anything to say before I start?"

"No. I'd just like to get out of here."

The ADA looked at Tanya. "You mentioned Hawaii and marriage. Are you aware that Mr. Rossini is married?"

"Of course." She flipped her dark hair over her shoulder. "He's divorcing her as soon as he can and then we're getting married in Hawaii, just like he promised."

"Mr. Rossini promised you marriage?"

"Yes."

"For what?"

Tanya blinked. "What do you mean?"

"Why couldn't he divorce her six months ago, a year ago or even two years ago? All he had to do was ask her for a divorce, but he didn't. Why all of a sudden is he going to ask his wife for a divorce?"

"Because he realized how much he loved me and

not that old crow." Tanya glanced at Sharon, but she remained stone-faced.

The ADA pulled a file from a folder and slid it across the table to Tanya. "Sharon Rossini filed for divorce yesterday, and to have all the evidence she needed, she hired a PI to follow Mr. Rossini for the last four months." She held up a CD. "On this CD is just about everything he's done during that time."

Tanya paled significantly. "What…? What…? Lou?"

"Don't worry, baby," Rossini told her with a sneer on his lips. "I got this. My wife, or soon-to-be ex-wife, is not intelligent enough to outsmart me." He faced his wife. "You know that PI you hired? I offered him a lump sum of money for his information and he took it. He wasn't very loyal to you. So, my sweet wife, you have nothing and you'll be out of my office by tomorrow."

"This is highly irregular," Mr. Harris complained. "And I will be talking to the DA."

"Go ahead, but first, let's go over some things. Mr. Harris, you've been asking me if I can place Mr. Rossini at the gallery. No, I can't, but I can place someone he's very close to there."

Tanya stood. "I really have to go…"

Richards jumped up and blocked the doorway.

"Sit down, Ms. Wilcox," the ADA said. "I'll show you some interesting pictures and videos."

"What's going on?" Rossini asked.

"You'll find out soon enough."

The ADA removed the CD from its holder and pushed it into the recorder beneath the TV. Picking up the remote control, she went back to her seat. Everyone scooted their chairs around and Richards stood at the door.

"I haven't seen this before, but I'm assured of what's on it." She clicked the remote control. Nothing happened. She clicked it again. Nothing but a whirling sound.

Rossini laughed, a sickening sound. "It's blank. I told you, you stupid cow. I bought everything he had. You have nothing. You'll never outsmart me. You're just a dumb bitch who's worth nothing and..."

Carter got up and grabbed Mr. Rossini around the neck and squeezed as hard as he could. The man's face turned red and he spluttered.

"You say one more word and I'll snap your neck." Carter released him.

Rossini rubbed his neck. "That's police brutality. I'm suing the Chicago Police Department and Mr. Finch."

"Mr. Finch does not work for the Chicago Police Department," the ADA told him. "I'd advise you to tone it down." She turned her attention to Tanya. "Ms. Wilcox, are you sure Mr. Rossini has plans to marry you?"

"Of course he does. We talk about it all the time. He hates his life with her." She pointed to Sharon.

Sharon sat between Lila and Carter. Her head was bent, and she gripped her hands tightly in her lap. It was the final blow in her life with Rossini. She finally stood up for herself and he had humiliated her beyond belief. Lila wanted to touch her hands or something to make her realize she wasn't alone. But she didn't want to embarrass her more.

"This has all been very interesting," Mr. Harris said, "but can we move on and get to a hearing?"

Sharon moved and Lila thought she was leaving the room, but she reached down and pulled out a big folder from her purse. She held it in her hand as she started to speak. "It seems very ironic that no one has thought of the real motive for the gallery fire."

Real motive? That puzzled Lila. How many motives could there be?

"It was because of the wiring," Richards said.

Sharon shook her head. "That was only part of it. Lou bought the building many years ago. The roof had a leak, but Lou never fixed it. There were steel beams in the roof to make the dome of the gallery. Chicago has lots of rain, and water leaked onto the beams, causing them to rust. Lou decided to sell the place, but it didn't pass inspection because of the rusted beams and the wiring. The inspector put a lock on the door. Until the repairs were done, Lou couldn't sell the place. So Lou does what he always does. He hired an inspector for a false report and rented the place to Ms. Colton."

Lila listened to this in shock. "No, that can't be right. I had an inspection done before I rented and the guy said everything was okay. I have the report in my files."

"I'm sorry, Lila. It was another fake inspection. When the wiring problem came up again, I decided to look for the first file and found Lou hadn't done any of the repairs as he'd told me and the city of Chicago." She waved the file toward the ADA. "It's all in there."

"You mean the roof could have come crashing down at any moment?"

"Yes, I'm afraid so."

A chill ran through Lila. So many people could have been hurt, some killed. It was a horrible thought.

Sharon reached for her purse and took out something that looked like a photo. She walked to the ADA and slipped it inside the file. "In case you need it." She then eased her purse strap over her shoulder and stared at her husband. "Lou wanted the building gone, but he didn't have the guts to do it himself. He tried to frame Sapp and Fox. He finally found the perfect pigeon to do his dirty work." She glanced at Tanya and walked out of the room with her power intact.

"What did she mean by that?" Tanya asked. She got up out of her chair as the truth hit her. "Oh, no, no! I'm not taking the blame for this."

"Sit down, Ms. Wilcox," the ADA ordered.

"I'm not going to be set up."

"Just shut up, Tanya," Lou said. "Trust me on this."

"If you have anything to tell us, you better tell us now. I tend to be lenient when people are honest."

They waited, but Tanya didn't budge.

"This might help." The ADA laid the photo in front of Tanya. Carter and Richards got up to view it and the lawyer and Rossini leaned over, as did Lila. It didn't take long for Lila to figure it out. There was a large photo of three children on a dresser, and in front of the photo lay a steel-like object about two and a half inches long and bigger than a tube of lipstick. Rossini stood at the mirror putting on cuff links.

"Mr. Rossini, can you identify the children in the photo?"

"They're mine."

"Where was the photo taken?"

"Looks like our bedroom."

"Who took the picture?"

"I have no idea. This is the first time I've seen it. Obviously, some of Sharon's handiwork," Rossini said.

Carter pointed to the person who could be seen in the mirror lying in the bed. "Who is that?"

Rossini swallowed. "You know who that is."

"Say it."

"It's Tanya."

Carter placed his finger on the object in front of the photo. "What is that?"

"You don't need to answer," the lawyer whispered.

"No, he doesn't," the ADA said. "Donald Sapp made it and I'm guessing he knows what it looks like."

"I'll have all of this thrown out," the lawyer said.

"I don't think so, Mr. Harris." She tapped the device on the photo. "I can almost put it in his hands. Wait— no. He put it into Ms. Wilcox's hands for a promise of marriage. Am I right, Mr. Rossini?"

"I refuse to answer."

"Do you have plane tickets to Hawaii? Do you have a wedding ring?" The ADA directed the questions at Tanya.

It took a moment for the answers to sink in for Tanya. She leaped toward Rossini and slapped his face and kept on slapping until Richards and Carter pulled her off. "You bastard. You used me. I'll bury your ass."

The ADA motioned for Richards to get Rossini out of the room. He read him his Miranda rights as he arrested him, leading him out the door.

As the room emptied, Rossini shouted to Tanya,

"Babe, don't tell them anything. It's you and me, babe, all the way."

For the next thirty minutes, Tanya told her story. She'd placed the device for Rossini on the promise of marriage and a future. She'd done it during the showing when it was busy. No one had noticed her. An officer led her out, no sass left in her. The ordeal was over.

Lila hugged the ADA. "Thank you. And thanks to Sharon. We could have never proved that Tanya was the one who set the device."

"You're right about that." The ADA gathered her things. "It's been the weirdest interview I've ever taken and I never want to have one like that again. Have a good evening."

Lila and Carter walked to the car without saying a word, both shell-shocked at the outcome of the interviews. Now she had to concentrate on the morning and Carter's leaving. That would be even more gut-wrenching.

Chapter Nineteen

When they reached the town house, Carter grabbed bottled water for himself and Lila. They sat on the sofa, both consumed with what had happened today.

"I would never have guessed that it was Tanya." Lila took a sip of cold water.

"I thought Rossini had hired someone, but he knew Tanya would do anything for him at the mention of marriage. He tricked her and she'll spend a lot of time in prison for that."

"How much time do you think Sapp will get?"

"Not over two years and he might get a probated sentence. He got used, too."

"It's really sad. So many people got hurt because Rossini is a cheapskate. If he had just paid the money to fix the roof and the wiring, no one would've gotten hurt."

Carter studied her face. She appeared calm and serene, like she had the first time he'd met her. Maybe the wounds would disappear, too. "How are you feeling?"

"Great. We finally know who the arsonist is, and that's a load off of my mind." She sat up straight.

"Damn. I had my chance and forgot to jump on Rossini for locking me in the closet."

"I think he got the message. Don't mess with Lila."

Her cell buzzed and she got up to get it out of her purse with a smile on her face. She winked at him. "You got it."

He listened as she talked. It was mostly, "Sure.

"Okay.

"It was awesome.

"That sounds like fun. I'll see you then."

"Are you going somewhere?" He bit his tongue, but it didn't stop the words from spilling out.

"Savon and I are going out to celebrate."

"Shouldn't you rest?"

Lucky for him, her phone rang again. "Savon must've forgotten something."

It wasn't Savon. He could tell by her demeanor and her serious voice. She was happy to talk to this person and her voice echoed that. It took him a few minutes to figure out it was Heath.

"That was Heath," she said as she sat on the sofa. "He had good news about the will. It's the same as my dad told me. The experts found evidence of doctoring of the named heirs. The judge granted more time to investigate, so the trial date has been extended, and Heath and his family are happy about that. It's giving the other Coltons a little longer to hold on to their father's legacy. He said to tell you thank you."

"I hope it works out the way *you* want."

She looked down at the phone in her hands. "I would just like some peace between the families. And if the will is a fake, then we all have to be prepared for that.

If it's real, we have to be prepared for that, too. Now—" she got to her feet "—I need to take a shower and get dressed for an evening out. I'm not going to think about the arson or the will. I'm just going to have fun and drink a little and smile a lot."

"What about your dad?"

That stopped her in her tracks. "My relationship with my dad is what it's always been…not much. I do all the calling, but I won't be doing that anymore. I have to step back from the relationship. He's never going to change and I've finally accepted that." She headed toward the stairs and turned back. "I guess you'll be packing?"

"I don't really have that much, but yes, I'll be getting my things together. My flight leaves at eleven."

She held up her hand. "I know. You like to be there early."

Sitting on the sofa with an ankle resting on a knee, he felt more alone than he ever had in his life. He thought she would be upset. Maybe a little sad at his leaving, but she seemed fine. And he wanted her to be. It was just that…loneliness pressed down on his chest. Was this love? Was this what a man experienced when someone he loved moved on?

Why hadn't she asked him to go out with them? After the high tension of the day, he would have welcomed an evening out with her.

And there it was.

He would be leaving in the morning.

And she would be here alone.

He couldn't ask that of her. This had been a special time in his life and he would remember her forever.

She came downstairs talking on the phone and he just stared. The outfit was definitely a party dress. The black skirt looked satiny, as did the black-and-white-striped top. The silver heels made her look taller and her legs longer. A black jacket rested over her arm. Attraction stirred in his gut and made him very aware that every inch of her was woman.

She slipped the phone into a silver purse she was carrying. "I'll see you later."

"If you need someone to pick you up, just call."

"Problem solved. We're taking a cab and calling one later. We played it smart this time. Bye," she called as she dashed out the door to the waiting cab.

He watched until it was out of sight and then he closed the door and went to the refrigerator. It was empty again. He had to get something for supper. To keep his mind busy, he ran upstairs to change into shorts and a T-shirt. Then he hit the street, the same route he'd taken the first time he went jogging with Lila. He'd like to eat one more hot dog before he left. But it wasn't the same sitting there at the table without her. Nothing was ever going to be the same again... without her. He finally realized that.

It was dark when he made his way back to the town house. With the many streetlights, it didn't make a difference. Streets were lit up, just calling for people to come out and play. A small grocery store was one street over and he crossed without a problem. He was getting to know Chicago. He bought the usual stuff for breakfast and snacks for the night. He planned to watch a movie or something to kill time.

When he got back, he packed everything except his

shaving kit, and then he took a shower and dressed in pajama bottoms and a T-shirt. Lying on the sofa, watching a movie he couldn't get interested in, he jumped at every sound, thinking she was home. But she wasn't. The last time he looked at the clock it was 1:00 a.m. She wasn't going to miss him at all. She had a full life and he was happy about that. He just couldn't understand why he was conflicted about leaving.

WHEN LILA GOT HOME, she was very quiet, not wanting to wake Carter. Then she saw him sleeping on the sofa. What was he doing downstairs? The TV was on and she walked over and turned it off. Carter stirred.

"You're home."

"Yes, and why are you here and not in your bed?"

He yawned and stretched, and she watched the play of muscles as they lit a flame deep inside her. "I was watching a movie." He got to his feet. "I better go to bed. Did you have a good time?"

"We had a great time." She sank into a chair and pulled off her heels. "I'm probably going to have sores on my feet from dancing so much."

He frowned. "You and Savon danced?"

"No, silly. Richards was there with one of his detectives. They stopped by our table for a drink. We talked about the case and just had a good time. Richards is a good dancer and a nice person once you get to know him. He's not so brusque."

"And are you getting to know him?"

His voice bordered on jealousy and she didn't like it. "For the record, Richards and his wife are separated and he's ready to go home, but he doesn't know how to go about it. I gave him some advice. That's all."

"Like what?"

She drew a deep breath and started to tell him it was none of his business, but they both were edgy and she should give him credit for that. "I told him to buy something that she really likes, take it over and tell her you would like to talk without the resentment. I guess we waited for about thirty minutes for him to figure out something that his wife liked. He doesn't know anything about her. We laughed at him and he finally said jelly beans. His wife loved jelly beans. He left to go buy jelly beans, and it was almost midnight. Imagine a husband not knowing anything about his wife. Richards is a total cop."

Carter didn't say anything and his flash-in-the-pan jealousy seemed to be gone. He picked up the pillow from the sofa. "Why didn't you ask me to go tonight?"

She was shocked and had to swallow a couple of times to speak. "Excuse me? You're leaving in a few hours. That should have said it all."

"What are we doing, Lila?"

"I'm trying to get through this night the best way I can." She charged up the stairs and slammed her bedroom door. She didn't want to spend this night with him, with memories of what they'd shared all around them. She wasn't that strong.

THE NEXT MORNING, she overslept, the dancing and the laughter having taken all her energy. It was 8:30 a.m. and she rushed into the bathroom, wanting to be gone by the time Carter had everything packed. She heard him in the shower. Her plan hadn't worked. She would have to face him once again.

She changed into shorts and a T-shirt and sneakers. Her mom had called last night while she was in the cab and invited her for lunch. Myles and Jackson would be there and she wanted both her kids to be home. She said Jackson would be excited. He would have someone to play with in the dirt. Myles wasn't too fond of playing in the dirt. But Lila would welcome it. For the distraction.

"Breakfast is ready!" Carter called from downstairs.

What? He had cooked breakfast? Where did he get the food? Instead of running out the front door, she played the good-girl part and went down to eat breakfast with him one more time.

"You didn't have to do this," she said as she took a seat.

"I'd rather eat something here than at the airport."

She sipped her coffee and decided to be an adult about this. "I'll miss you. I don't know how our stars crossed here in Chicago, but I'll never forget you."

"I'll miss you, too," he replied, his voice hoarse. "I never dreamed that when I came here I would meet the most gorgeous woman in the world. I'm sorry if you're hurt. I never meant for that to happen."

"It's my own fault. You told me up front that marriage wasn't for you and happy-ever-after wasn't in your DNA. You'd rather be on the road traveling. You told me all that and my heart still got involved." She tilted her head to look at him closely and her heart beat a little faster at the sculptured features and beautiful gray eyes. "You saved my life a couple of times and I will always be grateful for that."

She got to her feet and carried dishes to the sink. "You know, I might spend the night at my mom's. I'm going to pack a bag." It would be good to spend time with the family, especially with Jackson. If she stayed busy, the first week wouldn't be so bad. She just didn't know how to remove the love from her heart. Carter seemed to have no problem. But it wasn't love for Carter. She was just a girl he'd met along the way.

CARTER HAD EVERYTHING in the car. He had to go back and say goodbye, and it would be difficult. Lila deserved all the best things in life and he couldn't give her that. He found her sitting on the bed and waiting for him to drive away. Her eyes glistened and he knew they were tears. He swallowed the constriction in his throat.

"This isn't easy for me, either."

Her eyes met his. "I know, so don't feel bad about it. You can't produce love by snapping your fingers. It just wasn't meant to be for us. Call me every now and then if you get a chance. But it's not mandatory."

"Are you going to open another gallery?"

"I think I'm out of the gallery business, but only time will tell. I have an appointment with the insurance agent next week and I should get my money soon. By then I should know what I want to do."

"Hmm…"

"I wonder if the insurance company will pay out to Sharon."

"I'm sure lawyers will tear into it like vultures and she'll probably get half of what the building is worth.

But I wish her the best. She really came through when we needed her."

"She's a nice lady. The nice ones always get stuck with the jerks. My personal opinion."

"Is that aimed at me?"

"I wish I could dredge up that much anger, but I can't. Have a good life, Carter."

He leaned over and kissed her forehead. He couldn't resist. He wanted to keep his lips against her warm skin, but time had run out for them. "You, too." Then he added the hardest word in the English language. "Goodbye."

DON'T CRY. DON'T *CRY.* Lila sat on the bed with that resolve in mind, but her strong willpower couldn't stop a tear from slipping out and running down her cheek. She reached for a Kleenex on the dresser and wiped away the emotions of the past couple of weeks. He was gone and soon he would be just a memory, a very good memory of a special man.

The front door opened and she paused. Was that Carter? Had he forgotten something? She threw the tissue in the trash can and waited for him to enter the room.

The lines on his face were drawn and his gray eyes were dark and troubled. "Did you forget something?"

"I couldn't start the car."

"Oh. I'll take you to the airport."

He shook his head. "I didn't mean that."

"What did you mean?"

"I couldn't physically make myself start the engine. Everything I love is here and I can't walk away from it. I can tell myself all kinds of stories, but they even ring hollow to my ears. If you're not going to open another gallery, come to London with me."

What did he say?

She shook her head to clear it of cobwebs. "You want me to go to London with you?" She said the words slowly to get it right.

"Yes."

"And then what?"

"We live our lives the way we want…together. If you get homesick and want to come home, we'll come home."

Her heart was beating so fast she had to stop and take a deep breath. "Is marriage on the table?"

"If you want it to be."

She ran a hand over her hair. "Carter, you're blowing my mind. Just a few minutes ago you said you had to go. You've been saying that since you've been here. Marriage, home and family weren't for you and all that stuff. What changed your mind?"

"You. I know you love me. I can see it in your eyes every day and yet you're willing to let me go because you think that's what I want. Slowly you've been changing my mind. I like waking up with you and fixing breakfast. I love everything about you. I was too stubborn to admit it. Just now I couldn't start the car. I couldn't forcibly make myself do it because I was leaving behind everything I wanted. Besides, what kind of woman would tackle a criminal for me—someone who loves me. I love you, Lila Colton. Come spend the rest of your life with me."

She placed her hands on her hips, trying to balance

herself, trying to believe everything he was saying. "Where would we live?"

"Anywhere you want to. We would have to sort it out down the road. I can't leave Neil on the spur of the moment. We have to talk about a lot of things."

"I'm listening."

"You could be my assistant searching out art fraud. We would be together a lot, but I don't think that's a problem."

"I'd like that. But I want you to be very sure about changing your mind."

"I am. I knew something was missing in my life and now I know what it was. It was you."

Not able to stand it anymore, she practically jumped into his arms and held on for the bliss that was to come. "I love you," she whispered. "For a lifetime."

He held her face in his hands. "I love you, too. I'm thinking about what kind of house we would like."

She buried her face in his neck and breathed in the masculine scent of him. "Let's leave that until later. First, you have to tell my mother you're taking me far, far away."

"That might be my biggest challenge."

She jumped back. "Oh, Carter, your plane is leaving at eleven. You have to hurry."

"I canceled the flight and now I have to make a new one. I just wanted to make sure you'd say yes."

"Yes. Definitely yes." She put her hand over her mouth. "First problem."

"What?"

"I planned lunch with my mom, and Jackson will be

there. He knows I will be there. I can't break his heart. What are we to do?"

He pulled out his phone. "Let me see when I can get the latest flight out. You do have a passport, right?"

"Yes. I'll get it." She hurried upstairs, found it and rushed back to Carter. "It's up to date." Her heart was about to burst with happiness.

Carter laid his phone on the bar. "How does eight o'clock tonight sound? First-class."

"Wonderful. Thank you." She slid into his arms.

AN HOUR LATER, they were in the car and on their way to the suburb of Wheaton.

"You're a long way from your mother," Carter remarked.

"Sometimes that's a plus." She winked at him. "My mom tends to still baby me, and I'm the oldest—at least, by a few months. Myles and I have always been close. I just wish he and Faith would get back together."

"They'll work it out."

"Turn right."

"Is this it?"

"Yes. The big building is the nursery and the house is in the back. It's a two-story green Craftsman with tons of light and fresh flowers and airy windows. They sell everything from fresh flowers to fruit trees to prickly cactus, which I have a few scars from."

"I'll check later."

She chuckled. "You already have."

"This is a big place."

"Landscapers buy a lot from them and they're busy all the time. They work hard and that is just one of the little things I love about them." She pointed to an area near the house. "Park there."

They went into the house arm in arm. "The smell is intoxicating," Carter said.

Her mother met them at the back door with hugs. "I thought Carter was leaving?"

"Mom, I have some news." She told her about London.

"That's so far away. I'll never get to see you."

Rick placed an arm around his wife's shoulders. "Now, honey, she's grown. Let her live her own life. We'll miss her, but we'll celebrate twice as hard when she comes home." Rick shook Carter's hand. "It will just take some adjusting."

Myles walked in with Jackson, who had two big trucks under his arms. "Look, Li, I brought trucks to play with."

Lila rubbed his hair. "Yes, you did. We'll do that after lunch. Grandma is waiting for us to eat."

"Okay."

They gathered around the dining room table and Lila breathed in the scent of fresh flowers that were sitting in the center of the table. That would be a memory of home for the rest of her life. Her mom always had flowers on the table when they ate. The whole house smelled like a broken perfume bottle. That was what she used to think. Now she thought of how lucky she was to have that treat in her life.

Her mom and Rick brought the pot roast and all the trimmings to the table. Two chocolate pies were on the buffet.

"Everyone is very quiet," Myles said.

Rick told him about London. "Your mom is a little down."

"Mom." Myles shook his head. "How old is she now? It's time to let go."

"Where she going?" Jackson asked.

"London," he told his son.

"Is that far away?"

"Yes, it's far away."

Jackson's face crumbled into a baby-cry expression. "I don't want her to go."

Lila pulled him into her arms. "I'm not going to be gone forever. I will call you and talk to you on the phone. And we can see each other on the iPad. We can do all sorts of things. It's just like talking in person."

"Can I get a cell phone of my own?"

"You walked right into that one," Myles said to Lila. "And the answer is no, in case you're wondering."

Lila made a face at her brother.

Her mother began to remove the plates and Lila hurried to help. She put an arm around her mother. "Why are you so upset? Don't you want me to be happy?"

Vita turned and hugged her. "Of course I want my kids to be happy. Myles and Faith are separated and you're moving away. I feel like an old woman clinging to my babies."

"You love too much."

"Yes, I do, and you're a lot like me. I'm just hoping your feelings for this man are real, the lasting-forever kind."

"They are, Mom."

She reached for a dish towel and wiped her hands. "I felt the same way about your dad. It didn't take me long to figure out he wasn't my knight in shining armor. I don't want you to get hurt."

"Carter?" Lila called.

He came into the kitchen looking a little startled. She was startled, too, at her mother's reaction.

"Tell Mom our future plans."

"Um… We're going to London so I can validate a painting, and from there I suppose we'll come back to Chicago so Lila can finish up all the paperwork with the fire. Lila's going to be my assistant and we'll be working together like you and Rick. Eventually we plan to build a home somewhere in Chicago or somewhere close to her mother."

Her mother's whole demeanor changed. "You're coming back?"

"Yes," Carter replied. "What did you think?"

"I thought you would be living there."

Carter shook his head. "No, ma'am. Lila's roots are here and I would never take her away from that. We'll be in and out for the next couple of years."

Her mom patted his cheek. "Oh, you sweet boy."

Myles poked his head around the door. "All clear?"

"Yes," her mother said. "Now let's eat chocolate pie. Where's Jackson?"

Jackson wolfed down his pie and then played with his trucks.

"Heath called me, Myles. I haven't had a chance to tell you."

"I already know. Dad called. Carin called. Enough said."

"How do you feel about it? Dad said it was all my fault because I told Heath about the experts. And ruined his life. He won't be invited to any poker games because of what I did. Carin is very distraught and upset, and I'm supposed to call and apologize."

"Are you thinking about that?"

"No. I want to know if the will is a fake or not. I think we'll sleep better if we know. That's just my opinion, it seems."

Myles wiped his mouth with a napkin. "Sometimes I think about how good it would be to have that much money. Faith and I are arguing about money and how important it is to me. She thinks family is more important. If I inherited a lump sum of money, it would certainly make my life easier. But then I remind myself that Carin has never given me or you anything that I can recall. She's not going to share that money with anyone."

"You would side with Carin for the money?" Lila was appalled.

"I said *sometimes* I think about it, especially when I'm really down about Faith. That's it. Let me be clear in case you're not. I don't plan on sharing anything from the grandmother from hell. I haven't forgotten that she said I would never amount to anything and she wasn't going to spend one dime on a needless education."

Lila placed her hand on Myles's. "Money is not going to solve your problem. Only you can."

Jackson came into the room with trucks in his arms. "Is it time to play?"

"Yes, son."

For the next hour, they all sat out in the backyard watching Jackson play. He had a motorized dump truck that he could drive. He would fill it up with the smaller truck and dump the dirt to help Rick. Sometimes he wanted Lila to help put dirt in the truck with her hands.

"Carter, come play with us," Jackson shouted.

Without pausing, Carter removed his shoes and socks and rolled up his slacks. And then he pulled off his dress shirt and laid it on the porch.

"We have to load my truck with dirt."

They played in the sand, moving it from one spot to the other. Finally, Carter put his truck and sand in the bed of Jackson's truck. Lila followed suit.

Jackson got out of the truck shaking his finger at them. "You're doing it wrong."

Carter got to his feet and chased Jackson around the yard. "I'm doing it wrong? Wait until I catch you." Jackson's screeches echoed around the neighborhood. They laughed and played and it was a nice family afternoon.

Her mom had a gardenia bush blooming at the end of the house. The decadent white blooms were heavenly. She sat in a swing with Carter since Jackson was busy avoiding them.

"I've never seen a place like this. It looks all dressed up and just waiting for somewhere to go, but it has that feel of home. Raising a kid in an apartment in New York wasn't my parents' best idea. Kids need to be raised here in the open with all the flowers and the trees and lots of space."

She leaned over and kissed him. "It's getting late and we better go. I have to pack a few more things."

They got to their feet and Carter found his shoes and socks and put them on. They hugged and kissed everyone.

"When you coming back?" Jackson asked.

"Soon, and I'll bring you a gift."

"A gift?" He clapped his hands and then looked at Myles.

"Okay."

Her mom insisted they have another piece of chocolate pie before they left. They were sitting at the kitchen table when a young girl walked in with a red clay pot in her hands.

Her mom waved her over. "Sara, come on in."

"I didn't know you had company."

"That's okay. I'd like for you to meet my beautiful daughter and her boyfriend, Lila and Carter Finch. And this is Sara Sandoval. She's helping with marketing."

The pot crashed to the floor, splintering into many pieces. "Oh, I'm so sorry."

"Calm down," Rick told her, and he had the mess cleaned up in no time.

"Did you need something?" her mother asked.

"Oh, yes. A truck driver came into the office and said he has five hundred of—" she glanced down at the floor "— those and wanted to know where to put them."

"I'll take care of it," her mother said. Then she hugged Lila so tight she could barely breathe. "Take care of yourself. I love you, baby."

The trio made it out the door, and the young girl looked back and said, "Nice to meet you."

Lila and Carter made it back to the car.

"You seem deep in thought," Carter said.

"That girl. Who did my mom say she was?"

"Sara Sandoval."

"She seemed nervous. Did you think that?"

"A little. I think it was just seeing strangers when she only expected your mom and Rick."

"It's a little strange that Rick hired her. Rick says he'll hire family if he needs help. We have all worked there from time to time when we were in college or needed money. He was adamant about outsiders for some reason. That girl looked vaguely familiar."

Carter reached over and took her hand and squeezed it. "Let it go. Your mom will tell you if she's someone you need to know. Let's think about our future. It's going to be the best times of our lives."

"An adventure." She squeezed his hand, and every problem she ever had vanished with the feelings inside her. Life with Carter Finch would be an adventure.

* * * * *

COMING SOON!

We really hope you enjoyed reading this book.
If you're looking for more romance, be sure to
head to the shops when new books are
available on

Thursday 14th October

LET'S TALK
Romance

For exclusive extracts, competitions
and special offers, find us online:

 facebook.com/millsandboon

 @MillsandBoon

 @MillsandBoonUK

Get in touch on 01413 063232

For all the latest titles coming soon, visit
millsandboon.co.uk/nextmonth

MILLS & BOON

Desire

Indulge in secrets and scandal, intense drama and plenty of sizzling hot action with powerful and passionate heroes who have it all: wealth, status, good looks…everything but the right woman.

MILLS & BOON
MEDICAL
Pulse-Racing Passion

Set your pulse racing with dedicated, delectable doctors in the high-pressure world of medicine, where emotions run high and passion, comfort and love are the best medicine.